The Chestnut Man

A Novel

Søren Sveistrup

Translated by Caroline Waight

HARPER LUXE

An Imprint of HarperCollinsPublishers

To my beloved boys,
Silas and Sylvester

Originally published as *Kastanjemanden* in Denmark in 2018 by Politikens Forlag.

THE CHESTNUT MAN. Copyright © 2018 by Søren Sveistrup. English translation copyright © 2019 by Caroline Waight. All rights reserved. Printed in the United States of America. No part of this book may be used or reproduced in any manner whatsoever without written permission except in the case of brief quotations embodied in critical articles and reviews. For information, address HarperCollins Publishers, 195 Broadway, New York, NY 10007.

HarperCollins books may be purchased for educational, business, or sales promotional use. For information, please e-mail the Special Markets Department at SPsales@harpercollins.com.

FIRST HARPERLUXE EDITION

ISBN: 978-0-06-291160-5

HarperLuxe™ is a trademark of HarperCollins Publishers.

Library of Congress Cataloging-in-Publication Data is available upon request.

19 20 21 22 23   LSC   10 9 8 7 6 5 4 3 2 1

Tuesday,
October 31st, 1989

1

Red and yellow leaves drift down through the sunlight onto the wet asphalt, which cuts through the woods like a dark and glassy river. As the white squad car tears past, they're spun briefly in the air before coming to rest in sticky clumps along the edge of the road. Marius Larsen takes his foot off the accelerator and eases up for the bend, making a mental note to tell the council they need to come out here with the sweeper. If the leaves are left too long, they'll make the surface slippery, and that sort of thing can cost lives. Marius has seen it many times before. He's been on the force forty-one years, senior officer at the station for the last seventeen, and he has to prod them about it every single autumn. But not today—today he has to focus on the conversation.

Marius fiddles irritably with the frequency on the car radio, but he can't find what he's looking for. Only news about Gorbachev and Reagan, and speculation about the fall of the Berlin Wall. It's imminent, they're saying. A whole new era may be on its way.

He's known for a while that the conversation has to happen, yet he's never been able to screw up his courage. Now there's only a week until his wife thinks he's retiring, so the time has come to tell her the truth: That he can't cope without his job. That he's dealt with the practical side of things and put off the decision. That he isn't ready yet to settle on the corner sofa and watch *Wheel of Fortune*, to rake leaves in the garden or play Old Maid with the grandkids.

It sounds easy when he runs through the conversation in his head, but Marius knows full well she'll be upset. She'll feel let down. She'll get up from the table and start scouring the stove in the kitchen, and tell him with her back turned that she understands. But she won't. So when the report came over the radio ten minutes ago he told the station he'd handle it himself, postponing the conversation a little longer. Normally he'd be annoyed about having to drive all the way out to Ørum's farm through fields and forest merely to tell them they need to keep a better eye on their animals. Several times now, pigs or cows have broken through the fence and gone roaming the neighbors' fields until Marius or one of his men made Ørum sort it out. But today he isn't annoyed. He asked them to call first, of course, ringing Ørum's house and the ferry terminal, where he has a part-time job, but when nobody picked up at either place he turned off the main road and headed for the farm.

Marius finds a channel playing old Danish music. "The Bright Red Rubber Dinghy" fills the old Ford Escort, and Marius turns up the volume. He's enjoying the autumn and the drive. The woods, their yellow, red, and brown leaves mixing with the evergreens. The anticipation of hunting season, which is just beginning. He rolls down the window, the sunlight casting its dappled light onto the road through the treetops, and for a moment Marius forgets his age.

There's silence at the farm. Marius gets out and slams the car door, and as he does so it strikes him that it's been ages since he was last here. The wide yard looks dilapidated. There are holes in the windows of the stable, the plaster on the walls of the house is peeling off in strips, and the empty swing set on the overgrown lawn is nearly swallowed up by the tall chestnut trees encircling the property. Littered across the gravel yard are leaves and fallen chestnuts, which squelch beneath his feet as he walks up to the front door and knocks.

After Marius has knocked three times and called out Ørum's name, he realizes nobody will answer. Seeing no sign of life, he takes out a pad, writes a note, and slips it through the mailbox, while a few crows flit across the yard and vanish behind the Ferguson tractor parked in front of the barn. Marius has driven all the way out here on a fool's errand, and now he'll have to stop by the ferry terminal to get hold of Ørum. But he's not annoyed for long: on the way back to the car, an idea pops into his head. That never usually happens to Marius, so it must be a stroke of luck that he drove out here instead of heading straight home to the conversation. Like a Band-Aid on a cut, he'll offer his wife a trip to Berlin. They could run down there for a week— well, at least a weekend, say, as soon as he can take time off. Do the drive themselves, witness history in the making—that new era—eat dumplings and sauerkraut like they did before in Harzen, on that camping trip with the kids far too long ago. Only when he's almost reached the car does he see why the crows are settling behind the tractor. They're hopping around on something pallid and formless, and not until he gets closer does he realize it's a pig. Its eyes are dead, but its body jerks and shivers as though trying to frighten off the crows, which are feeding from the gunshot wound at the back of its head.

Marius opens the front door. The hallway is dim, and he notices the scent of damp and mold, and something else he can't quite put his finger on.

"Ørum, it's the police."

There's no reply, but he can hear water running somewhere in the house, so he steps into the kitchen. The girl is a teenager. Maybe sixteen, seventeen. Her body is still sitting in the chair by the table, and what's left of her ruined face is floating in her bowl of porridge. On the linoleum on the other side of the table is another lifeless figure. He's a teenager too, a little older, with a gaping bullet wound in his chest and the back of his head tilted awkwardly against the stove. Marius goes rigid. He's seen dead people before, of course, but never anything like this, and for a brief moment he's paralyzed, until he takes his service pistol out of the holster on his belt.

"Ørum?"

Marius proceeds farther into the house as he calls Ørum's name, this time with his pistol raised. Still no reply. Marius finds the next corpse in the bathroom, and this time he has to clap his hand to his mouth so he doesn't throw up. The water is running from the tap into the bathtub, which has long since filled to the brim. It's spilling onto the terrazzo flooring and down the drain, intermingled with the blood. The naked woman—she must be the teenagers' mother—is lying tangled on the floor. One arm and one leg have been separated from the torso. In the subsequent autopsy report, it will emerge that she has been struck repeatedly with an axe. First as she lay in the bathtub and then as she tried to escape by crawling onto the floor. It will also be established that she tried to defend herself with her hands and feet, which is why they have split open. Her face is unrecognizable, because the axe was used to cave in her skull.

Marius would have frozen at the sight if he hadn't glimpsed a faint movement out of the corner of his eye. Half-hidden beneath a shower curtain dumped in the corner, he can make out a figure. Cautiously, Marius pulls back the curtain a little. It's a boy. Disheveled hair, about ten or eleven. He's lying lifeless in the blood, but a corner of the curtain is still covering the boy's mouth, and it vibrates weakly, haltingly. Marius swiftly leans over the boy and removes the curtain, picking up his limp arm and trying to find a pulse. The boy has cuts and scratches on his arms and legs, he wears a bloody T-shirt and underwear, and an axe has been dropped near his head. Finding a pulse, Marius leaps to his feet.

In the living room he grabs feverishly at the telephone beside the full ashtray, sending it tumbling to the floor, but by the time he gets hold of the station his head is clear enough to deliver a coherent message. "Ambulance. Officers. ASAP. No trace of Ørum. Get going. Now!" When he hangs up his first thought is to hurry back to the boy, but then abruptly he remembers that there must be another child: the boy has a twin sister.

Marius heads back toward the front hall and the staircase up to the first floor. As he passes the kitchen and the open basement door, he stops short. There was a sound. A footfall or a scrape, but now there's silence. Marius draws his pistol again. Opening the door wide, he shuffles gingerly down the narrow steps until his feet find the concrete floor. It takes his eyes a moment to adjust to the dark, and then he sees the open door at the end of the corridor. His body hesitates, telling him he ought to stop here, wait for the ambulance and his colleagues, but Marius thinks of the girl. As he approaches the door he can see it's been forced open. The lock and bolt are discarded on the ground, and Marius enters the room, which is lit only dimly by the grime-smeared windows above. Yet he can still make out a small shape hidden well back beneath a table in the corner. Hurrying over, Marius lowers his gun, bends down, and peers underneath it.

"It's okay. It's over now."

He can't see the girl's face, only that she's shaking and huddled into the corner without looking at him.

"My name is Marius. I'm from the police, and I'm here to help you."

The girl stays timidly where she is, as though she can't even hear him, and suddenly Marius becomes aware of the room. Glancing around, he realizes what it's been used for. He's disgusted. Then he catches a glimpse of the crooked wooden shelves through the door to the adjoining room. The sight makes him forget the girl, and he walks across to the threshold. Marius can't see how many there are, but there are more than he can count with the naked eye. Chestnut dolls, male and female. Animals too. Big and small, some childish, others eerie. Many of them unfinished and malformed. Marius stares at them, their number and variety, and the small dolls on the shelves fill him with disquiet, as the boy steps through the door behind him.

In a split second Marius realizes he should remember to ask Forensics whether the basement door was broken down from the inside or the outside. In a split second he realizes something monstrous may have escaped, like the animals from their pens, but when he turns toward the boy his thoughts swim away like tiny, puzzled clouds across the heavens. Then the axe strikes his jaw, and everything goes black.

Monday, October 5th.
The Present Day

2

The voice is everywhere in the darkness. It whispers softly and mocks her—it picks her up when she falls and it whirls her around in the wind. Laura Kjær can't see anymore. She can't hear the whistling of the leaves in the trees, or feel the cold grass beneath her feet. All that is left is the voice, which keeps whispering between the bludgeon's blows. If she stops resisting, she thinks, the voice might go quiet, but it doesn't. It keeps going, and so do the blows, until at last she can't move. Too late she feels the sharp teeth of the saw bite hard around one of her wrists, and before she loses consciousness she hears the mechanical noise of the saw blade and her own bones being severed.

Afterward, she doesn't know how long she's been gone. The darkness is still there. So is the voice, and it's as though it has been waiting for her return.

"Are you okay, Laura?"

Its tone is soft and affectionate and much too close to her ear. But the voice doesn't wait for an answer. For a moment it removes the thing that was stuck over her mouth, and Laura hears herself begging and pleading. She doesn't understand anything. She'll do anything. Why her—what has she done? The voice says she knows that perfectly well. It bends down very close and whispers into her ear, and she can tell it has been looking forward to exactly this moment. She has to concentrate to hear the words. She understands what the voice is saying, but she can't believe it. The pain is greater than all her other injuries. It can't be that. It *mustn't* be that. She pushes the words away, as though they're part of the madness that engulfs her in the blackness. She wants to stand up and keep fighting, but her body gives in, and she sobs hysterically. She's known it for a while, yet somehow not—and only now, as the voice whispers it to her, does she understand that it's true. She wants to scream as loudly as she can, but her guts are already halfway up her throat, and when she feels the bludgeon stroke her cheek she flings herself headlong with all her strength and staggers deeper into the gloom.

Tuesday, October 6th

3

It's beginning to grow light outside, but as Naia Thulin reaches down and guides him into her, he's only gradually emerging from sleep. She feels him inside and begins sliding backward and forward. She takes hold of his shoulders and his hands awaken, but slowly and fumblingly.

"Hey, wait . . ."

He's still drowsy, but Naia doesn't wait. This is what she wanted when she opened her eyes, and she moves more insistently, sliding backward with greater intensity, putting one hand against the wall. She is aware he's lying awkwardly, that his head is banging against the headboard, and she's aware of the sound of the headboard banging against the wall, but she doesn't care. She continues, feeling him give in, and as she comes she digs her nails into his chest and senses his pain and pleasure as they both stiffen.

A moment later she's lying there breathlessly, listening to the garbage truck in the courtyard behind her building. Then she rolls away and gets out of bed before his hands are finished stroking her back.

"It's best you go before she wakes up."

"Why? She likes it when I'm here."

"Come on. Get up."

"Only if you two move in with me."

She chucks his shirt at his head and vanishes into the bathroom, while he falls back onto the pillow with a smile.

4

It's the first Tuesday in October. Autumn came late, but today the sky above the city is a low ceiling of dark gray clouds, and it's pouring with rain as Naia Thulin dashes out of the car and through the street traffic. She can hear her mobile ringing, but she doesn't reach into her coat pocket for it. She has her hand on her daughter's back so she can hurry her through the small gaps in the rush-hour jam. The morning has been busy. Le was mostly interested in talking about the League of Legends computer game, which she's much too little to know anything about yet still knows *all* about, and she named a Korean professional gamer called Park Su as her big hero.

"You've got your rain boots, in case you're going to the park. And remember Granddad's picking you up, but you've got to cross the road yourself. You look left, right, then—"

"Then left again, and I've got to remember to put my jacket on, so they can see the reflective bits."

"Stand still so I can tie your shoelaces."

They've reached the front of the school, standing underneath the roof of the bike shed, and Thulin bends down as Le tries to stand still with her boots in the puddles.

"When are we moving in with Sebastian?"

"I haven't said we're moving in with Sebastian."

"Why isn't he there in the morning when he's there in the evening?"

"Grown-ups are busy in the morning, and Sebastian has to rush off to work."

"Ramazan's had a little brother and now he's got fifteen pictures on the family tree, and I've only got three."

Thulin glances curtly up at her daughter and curses the sweet little posters of the family trees, which the teacher decorated with autumn leaves and displayed on the classroom wall so that parents and children can stop and examine them. On the other hand she's always grateful when Le automatically counts Granddad as part of the family, even though technically speaking he isn't her grandfather.

"It's not about that. And you have five pictures on the family tree, if you count the parakeet and the hamster."

"The others don't have animals on their trees."

"No, the other children aren't that lucky."

Le doesn't answer, and Thulin stands up.

"I know there's not a lot of us, but we're doing all right, and that's the important thing. Okay?"

"Can I get another parakeet, then?"

Thulin gazes at her, wondering how this conversation started and whether her daughter might be sharper than she thinks.

"We'll discuss that another time. Just wait a bit."

Her mobile has begun to ring again, and she knows she has to answer it this time.

"I'll be there in fifteen minutes."

"No rush," says the voice on the other end of the line, and she recognizes it as one of Nylander's secretaries. "Nylander can't make your meeting this morning, so it'll be Tuesday next week instead. But I'm supposed to tell you he wants you to take the new guy with you today, so he'll be good for something while he's here."

"Mom, I'm going in with Ramazan!"

Thulin watches her daughter scamper over to the boy called Ramazan. She falls in quite naturally with the rest of the Syrian family, a woman and a man, the man with a newborn in his arms, and two other children. To Thulin they look like they've just stepped out of a women's magazine article about a model family.

"But that's the second time Nylander's canceled, and it'll only take five minutes. Where is he right now?"

"I'm afraid he's on his way to the budget meeting. And he'd like to know what your chat is going to be about?"

For a moment Thulin considers telling her that it's going to be about how her nine months at the Major Crimes Division, known as the murder squad, have been about as exciting as a visit to the police museum. That the assignments are tedious, the standards of technology at the department barely more impressive than a Commodore 64 computer, and that she's desperately looking forward to moving on.

"Nothing major. Thanks."

She hangs up and waves at her daughter, who is running into the school. She can feel the rain beginning to seep through her coat, and as she heads toward the road she realizes she can't wait until Tuesday for the meeting. She dodges through the traffic, but as she reaches the car and opens the door, she gets the sudden sensation that she's being watched. On the other side of the crossing, through the endless rows of cars and trucks, she glimpses the outline of a figure—but by the time the queue has passed the figure is gone. Shaking off the feeling, Thulin gets into her car.

5

The spacious corridors of the police station echo with the steps of the two men as they pass a pack of detectives going in the opposite direction. Nylander, head of the Major Crimes Division, loathes conversations like this one, but he knows it will probably be the only chance he'll get all day, so he swallows his pride and keeps pace with the deputy commissioner as one dull sentence follows another.

"Nylander, we need to tighten our belts. It's the same with all our departments."

"I was given to think I'd have more officers—"

"It's a question of timing. Right now the Ministry of Justice is prioritizing departments other than yours. They've got ambitions for NC3 to become the best cyber-crime unit in Europe, so they're cutting back on resources elsewhere."

"That doesn't mean my department should suffer. We've needed twice the manpower these last—"

"I've not given up, but you have just had some of the pressure taken off, you know."

"I haven't had any pressure taken off. A single investigator who'll be here a few days because Europol have chucked him out on his ass doesn't really count."

"He'll probably hang around a bit longer, depending on the situation. But the ministry could actually have *cut* the number of staff, you know, so right now it's about making the best of a bad job. All right?"

The deputy commissioner pauses, turning toward Nylander to emphasize his words, and Nylander is about to answer that no, it damn well isn't all right. He needs more manpower like he was promised, but instead he's been passed over in favor of the twats at NC3, to use the fancy-pants abbreviation for the National Cyber Crime Center. On top of that, it's a monumental bureaucratic slap in the face that he should have to make do with some washed-up detective who's fallen out of favor at the Hague.

"Do you have a moment?" Thulin has appeared in the background, and the deputy commissioner uses the interruption to slip through the meeting-room door and shut it behind him. Nylander stares briefly after him before starting to head back the way he came.

"Not now, and nor do you. Check with the duty officer about the report that's come in from Husum. I want you to take that Europol chap and get cracking."

"But it's about—"

"I don't have time for this conversation right now. I'm not blind to your abilities, but you're the youngest detective ever to set foot in this department, so I don't want you setting your sights on becoming team leader or whatever it is you're itching to meet about."

"I don't want to be team leader. I need a recommendation for NC3."

Nylander judders to a halt.

"NC3. The department for cyber crime—"

"Yeah, I *know* what department it is. Why?"

"Because I think the assignments at NC3 are interesting."

"As opposed to?"

"As opposed to nothing. I'd just like to—"

"You've basically only just started. NC3 doesn't take people who apply on the off chance, so there's no point trying."

"They've specifically asked me to apply."

Nylander tries to conceal his surprise, but he knows instantly she's telling the truth. He looks at the slight woman standing before him. How old is she? Twenty-nine, thirty, thereabouts? An odd little thing, not much to look at. He clearly remembers underestimating her—before he knew better. In his staff assessment he recently split his detectives into an A and a B team, and Thulin, despite her age, was one of the first names he put onto the A team alongside seasoned investigators like Jansen and Ricks, whom the department was supposed to consolidate around. And Nylander *did* actually consider her for team leader. He isn't overfond of female investigators, and her general air of aloofness rubs him the wrong way, but she's highly intelligent and has breezed through her cases at a pace that made more experienced detectives look like they were standing still. Thulin probably thinks the level of technology at the department is out of the Stone Age, and it's because he shares her opinion that he knows how much he needs tech geeks like her. The department has to keep up with the times. Hence why he's used a few of their conversations to remind her that she's still wet behind the ears: he's trying to make sure she doesn't do a runner.

"Who asked you?"

"The boss, what's-his-name. Isak Wenger."

Nylander feels his face darken.

"I've been happy here, but I'd like to send off my application by the end of the week at the latest."

"I'll think it over."

"Can we say Friday?"

Nylander has already stalked off. For a moment he senses her eyes on the back of his neck, and knows she'll be after him on Friday to get that recommendation. So it's come to this. His department has become a seed bed for the elite, for the ministry's new darling, NC3. When he goes into the budget meeting in a few minutes' time, that priority will be brought home to him once again in the form of figures and hard caps. Christmas will mark three years since Nylander accepted the top job in Homicide, but now things have come to a grinding halt, and if something doesn't change, the promotion won't be the career opportunity he once imagined.

6

The windshield wipers chuck the streaming water aside. When the traffic light changes to green, the police car swings out of the line—away from the bus-side ads for private hospitals offering new breasts, Botox, and liposuction—and sets off for the suburbs. The radio is on. The hosts, chatting and playing the latest pop songs about sex, ass, and lust, are briefly interrupted by the news, and the newscaster announces that today is the first Tuesday in October: the opening of parliament. The top story, unsurprisingly, is about Rosa Hartung, minister for social affairs, returning to her post after the tragic episode involving her daughter nearly one year earlier, which everybody across the nation followed with bated breath. But before the newscaster can finish, the stranger beside Thulin turns down the sound.

"Do you have a pair of scissors or anything?"

"No, I don't have any scissors."

For a moment Thulin lets her eyes flit from the traffic and toward the man sitting beside her, who is struggling to open the packaging on a new mobile phone. He was standing smoking a cigarette not far from the car when she arrived at the garage opposite the station. Tall, upright, yet somehow a little down at heel. Unkempt, rain-soaked hair, worn and sopping Nike shoes, thin, baggy pants, and a short black quilted jacket that also looked like it was thoroughly drenched. The man isn't dressed for the weather. *He must have come straight from the Hague*, thinks Thulin. The small, battered holdall at his side lends weight to that impression. Thulin knows he arrived at the station less than forty-eight hours ago, because she overheard colleagues gossiping about him as she fetched her morning coffee from the canteen. A "liaison officer" stationed at Europol's headquarters in the Hague, he'd been suddenly relieved of duty and ordered to Copenhagen as penance for some blunder or other. It prompted a few derisive remarks from her colleagues. The relationship between the Danish police and Europol had been strained ever since the Danes refused to relinquish one of their opt-outs from the EU in a referendum some years before.

When Thulin bumped into him in the parking garage he was lost in thought, and when she introduced herself he simply shook her hand and said, "Hess." Not especially chatty. Normally neither is she, but the conversation with Nylander went as planned. She feels certain her days at the department are coming to an end, so it can't hurt to show a bit of friendliness toward an embattled colleague. After they got into the car, she rattled through everything she knows about the assignment, but the man simply nodded with a minimum of interest. She puts him somewhere between thirty-seven and forty-one, and his shabby street-urchin look reminds her of an actor, but she can't think whom. He wears a ring on his finger, possibly a wedding band, but her instinct tells her the man is long divorced—or at least in the process thereof. Meeting him felt like kicking a ball against a concrete wall, but it hasn't spoiled her good mood, and her interest in transnational police cooperation is genuine.

"So how long are you home?"

"Probably just a few days. They're figuring it out."

"Do you like being at Europol?"

"Yeah, it's fine. Weather's better."

"Am I right in saying their cyber-crime unit has begun recruiting hackers they themselves have tracked down?"

"No idea, not my department. You mind if I duck out for a minute after we're done at the scene?"

"Duck out?"

"Just for an hour. I need to pick up the keys to my apartment."

"Of course."

"Thanks."

"But you're usually based at the Hague?"

"Yeah, or wherever they need me."

"Where might that be?"

"It varies. Marseille, Geneva, Amsterdam, Lisbon . . ."

The man is concentrating on his mobile phone packaging again, but Thulin guesses he could have kept listing cities for a while. There's something cosmopolitan about him. A kind of traveler without baggage, although the sheen of the big city and distant skies has long since rubbed off. If it was ever there.

"How long have you been gone?"

"Nearly five years. I'm just going to borrow that."

Hess snatches a ballpoint pen from the cup holder between the seats and begins to lever open the packaging.

"Five years?"

Thulin is surprised. Most liaison officers she's heard of are contracted for two years at a stretch. Some extend it to four, but she's never heard of a liaison officer being away for five.

"The time goes quickly."

"So it was because of the police reform."

"What was?"

"That you left. I heard lots of people left the department because they weren't happy with—"

"No, that wasn't why."

"What, then?"

"Because I just did."

She looks at him. He glances fleetingly back, and for the first time she notices his eyes. The left is green, the right blue. He didn't say it in an unfriendly way, but it's a line in the sand, and he doesn't comment further. Thulin puts on her blinker and turns off into a residential area. If he wants to play the macho agent with a mysterious past, so be it. There are enough guys like that at the station to form their own soccer team.

The house is a white, modernist home with its own garage. It's situated in the middle of a family neighborhood in Husum, among privet hedges and trim rows of mailboxes facing the road. This is where middle-income earners move once they've made the nuclear family a reality, and if their means stretch that far. A safe neighborhood, where sleeping policemen ensure nobody exceeds the thirty-mile-per-hour speed limit. Trampolines in the gardens and traces of chalk on the wet asphalt. A few schoolchildren wearing helmets and reflective jackets go cycling past in the rain as Thulin pulls up next to the patrol cars and Forensics vehicles. A few scattered residents stand murmuring under umbrellas a little way behind a barrier.

"I've just got to answer this." Less than two minutes ago, Hess stuffed a SIM card into his mobile and sent a text, and it's already buzzing.

"That's fine, take your time."

Thulin gets out into the rain while Hess remains sitting in the car and begins a conversation in French. As she jogs down the little garden path over its traditional concrete paving stones, it occurs to her that she might have found another reason to look forward to leaving the department.

7

The voices of the two morning TV hosts echo through the large, fashionable villa in Outer Østerbro as they prepare for another conversation over coffee on the studio's comfy corner sofa.

"So today parliament opens, and we're kicking off a new year. It's always a very special day, but this time it's *especially* special for a certain politician, and by that I mean Minister for Social Affairs Rosa Hartung, who lost her twelve-year-old daughter on October 18th last year. Rosa Hartung has been on leave since her daughter was—"

Steen Hartung reaches out and switches off the flat-screen, which hangs on the wall beside the fridge. He picks up his architectural drawings and writing implements from the wooden floor in the spacious

French-inspired country kitchen where he's just dropped them.

"Come on, get ready. We're setting off as soon as your mother's left."

His son is still sitting at the large table, scribbling in his math book, surrounded by the leftovers from breakfast. Every Tuesday morning Gustav is scheduled to meet in school an hour later than usual, and every Tuesday Steen has to tell him it's the wrong time to be doing homework.

"But why can't I go on my bike?"

"It's Tuesday; you've got tennis after school, so I'm picking you up. Have you packed your clothes?"

"I have."

The petite Filipina au pair comes into the room and puts down a sports bag, and Steen watches her gratefully as she starts clearing up.

"Thanks, Alice. Come on, Gustav."

"All the other kids cycle."

Through the window Steen sees the big black car roll up the driveway and park in the puddles outside.

"Dad, just for today?"

"No, we'll do the usual. The car's here. Where's your mom?"

8

Steen is on his way up the stairs to the first floor when he calls out to her. The hundred-year-old patrician villa is nearly four hundred square meters, and he knows every single nook and cranny, having renovated it himself. At the time they bought it and moved in, it was important to have plenty of space, but now it's too big. Much too big. He looks for her in the bedroom and the bathroom before realizing the door opposite him is ajar. Hesitating a moment, he pushes it open and peers into the room that was once his daughter's.

His wife is sitting in her coat and scarf on the bare mattress by the wall. His eyes dart around the room. Across the empty walls and the cardboard boxes stacked in the corner. Then back at her.

"The car's here."

"Thanks . . ."

She nods quickly, still seated. Steen takes another step forward and feels the chill in the room. He notices she's kneading a yellow T-shirt between her hands.

"Are you okay?"

It's a stupid question—she doesn't look okay.

"I opened the window yesterday then forgot to close it, and I only just realized."

He nods sympathetically, although her words didn't answer the question. From far down the hall they can hear their son shouting that Vogel has arrived, but neither reacts.

"I can't remember what she smelled like anymore."

Her hands caress the yellow fabric, and she looks at it as though searching for something hidden in its woven threads.

"I just had to try. But her scent isn't there. Or in any of the other stuff."

He sits down next to her.

"Maybe that's okay. Maybe it's better this way."

"How could it be better . . . it's *not* better."

He doesn't reply, and he can tell she regrets snapping at him when her voice grows gentler.

"I don't know if I can do this . . . it seems wrong."

"It's not wrong. It's the only right thing to do. You told me that yourself."

Their son calls again.

"She would have told you to go. She would have told you it would all work out. She would have told you you're amazing."

Rosa doesn't answer. For a moment she just sits there with the T-shirt. Then she takes his hand and squeezes it and attempts a smile.

"Okay, great, see you soon." Rosa Hartung's personal advisor hangs up his phone as he sees her coming down the stairs toward the hall.

"Did I get here too early? Should I ask the royal family to postpone the opening until tomorrow?"

"No, I'm ready now."

Rosa smiles at Frederik Vogel's energy, thinking it makes a nice change. When Vogel's around, there's no room for sentimentality.

"Good. Let's run through the program. We've had a lot of questions come in—some of them good, some of them predictable and tabloid-esque—"

"We'll do that in the car. Gustav, remember it's Tuesday and Dad is picking you up. And call if you need anything. All right, love?"

"I know that."

The boy nods wearily, and Rosa barely has time to ruffle his hair before Vogel opens the door for her.

"You've also got to say hello to the new driver, and we really need to discuss how we're going to order these negotiations . . ."

Steen watches them through the window in the kitchen, trying to smile encouragingly at his wife as she greets the new driver and climbs into the back of the car. As they leave the driveway, Steen feels relieved.

"Are we going or what?"

His son is asking, and Steen can hear him putting on his coat and boots in the hall.

"Yeah, I'm coming now."

Steen opens the fridge, takes out the pack of small liquor bottles, unscrews the cap from one, and empties it into his mouth. He feels the spirits rake their way down his gullet and into his belly. Then he puts the remaining bottles in his bag, shuts the fridge, and remembers to grab the car keys, which are lying on the kitchen table.

9

There's something about the house Thulin doesn't like. The feeling began to set in as she stepped, clad in gloves and blue plastic overshoes, into the dark front hall, where the family's footwear is neatly arrayed beneath the coatrack. Delicate framed pictures of flowers hang on the walls in the corridor, and when she enters the bedroom the room strikes her immediately as feminine and innocent, everything in shades of white apart from the pink pleated blinds, which are still drawn down.

"The victim's name is Laura Kjær, thirty-seven years old, nurse at a dental practice in central Copenhagen. Looks like she was surprised after she went to bed. Her nine-year-old boy was sleeping in the room at the end of the hall, but apparently he didn't see or hear anything."

Thulin is staring at the double bed, which has only been used on one side, as she's briefed by the older, uniformed officer. A bedside lamp has toppled off the nightstand and lies cushioned on the thick white carpet.

"The boy woke up to find the house empty, nobody around. He made breakfast for himself, got dressed, and waited for his mother, but when she didn't show up he went to the neighbor's. The neighbor went back to the house, found it empty, then heard a dog barking out in the play area, where she subsequently found the victim and called us."

"Has the father been contacted?"

Thulin walks past the officer, glancing briefly into the child's room before returning down the corridor, the officer in her wake.

"According to the neighbor, the father died of cancer a couple of years ago. The victim met someone new six months later, and they moved in here together. Guy's at a trade fair somewhere in Zealand. We called him when we arrived, so he should be here soon."

Through the open bathroom door, Thulin can see three electric toothbrushes in a row, a pair of slippers ready on the tiled floor, and two dressing gowns hanging from pegs. She leaves the corridor and enters the open-plan kitchen, where white-clad Forensics techs are busy checking for trace evidence and fingerprints. The furnishings are as ordinary as the neighborhood. Scandinavian design, probably mostly from IKEA and ILVA, three empty place mats on the table, a little autumn bouquet of decorative sprigs in a vase, cushions on the sofa, and on the kitchen island a single deep bowl containing the remains of milk and cornflakes, which she guesses must be the boy's. In the living room is a digital photo frame displaying a constant flow of images of the little family to the empty armchair next to it. Mother, son, and presumably the live-in boyfriend. They're smiling and looking happy. Laura Kjær is a beautiful, slender woman with long red hair, but there's a vulnerability in her warm, sympathetic eyes. It's a nice home, yet there's definitely something about it Thulin doesn't like.

"Signs of forced entry?"

"No. We've checked the windows and doors. Looks like she watched TV and drank a cup of tea before she went to bed."

Thulin skims the kitchen noticeboard, but all that hang there are school timetables, calendars, the schedule for the local pool, a tree surgeon's flyer, an invitation to the residents' association's Halloween party, and a reminder letter about a checkup at the Rigshospital's pediatric department. Normally, this is where Thulin excels: at noticing the little things that prove significant. Once upon a time she was used to it. Used to coming home, unlocking the front door, and reading the signs that augured whether it would be a good day or a bad day. But in this case there's nothing to notice. Just an ordinary family and their idyllic day-to-day life. The kind of thing she'll never be able to accept, and for a moment she tries to tell herself that maybe *that's* all she dislikes about the house.

"What about computers, tablets, mobiles?"

"As far as we can see, nothing's been stolen, and Genz's people have already packed up the gizmos and sent them in."

Thulin nods. Most assaults and murders can be cleared up that way. As a rule there are always texts, calls, emails, or Facebook messages to indicate why things ended as they did, and she's already itching to get her hands on the material.

"What's that smell in here? Vomit?"

Thulin has suddenly become aware of the harsh, unpleasant stench following her around the house. The older officer looks shamefaced, and Thulin registers that he's pale.

"I'm sorry. I've just come from the scene. I thought I was used to . . . but I'll show you the way."

"I'll manage. Just let me know when the boyfriend shows up."

She opens the terrace door to the back garden while the officer nods gratefully.

10

The trampoline has seen better days, as has the tiny overgrown greenhouse to the left of the terrace door. To the right, the wet grass extends to the rear wall of a shiny metal garage; although immensely practical, it doesn't really suit the white, modernist house. Thulin walks toward the far end of the garden. On the other side of the hedge she can see floodlights, uniformed officers and white-clad Forensics techs, and she edges through the trees and bushes with their fire-red and yellow leaves until she reaches a playground. A bulb flashes repeatedly in the rain near a battered playhouse, and from a distance she sees Genz animatedly photographing details of the crime scene while he directs his team.

"Got anywhere?"

Simon Genz glances up from his camera's view-finder. His face is serious, but when he sees her it lightens into a brief grin. Genz is probably in his midthirties, and an active guy: rumor has it he's run five marathons this year alone. He's also the youngest boss the Forensics Department has ever had. Thulin considers him one of the few people worth listening to. Sharp, nerdy—and quite simply she trusts his judgment. If she keeps him at arm's length, it's only because he asked her whether she wanted to go on a run together one day, and she didn't. During the nine months Thulin has been with the murder squad, Genz is the only person with whom she's developed any sort of relationship, but the least sexy thing she can imagine is a romance with a colleague.

"Hi, Thulin. Not far. The rain makes things tricky, and it's been quite a few hours since it happened."

"Have they said anything about a time of death?"

"Not yet. The coroner's just around the corner. But the rain started about midnight, and my guess is that's roughly when it happened. If there were obvious tracks in the soil, they've been thoroughly washed away, but we're not giving up. Do you want to see her?"

"Yes, please."

The lifeless figure on the grass has been covered with a white sheet from the Forensics Department.

It's leaning against one of two poles supporting the roof above the playhouse's front porch, and the scene looks almost peaceful: in the background, red-and-yellow climbing plants are exploding with color in the dense shrubbery. Carefully Genz draws back the white sheet to reveal the woman. She's slumped like a rag doll, naked apart from underpants and a camisole that was once beige but is now soaked with rain and blotches of dark blood. Thulin steps closer, squatting down to get a better look. Laura Kjær has black gaffer tape wrapped all the way around her head. Cutting into her rigid, open mouth, it has been wound several times around the back of her skull and wet red hair. One eye has been caved in, so that you can see deep into the socket, while the other stares blindly into space. Her bluish skin is marred with countless scratches, tears, and bruises, and her bare feet have been scraped bloody. Her hands are buried in a little heap of leaves in her lap, bound tightly at the wrists with broad plastic strips. Thulin needs only a single glance at the body to understand why the older officer cracked. Usually she has no problem with examining dead people. Working in Homicide demands an unsentimental approach to death, and anyone who can't examine a corpse is better off elsewhere. But Thulin has never seen anyone as brutalized as the woman leaning against the playhouse pole.

"You'll hear it from the coroner, of course, but in my opinion some of the injuries suggest that she tried to run off among the trees at some point. Either away from the house or back to it. But it was pitch-black, and she must have been badly weakened after the amputation, which I'm certain was done before she was arranged like this."

"The amputation?"

"Hold this."

Genz absentmindedly hands her the heavy camera and flash. Approaching the body, he crouches down on his haunches and gently uses his flashlight to lift the woman's bound wrists a fraction. Rigor mortis has set in, and her stiff arms mechanically follow: Thulin can see now that Laura Kjær is missing her right hand. It isn't buried in the leaves, as she supposed. The arm stops grotesquely just beneath the wrist, where a slanting, jagged cut exposes the bone and sinews.

"For the time being we're assuming it must have happened out here, because we didn't find a drop of blood in the garage or the house. I've asked my people to check the garage thoroughly, of course, especially for tape, gardening tools, and cable ties, but so far we've come up with nothing obvious. Needless to say we're also wondering why we haven't found the hand yet, but we're still looking."

"Could be a dog ran off with it."

Hess's voice; he has emerged from the garden and the hedge. He glances around briefly, his shoulders giving a shudder in the rain, and Genz gazes at him in surprise. For some reason the remark irritates Thulin, although she knows he might be right.

"Genz, this is Hess—he's joining us for a few days."

"Good morning. Welcome." Genz moves to shake hands with Hess, but Hess merely nods toward the house next door.

"Anybody hear anything? Neighbors?"

There's a thunderous clatter, and a train abruptly shoots along its wet tracks on the other side of the playground, so Genz has to shout his reply.

"No, as far as we know nobody heard anything! The S-trains don't run as frequently at night, but on the other hand there are quite a few freight trains on this line!"

The sound of the train vanishes, and Genz looks at Thulin again.

"I wish I had loads of evidence for you, but right now there's nothing else I can say. Only that I've never seen anyone this savagely beaten before."

"What's that?"

"What?"

"There."

Thulin is still squatting beside the body, but now she's pointing at something Genz has to twist around to see. Behind the dead woman, from the beam above the playhouse porch, there's something dangling in the wind, something caught in its own string. Genz reaches a hand underneath the beam and unwinds the object so that it hangs freely, swinging back and forth. Two dark brown chestnuts placed on top of each other, the top one small and the bottom one large. Two holes have been scratched into the smaller chestnut to make eyes. Matchsticks have been poked into the larger one, representing arms and legs. It's a simple doll consisting of two spheres and four sticks, but briefly, for some reason she can't explain, it makes Thulin's heart stop.

"A chestnut man. Shall we bring him in for questioning?"

Hess is gazing at her innocently. Evidently cop humor of the classic style is favored at Europol too, and Thulin doesn't reply. She and Genz only have time to exchange a glance before Genz is interrupted with a question by one of his people. Hess reaches into his jacket for his phone, which has begun to ring again, and at that moment there's a whistle from the house. It's the officer from before, signaling to Thulin from the garden. She gets to her feet and casts her eyes across the playground, which is surrounded by bronze-leafed trees, but there's nothing else to see. Only wet swing sets and climbing frames and a parkour course, desolate and sad despite the army of officers and techs wading around in the rain as they search the area. Thulin returns to the house. When she passes Hess, he's speaking French again, as yet another train goes rumbling by.

11

On their way into the city center in the ministerial car, Vogel runs through the day's schedule. All the government ministers are meeting at Christiansborg before heading around the corner to the Palace Chapel for the traditional service. Once that's over, Rosa will be greeting her staff at her offices, which are located on Holmens Kanal opposite Christiansborg Palace Square, and then rushing back over to Christiansborg in time for the official opening of parliament.

The rest of the day is also tightly scheduled, but Rosa interjects a few corrections and updates the calendar on her iPhone. She doesn't need to, because her secretary keeps track of everything on her behalf, but Rosa prefers it like this. It helps her get a sense of the details, to keep a grip on reality and feel like she's in control.

Especially today. But by the time the car swings into the courtyard outside parliament, she's no longer listening to Vogel. Danish flags wave from the central spire, and there are media vans all over the courtyard; she watches people getting ready or recording pieces on camera underneath umbrellas, lit by their photographers.

"Asger, we'll keep driving, head around to the back entrance."

The new driver nods at Vogel's words, but Rosa doesn't like the suggestion.

"No. Let me out here."

Vogel turns toward her in surprise, and the driver glances at her in the rearview mirror. Only now does she notice that despite his young age there are grave lines drawn around his mouth.

"If I don't do it now, they'll keep at it all day long. Drive right up to the entrance and let me out there."

"Rosa, are you sure?"

"I'm sure."

The car glides up to the curb, and the driver jumps out and opens the door for her. As she climbs out and begins walking toward the broad steps of the parliament building, everything seems to move in slow motion: cameramen turning, journalists beginning to stampede her way, faces with mouths open and words twisted.

"Rosa Hartung, a moment!"

Reality strikes her. The crowd around her explodes, cameras are thrust into her face, and the journalists' questions come hailing down. Rosa makes it up two steps before turning to gaze out over the crowd, noting everything. The voices, the lights and microphones, a blue hat drawn down over a furrowed brow, an arm waving, a pair of dark eyes trying to follow along from the back row.

"Hartung, do you have a statement?"

"What's it like to be back?"

"Could you just give us two minutes?"

"Rosa Hartung, over here!"

Rosa knows she has been a topic of discussion at various editorial meetings over the last few months—the last few days, especially—but nobody saw this move coming: they are unprepared, and that's why Rosa has done it.

"Move back! The minister has a statement."

Vogel has elbowed his way in front of her, making sure the crowd keeps its distance. Most do as they're told, and Rosa studies their faces. Many she already knows.

"As you're all aware, this has been a difficult time. My family and I are grateful for all the support we have been given. We're at the start of a new parliamentary year, and it's time now to look to the future. I want to thank the prime minister for his faith in me, and I'm looking forward to getting stuck into the political tasks ahead. I hope you will all respect that. Thank you."

Rosa Hartung continues walking up the steps after Vogel, who tries to clear a path.

"But, Hartung, are you ready to come back?"

"How are you feeling!?"

"What's it like to know the killer never revealed the location where your daughter—"

Vogel manages to get her up to the big doors, and when they reach her secretary—waiting on the threshold, stretching out a hand—it's like being rescued ashore from a foaming sea.

12

"As you can see, we've made a few adjustments to the layout because of the new sofas, but if you'd rather have the others back—"

"No, this is fine. I like that it's new."

Rosa has just stepped into her office on the fourth floor of the Ministry for Social Affairs. Arriving at Christiansborg and at the church service she bumped into many of her colleagues, and it feels nice to get some distance from all the attention. Some gave her a hug, others nodded kindly and with compassion, and she tried to keep moving—except at the service, when she did her best to focus on the bishop's sermon. Afterward, Vogel stayed behind to speak to various MPs; she was met by her ministerial secretary and a few assistants, and together they crossed the palace square and entered the large gray-brown building that housed the Ministry for Social Affairs. Vogel's absence suits her just fine; now she can concentrate on greeting her staff and chatting to her ministerial secretary.

"I don't know how to put this, so I'm just going to ask straight out. How are you doing?"

Rosa knows her secretary well enough to understand that she has her best interests at heart. Liu is of Chinese heritage, married to a Dane, mother of two, and one of the kindest people Rosa knows, but she still feels compelled to dodge such a personal question.

"It's all right to ask. I'm doing well, given the circumstances, and now I'm looking forward to getting started. What about you?"

"Oh yes, all fine. The younger one has colic. And the older . . . but it's all fine."

"That wall looks a bit bare, doesn't it?"

As Rosa points, she senses Liu straining not to put her foot in her mouth.

"Well, that's where the pictures were. But I think you should make up your own mind. There were some of—of all of you together—and I wasn't sure whether you'd want to put them up again."

Rosa looks down at the box beside the wall and recognizes the corner of a photograph with Kristine.

"I'll see about that later. Tell me how much time I have for meetings today."

"Not much. You'll greet the staff in a moment, then there's the official opening with the prime minister's speech, and afterward—"

"That's fine, but I'd like to get the meetings underway today. Nothing major, just between sessions, quite unofficial. I tried emailing a few people on my way in, but the system was down."

"It still is, I'm afraid."

"Okay, then send Engells in so I can start explaining who I want to talk to."

"Engells is out running an errand at the moment, unfortunately."

"Now?"

Rosa looks at her, and all of a sudden it hits her there must be another reason for her secretary's uncertainty and nerves. The chief of staff would normally be ready and waiting for her on a day like today, and the fact that he isn't suddenly seems ominous.

"Yes. He had to go because . . . but he can tell you himself when he gets back."

"Back from what? What's going on?"

"I don't know exactly. And I'm sure it will all be sorted out, but as I said—"

"Liu, what's happening?"

The ministerial secretary hesitates, looking deeply unhappy.

"I'm really sorry. We've had so many lovely emails from people supporting you and wishing you well, and I don't understand how anybody could send something like that."

"Send what?"

"I haven't seen it myself. But I believe it's a threat. From what Engells told me, it was something about your daughter."

13

"But I spoke to her last night . . . I ate, and then I called home, and there was nothing out of the ordinary."

Laura Kjær's forty-three-year-old partner, Hans Henrik Hauge, is sitting on a chair in the kitchen, still in his damp overcoat and clutching his car keys in his hand. His eyes are red and puffy, and he's staring through the window in confusion at the white-clad figures in the garden and down by the hedge before he looks back at Thulin.

"How did it happen?"

"We don't know that yet. What did you talk about on the phone?"

There's a clatter, and Thulin shoots a sidelong glance at the man from Europol, who's wandering around opening drawers and cupboards. She's discovered he has the power to exasperate her even when he isn't talking.

"Nothing special. What did Magnus say? I'd like to see him."

"In a moment. Did she say anything that made you wonder, or was she anxious, or—"

"No. We just talked about Magnus, and then she said she was going to bed because she was tired."

Hans Henrik Hauge's voice is cracking. He's tall, powerfully built, and well dressed, but he also seems like a soft man, and Thulin thinks it might be difficult to get through the interview if she doesn't pick up the pace.

"Tell me how long you've known each other."

"Eighteen months."

"Were you married?"

Thulin's eyes are on Hauge's hands, where he's begun to fiddle with a ring.

"Engaged. I'd given her a ring. We were going to go to Thailand and get married in the winter."

"Why Thailand?"

"We'd both been married before. So we decided this one should be different."

"Which hand did she wear her ring on?"

"What?"

"The ring. Which hand did she wear it on?"

"The right one, I think. Why?"

"I'm just asking questions, but it's important that you answer them. Tell me where you were yesterday."

"Roskilde. I'm an IT developer. I drove down there yesterday morning, and I was only supposed to be at the fair until this afternoon."

"So you were with someone last night?"

"Yes, with my boss. Well, I drove to the motel about nine or ten. That was where I called her from."

"Why didn't you just drive home?"

"Because the company had asked us to stay the night. We had early-morning meetings."

"How were things between you and Laura? Were you having any problems, or—"

"No. Things were great. What are they doing in the garage?"

Hauge's tearstained gaze has strayed back out through the window, this time toward the rear of the garage, where a couple of Forensics techs are standing by the door.

"They're looking for evidence, if there is any. Can you think of anyone who would have wanted to harm Laura?"

Hauge looks at her, but it's as though he's somewhere else entirely.

"Perhaps there was something you didn't know about her? Could she have been seeing another man?"

"No, no way. Now I'd like to see Magnus. He needs his medication."

"What's wrong with him?"

"We don't know. I mean . . . he's been treated at the Rigshospital, and they think he's got some form of autism. They gave him something for anxiety. Magnus's a good boy, but he's very withdrawn, and he's only nine . . ."

Hans Henrik Hauge's voice cracks again. Thulin is about to ask another question, but Hess beats her to the punch.

"Things were good, you said? No problems?"

"That's what I already *said*. Where's Magnus? I want to see him now."

"Why did you get the lock changed?"

The question comes out of the blue, and Thulin stares at Hess. He asked innocently, almost offhandedly, as he held up something from a kitchen drawer. A slip of paper with two shiny keys stuck to it.

Hauge gapes blankly at him and the piece of paper.

"This is a receipt from a locksmith. It says the lock was changed on October 5th at three thirty p.m. That's yesterday afternoon. In other words, after you'd gone to the trade fair."

"I don't know. Magnus had thrown his keys away a few times, so we'd talked about it. But I didn't know Laura had done it . . ."

Thulin stands up to look at the receipt, taking it from Hess's hand. She would have found it later when she searched the house, but she decides to use the momentum despite her irritation.

"You didn't know Laura had had the lock changed?"

"No."

"She didn't mention it when you spoke on the phone?"

"No . . . I mean, no, I don't think so."

"Could there be another reason why she didn't tell you?"

"She was probably just going to tell me later. Why does it matter?"

Thulin looks at him without answering. Hans Henrik Hauge stares back with wide, uncomprehending eyes. Then he jerks to his feet and the chair flips onto the ground.

"You can't just keep me here. I have a right to see Magnus. I want to see him now!"

Thulin hesitates, then nods to an officer waiting in the background by the door.

"Afterward, you'll have to be swabbed and finger-printed. That's important, so we can distinguish between the prints that are supposed to be here and those that aren't. Do you understand?"

Hauge nods distractedly and disappears with the officer. Hess has taken off his latex gloves, zipped up his jacket, and picked up the little holdall, which he'd set down on a piece of plastic in the hallway.

"See you at the coroner's office. Probably a good idea to check that guy's alibi."

"Thanks, I'll try to remember that."

Hess nods, unfazed, and leaves the kitchen as another officer steps inside.

"Will you speak to the boy now? He's at the neighbor's; you can see him from the window."

Thulin walks across to the window that overlooks the neighbor's house and peers through the patchy hedge into a conservatory. The boy is sitting on a chair by a white table, playing on something that looks like a gaming console. She can only see him in profile, but it's enough to grasp that there's something mechanical and vacant about his face and movements.

"He doesn't say much, seems a bit backward, really. Talks almost entirely in one-syllable words."

Thulin is observing the boy as she listens to the officer, and for a moment she recognizes herself and the yawning loneliness she knows the boy will feel today and for many years to come. But then he disappears behind an older woman, presumably the neighbor, who enters the conservatory followed by Hans Henrik Hauge. Hauge begins sobbing at the sight of the boy; he squats down and puts his arm around him while the boy continues to sit bolt upright with his hands on the console.

"Shall I fetch him?"

The officer is looking impatiently at Thulin.

"I asked—"

"No, give them a moment. But keep an eye on the boyfriend and find someone to check his alibi."

Thulin turns away from the window. She hopes the case is as straightforward as it seems. For a moment the image of the little chestnut doll from the playhouse flickers across her mind's eye. NC3 can't come fast enough.

14

The panoramic windows at the architectural firm offer an expansive view across the city. The desks are arranged in small islands throughout the large skylit room, but it looks as though the place is capsizing, since most of the employees have converged around the flat-screen TV hanging from the ceiling on one side of the space. The drawings in his arms, Steen Hartung walks up the stairs as the screen, tuned to the news, finishes playing the clip of his wife arriving at Christiansborg. Most of his employees notice his presence and hurriedly pretend to be hard at work as he makes for his office. Only his partner, Bjarke, looks at him and beams an embarrassed smile.

"Hey there, do you have a second?"

They go into Steen's office, and Bjarke shuts the door.

"She's dealing with it brilliantly, I think."

"Thanks. Have you spoken to the client?"

"Yes, they're happy."

"Then why haven't we sealed the deal?"

"Because they're playing it very safe. They want more drawings, but I told them you need more time."

"More drawings?"

"How's it going at home?"

"I can get them done quickly, that's not a problem."

Steen clears his drafting table to make space for the brochures, his frustration escalating as his partner continues to stand and stare.

"Steen, you're pushing yourself too hard. We'd all understand if you took your foot off the pedal and gave yourself a bit of time. Let the others take the strain. I mean, that's the whole point of hiring them."

"Just tell the client I'll clarify the proposal in a few days. We need to land this order."

"But it's not what matters most. Steen, I'm worried about you. I still think—"

"This is Steen Hartung."

Steen picked up his phone at the very first ring. The voice on the other end introduces itself as his lawyer's secretary, and Steen turns his back to his partner, hoping he'll take the hint.

"Now's convenient. What's it about?" In the reflection in the large pane of glass, Steen sees his partner plod out of the office as the voice on the line continues speaking.

"Just following up on the information you've already been given, and you certainly don't need to answer now. There may be many good reasons to wait, but now the anniversary of the incident is coming up, we just want to remind you that you're entitled to start proceedings toward having her declared dead."

For some reason this isn't what Steen Hartung was expecting to hear. He feels a wave of nausea, and for a moment he's unable to move, caught staring at his face in the rain-spattered window.

"As you know, there are steps we can take in cases where the missing person hasn't been found but there's no doubt about the outcome. Of course, it's up to you whether you want to draw a line under it now. We're just letting you know so you can discuss it with—"

"We want to."

The voice on the line falls silent a moment.

"As I said, this isn't something you need to—"

"If you care to send me the papers, I'll sign them and tell my wife about it myself. Thanks."

He puts down the phone. Two damp pigeons are mincing around on the cornice outside the window. He looks at them without seeing them, and when he stirs the pigeons rise and flap away.

Steen takes a bottle out of his bag and pours it into his coffee cup before getting down to work on the brochures. His hands shake, and he has to use them both when he takes out his gauge. He knows it's the right decision, and he wishes he could get it done and dusted straightaway. It's a small thing, but important. Mustn't let the dead overshadow the living. That's what they said, the psychologists and the therapists, and every single fiber in his body is telling him they're right.

15

"It arrived for you early this morning, sent to your official parliamentary email address. Intelligence are trying to trace the sender, and I'm sure they'll get there, but it may take some time. I'm really very sorry," says Engells gently.

When Rosa returned to her office after greeting her staff, she found Engells waiting for her. Now, as she stands by the window behind her desk, she's aware that her chief of staff is watching her with the sympathetic gaze she finds unbearable.

"I've had hate mail before. It's usually from sad people who can't help themselves."

"This is different. More spiteful. They've used images from your daughter's Facebook page, which was deleted more than a year ago, when she . . . when she went missing. That means it's from someone who's been interested in you for a long time."

The information shakes Rosa, but she's determined to suppress the shock.

"I'd like to see it."

"It's been handed over to Intelligence and the Security lot, and they're currently—"

"Engells, you never do anything without making about seven copies. I'd like to see it."

Engells looks at her dubiously, but then opens the folder he brought with him when he arrived and draws out a sheet of paper, placing it on the table. She picks up the sheet. At first Rosa can make nothing of the tiny, colorful fragments scattered clumsily across the page. But then she understands. She recognizes the selfies Kristine took: lying on the floor of the sports hall, laughing and sweaty in her handball clothes; on the way to the beach on her new mountain bike; during a snowball fight with Gustav in their garden; dressed up in front of the bathroom mirror, pretending to be a model. So many photographs, smiling and happy. Rosa feels a surge of loss and grief, until her eyes fall on the sentence directed at her. *"Welcome back. You're going to die, slut."* The words are arranged above the images in an arc of red lettering, and the message seems all the more malevolent because it's written in an uncertain, childish hand.

When Rosa speaks again, she struggles to sound normal. "It's not the first nutter we've seen. Usually it's no big deal."

"No, but this . . ."

"I won't let myself be intimidated. I'll do my job and Intelligence can do theirs."

"We all think you should put in a request for body-guards. They can protect you, if—"

"No, no bodyguards."

"Why not?"

"Because I don't believe there's any need. The message is an end in itself. It was written by some sad sack who wants to stay hidden behind a screen, and anyway, we could really do without that at home right now."

Engells looks at her in mild astonishment, the way he always does on the rare occasions when she mentions her private life.

"We need things to be normal if we want to move on."

The chief of staff is about to say something, and Rosa can see he doesn't agree.

"Engells, I appreciate your concern, but if there's nothing else I'd like to head into the chamber for the prime minister's opening speech."

"Of course. I'll pass on your instructions."

Rosa walks over to the door, where Liu is waiting. Engells watches her leave, and Rosa senses he will remain standing there long after she has gone.

16

The long rectangular building with its adjoining chapel is situated on the traffic-choked artery between the districts of Nørrebro and Østerbro. Not far from the entrance the city is full of life, teeming with cars and busy pedestrians, and only a stone's throw away, happy voices can be heard from the playgrounds and skate parks on the Common—yet in the oblong building with its four sterile autopsy rooms and basement cold stores it's impossible not to be reminded of death and the ephemerality of all things. There is a sense of unreality about the place. Thulin has been to the Department of Forensic Medicine plenty of times, but she's never gotten used to it, and she always looks forward to reemerging through the swing doors at the end of the much-too-long corridor she's walking down now. She has just watched the coroner examine Laura Kjær's body, and she's trying to get hold of Genz. His voicemail begins to repeat its automatic invitation to leave a message, but Thulin cuts it short and tries again impatiently. Genz promised her the preliminary transcripts of Laura Kjær's email correspondence as well as her texts and call history by three p.m., but it's now half past and still she's heard nothing. Normally you can set your watch by him, and Thulin has never known him to fail to deliver on time. Nor, in fact, has he ever not answered his phone when she wants to speak to him.

The examination of the body brought no crucial new evidence to light. Their guest from Europol, or wherever he now calls home, did not—of course—turn up as agreed, and Thulin didn't bother to wait more than half a second. She simply asked the coroner to start. The earthly remains of Laura Kjær lay on the autopsy slab while the coroner scrolled through his notes on a screen and chatted about his unusually busy day. There had been several traffic accidents, he informed her, presumably due to the heavy rain. Anyway, he continued, starting systematically, her stomach contents revealed an evening meal of squash soup and chicken-and-broccoli salad, possibly washed down with a cup of tea—although that may have been ingested slightly earlier. Thulin asked him impatiently to fast-forward to the useful bit. The coroner always reacted testily to that sort of request—"Thulin, that's like asking Per Kirkeby to explain his paintings!"—but she insisted. The day hadn't yet brought her the answers she was hoping for, and while the coroner read aloud from his notes she heard the rain beat against the roof as though drumming down onto a coffin.

"There are a number of puncture wounds and lacerations, and she has been struck up to fifty or sixty times with a bludgeon made of steel or aluminum. What kind of bludgeon I can't say, but judging by the marks it's fitted with a ball the size of a fist, which is densely studded with small spikes approximately two or three millimeters in length."

"Like a mace?"

"In principle, yes, but it's *not* a mace. I've been wondering whether it might be a tool used for gardening, but I haven't got anywhere with that. The cable ties around her wrists left her unable to defend herself. She also fell repeatedly onto the ground, which caused additional injuries."

Thulin knew most of that already, after the morning's conversation with Genz: she was more interested in whether there was any evidence pointing to the boyfriend, Hans Henrik Hauge.

"Yes and no," came the infuriating answer. "So far my examination has revealed his DNA on her underpants, camisole, and body, but no more of it than one might expect if she'd been sleeping in the double bed they shared."

"Raped?"

But the coroner dismissed that possibility—so much for a sexual motive. "Unless one takes the view that there's some sexual urge behind sadistic punishment." Thulin asked him to expand on that remark, and the coroner pointed out that Laura Kjær had been tortured.

"He must have seen that she was in pain as he was inflicting it. If he'd merely wanted to kill her, he could have done so very quickly. She would have lost consciousness several times during the attack, and my guess is that she was assaulted for roughly twenty minutes before the blow to the eye, which was the proximate cause of death."

Nor did the wound left by the missing right hand, which had still not been found, offer any new evidence. The coroner couldn't say what kind of tool had been used to amputate it, but it prompted him to muse that amputations were most often seen among biker gangs—although as a general rule they stuck to individual fingers, collected in lieu of money owed, and their instruments of choice were usually meat shears, samurai swords, or the like. He couldn't confirm whether that was the case here.

"Hedge clippers? Shears?" Thulin asked, thinking of the tools in the garage at Husum.

"No, it was definitely some kind of saw. Possibly a circular saw or a plunge saw. Most likely battery-powered, given that the killer was sawing freehand in the middle of a playground. On the face of it I'd say a diamond blade or similar."

"A diamond blade?"

"There are various types of saw blade, depending on what they're used for. Diamond ones are the most robust. Typically they're used for cutting tiles, concrete, or brick, and can be purchased at most DIY stores. This cut was made quickly. On the other hand, the blade was evidently coarse-toothed, because the laceration was jagged and more haphazard than we'd see with a fine-toothed blade. Either way, the amputation would have weakened her considerably."

So Laura Kjær had been alive during the amputation: the idea was so unpleasant that Thulin barely heard the next few sentences, and had to ask the coroner to repeat them. Judging by her other injuries, Laura Kjær had then tried to flee again, woozy and increasingly incapacitated by loss of blood, until she'd apparently become so weak the killer was able to take her to the execution site outside the playhouse without a fight. For a moment Thulin pictured the woman running through the pitch-dark, her pursuer at her heels, and into her mind's eye popped a scene she'd witnessed one summer as a child: a headless chicken darting panic-stricken around a friend's farmyard. Forcing the image aside, Thulin asked about the victim's nails, mouth, and skin abrasions, but besides the injuries the coroner had already mentioned there was no evidence of physical contact with the killer. He did, however, point out that the rain might have had something to do with that.

Thulin gets Genz's voicemail for the third time as she reaches the swing door. This time she leaves a terse message, making it clear that Genz should call back as soon as possible. The rain is still bucketing down outside, and as Thulin shrugs on her coat she decides it would be best to drive back to the station while she waits. By now they have confirmed that Hans Henrik Hauge left the trade fair the previous evening around nine thirty p.m. in his car, after having drunk a glass of white wine with one of his bosses and two colleagues from Jutland while they discussed a new firewall. After that, however, Hauge's alibi is shaky. He indeed checked into the motel, but nobody could say for sure whether his black Mazda6 was parked there all night. He could, in theory at least, have driven to the house in Husum and back, but as yet they don't have enough evidence to justify investigating Hauge and his car more thoroughly—hence why she needs Genz and the results of his forensic tests promptly.

"Sorry. Took a while."

Hess has arrived at the morgue, emerging through the swing door. His clothes drip small puddles onto the floor, and he gives his soaking-wet jacket a shake.

"I couldn't get hold of my property manager. Everything okay?"

"Yep, all fine."

Thulin strides through the swing door without glancing back. Emerging out into the rain, she jogs over to her car, trying to avoid getting wetter than absolutely necessary. She can hear Hess's voice behind her.

"I don't know where you've got to, but I can take statements from the victim's workplace, or—"

"Nope, already done, so no need to worry about that."

Thulin unlocks her car and climbs in, but before she can slam the door Hess catches up and blocks her. He shivers in the rain.

"I don't think you understood what I said. I'm sorry about the delay, but—"

"I *do* understand. You screwed things up at the Hague. Somebody told you to clock in at the station here until you get the green light to come back, but you couldn't care less about the job, so you're just marking time while you do as little as possible."

Hess doesn't move. He just stands and stares at her with the eyes she still isn't used to. "Well, today's wasn't exactly the toughest assignment."

"I'm trying to make things easy for you. You concentrate on the Hague and your apartment, and I won't say anything to Nylander. Okay?"

"Thulin!"

Thulin glances toward the entrance, where the coroner has come outside and is standing under an umbrella.

"Genz says he can't get through to you, but you're to head to Forensics straightaway."

"Why? Can't he just call me?"

"There's something you've got to see. He says you need to see it or you'll think he's pulling your leg."

17

The new, cube-shaped headquarters of the Criminal Forensics Department is located in the northwest part of the city. It has begun to grow dark outside among the birch trees in the parking lot, but in the labs on the story above the large garage they're still hard at work.

"Texts, emails, phone calls, have you checked all that?"

"The IT guys haven't found anything significant yet, but anyway, that's not as important as what I've got to show you."

Thulin follows Genz, who has just fetched them from reception and confirmed that she and Hess are his guests. Hess insisted on coming along, but probably only so she can't say he's neglecting the investigation.

In the car on the way over the man skimmed the autopsy report without much interest, and Thulin didn't deem it necessary to discuss the case with him. The drive has put her on edge, and so has Genz's cryptic reply, but he gives no sign of explaining further until they reach his lab.

There are large, frosted glass partitions everywhere. Forensics techs are swarming around their desks like small white bees, and a plethora of air-conditioning units and thermostats on the walls ensure that the temperature and humidity are kept at the correct level for the tests being conducted in the various glass compartments. It's at the Forensics Department that material gathered from any and every crime scene is examined and assessed. It's often the forensic evidence that determines the direction of a case, and during her short tenure on the murder squad Thulin has seen the Forensics Department carry out meticulous examinations of such various items as clothing, bed linen, carpets, wallpaper, food, vehicles, vegetation, and soil; in principle the list is endless. The coroner's office and the Forensics Department are the two scientific legs of any investigation, and both identify the evidence that the prosecutor will later use to secure a conviction.

Since the 1990s, the Forensics Department has also been responsible for digital evidence, incorporating a subdepartment that investigates technological items belonging to victims and suspects. With the increasing focus on global cyber crime, hacking, and international terrorism, since 2014 its responsibilities have gradually been transferred to NC3, but for practical reasons the department still carries out smaller, local tasks itself, such as the examination of the computers and mobile phones from Laura Kjær's home.

"What about other evidence? The bedroom, the garage?" Thulin stands impatiently in the big lab where Genz has taken them.

"No. But before I say more, I need to know whether we can trust him."

Genz shuts the door and nods at Hess. Although Thulin is rather gratified that Genz is suddenly being so explicitly cautious about the stranger, it also takes her by surprise.

"What do you mean?"

"What I have to say to you is big news, and I don't want to risk the information getting out. It's not personal, I hope you understand." The latter remark is addressed to Hess, who remains expressionless.

"He's been taken on as an investigator by Nylander. And since he's actually here, I'd say we can trust him."

"I mean it, Thulin."

"I'll take responsibility. Tell me what you've got."

Genz hesitates a moment before turning to his keyboard and rapidly typing in an access code, while with his other hand he reaches for his reading glasses on the table. Thulin hasn't seen Genz like this before, earnest and exultant at the same time. And she expected a more sensational reason for his peculiar mood than the ordinary-looking fingerprint that now appears on the HD screen on the wall above the imposing desk.

"I found it quite by chance. We decided to brush the playhouse for fingerprints where the body had been placed, just in case the killer had supported himself on the posts, maybe cut himself on a nail or something. A waste of time, of course. It was teeming with prints, probably from all the children who use the playhouse. But for the same reason we did a routine check of the little doll, the chestnut man, because it was hanging so close to the body."

"Genz, what is it that's so important?"

"The print was on the bottom chestnut. On the bit you might call the body, I mean. It was the only one on the doll. I don't know whether you're aware of this, but when it comes to identifying fingerprints we normally look for ten points of comparison. With this print, unfortunately, it was only possible to establish five points, because it's smeared. But five points ought in principle to be enough. Certainly it's been sufficient in several court cases where—"

"Enough for what, Genz?"

As he spoke Genz was pointing out the five points on the fingerprint with his electronic pen and the digital tablet on the desk, but now he puts down the pen and looks at Thulin.

"Sorry. Enough to establish that the fingerprint on the chestnut man—at least, five points on it—are identical with Kristine Hartung's fingerprints."

For a brief moment Thulin forgets to breathe. She doesn't know what bombshell she expected Genz to drop, but at least something in roughly the same solar system as hers.

"The match came from the computer as it gradually identified the five points. It happens completely automatically, because the material is connected to the database with thousands of prints from previous cases. Normally, of course, we'd like to see more points. Ten is most common, but as I say, five points is enough to—"

"Kristine Hartung is presumed dead." Thulin has regained her poise, and when she continues her voice is exasperated. "The investigation concluded she was killed about a year ago. The case is solved, and the killer has been convicted."

"I know that."

Genz removes his reading glasses and studies her.

"All I'm saying is the print—"

"But it must be a mistake."

"No mistake. I've been going over it again and again for the last three hours because I didn't want to say anything until I was certain. But now I am. Going on five points of comparison, it's a match."

"What program are you using?"

Hess has risen from his seat in the background, where he's been fiddling with his phone, and Thulin notices the new, alert expression on his face. She hears Genz guardedly explaining the dactyloscopic system he used, and she hears Hess confirm that it's the same system used at Europol to identify prints.

Genz perks up, surprised and pleased to find his guest knows the system, but Hess doesn't return his enthusiasm.

"Who *is* Kristine Hartung?" he asks instead.

Thulin looks up from the fingerprint on the screen and gazes into the blue-and-green eyes.

18

The rain has stopped and the soccer fields are deserted. He sees the lone figure emerge through
the trees and cross the pitches, the wet astroturf glit-
tering beneath the floodlights. Not until she passes
the last goalpost and approaches the concrete barrier
to the empty parking lot does he begin to grasp that
it's genuinely her. She's wearing the same clothes as
the day she disappeared and walking with the gait he
knows so well; he'll always be able to tell her from
thousands of other children by the way she walks.
When she notices the car she starts to run, and he
watches her smile broaden as her hood falls back and
the light hits her face. Her cheeks are red with cold;
he can already smell her, and he knows exactly how
she will feel in his arms when he squeezes her close. She

laughs and calls to him as she's done so many times before, and his whole body feels about to explode as he flings the door open and hugs her, beginning to swing her around and around.

"What are you doing? Drive!"

The back door slams hard. Steen Hartung wakes in confusion. He's been asleep, resting against the side window. His son is sitting in his training gear on the backseat amid bags and racquets, while outside other children are cycling away, staring at Steen and laughing to one another.

"Are you done with—"

"Just drive."

"I've got to find the key."

Steen looks for the key, opening the car door into the darkness to make the light come on, and eventually finds it lying on the mat beneath the wheel. His son shrinks down into the seat as the last few children go by.

"Aha . . . *there* it is."

Steen shuts the door.

"Did it go well, your—"

"I don't want you picking me up anymore."

"What do you mean—"

"The whole car stinks."

"Gustav, I don't know—"

"I miss her too, but I don't drink!"

Steen freezes. He stares out at the trees and feels the weight of a thousand dead, drenched leaves, burying him. In the rearview mirror he can see his son gazing out of the window, his eyes hard. He's only eleven years old, and his words should sound comical, but they don't. Steen wants to say something, to say it isn't true, that the boy is mistaken, to laugh loudly and heartily and crack some joke that will get his son to laugh, because he never laughs anymore, and it's been so long since the last time.

"Sorry . . . you're right."

Gustav's face doesn't change. He just stares out into the empty parking lot.

"It was a mistake. I'll pull myself together . . ."

Still no reply.

"I understand you don't believe that, but I mean it. This won't happen again. The last thing I want is to make you unhappy. Okay?"

"Can I play with Kalle before we eat?"

Kalle is Gustav's best friend, and he lives on their way home. Steen takes a final glance in the rearview mirror before turning the key and starting the engine.

"Yeah. Of course."

19

"And? What happened then?"

"Well, then the opposition got started. It all went nuts—remember that pretty woman from the Red–Greens with the horn-rimmed glasses?"

Steen is standing by the large gas stove, tasting the food and nodding with a smile. The radio is playing in the background, and Rosa is pouring a glass of wine. She's about to pour one for him too, but he waves her away.

"You mean the woman who drank too much at the Christmas party and got sent home?"

"Yeah, that's the one. She leapt up in the middle of the chamber and began hurling insults at the prime minister while the chairman tried to make her sit back down. Only then she started insulting the *chairman*.

And she'd already refused to stand when Her Majesty entered, so now half the chamber began to boo her, and finally she got so furious she threw down her notes and they went flying across the room along with her pen and glasses case."

Rosa is laughing, and Steen smiles along. He can't remember the last time they stood in the kitchen and chatted like this, but it feels like much too long ago. He pushes the other thing aside in his mind. The thing he can't think about—the thing that would make her sad. Their eyes meet in the wake of their smiles, and for a moment neither of them speaks.

"I'm glad you had a good day."

She nods and sips her wine—a little too quickly, he thinks, but she's still smiling.

"And you haven't even heard about the People's Party's new spokesperson yet." Her mobile has begun to ring on the kitchen table. "But I'll tell you later. I'll just go and change while I brief Liu about a memo for tomorrow."

She takes her phone and he hears her talking as she walks up the staircase to the first floor. Steen pours the rice into the boiling water, and when the doorbell rings in the hall he isn't surprised: it's bound to be Gustav, back from Kalle's and too lazy to fish out his key.

20

When the front door of the villa opens and Thulin looks into Steen Hartung's face, she instantly regrets being there. He has an apron around his waist and a measuring cup with a few grains of rice in his hand, and his eyes tell her he was expecting someone else.

"Steen Hartung?"

"Yes?"

"Sorry to disturb you. Police."

The man's face shifts. It's as though something breaks inside him, or as if he's been brought down to a reality momentarily forgotten.

"May we come in?"

"What's this about?"

"It'll only take a minute. Best we talk inside."

Thulin and Hess glance awkwardly around the spacious living room as they wait, not exchanging so much as a word. Beyond the glass patio doors, the garden is unlit. The dining table is laid for three people beneath a large Arne Jacobsen lamp, and the aromatic savor of a stew drifts in from the kitchen. Thulin has a sudden urge to bolt through the door before Steen Hartung comes back. She casts a sidelong glance at her companion, who is standing with his back turned to her; she knows she can expect no help from that quarter.

After their conversation with Genz at Forensics, she had phoned Nylander, who responded tetchily at being interrupted during a meeting. Nor did his mood improve when she explained the reason for her call. At first he was disbelieving, insisting that it had to be a mistake, but once he realized Genz had cross-checked the result a million times he'd gone quiet. Despite her generally negative impression of the department, Thulin knew Nylander was far from stupid, and it was clear he took the information seriously. He said there had to be a logical explanation, some simple connection they weren't aware of, so he dispatched them to see the Hartungs. Personally, Thulin can't imagine a logical explanation.

Hess hasn't said much. On their way over in the car, she gave him the gist of the Kristine Hartung business. She wasn't with the department at the time, but naturally the case was a topic of conversation at the station and in the media long after it was closed. For that matter, it still is. Kristine Hartung was the daughter of Rosa Hartung, politician and minister for social affairs, who has only just made her political comeback. The twelve-year-old girl went missing on her way home from sports practice less than a year ago. Her bag and bike were found dumped in the woods, and a few weeks later a young tech nerd, Linus Bekker, was arrested. He had several sexual offenses on his record, and the weight of evidence was overwhelming. During an interrogation at the station, Bekker confessed to sexually assaulting Kristine Hartung before strangling her and dismembering the body with a machete—stained with Kristine's blood—discovered in his garage. According to his own testimony, he then buried the various parts of her body at different locations in the forests of North Zealand, but Bekker, who had been diagnosed as a paranoid schizophrenic, was unable to show the police exactly where, and after two months of resource-intensive investigation they gave up when the frost set in and the task became impossible. Bekker was convicted in the spring under fierce media scrutiny and given the harshest possible punishment: detention in psychiatric care for an indefinite period of time. In reality, this meant the man would be locked up for at least fifteen to twenty years.

Thulin hears the radio being switched off, and Steen Hartung reemerges from the kitchen.

"My wife is upstairs. If this is because you've—"

Hartung stumbles, groping for the words.

"If something's been found . . . I'd like to hear about it before my wife finds out."

"We haven't. This has nothing to do with that."

The man looks at her. He's relieved, yet also puzzled and wary: he knows, of course, that there has to be a reason they're there.

"In the course of examining a crime scene earlier today, we happened across an object that most likely has your daughter's fingerprint on it. To be specific, the print is on a little doll made of chestnuts. I've brought a photo, and I'd like you to take a look."

Thulin holds out a photograph, but Steen Hartung merely glances at it in bewilderment before looking back at Thulin.

"It's not one hundred percent certain that it *is* her print, but it's probable enough that we need to explain why it's there."

Hartung picks up the photo, which Thulin has placed on the dining table.

"I don't understand. A fingerprint . . . ?"

"Yes. We found the doll at a play area in Husum. At 7 Cedervænget, to be precise. Does that playground or that address mean anything to you?"

"No."

"What about a woman named Laura Kjær? Or her son, Magnus, or a man by the name of Hans Henrik Hauge?"

"No."

"Is it possible that your daughter might have known the family? Or another family in the area—maybe she had playdates there, or visited someone, or—"

"No. We live here. I don't understand what this means?"

For a moment, Thulin doesn't know what to say.

"There's probably a logical explanation. If your wife is home, maybe we could ask her about—"

"No. You're not asking my wife." Hartung glares at them, his eyes hostile.

"I'm very sorry, but we need to get to the bottom of this."

"I couldn't give a fuck. You're not talking to my wife. My answers are just as good as hers. We have no idea about any fingerprint, and we don't know the place you're talking about, and I don't understand why the hell it's so important!"

Steen Hartung suddenly realizes that Thulin and Hess are staring at something behind him. His wife has come down the stairs and is looking at them from the hall.

For a moment, nobody says anything. Rosa Hartung enters the living room and picks up the photograph Steen has tossed angrily aside. Once again Thulin considers making a run for the door, and she's becoming increasingly ticked off with Hess, who is still wordlessly skulking in the background.

"I'm sorry to disturb you. We—"

"I heard you."

Rosa Hartung studies the picture of the chestnut man as if she's hoping to find something. Her husband begins shepherding them toward the front door.

"They're going now. I've told them we don't know anything. It's been a real pleasure."

"She sold them down by the main road . . ."

Steen Hartung pauses in the doorway and turns back toward his wife.

"Every autumn. With Mathilde, another girl in her class. They used to sit here and make piles of them . . ."

Rosa Hartung looks from the photo to her husband, and Thulin can see the memory suddenly cross his face.

"Sold them how?" Hess speaks up, treading closer.

"They had a little stall. For people walking past, or cars that stopped. They also baked cakes and made squash. You could buy them with one of these . . ."

"And they did that last year too?"

"Yeah . . . they sat at this table. They'd been gathering chestnuts in the garden, and they were having a lovely time. In the summer they did the flea market, but . . . but she liked it best in the autumn, if we had time to do it together. I remember, because it was the weekend before . . ." Rosa Hartung breaks off.

"Why does it matter?"

"It's just something we need to investigate. With regard to a different case."

Rosa Hartung says nothing. Her husband is standing only a step away, and it's as though both of them are in free fall. Thulin reaches for the photo as though for a lifeline.

"Thank you so much. We've got what we needed. Apologies again for the interruption."

21

Thulin glances at Hess in the rearview mirror as she accelerates and drives away. As she opened the car door in the driveway, he looked back at the house and said he'd rather walk, which suits her just fine. She takes the first side street out of the neighborhood and makes two calls on her way back into town. The first is to Nylander, and he picks up immediately. He's clearly been waiting for it. She can hear his wife and children in the background, and when she tells him the result of their visit to Kristine Hartung's parents he sounds satisfied with the explanation. Before hanging up, however, he impresses on Thulin that the information should be kept confidential—he doesn't want the media latching on to something irrelevant and creating a nuisance for the girl's parents—but

Thulin is only listening with half an ear. She's already figured that much out for herself.

Afterward, she calls the third photo on her family tree, the man her daughter calls Granddad: Aksel, always loyal and always sturdy, the person to whom she owes everything. It's good to hear his calm voice, and he informs her they're playing a very complex South Korean game he doesn't understand a thing about. Le asks in the background whether she can sleep over at Granddad's, and Thulin gives in, although she doesn't feel like being alone tonight. Aksel can hear it in her voice, and she hurriedly tells him everything is fine before she hangs up. Through the car window she can see families plodding home with their shopping bags, and she feels a rising unease that she struggles to quell.

A girl sells a chestnut man at a stall by the road, and it happens to end up at a playhouse somewhere in Husum. Finished, end of story. She makes a decision and turns down Store Kongensgade.

An elderly man in a fur coat and carrying a dog in his arms comes out of the front door and eyes her mistrustfully as she enters the lobby without ringing the bell. She walks up the wide staircase past large, luxurious apartments, and when she reaches the second floor she can hear music coming from inside Sebastian's place.

She knocks once but opens the door without waiting. Sebastian is standing holding his phone. He gives a smile of surprise, still in his suit, which seems to be the only acceptable uniform in his industry.

"Hi?"

Thulin lets her coat fall.

"Take off your clothes, I have half an hour."

Her hands have unzipped his pants and are busy with his belt before she hears the sound of footsteps.

"Where do you keep your corkscrew, my lad?"

An older man with sharp features appears in the doorway holding a bottle of wine, and at a break in the music Thulin becomes aware of the cacophony of voices from the living room.

"This is my father—Dad, this is Naia." Sebastian introduces them with a grin, as a couple of children playing catch race through the hall and out into the kitchen.

"Pleasure to meet you. Sweetheart, come here!"

Before she knows what's happening, Thulin finds herself encircled by Sebastian's mother and the rest of his family. After her third attempt to turn down the invitation, it becomes clear she'll be joining them for dinner.

22

I t's drizzling, and the fluorescent tubes in the bike sheds illuminate one end of the basketball court. The wet children pause to watch the figure before they continue their game. Odin Park in Outer Nørrebro doesn't have many white residents, so when one does show up people take notice. Usually they'll be police, uniformed or plainclothes, but police came in pairs, never alone like this figure, which is ambling toward a block on the edge of the complex with takeout in its hand.

Hess climbs up the external staircase to the third floor, then goes down the walkway toward the last door. In front of the other doors are trash bags and bikes and junk, and from a slightly open window drift Arabic voices and spices that remind Hess of the Tunisian neighborhood in Paris. In front of the final door, 37C, is a weather-beaten old garden table and an unsteady white plastic chair. Hess pauses to fish out his key.

The apartment is dark, and he switches on the light. There are two rooms; his dirty holdall sits by the wall, where he put it down after being given the key by the property manager earlier in the day. The apartment was most recently let to a Bolivian student, but the young man went home in April, and according to the manager it has proved impossible to rent out Hess's apartment since. Which perhaps isn't all that strange. In the front room there are a table, two chairs, a kitchenette with two hot plates, a hole-ridden, uneven floor, and four bare, blotchy walls. Nothing personal, only the battered old TV in the corner, which despite its analogue appearance still works, because it's hooked up to the residents' association's cable package. There has never been any reason to do up the place because Hess is never there, but over the years the mortgage has been paid off by renters, so he's kept the apartment. Hess takes off his jacket, removes his holster and his cigarettes, and hangs his jacket over the back of a chair to dry. For the third time in half an hour, he calls François on the number they agreed, but again the call goes unanswered, and Hess doesn't leave a message.

As he sits at the table and opens the carton of Vietnamese food, he switches on the TV. He eats chicken and noodles without appetite, flicking restlessly through the cornucopia of channels until he reaches the news. They're showing images of Rosa Hartung taken that day at Christiansborg, while a voice-over recounts the story about her daughter. Hess keeps flicking through the channels, ending up on a nature program about South African spiders that are notable for eating their mother as soon as they're hatched. The program doesn't interest him, but neither does it disturb his train of thought as he tries to figure out how he can get back to the Hague as quickly as possible.

It has been a dramatic few days for Hess. Out of the blue this past weekend he was relieved of duty by his German boss at Europol, Freimann—effective immediately. Well, maybe it wasn't completely unexpected, but it was certainly an overreaction. In Hess's eyes, at least. The decision made its way through the system, the rumor swiftly reaching Copenhagen, and on Sunday evening he was ordered home to face the music. At Monday's meeting at the station, his Danish bosses refused to accept his reading of the situation and reminded him that his actions were particularly unfortunate given the Danish police's already troubled relationship with Europol, which had been strained ever since the notorious referendum. Hess, in other words, was not helping matters, and their collaboration hinged on staying in Europol's good graces. In fact, one of the bosses emphasized that it bordered on the embarrassing, and Hess tried to look chastened. After that they ran through the checklist of his sins: disciplinary issues involving arguments with his superiors; absences; generally slipshod work; accusations of drunkenness and partying in European capitals; and then the overarching umbrella theory about burnout. He objected that it was a storm in a teacup, and he was sure the evaluation would end up finding in his favor. In his head he was already on the 3:55 flight to the Hague—his ticket was already booked—and unless the plane was delayed he'd be back at his second-floor apartment in Zeekantstraat in time to plump down on the sofa and watch the postponed Champions League match between Ajax Amsterdam and Dortmund. But then the bomb had dropped. Until things were straightened out, Hess was relegated to his former division, Major Crimes. Starting the very next morning.

Hess had brought almost nothing to Copenhagen. He'd chucked the bare necessities into his holdall before setting off, and after the disastrous meeting he went to recover at the Methodist hotel near the railway station, although he'd only just checked out. As a first step he'd called his partner, François, to explain the situation and to get an update on the outlook in the Hague. François was a bald forty-one-year-old Frenchman from Marseille, a third-generation policeman, hard-boiled but with a heart of gold, and the only one among his colleagues Hess liked and trusted. François explained that the evaluation had been set in motion and he'd keep Hess in the loop, covering for him as much as possible, but that they needed to coordinate who said what so that it didn't look like they'd colluded in their respective reports. If it became a disciplinary matter, their telephone conversations might be tapped, so it seemed like a good idea to get new phones. After the call, Hess downed a can of beer from the minibar and tried to get hold of the property manager who had the key to his apartment: no need to pay for more nights at the hotel than absolutely necessary. But the office was closed, and Hess dozed off fully clothed on the hotel bed to Ajax Amsterdam's ignominious three–nil defeat by the Germans.

The spiders have finished devouring their mother by the time his new phone rings. François's English isn't quite smooth, so Hess prefers to speak French with him, although his French is broken and self-taught.

"How was your first day at work?" is what François wants to know.

"Super."

They coordinate briefly, Hess bringing François up to speed on what he's writing in his report, and François updating him on the latest developments. When they're done, Hess senses there is something weighing on the Frenchman's mind.

"What?"

"You don't want to hear it."

"Spit it out."

"I'm just thinking out loud, here: Why don't you just relax and stay in Copenhagen for a bit? I'm sure you'll be back, but maybe this is good for you. Getting away from it all. Recharging your batteries. Meeting a few sweet Danish girls, and—"

"You're right. I don't want to hear it. Just concentrate on your report and have it on Freimann's desk ASAP."

Hess hangs up. The prospect of remaining in Copenhagen has become increasingly unbearable over the course of the day. His nearly five years at Europol

were no picnic, but anything is better than here. As
a liaison officer representing the Danish police, he
could in principle have contented himself with sitting in front of a computer screen in his office at HQ,
but soon after his arrival Hess had been headhunted
as an investigator for their transnational mobile task
force. On average, he'd probably spent 150 days out of
the year traveling, as one case was superseded by the
next. Berlin become Lisbon, Lisbon became Calabria,
Calabria became Marseille, and so it had continued,
the only interruptions brief stays at the Hague, where
he'd been provided an apartment. He kept in tenuous
touch with the Danish system via occasional reports,
which were supposed to summarize the connections
of organized crime to Northern Europe—Scandinavia
and Denmark especially. Via email, as a rule, and on
rare occasions via Skype. This peripheral contact had
suited Hess perfectly. So did the feeling of rootlessness.
In time he'd even learned to live with the machinery
of the European police, a colossus with feet of clay and
a thousand legal and political hurdles, which seemed
more and more insurmountable each time he encoun-
tered them. Did he burn out? Yeah, maybe. As an
investigator he saw fresh examples of organized in-
justice, malice, and death all the time. He followed
leads, gathered evidence, and interrogated people in

countless different languages, but often the charges were shelved by politicians who couldn't come to an agreement across national lines. On the other hand, Hess was left mostly to his own devices. The system was so vast and labyrinthine you could get away with anything. Until recently, at least, with the arrival of a new boss to his department: Freimann, a young bureaucrat from former East Germany who believed in pan-European police cooperation and had diligently begun to streamline operations and clean house. But even a long weekend on a desert island with Freimann had sounded tempting after his first day on the job in Copenhagen.

To be fair, the day had gotten off to a tolerable start. He'd avoided bumping into old acquaintances at the station and was sent out on assignment from early morning onward. The female investigator he'd been partnered with was sharper than most and clearly uninterested in his presence, which could only play to his advantage. But then an apparently simple killing in suburban dullsville was complicated by a fingerprint, and before he could blink he was standing in a house where grief clung to the walls like thick tar, which always made him want to run screaming from the room.

After their visit to the Hartungs', he'd needed some air. There was something nagging him, and it wasn't just the grief. It was a detail. Something that hadn't yet become a thought; or maybe it had, but it had brought with it a blizzard of questions that his conscious mind rushed to dismiss—he simply didn't want to act on them.

Hess walked through the dripping streets, taking a detour into the city he no longer knew. Structures of glass and steel were everywhere, construction that testified to a city under transformation, in principle a European capital like all the others, yet still smaller, lower, and safer than most of the capitals to the south. Happy families with children had defied the autumn and the rain for the attractions of Tivoli, but the piles of fallen leaves underneath the chestnut trees by the lakes made him think of Laura Kjær. The picture-postcard image of this safe fairy-tale land had once more begun to crack, and by the time he reached Queen Louise's Bridge, memories of his own had begun to materialize, like small, teasing ghosts, refusing to vanish until he came to Outer Nørrebro.

Hess knows it doesn't have to concern him. It isn't his responsibility. There are nutcases all over the place, and parents lose their children every single day, just as children lose their parents. He's seen it so many times before in so many different cities and nations, in more faces than he cares to remember. In a few days, there will be a conciliatory call from the Hague, so it doesn't matter what he's seen today. He will board a flight or a train or get into a car with another clear-cut task, and until then he simply has to pass the time.

Hess realizes he's staring apathetically at one of the discolored walls, and before the sense of unease can pluck at him again he chucks the box of leftover noodles into the trash and heads for the door.

23

The sound of Bob the Builder's voice fills Nehru Amdi's living room, where his youngest child seems especially absorbed by the screen. Nehru is busy preparing curried lamb and spinach for his wife and four kids when there's a knock at the door. His wife yells that she's talking business on the phone with her cousin, so Nehru has to get it. Irritably, an apron still around his waist, he opens the door to find the white man from 37C standing outside. Nehru already caught a glimpse of him earlier in the day.

"Yes?"

"Sorry to disturb you, but I'd like to paint my apartment. 37C."

"Paint your apartment? Now?"

"Yes, please. The manager said you're the caretaker, so you'd know where the painting supplies are kept." Nehru notices the man's eyes are two different colors, one green and one blue.

"But you can't just up and paint it. You need the owner's permission for that type of thing, and the owner's away."

"I *am* the owner."

"You're the owner?"

"Maybe you could just give me the key. Is the stuff down in the basement?"

"Yeah, sure, but it's dark. You can't paint now unless you've got lamps. Have you got lamps?"

"No, but it's only now I've got the time," the man replies impatiently. "I'm in Copenhagen for a few days, and I'd like to spruce up the apartment a bit so I can sell it. So if it's not too much trouble, could I have the key?"

"I'm not allowed to give out keys to the basement. Wait for me in the corridor, I'll be right there."

The man nods and leaves. Nehru's wife takes her phone from her ear and shoots Nehru a glance as he starts rummaging around for the key. No normal white man would voluntarily own anything at Odin, let alone live there, so there's good cause to be on his guard.

The roller trundles up and down the wall, spattering globs of paint across the cardboard-covered floor. As Nehru walks through the door with another pot of paint, the man is sloshing the roller around in the tray before returning to his task, sweat dripping down his face.

"There was one more tin, but I've got no time, so you'll have to check yourself whether it's the same color code."

"Doesn't matter, just has to be white."

"It does matter. It has to be the same code."

Nehru moves the man's jacket to make room for the tin so he can check the code. As he does so he exposes the gun holster, and Nehru freezes.

"It's all right. I'm a policeman."

"Right, of course," says Nehru, shuffling half a step backward toward the door as he remembers his wife's glance.

The man flips open his police badge with the tips of his fingers, which are already flecked with white.

"Seriously. I am."

Nehru feels only slightly reassured as he examines the badge, while the tall figure begins moving the roller up and down again.

"A plainclothes agent? You're using the apartment for surveillance?"

Odin is often accused of being a breeding ground for criminal gangs and Islamic terrorists, so Nehru's question is not unreasonable.

"Nah, it's just mine. No surveillance. But I work overseas, so now I'm looking to get it off my hands. Leave the door ajar when you go—I want to let the air in."

The reply disarms Nehru. He's still baffled as to why the man has taken it into his head to buy real estate in Odin, but being asked to leave is reassuring. Very Danish and normal. Eyeing the figure, Nehru can't resist. The tall man paints like a horse kicks. Like his life depends on it.

"You're doing that much too hard. Can I just see the roller—"

"No, it's fine."

"Well, you can't see a thing without light."

"It's fine."

"Stop, I'm telling you. If I don't help, you won't be happy with what you're doing."

"I won't be unhappy, I promise."

But Nehru has grabbed the handle and is surveying the roller, even as the man maintains his grip.

"I thought so. It needs to be changed. I'll just do that now."

"No, it's fine."

"It's not fine. I'm an old hand at painting, and I can't just stand by and watch you mess it up when I know better."

"Listen, I just want to paint—"

"I can't just stand and watch. One's obliged to help if one can. I'm very sorry, but there's nothing I can do."

The man slowly releases the handle. For a moment he stares into empty space, as though Nehru has deflated his life of meaning, and Nehru hurries off with the roller before he can change his mind.

Back at his apartment, Nehru swiftly hunts out a few work lamps and a new roller in a bucket at the back of the cupboard in the hall. His wife is sitting at the kitchen table with the children. She doesn't understand him; 37C can look after himself until they've eaten, surely. "The man could be lying, you know. Could be some poor nutter the council's housed in the complex?"

Nehru gives up trying to explain to her that when you paint, you've got to do it properly. Carrying the gear under his arm, he shuts the front door behind him and is about to pick up the roller handle from the newspaper on the doormat where he left it, when suddenly he notices the figure from 37C hurrying past the basketball court outside.

For a moment, Nehru is nonplussed. Then he tells himself that people these days have no respect for each other, and that his wife might be on to something about the nutter and the council. Either way, it's a good thing the man is selling.

24

To her surprise, Thulin is beginning to enjoy dinner. Sebastian belongs to a reputable, prosperous family of lawyers, of which his father is the all-imposing patriarch. Nearly ten years ago he was made a regional judge, and now Sebastian and his older brother lead the firm—although that certainly doesn't mean they see eye to eye on everything. That much is plain at dinner. His older brother's awkward, neoliberal observations about state and community tumble clunkily across the table, sharply pursued by Sebastian's quick rejoinders and his sister-in-law's sarcastic reminders that her husband's emotional life officially died when he finished his legal training. His father had asked Thulin about her role in the murder squad and praised her decision to apply to NC3, which he firmly believed was the future, not the fusty old Major Crimes Division. His older brother, meanwhile, insisted that none of the departments would still exist in twenty years' time, since by that time all police work would hopefully have been privatized. In the middle of the main course, however, his interest turns to why Sebastian apparently isn't attractive enough for Thulin to want to move in with him. "He's not man enough to give you what you want, eh?"

"No, he is. I'd just rather take advantage of him sexually than choke the life out of the relationship."

Her answer makes the man's wife splutter with laughter, so much so that red wine ends up on his white Hugo Boss shirt, which he immediately begins scrubbing with his napkin. "Cheers to that," she says, emptying her glass before the others can catch up. Sebastian shoots Thulin a smile, and his mother gives her hand a squeeze. "Well, we're certainly very pleased to meet you, and I know Sebastian is happy."

"Mom, give it a rest."

"I didn't say anything!"

She has Sebastian's eyes. The same warm, dark glow Thulin felt a little more than four months earlier in court, when she sat in the spectators' gallery while one of her cases was being heard by a judge. Witnessing Sebastian Valeur during this preliminary hearing was like seeing a factory-fresh Tesla at a classic car museum, but her knee-jerk judgment about his arrogance had been put to shame. As the court-appointed lawyer for the accused, a Somali, he defended his client without putting on airs and with such good sense that he convinced the man to plead guilty to the incident of domestic violence with which he'd been charged. Afterward, Sebastian caught up with her outside the building, and although he had no luck inviting her out, she was attracted to him. One late afternoon in early June, she showed up unannounced at his office in Amaliegade and tore off his pants as soon as they were alone. She hadn't thought it would develop into anything more, but the sex was surprisingly good, and Sebastian understood she wasn't looking for someone to go for long walks on the beach with. Now that she's actually sitting here and laughing along with his oddball family, that part doesn't seem quite as frightening as it usually does.

Suddenly a loud ringtone makes the table fall silent, and Thulin has to reach into her pocket and answer the call.

"Yes, hello?"

"It's Hess. Where's the boy now?"

Thulin stands up and slips into the hallway.

"The boy?"

"The boy from the house in Husum. There's something I've got to ask him, and it has to be now."

"You can't talk to him now. He was examined by a doctor who decided he was possibly in shock, so he's been taken to A&E."

"Which A&E?"

"Why?"

"Doesn't matter. I'll figure it out."

"Why do you—"

The line goes dead. For a moment Thulin stands there with the phone in her hand. The chatter of voices around the table continues, but she's no longer listening to what they're saying. By the time Sebastian appears to ask whether anything is wrong, she's already pulling on her coat and halfway out the door.

25

The corridors are deserted and only dimly lit when Thulin enters the Children's and Adolescent Psychiatric Centre at Glostrup Hospital. As she reaches the desk she sees Hess arguing with an elderly nurse in the back office. Their voices seep out under the door of the glass-partitioned room, and a few teenagers in slippers have stopped to watch. Thulin pushes past them, knocks, and opens the door.

"Come with me."

Hess, noticing Thulin, follows reluctantly after her while the nurse watches him with a peevish expression.

"I've got to speak to the boy, but some idiot promised them he wouldn't be disturbed again today."

"*I* promised that. What do you need to speak to him about?"

She looks at Hess, who for some reason has flecks of white paint on his face and fingers.

"The boy has already been questioned once today, and if you can't tell me what this is about, then it can't be that important."

"It's just a few questions. If you can persuade the nurse, I promise I'll call in sick tomorrow in exchange."

"Tell me what you want to ask him."

26

The ward at the Children's and Adolescent Psychiatric Centre is essentially identical to the one for
adults, except for a few scattered islands of toys and
books beside child-sized tables and chairs. They don't
make much difference—the interior still feels barren
and sad—but Thulin knows from experience that there
are places much worse than this.

At long last, the nurse emerges from the boy's room
and, ignoring Hess, looks directly at Thulin.

"I've told him you have five minutes. But he's not
saying much, and hasn't since he arrived. Don't force
him to. Agreed?"

"Thanks, that's fine."

"I'll be keeping an eye on my watch."

The nurse taps her wrist and shoots a disgruntled glance at Hess, who already has his hand on the door-knob.

Magnus Kjær doesn't look up as they enter. He's sitting in bed underneath the duvet with the head-board raised, and in his hands is a laptop with a large hospital logo on the back. It's a private room. The curtains are drawn and a single lamp glows on the bedside table, but it's the computer screen that lights the boy's face.

"Hi, Magnus. Sorry to disturb you. My name's Mark, and this is . . ."

Hess glances at Thulin, who is trying to get her head around the concept of Hess having a first name.

"Naia."

The boy doesn't respond, and Hess walks up to the bed.

"What are you doing? Mind if I sit down for a minute?"

Hess sits down on the chair beside the bed while Thulin lingers in the background. Something makes her want to keep her distance. She can't put it into words, but she senses it's the right thing to do.

"Magnus, I'd really like to ask you something. If I may. Is that all right, Magnus?"

Hess looks at the boy, who doesn't react, and Thulin decides they're wasting their time. Magnus is entirely focused on the screen, his fingers eagerly tapping across the keyboard. It's as though he's created a bubble around himself, and Hess could ask questions until he was blue in the face without receiving any answer.

"What are you playing? Is it going well?"

The boy still doesn't reply, but Thulin has instantly recognized League of Legends, familiar from her daughter's screen.

"It's a computer game. You have to—"

Hess raises his hand to silence Thulin, while he keeps his eyes fixed on the boy's screen.

"You're playing on Summoner's Rift. I like that map the best too. Is it Lucian the Purifier who's your champion?"

The boy doesn't answer, and Hess points at one of the symbols at the bottom of the screen.

"If you're Lucian, then you'll soon have enough for an upgrade."

"Already do. Waiting for the next level."

The boy's voice is mechanical and monotone, but Hess points at the screen again, undeterred.

"Watch out, there are minions coming. Nexus is going to be captured if you don't do something. Press magic or you'll fail."

"I'm not failing—I *have* pressed magic."

Thulin hides her astonishment. The other colleagues she's met at the station view computer games much as they view Cantonese—but evidently not Hess. She senses instinctively that this is the best conversation Magnus has had all day. It strikes her that the same might be true of the man sitting on the chair beside him, who appears genuinely engrossed.

"You're good at that. When you take a break, I'd like to give you another mission. It's a bit different from in LoL. You'll need all your skills."

Immediately, Magnus puts down the laptop and waits for Hess without meeting his eye. Hess takes three photos from his inside pocket and places them facedown on the duvet in front of the boy. Thulin steps closer.

"That wasn't what we agreed. You didn't say anything about photos."

Hess ignores her and looks at the boy.

"Magnus, in a moment I'm going to turn over the photos one by one. You'll have ten seconds to look at each picture and tell me whether anything is out of place. Something that shouldn't be there. Something weird, something that doesn't belong. Kind of like you're looking for a Trojan horse that's snuck into your compound. Okay?"

The nine-year-old boy nods, gazing resolutely at the back of the photographs lying on the duvet. Hess turns over the first picture. It's a section of the kitchen at Cedervænget, revealing a few shelves of spices and the boy's antianxiety medication. Taken by Genz and the Forensics guys, presumably. It suddenly occurs to Thulin that Hess must have dropped by the police station to pick up the photos before he got to the hospital, and the realization puts her further on her guard.

Magnus's eyes flick from detail to detail, mechanically analyzing the image, but then the boy shakes his head. Hess smiles approvingly and turns over a new picture. It's another random photo, this time of a corner in the living room, focused on a few women's magazines and a folded blanket on the sofa. In the background is a windowsill with a digital photo frame, frozen on a picture of the boy himself. Magnus repeats the process and again shakes his head. Hess turns over the final image. It's a section of the playhouse, and Thulin's stomach churns as she scans the photograph, making sure there's no trace of Laura Kjær. The picture has been taken from an angle that primarily shows the swings and the bronze-colored trees in the background, but no more than a second passes before the boy's finger is tapping the little chestnut man hanging from the beam in the top right corner of the photo. Thulin looks at his finger, and feels the silence knot in her belly until Hess speaks up.

"You're sure? You've never seen that before?"

Magnus Kjær shakes his head.

"Went to the playground with Mom yesterday before tea. No chestnut man."

"Great . . . you're brilliant. Do you also know who put it there?"

"No. Is the mission complete?"

Hess looks at the boy and straightens up again.

"Yes. Thank you . . . you've been a huge help, Magnus."

"Isn't Mom coming back?"

For a moment, Hess clearly doesn't know what to say. The boy still isn't looking at them, and the question hangs in the air too long before Hess takes the boy's hand, which is lying on the duvet, and gazes at him.

"No, she isn't. Your mom's in another place now."

"In Heaven?"

"Yes. She's in Heaven now. A good place."

"Will you come back and play with me?"

"Yeah, of course. Another day."

The boy opens his computer again, and Hess has to release his hand.

27

Hess stands with his back to the exit, smoking, while the wind swirls the smoke among the buildings and the trees. In front of him are the gloomy parking lot and the old black trees, their roots twisting and bulging beneath the asphalt. Thulin glimpses an ambulance bumping across the pavement and down into the underground garage as the automatic glass doors open for her.

Thulin needed to wrap things up with the nurse afterward, and to reassure herself that the boy would be given the best possible care. By the time they finished talking, Hess was gone, and as she steps out into the parking lot she realizes she's glad he waited for her.

"What's going to happen to him?"

The question feels strangely intimate, given that she's known Hess for less than twenty-four hours, but there's no doubt what he means.

"It's up to the social workers now. He doesn't have any other relatives, unfortunately, so they'll probably figure out a solution with the stepfather. Unless the stepfather's guilty, of course."

Hess looks at Thulin. "Do you think he is?"

"He doesn't have an alibi. And in ninety-nine percent of cases it's the husband who did it. We didn't get anything new in there."

"Didn't we?" Hess holds her gaze as he continues. "If the boy's telling the truth, then the doll with the fingerprint was probably brought to the crime scene the same night the killing took place. That's odd, to put it mildly, and I don't think we can explain it away by saying someone just happened to buy the doll at a roadside stall a year ago, do you?"

"Things don't necessarily have to be connected. The partner could easily have killed the woman, and the boy could be mistaken about the doll. I mean, nothing else makes much sense."

Hess is about to say something, but then he thinks better of it and stamps out the cigarette beneath his foot. "No. Perhaps not."

He nods an abrupt goodbye, and Thulin watches him trudge across the parking lot. She opens her mouth to ask whether he wants a lift back into town, but as she does so a gust of wind kicks up and something drops to the ground behind her. Turning around, Thulin sees a prickly, greenish-brown ball roll down into the hollow by the cigarette bin, where others like it have collected. She realizes what it is. Peering up into the chestnut tree, she contemplates its swaying branches and all the other prickly, greenish-brown balls waiting to hatch, and for a moment she sees Kristine Hartung making chestnut men at the table in her living room. Or somewhere else entirely.

Monday, October 12th

28

"I'm sick of saying it. I drove back to the motel and went to bed, and now I want to know when I can go home with Magnus!"

The small room at the end of the Homicide Department's long corridor is overbright and stuffy, and Hans Henrik Hauge is sobbing and kneading his hands. His clothes are crumpled, and he reeks of sweat and urine. Six days have passed since the discovery of Laura Kjær's body, and for nearly two days Thulin has kept him in custody. The judge has given the department forty-eight hours to find enough evidence to charge him—thus far with no luck. Thulin is convinced Hauge knows more than he's letting on, but the man is no fool. A computer scientist trained at the University of Southern Denmark, he's old-fashioned and predictable in his work, but not unskilled. He's moved around a lot and claims to have been a freelance IT developer until he met Laura Kjær and found a permanent job at a medium-sized IT company on the waterfront at Kalvebod Quay.

"Nobody can confirm you stayed at the motel Monday evening, and nobody noticed your car in the motel parking lot until seven the next morning. Where were you?"

When Hauge was taken into custody, he'd exercised his right to an appointed attorney. A young woman, sharp and fragrant, wearing clothes Thulin will never be able to afford. She's the one to speak up.

"My client maintains that he was at the motel all night. He has patiently repeated that he had nothing to do with the crime, so unless you have new information I'd like him released as soon as possible."

Thulin looks only at Hauge.

"The fact is you have no alibi, and the day you left for the trade fair, Laura Kjær had the locks changed without your consent. Why?"

"I *told* you. Magnus threw a set of keys away—"

"Was it because she'd found somebody else?"

"No!"

"But you got angry when she told you on the phone that she'd changed the locks—"

"She *didn't* say she'd changed the locks—"

"And Magnus's disorder must have put a strain on your relationship. I can easily understand why you'd be angry if she suddenly told you she was turning elsewhere for comfort."

"I know nothing about anyone else, and I've never been angry with Magnus."

"So you *were* angry with Laura?"

"No, I *wasn't* angry with—"

"But she changed the locks because she didn't want you anymore, and that was what she told you on the phone. You felt let down, you'd done so much for her and the boy, so you went back to the house—"

"I didn't go back to the house—"

"You knocked on the door or the window, and she opened up because she didn't want you waking the boy. You tried to talk to her. You reminded her of the ring on her finger—"

"That's not true—"

"—the ring you'd given her, but she was cold and indifferent. You took her outside, but she kept telling you to go to hell. It was over between you— you had no right to anything—you weren't allowed to see the boy, because you meant nothing, and finally—"

"It's not true, I'm telling you!"

Thulin can feel the lawyer's peevish gaze, but she's looking only at Hauge, who is once more wringing his hands and fiddling with his ring.

"This isn't going anywhere. My client has lost his fiancée, and there's also the boy to think of, so it seems inhumane to keep him here any longer. My client would like to return to his house as soon as possible so that he can provide the boy a sense of security and routine, just as soon as he's discharged from—"

"We just want to go home, for Christ's sake! How long are you going to be in our house? Surely you must be finished with us by now!"

There's something about Hauge's outburst that baffles Thulin. It isn't the first time the forty-three-year-old IT developer has expressed impatience at their continued examination of the house and their refusal to permit him entry, although logically Hauge ought to be interested in the police taking their time to secure all the evidence there. On the other hand, every nook and cranny of the house has already been checked so many times that if Hauge were trying to hide something they would already have found it, so she has to resign herself to the idea that he's simply thinking of the boy's welfare.

"My client shall of course be accommodating of your investigation. But is he free to go?"

Hans Henrik Hauge gazes tensely at Thulin. She knows she has to let him go, and soon she will have to inform Nylander that they're still treading water in the Laura Kjær murder case. Nylander will doubtless be waspish, asking her to pull her finger out and avoid wasting more time and resources, and he'll probably ask her where the hell Hess has gotten to. Thulin has no answer to that, for good reason. Since they went their separate ways at Glostrup Hospital last Tuesday evening, he's done the bare minimum and has largely come and gone as he pleases. Over the weekend he called and asked about the case from somewhere that sounded like a DIY store; someone was prattling about paint and color codes in the background. After the call she got the sense he had simply clocked in to give the impression that he was still on the case. She has no intention of telling Nylander that, of course, but the man's absence will probably annoy him almost as much as her abortive detention of Hauge, and none of it will do Thulin any favors when she finishes the conversation by jogging his memory about the recommendation to NC3, which he didn't have time to discuss on Friday as they'd agreed.

"He's free to go, but the house is out of bounds until our examination has concluded, so your client will have to find another solution."

The lawyer shuts her briefcase with a satisfied expression and rises to her feet. For a brief moment, Thulin can tell Hauge wants to protest, but a glance from his lawyer keeps him quiet.

29

The tall, yellow-leafed birch trees sway menacingly in the wind as Hess pulls up and parks his squad car directly outside the main entrance to the Forensics Department. Reaching the reception on the first floor, he forestalls any protests by flashing his badge and declaring that he has an appointment. When Genz appears a moment later, clad in a white coat, he stares at Hess in surprise.

"I need your help with a little experiment. It won't take long, but I need a reasonably sterile room and a tech who can use a microscope."

"That's most of us. What's this about?"

"First I need to know whether I can trust you. It's most likely a fool's errand, and not worth spending time on, but I don't want to risk the information getting out."

Genz, who so far has been eyeing Hess skeptically, grins.

"If you're alluding to what I said the other day, I hope you understand I had to be careful."

"Well, now I'm the one who has to be careful."

"You mean it?"

"I mean it."

Genz glances swiftly over his shoulder, as though remembering the mound of work on his desk.

"If it's relevant, and if it's within the bounds of the law."

"I believe so. Unless you're a vegetarian. Now, where can I drive the car inside?"

The last of the electronic gates alongside the building slides open, and once Hess has backed the car inside, Genz presses a button and the gate slides shut before the fallen leaves can follow. The room is about the size of a mechanic's workshop. It's one of the department's vehicle examination rooms, and although the car isn't what Hess wants to examine, it suits him just fine. It has powerful neon ceiling lights and a drain in the floor.

"What is it you want to test?"

"If you could grab that end."

Hess opens the trunk and Genz gasps in shock as he

finds himself staring down at a pale body swathed in thick, transparent plastic.

"What is that?"

"A pig. About three months old. Bought it at the meat market, where it was hanging in cold storage until an hour ago. Let's put it on the table over there."

Hess takes the pig's hind legs while Genz hesitantly lifts its front trotters. Together they manhandle the pig onto the steel table along one side of the room. The belly has been opened and all the organs removed; its eyes stare lifelessly at the wall.

"I don't think I understand. This can't be relevant, and if it's a joke I simply don't have time."

"It's not a joke. This guy weighs forty-five kilograms—roughly the same as a preteen, in other words. It has a head and four limbs, and although its cartilage, muscles, and bones are slightly different from those of a human being, it'll do a decent enough job for comparing tools. After the dismemberment."

"The *dismemberment*?"

Genz gawps in disbelief at Hess, who has returned to the car and is removing a case file and a long, wrapped object from the backseat. Tucking the file under his arm, he tears the thick packaging off the long object to reveal a machete nearly a meter in length.

"This is what we've got to examine once we're done. The machete is virtually identical to the one found at the perpetrator's home in the Hartung case, and as far as possible I'd like us to dismember the pig using the description he gave during the interrogation. I'll just borrow an apron."

Hess places the weapon and the Hartung case file on the steel table next to Genz before taking down one of the aprons from the row of pegs. Genz looks at the report then back to Hess.

"But why? I thought the Hartung case wasn't relevant. Thulin told me—"

"It *isn't* relevant. If anybody asks, we're just butchering a Christmas pig for the freezer. Will you start, or shall I?"

This time last week, Hess would not in a million years have pictured himself dismembering a pig, but then something happened that gave him an entirely different perspective on the Laura Kjær killing. It had nothing to do with the unease he'd felt after visiting Magnus at Glostrup Hospital. If a chestnut man with Kristine Hartung's fingerprint had been left at the crime scene around the same time as the murder, then it had to be an extraordinary coincidence, but on the train on the way home from Glostrup he'd found himself reviewing the case again. He wasn't questioning that the Hartung girl had been killed and dismembered a year earlier, as Thulin had told him. Working on the Danish police force wasn't the easiest job—he knew that from his own experience—but the murder squad's thoroughness and clear-up rate had been among the European elite for years. Human life still meant something in this country—especially when it came to children—and most of all when it came to the child of a prominent MP. The fact that Kristine Hartung was the daughter of a minister would have meant a full-scale, meticulous investigation, with detectives, Forensics techs, geneticists, SWAT teams, and intelligence services working round the clock. The crime against the girl had probably been seen as a potential attack on democracy, so they would have pulled out all the stops. Fundamentally, Hess did have confidence in the investigation and its results. Yet there was still that random coincidence, and the unease that niggled even after he got back to his Odin hideout.

As the days had passed, suspicion logically fell on the boyfriend, Hans Henrik Hauge, and Hess resigned himself to that. The investigation was in Thulin's hands, and she seemed both thorough and persistent, clearly on her way out of the department and up the career ladder. She also came across as distinctly chilly, but on the other hand his efforts—apart from the spontaneous visit to Magnus Kjær—were negligible, and he took every opportunity to make himself scarce. He spent most of his time crafting a report to his boss at Europol, which he'd shared with François. After a few adjustments, both submitted their reports to Freimann, and while Hess awaited the judgment of his German boss he began to do up his apartment. Given that he'll be back on the treadmill soon—he hopes—Hess even contacted a real estate agent. Several, in fact. The first three he called didn't want the apartment on their books. The fourth did, but he warned Hess not to expect a speedy outcome. As he knew, the area didn't have the best reputation. "Unless you're an Islamist or generally sick and tired of life," he added. The overzealous caretaker, of course, inveigled himself into the redecoration, and the little Pakistani man gave Hess an earful while he painted the apartment, but the project was nonetheless going reasonably well.

Then, last night, something happened. First he had a call from the Hague. A cold-voiced secretary told him in English that Freimann wanted a telephone meeting with him at three p.m. the following day, and the prospect of communication made Hess more cheerful. He used the positive development to perk himself up into painting the ceiling, which he wouldn't otherwise have bothered with. Unfortunately he'd run out of cardboard, so instead the caretaker gave him a pile of old newspapers from the basement to spread out on the floor, but just as Hess was finishing off the ceiling in the kitchenette, he glanced down from his ladder to find Kristine Hartung gazing up at him from one of the pages.

The temptation was too much, and he picked up the page with paint-spattered fingers. WHERE IS KRISTINE? the headline read, and he soon found himself searching for the continuation of the article, which turned out to be among the pages on the floor by the toilet. It was a feature piece dated December 10th last year, summarizing the case and the still-fruitless search for Kristine Hartung's body. Though by that point the police had established what had happened to Kristine, the article took a mysterious and lurid tone. The killer, Linus Bekker, had confessed to her sexual assault, murder, and dismemberment during interrogation a month earlier, but the body parts still had not been found, and the article was accompanied by atmospheric black-and-white photographs of officers combing the woods. Various anonymous police sources were quoted as saying it was possible that foxes, badgers, or other animals had dug up the body parts and eaten them, which might explain why nothing had been found.

Nylander, however, had sounded an optimistic note, although he also remarked that the weather might put a spanner in the works. The journalist had asked him whether it was possible that Linus Bekker's confession was false, since they'd had no luck with the search, but Nylander had dismissed the idea: in addition to Bekker's confession they had clear proof of the murder and dismemberment, although Nylander wouldn't offer any details.

Hess tried to keep painting, but at last he was forced to accept that a visit to the station might be required. Partly to fetch a squad car, which he needed in order to pick up a floor sander at the DIY store the following day, but partly to put his mind at rest.

The corridors were empty—it was nearly ten on a Sunday—and he was lucky to catch the last member of the administrative staff on duty. On a screen at the far end of the dimly lit department, he logged onto the database, explaining that he needed to read up on the Laura Kjær case, but as soon as the staff member disappeared he looked up Kristine Hartung instead.

The material was exhaustive. Nearly five hundred people had been questioned. Hundreds of places had been searched and countless items sent for forensic examination. Hess, however, was seeking only the summary of the evidence against Linus Bekker, and that made his search easier. The only problem was that reading it did not give him the peace of mind he was after. It had the opposite effect.

The first thing that stuck in his craw was finding that Linus Bekker had only become a person of interest off the back of an anonymous tip. As a convicted sex offender, of course, he'd already been put through a routine interrogation, but it hadn't led anywhere until the anonymous tip came in—and they'd never determined who was behind that. The other thing still troubling Hess was Bekker's insistence that he couldn't remember the exact locations where he'd buried the girl's dismembered body, apparently because it had been dark and he'd been in a seriously disturbed frame of mind at the time.

As for proof against Bekker, they had found the weapon apparently used to dismember Kristine Hartung during a search of the garage at his residence, a ground-floor apartment in Bispebjerg; evidently this was the conclusive evidence Nylander had alluded to in the article. The weapon, a ninety-centimeter-long machete, had been examined by forensic geneticists, and—confronted with the fact that blood found on the weapon was a one hundred percent match to Kristine Hartung—Bekker had confessed to the killing. He described following the girl in his car into the woods, where he'd overpowered, molested, and strangled her. After wrapping the body in black plastic bags from his trunk, he'd then driven home to fetch the machete and a shovel from the garage. He insisted, however, that he'd had blackouts and could only recall the event in flashes. Darkness had fallen, he told them, as he was driving around with the body, until he ended up at a forest in North Zealand. There he'd dug a hole, cut up the body, and buried some of it, probably the torso, before continuing through the forest and burying the limbs elsewhere. On top of the forensic geneticists' analysis, which left no question that the machete had been used to attack Kristine Hartung, the case was solved.

Yet it was the analysis of the weapon that sent Hess to the meat market that morning. On his way through the city he stopped at a hunting and fishing store near Gammeltorv, which he remembered from his time with the murder squad. The shop still sold exotic weaponry, and Hess couldn't help wondering whether it was legal. There he found the machete, which though it wasn't precisely identical to the one from the Hartung case did have roughly the same blade length, weight, and curvature and was made from the same material. He dithered about which forensics expert he ought to ask for help with his experiment, but because he knew Genz had a good reputation—acknowledged, even, among Europol's own experts—the choice had fallen on him. As an additional upside, it meant Hess could avoid talking to any of his old acquaintances.

They have nearly finished dismembering the pig. Once Hess has separated another leg, this time the front one, with two hard, precise blows to the joint beneath the shoulder blade, he wipes his forehead and steps back from the steel table.

"What now? Are we done?"

Genz, who has been holding the pig for Hess, releases the front leg and body and looks at his watch, while Hess holds up the blade to the light to assess the effect of contact with the bone.

"Not yet. We just need to scrape it clean, then I hope you've got a really strong microscope."

"For what? I still don't get what we're doing here."

Hess doesn't respond. Gingerly, he runs the very tip of his index finger along the machete's blade.

30

Thulin scrolls in frustration through the material on the flat screen in front of her, watching Laura Kjær's electronic remains zoom past. The computer techs from Forensics have prepared three folders for her with Kjær's texts, emails, and Facebook updates. Over the past week she's already gone through the material several times, but Hauge has just been released, and the investigation lacks direction. On coming into the office a moment earlier, she asked the two male detectives assigned to help her to summarize the alternatives to Hauge so that she can present all the information to Nylander.

"The boy's learning-support teacher is a possibility," says one. "He had plenty of contact with Laura Kjær because the boy swings between total withdrawal and sudden aggression and violence. He says he suggested to the mother at several meetings that the boy should be put into a special school, but it's possible their relationship developed from there."

"Developed how?" Thulin wants to know.

"Maybe Mommy started spreading her legs for the teacher, but then one evening he turns up unannounced at her house looking for another ride, and we've got trouble."

Thulin ignores the suggestion, and tries to focus on the myriad of letters and sentences swarming furiously past on her screen.

The computer techs were right that Laura Kjær's network traffic during the period up to the killing was uninteresting in the sense that it didn't provide the smoking gun. Just lots of trivial junk, especially between her and Hans Henrik Hauge. So Thulin asked to see her texts, email inbox, and Facebook updates from all the way back to her husband's death two years earlier. From her screen at the police station she logged in to the cache of data using the code Genz had given her over the phone, and he took the opportunity to ask how the astonishing discovery of Kristine Hartung's fingerprint had affected the case. Although Genz was well within his rights to inquire, the reminder annoyed Thulin, and she informed him curtly that since there was a logical explanation it wasn't worth them spending any time on it. Afterward, she regretted her response. Genz was one of the few techs who bothered to follow up on cases at all, and she decided to reconsider going on a run with him.

Thulin didn't read through the entire cache of data, but spot tests were enough to form a picture of the deceased woman. The problem was that this didn't help much, so she visited Laura Kjær's workplace. But at the sterile dentist's office located on one of the city center's polished pedestrian streets, her dismayed and mournful coworkers had merely confirmed that Laura was a family-oriented woman primarily concerned with her son, Magnus. After losing her husband a couple of years ago, she'd been unhappy, particularly so because the death had turned her previously cheerful seven-year-old into a virtually mute and highly introverted child. She hadn't been good at being alone, so a young, female colleague had introduced her to various dating sites where she might find love again. She'd tried dating several men, initially via hookup apps like Tinder, Happn, and Candidate, which Thulin already knew from her emails. Yet Laura had been unable to find a man who was interested in a lasting relationship, so she'd turned to the dating site

My Second Love, where after a few frogs she'd stumbled across Hans Henrik Hauge. Unlike the previous candidates, Hauge had been flexible enough to accept her son, and Laura had apparently been very much in love and very pleased to settle back into family life. As Magnus's difficulties with social interactions grew more pronounced, however, that had become the main topic of watercooler chat between root canals and tooth bleachings, and Laura had become increasingly obsessed with finding specialists who could help the boy, whose condition had by then been diagnosed as a form of autism.

It was impossible to get Laura's colleagues to say a bad word about Hauge, who had occasionally picked her up after work. Hauge had apparently been a huge support, patient and dedicated to the boy's well-being, and several colleagues believed Laura would have fallen apart without him. That said, over the past few weeks she'd been a little less communicative about her son than usual. The Friday before the murder, she'd asked for the day off so she could spend some time with him, and she'd also canceled plans with a few colleagues: an overnight trip to Malmö for a training course.

Thulin knew all that from Laura's texts. Hauge had messaged her from work, worried that she was isolating herself and pushing people away to be with her son, but Laura had replied only sparingly or not at all. Yet Hauge showed no signs of anger. In his repeated attempts to get her attention via text, he stoically continued to call her "the love of my life," "darling," "cutie pie," and other things that made Thulin want to vomit.

Thulin had been expecting, and probably also hoping, that her warrant to check Hauge's network traffic during his stint in custody would reveal a different side to him, but there too she was disappointed. The material painted a picture of a man dedicated to his job, a valued employee at the tech company on Kalvebod Quay, whose primary interest—apart from Laura and Magnus—was his house and garden, including the garage. He'd evidently dug the foundations and built the structure himself. Hauge's Facebook page was largely neglected, displaying little more than a picture of himself wearing overalls in the garden, standing next to a wheelbarrow with Laura and Magnus. Nothing about it seemed suspicious. There weren't even the usual porn searches on the web. Thulin had asked Hauge about his lack of interest in social media during one of the initial interrogations, and the man had countered that he got plenty of screen time at work, so much preferred to focus on other things in his free time. This general impression of harmlessness was backed up by his coworkers and small circle of friends, none of whom had noticed anything amiss, either at the trade fair or beforehand.

Next Thulin put her faith in Genz and the forensic examination: Hauge's car, plus various items of his clothing and footwear, were seized and scrutinized for traces of Laura Kjær's blood or other evidence from the night of the murder. Nothing. And when Genz assured Thulin that neither the gaffer tape over Laura's mouth nor the cable ties around her wrists matched the kind found on the shelves in Hauge's garage, she began to lose hope.

The bludgeon, as well as the saw used to amputate the woman's hand, was still missing—as was the amputated hand.

Logging off, Thulin makes a decision: Nylander will just have to cool his heels. Rising and picking up her coat, she interrupts the two detectives, who are still swapping theories about the support teacher.

"Drop the teacher, stay on Hauge. Go through the traffic-cam footage again and see if you can find Hauge's car on the route between the convention center and Husum between ten that night and seven the next morning."

"Hauge's car? But we've already done that?"

"Then do it again."

"Didn't we just release Hauge?"

"Call me if you find anything. I'm going to talk to Hauge's employer again."

Thulin is striding away from their protests when Hess suddenly appears in the doorway.

"Got a minute?"

He looks hassled and shoots a glance at the officers in the background. Thulin walks past.

"No, not really."

31

"Sorry I wasn't there this morning. I understand you've let Hauge go, but it might not matter. We need to talk about that fingerprint again."

"The fingerprint isn't important."

As Thulin stalks down the long corridor, she hears Hess behind her.

"The boy said the doll wasn't there before the murder. You need to investigate whether anyone else can confirm that. People who live out there, people who might have seen something."

Thulin has nearly reached the spiral staircase leading down to the central courtyard. Her mobile rings, but she doesn't want to lose speed, so she lets it ring as she swings down the stairs with Hess on her heels.

"No, we've already explained that. In this department we generally take the view that time is best spent on cases that *aren't* solved rather than on ones that *are*."

"That's what we need to talk about. Hang on a minute, for Christ's sake!"

Thulin has reached the bottom of the stairs and emerged into the deserted central courtyard when she feels Hess grab her shoulder, forcing her to a halt. She twists free and glares at him, while he jabs his finger at a folder she recognizes as a case summary.

"According to the original analysis, there was no trace of bone dust found on the weapon Linus Bekker used to dismember Kristine Hartung. It had traces of her blood, and they assumed that that plus Bekker's statement was enough to make dismemberment sound plausible."

"What the hell are you on about? Where did you get that report?"

"I've just come from Forensics. Genz gave me a hand with an experiment. When you cut through bone, doesn't matter what bone, you get microscopic bone dust left in the cracks and notches in the blade. Look at this blowup of the machete we used in the experiment. It's pretty much impossible to remove the particles, no matter how thoroughly you clean the weapon. But the original forensic genetic analysis only found traces of blood. *Not* bone dust."

Hess hands Thulin a few loose sheets of close-up photographs of what looked like small particles on a metallic surface, presumably the machete. But it is the severed limbs in one of the other images that catch her eye.

"What's that in the background? A pig?"

"It was an experiment. It's not proof, but the important thing is—"

"If this were relevant, they'd probably have mentioned it before, don't you think?"

"It wasn't important then, but it might be now—now we've found the print!"

The main door opens and the cold wind whirls inside, carrying with it two laughing men. One is Tim Jansen, a towering and solidly built investigator who is usually seen only in the company of his partner, Martin Ricks. Jansen has a reputation as a sharp and experienced detective, but Thulin knows him as a chauvinist pig, and she remembers clearly how he rubbed his groin against her during combat training that winter, only letting go when she buried an elbow in his solar plexus. Jansen is also the investigator who, along with his partner, wrung a confession out of Linus Bekker, and Thulin has the feeling their position in the department is unassailable.

"All right, there, Hess. Back on sabbatical?"

Jansen accompanies the greeting with a smirk, and Hess does not respond. He waits until they've passed through the courtyard before saying anything else, and Thulin feels like telling him his caution is absurd.

"Maybe it's nothing. Her blood was there, after all, and personally I couldn't care less one way or the other, but you need to go to your boss and find out where to go from here," he says, holding her gaze.

Thulin doesn't want to admit it, but after visiting Magnus at Glostrup Hospital, she too logged on to the archive and read up on the Hartung case, just to reassure herself that there really wasn't anything she should bear in mind—and as far as she is concerned, there isn't. Besides the reminder of how painful it must have been for the parents when she and Hess showed up at their house the other day.

"And you're telling me this because your work at the Hague makes you an expert in murder cases?"

"No, I'm telling you because—"

"Then keep out of it. I don't want you making a fuss and clumping around in people's grief because somebody else did their job while you weren't doing yours."

Hess looks at her. She can see in his eyes that he's taken aback. It's a mitigating factor that he's been so far along his train of thought he hasn't realized he's doing more harm than good, but that doesn't change anything. She's about to head for the door when a voice echoes across the courtyard.

"Thulin, the IT techs are trying to get hold of you!"

Thulin peers up the staircase at the officer walking toward her, a mobile phone in his hand.

"Tell them I'll call back in a minute."

"It's important. Laura Kjær's mobile has just received a message."

Thulin senses Hess becoming alert, turning to face the officer, and she takes the phone he hands her.

There's a computer tech on the other end. A young guy whose name she doesn't catch. He speaks quickly, gabbling as he attempts to explain the situation.

"It's about the victim's mobile. We always cancel it with the phone company once we've finished examining it, but that takes a couple of days, so it's still active, and you can still—"

"Just tell me what the message said."

Thulin gazes at the columns around the courtyard, the bronze-colored leaves swirling through the air, and senses Hess's eyes on the back of her neck while the tech reads the message aloud. A chill draft blows through the loosely latched doors, and she hears herself ask whether they can trace the sender.

32

She is only fifteen minutes into her meeting with Gert Bukke, the leader of their supporting party, but already Rosa Hartung is beginning to realize that something is seriously wrong.

The last few days at Christiansborg have been busy, and suggestions for various additions to the social policy budget for next year's finance bill have been passed back and forth between her ministry and Bukke's office. She and Vogel have worked day and night to pull together a compromise that will satisfy both the supporting party and the government, but being busy suits Rosa just fine. For six days she's been trying to forget the hope the two police officers briefly gave her, instead pouring all her energy into reaching an agreement on social policy, as the prime minister expected. It is extremely important for her to live up to the PM's confidence in her, especially because Rosa has given him her own personal assurance that she's ready to take up a ministerial role once more. That isn't quite true, perhaps, but it has been crucial in getting Rosa back to work. Luckily there had been no more threats or interruptions last week, and she's been feeling as though things were headed in the right direction—until now, anyway, as she sits in the meeting room next to the chamber and surveys Gert Bukke. Bukke is nodding along politely as Vogel explains the suggested amendments, but Rosa can tell he is paying more attention to the doodles on his pad of graph paper. When he speaks, she's astonished.

"I hear what you're saying, but I'll have to discuss it with the group."

"But you've already done so. Several times?"

"Now I'm doing it again. Why don't we put it like that?"

"But the group just does whatever you tell them, Bukke. I need to know whether there's any chance of coming to an agreement before—"

"Rosa, I know the procedure. But as I said."

Rosa looks at him as he stands up. She knows that, freely translated, Bukke's words mean that he is playing for time, but she doesn't understand why. His political backing and general electoral support aren't in great shape, and if he could reach an agreement with her then in theory it ought to put him back on track.

"Bukke, we're happy to meet you halfway, but we can't let ourselves be blackmailed anymore. We've been negotiating for nearly a week, and we've given you concessions, but we cannot—"

"As I see it, it's the prime minister putting *us* under pressure, and I don't appreciate that, so I'm going to take all the time I need."

"What pressure?"

Gert Bukke sits back down and leans forward.

"Rosa, I like you. And I'm sorry for you and your loss. But if I'm being honest, it seems like you've been yanked back into the ring to make the pill go down more easily, and that's just not right."

"I don't understand what you mean."

"In the year you've been gone, the government has stumbled from one shitstorm to the next. They're tanking in the opinion polls, and the prime minister is desperate. Now he's trying to turn the finance bill into one massive handout, and he's deliberately hauled in his most popular minister—i.e., you—to play Santa, so that they can bring the voters back into the fold in time for reelection."

"Bukke, I wasn't 'hauled in.' I asked to come back."

"If you say so."

"And if you think the proposal is a handout, then we should discuss that. We're in the middle of a parliamentary term. We need to stick together for another two years, so all I'm interested in is finding a solution that satisfies both sides. But it just seems like you're dragging things out."

"I'm not dragging things out. I'm just saying there are challenges here: I've got mine, and obviously you've got your own stuff to contend with, so of course it's understandable this is proving tough."

Bukke gives a diplomatic smile, and Rosa stares at him. Vogel has been attempting in vain to soften the tone, and now he tries again.

"Bukke, if we just make a few more cuts to—"

But Rosa gets abruptly to her feet.

"No, we're finished here. Let's give Bukke time to discuss it with the group."

She nods goodbye and strides through the door before Frederik Vogel can say another word.

The main lobby at Christiansborg is filled with visitors and their enthusiastic guides, who are pointing at the ceiling paintings of various past heads of state. Rosa noticed the busses when she arrived that morning, and although she's all for democratic transparency, she navigates her way through the throng and up the steps with a strained expression. Vogel catches up with her halfway.

"Just to remind you, we're dependent on their support. They're the government's parliamentary bedrock. You can't react like that. Even if he did mention your—"

"It has fuck all to do with that. We've frittered away a whole week. His plan is to make me look like I'm not up to the job, so he has an excuse to give his support base when the negotiations break down and we're forced to call an election."

It's clear to Rosa that Bukke is sick of cooperating with the government. He's probably already received a more attractive offer from the opposition. If he forces an election, Bukke's center party will be free to enter into a new alliance, and that last remark—"obviously you've got your own stuff to contend with"—probably indicates that he will do his best to make the fuckup Rosa's responsibility.

Vogel glances at her as they walk.

"You think he's had an offer from the opposition? If so, you're giving him good reason to consider it by walking out of negotiations like that. I'm not sure the prime minister will be best pleased."

"I didn't walk out of anything. But if he's trying to pressure us, we need to do the same."

"How?"

It strikes Rosa that she's made a big mistake. Since returning to office she's avoided the media, asking her staff to kindly but firmly refuse all requests for interviews. Partly because she knows what they would really be about and partly because she'd rather spend the time negotiating. But mainly the former, perhaps. Vogel had tried to change her mind, but she'd stuck to her decision; now, viewing the situation from outside, she realizes her low profile might be confused with weakness if negotiations end in collapse.

"Arrange some interviews. As many as we can fit in today. Let's get our social-policy suggestions out there so as many people hear them as possible—that'll turn up the pressure on Bukke."

"Agreed. But it will be difficult to keep the focus solely on the politics."

Rosa doesn't get a chance to reply. She feels a hard shove as a young woman bumps into her shoulder, and she has to steady herself against the wall so she doesn't fall.

"Hey, what are you doing?!"

Vogel takes her arm, glaring indignantly at the woman, who shoots them a backward glance without bothering to slow down. She's wearing a vest and a red hoodie, the hood drawn up around her head. Rosa catches only a brief glimpse of the woman's dark eyes before she vanishes, apparently to catch up with a group of visitors.

"Idiot. Are you all right?"

Rosa nods and keeps walking, while Vogel takes out his mobile phone.

"I'll get on it right now."

As Vogel gets through to the first journalist, they reach the stairs. Rosa glances over her shoulder, but she can no longer see the woman among the group of visitors. It strikes her that there was something familiar about her, but she can't remember where or when she's seen her before.

"Will you be ready for the first interview in fifteen minutes?"

Vogel's voice jerks her back to reality, and the thought is soon forgotten.

33

The autumn wind tugs and plucks menacingly at the fluttering tarpaulins over the scaffolding at Jarmers Square, which is choked with traffic. The white squad car, lights flashing and sirens blaring, speeds across the cobbles and past the medieval ruins before getting stuck behind a local-authority flatbed piled high with wet leaves.

"Be more precise. Where's the signal now?!"

Thulin is sitting behind the wheel, impatiently waiting for the tech to respond over the radio while she tries to steer around the council vehicle.

"The phone signal has left Tagensvej and the lakes and it's heading down Gothersgade now, most likely in a car."

"What about the sender's details?"

"We haven't got any. The message was sent from a mobile phone with an unregistered prepaid card, but we've sent you the message so you can see for yourself."

Thulin honks the horn violently, flooring the accelerator the moment she finds a gap in the jam, while Hess, in the passenger seat, reads the text aloud from the display on his phone.

"'Chestnut man, do come in. Chestnut man, do come in. Have you any chestnuts that you've brought for me today? Thank you kindly, won't you stay . . .'"

"It's from a children's song. 'Apple Man, Do Come In.' But kids can swap out 'apple man' for 'plum man,' 'chestnut man,' whatever they feel like. Move it, for fuck's sake!"

Thulin slams her palm against the horn again, overtaking a van. Hess eyes her.

"Who knew we found the chestnut man at the crime scene? Was it mentioned anywhere, in a report or analysis or—"

"No. Nylander shut it down, so it wasn't mentioned anywhere."

Thulin knows why Hess is asking. If it has leaked out that they've found a chestnut doll with Kristine Hartung's fingerprint on it, they could be getting messages from any old loony. But that doesn't seem likely here. Not when the text has been sent directly to

Laura Kjær's phone. The thought makes her bark into the radio again.

"What now? Where are we going?"

"The signal's heading down Christian IX's Gade, seems to be vanishing into a building. It's getting weaker."

The light is red, but Thulin mounts the pavement and rams the pedal to the floor. She hurtles through the crossing, looking dead ahead.

34

As they leap out of the car and sprint down the ramp, they pass a line of cars queuing behind the barrier to get inside the parking garage. According to the last update, the phone was heading that way before the signal cut out. But the parking lot is nearly full. It's midafternoon on a Monday, and people are wandering among the vehicles. Families with hefty shopping bags and pumpkins ready to be carved for Halloween. Muzak plays over the loudspeakers, interrupted only by an enthusiastic voice announcing unbeatable autumn deals waiting to be snapped up on the ground level of the department store.

Thulin makes a beeline for the parking attendant's glass booth at the far end of the garage. A young man is sitting side-on, putting a couple of files back on a shelf.

"This is the police. I need to know—"

Thulin notices the attendant's headphones, and he only reacts when she bangs on the window and shows her badge.

"I need to know what cars arrived within the last five minutes!"

"Not a clue."

"You've got it on the screen—come on!"

Thulin points at the wall of small screens behind the man, who is slowly beginning to grasp the urgency.

"Run it back, hurry up!"

There has been no trace of the signal since it vanished into the building, but if Thulin can see which cars had arrived within the last five minutes, she can also see the registration numbers and use them to narrow down the pool. Meanwhile, however, the parking attendant is rummaging around for the remote control.

"I do remember a Mercedes and a courier and some ordinary cars—"

"Come on, come on, come on!"

"Thulin, the signal's headed for Købmagergade!"

Thulin glances back at Hess, who has his phone pressed to his ear and is following the information

relayed from the tracking device. He's zigzagging between the cars toward the exit. Thulin turns back to
the parking attendant in the glass booth—he's finally
located the remote.

"Doesn't matter. Show me the cameras in the department store—the ones on the ground floor, pointing
toward the Købmagergade exit!"

The attendant points at the uppermost three
screens, and Thulin keeps her eyes glued to the black-
and-white images. A horde of people are milling
around the department store like ants in an anthill.
It seems impossible to focus on any single individual, until suddenly she catches a glimpse of a lone
figure. More purposeful than the rest, and crossing
the shop floor in the direction of the Købmagergade
exit. Keeping its back to the CCTV cameras. As the
dark-haired, suited figure disappears behind a pillar,
Thulin breaks into a run.

35

E rik Sejer-Lassen is walking just three paces behind the woman, and he can smell her perfume. She's in her early thirties, wearing a black skirt and black stockings, and he finds the click of her high-heeled Louboutins nearly unbearable as he follows her through the Victoria's Secret concession. She is well-groomed, with the proportions he favors, the large breasts and narrow waist, and he guesses she works someplace with mirrors, oils, hot stones, and shit like that—some job she uses to pass the time while she waits for a rich man to take her home and keep her there like a piece of decorative furniture. He thinks about what he wants to do to her, to shove her through a door, force up her skirt, and stick it in her from behind as he grabs her long bleached-blond hair and jerks it back until she screams. He could probably gain access to the promised land by inviting her to some fancy restaurant and a fashionable club, where she'd be giggly and impressed, and her panties would get wet every single time he ran his platinum card through the machine, but that isn't what he wants—that isn't what she deserves. He notices his mobile ringing, and when he reaches into his shoulder bag and hastily checks the display, it jolts him out of the fantasy.

"What?"

His voice is frosty, and he knows his wife will hear it in his reply, but it's her own fucking fault he's like this. He pauses and looks for the woman in the Louboutins, but she has already vanished into the crowd.

"Sorry if I'm disturbing you."

"What do you want? I can't talk now. I *told* you so."

"I just wanted to find out if it's okay for me to take the girls up to Mom's today. For the night."

He's suspicious.

"Why would you want to do that?"

She's silent a moment.

"It's just ages since I've seen her. And if you're not home anyway."

"Do you want me to come home, Anne?"

"Yes, of course I do. It's just, you said you were working late today, so—"

"So what, Anne?"

"Sorry . . . we'll stay home, then . . . if you don't think it's a good idea . . ."

There's something about her that irritates him. Something about her voice—something he doesn't trust. He wishes it wasn't like that; he wishes so much he could rewind the whole thing and redo it altogether differently. Then suddenly he hears the sound of heels on marble flooring, and when he turns around he sees the woman in the Louboutins emerge from a cosmetics stand with a chic little bag in her hand and strut toward the elevator beside the Købmagergade exit.

"That's fine. Whatever, go."

Breaking off the call, Erik Sejer-Lassen just makes it to the elevator before the doors close.

"May I ride with you?"

She is standing alone with her doll-like face, staring at him in surprise. She takes the measure of him swiftly—he can sense her gaze on his features and dark hair, on his expensive suit and shoes—and then her face breaks into a beaming smile.

"Of course."

Erik steps into the elevator. He has just returned the smile, pressed the button, and turned to the woman when a man with a wild expression thrusts his arm between the doors and slams him against the mirrored wall, flattening his nose against the cold glass. The woman squeals in terror. He feels the weight of the man at his back, his hands frisking him, and for a brief moment he catches a glimpse of the man's eye color and thinks he must be insane.

36

It's clear to Steen that the client doesn't have a clue when it comes to the drawings. He's seen it many times before, but in this instance it's immensely annoying, because the client is also making a virtue of his ignorance and insisting that it means his ideas are "original" and "lateral" and "outside the box."

They're waiting in the large meeting room, he and his partner, Bjarke, for the client to finally stop staring at yet another drawing and deign to give them an opinion. Steen glances at his watch. The meeting has dragged on and on. He should have been in the car five minutes ago, on his way to the school. But the client is twenty-three, a tech multimillionaire, dressed like a fifteen-year-old in a hoodie, ripped jeans, and white sneakers, and Steen knows instinctively that the guy would only be able to spell *functionalism* with the aid of the autocorrect on his brand-new iPhone, which he's placed on the table and can't stop fiddling with.

"Lads, there's not a lot of *detail* on this."

"No. Last time you said there was too much detail."

Steen senses Bjarke wince, and his partner hurries to smooth over the remark.

"We can always add more, no problem."

"Either way, it just needs more *pang*, more *kapow*."

Steen, who has been waiting for that very comment, pulls out the stack of old drawings.

"These are the most recent drawings. They had *pang* and *kapow*, but you said it was too much?"

"Yeah, it was. Or too little, maybe."

Steen looks at the man, who returns his gaze with a wide smile.

"Maybe the problem is that it's all too in-between. You keep coming with one drawing after another—you know your shit, but it's too nuanced, and it needs to be much more no-strings-attached. You follow me?"

"No, I don't follow you. But maybe we can put red plastic animals along the driveway and turn the lobby into a pirate ship, if that's any better."

Bjarke gives a yap of laughter, much too loud, in an attempt to defuse the situation, but the young Sun King isn't having it.

"That might be a good idea. Or I could ask your competition, if you don't have a better take on it before your deadline this evening."

When Steen is in his car on the way to the school a few minutes later, he phones his lawyer's office and says he still hasn't received the certificate confirming presumption of death. The secretary sounds surprised and apologizes, and Steen cuts her off a little too quickly—but she gets the message and promises to chase it down.

By the time he's pulled up outside the school he's already downed three of the small liquor bottles, but this time he's remembered his chewing gum and driven several kilometers with the windows rolled down. Seeing that Gustav isn't waiting under the trees as usual, he tries his mobile. Suddenly he isn't sure whether he's arrived too early or too late. The schoolyard is empty. Steen looks at his watch. He rarely goes inside the school these days; in fact, he can't remember the last time he did so. It's as though both he and his son know it's better he remain outside. But now his son isn't there, and in half an hour Steen has to be back at the office to revise the drawings for the Sun King. Too restive to help himself, he opens the car door.

37

The door to Gustav's classroom is ajar, but the room is empty. Steen hurries onward, counting himself lucky that lessons are in progress: the corridors are free of inquiring glances. As he passes the doors leading to the buzzing kindergarten classes, he almost manages to ignore the decorative autumn twigs and animals made of chestnuts. The police visit the other day had been a nightmare. The fingerprint. The feeling awoken inside him when he realized what they were saying. The hope, welling up and mingling with bewilderment. It had happened to them many times before—being smacked back to square one—but this time it had been more unexpected. They'd discussed it afterward— that it just was what it was, and that for Gustav's sake, at least, they should try to be strong enough to meet head-on the knocks and pitfalls these reminders of their daughter would always be. Regardless of what form they took. They'd promised each other that they would move on, in spite of everything, and although Steen can almost feel the chestnut animals following him with their eyes as he turns the corner toward the common area, he's determined not to let it affect him.

Steen stops short. It takes him a moment to realize the children sitting in the common room are her class-mates. It's ages since he's seen them, but he recognizes their faces.

They are sitting peacefully around the white tables arranged on the brown carpet, working in groups, but as soon as the first pupil catches sight of him, there is a ripple of attention across the room, and all faces turn toward him. No one speaks. For a second he doesn't know what to do, but then he begins to retreat the way he came.

"Hi."

Steen turns to the girl sitting alone at the nearest table, her schoolbooks piled neatly in front of her, and realizes it's Mathilde. She looks older. Graver, clad in black. She gives him a friendly smile.

"Are you looking for Gustav?"

"Yeah."

He's seen her thousands of times; she'd been in their home so often it had become almost customary for him to speak to her as though to his own daughter, but it isn't anymore, and he can't find the words.

"His class went past a little while ago, but they'll probably be back soon."

"Thanks. Do you know where they went?"

"No."

Steen checks his watch, although he knows the time.

"Okay, I'll wait for him in the car."

"How are you doing?"

Steen looks at Mathilde and tries to smile. It's one of the dangerous questions, but he's heard it so often that he knows all he has to do is answer quickly.

"Fine. Bit busy, but that's all good. And you?"

She nods and forces a smile, but she looks sad.

"I'm sorry I haven't come to visit more."

"Don't be. We're all right."

"Hi, Steen. Anything I can help you with?"

Steen turns to find the teacher, Jonas Kragh, approaching them. He's in his midforties, dressed in jeans and a tight black T-shirt. His eyes are kind, but also vigilant and probing, and Steen knows exactly why he's looking at him that way. The whole class has been affected by what happened, and the school has been trying to help the pupils get through it ever since. Kragh was one of the staff who thought it was better for the students not to take part in the memorial ceremony, which for logical reasons was held a few months after Kristine's disappearance. It would do more harm than good, he believed, reopening a wound that was beginning to heal, and he'd made that clear to Steen at the time. Meanwhile the school board had decreed that the students could make up their own minds whether to take part, and more or less all Kristine's classmates had turned up.

"No, it's fine. I'm just leaving."

As Steen reaches the car, the bell rings. He shuts the door and tries to concentrate on finding Gustav's figure among the kids streaming out of the main doors. He knows he's done the right thing, but the sight of Mathilde has brought the visit from the police crowding back to the forefront of his mind, and he reminds himself of his most recent therapist's words: that grief is love made homeless, that one needs to live with grief and force oneself on.

He hears Gustav get into the passenger seat beside him, and hears him explain that the Danish teacher dragged them all down to the library and made them borrow books to read in their free time, which is why he's a bit late. Steen wants to nod understandingly, start the engine and pull away from the curb, but he sits where he is, and knows he needs to go back inside the school. The bell rings, and he fights the urge. He knows to obey it will take him over the line he's drawn for himself, but if he doesn't do it now he might never ask Mathilde, and there is something about the question that matters, that matters perhaps more than anything else in the world.

"Is something wrong?"

Steen opens the car door.

"Just something I have to do. You stay put."

"What are you doing?"

Steen slams the door and heads for the main entrance, the leaves whirling around him.

38

"What the *hell* are you doing? I demand an explanation," roars Erik Sejer-Lassen.

Thulin presses the messages icon on his Samsung Galaxy phone and skims his texts while Hess empties the contents of Sejer-Lassen's bag onto one of the white leather sofas, which are arranged like a lounge.

They're in the man's office on the top level of the building. While department-store Muzak and hordes of people battle for space on the floors below them, the story nearest the sky is dedicated to the impressive offices of Sejer-Lassen's investment firm. The daylight is fading, and beyond the glass partition between the office and the hall, employees with worried faces have gathered to watch their CEO, who moments earlier had been frog-marched out of the elevator in unmistakable fashion.

"You have no right to do this. What are you doing with my phone?"

Ignoring him, Thulin switches off his phone and glances at Hess, who is rummaging through the contents of the bag again.

"The message isn't there."

"He could have deleted it. They're saying the signal is still coming from here."

Hess grabs a white 7-Eleven bag out of the satchel, while Erik Sejer-Lassen takes a step toward Thulin.

"I haven't done anything. Either you get the fuck out of here, or you tell me—"

"What is your relationship with Laura Kjær?"

"Who?"

"Laura Kjær, thirty-seven years old, dental nurse. You just sent a message to her phone."

"I've never heard of her!"

"What have you done with your other mobile?"

"I only have one!"

"What's in the package?"

Thulin sees that Hess has removed a padded white A5 envelope from the carrier bag and is holding it out toward Sejer-Lassen.

"No idea—I only just picked it up! I was coming out of a meeting and got a text from a courier to say there was a package for me at 7-Elev . . . hey!"

Hess is tearing open the padded envelope.

"What are you doing? What the hell *is* this?!"

Hess abruptly lets the package drop onto the white leather. The opening is big enough for Thulin to glimpse a transparent plastic bag clotted with dark stains and an old, flashing Nokia mobile phone. The Nokia is gaffer-taped to a strange gray lump, and it isn't until Thulin recognizes the ring on the finger that she realizes they are staring at Laura Kjær's amputated hand.

Erik Sejer-Lassen goggles at it.

"What the fuck is *that*?"

Hess and Thulin exchange a glance, and Hess takes a step closer.

"I want you to think very carefully. Laura Kjær—"

"Hey, look, I don't know anything!"

"Who sent you the package?"

"I only just got it! I don't know—"

"Where were you last Monday evening?"

"Monday evening?"

Thulin tunes out their voices as she surveys the man's office. She knows instinctively their conversation is irrelevant. The confusion feels intentional. Like someone is already laughing at them as they bumble around like insects in a bottle, and she tries to focus on why they are there, why the place seems somehow right and wrong.

Somebody has deliberately sent a text to lure them here. Somebody wanted them to follow the signal from the Nokia and find Laura Kjær's right hand in Erik Sejer-Lassen's office. But why? Not to help, and apparently not because Sejer-Lassen could shed any light on the case. Yet why lead them straight to him?

Thulin's eyes come to rest on the beautifully framed photograph of Erik Sejer-Lassen and his wife and children on the Montana shelves behind the desk, and it dawns on her what the most appalling reason would be.

"Where is your wife?"

At Thulin's interruption, Hess and Erik Sejer-Lassen fall silent and turn to look at her.

"Your wife! Where is she right now?"

Sejer-Lassen shakes his head incredulously, while Hess glances from Thulin to the family photo on the shelf. She can tell he's had the same thought. Sejer-Lassen shrugs his shoulders and laughs.

"How the hell should I know? Home, probably. Why?"

39

The house is one of the biggest in Klampenborg, and ever since Anne Sejer-Lassen, her husband, and their two children moved in a few months earlier it has been her habit to finish her run outside the imposing electronic metal gates and walk the final stretch across the gravel to the front door, getting her breath back and her pulse down. But not today. After she screwed up her courage and called Erik she ran hard to get home, continuing over the gravel, past the neatly pruned bushes, the alabaster fountain, and the Land Rover. She doesn't care that she's left the gate open, because she knows in a minute she'll be driving out through it for the last time in her life. She's already called the au pair and said she will be picking up Lina and Sofia from kindergarten and the after-school club herself. When she reaches the stone front step, the dog bounces up and barks at her playfully as usual, but she pats it distractedly, takes the key from underneath the stone pot, and unlocks the door.

Inside the house, darkness is beginning to settle, and she switches on the light before disarming the security system, still out of breath. She kicks off her running shoes and walks purposefully up the stairs with the dog at her heels. She knows exactly what she needs, because in her head she's packed her bags many times before. From the children's room on the first floor she takes the two piles she has ready at the back of the wardrobe, and in the bathroom she remembers to grab their toothbrushes and toiletry bags. When her mobile rings, she can see on the screen that it's her husband, but she doesn't pick up. If she hurries now, she can call him later and say she couldn't answer because she was driving, and then he probably won't figure out what's going on until tomorrow morning, when he finds out they aren't at her mother's. She speeds up, stuffing the girls' clothes into the black holdall in the master bedroom, which is already full of her own clothes and their three beetroot-colored passports. She zips the bag shut and rushes down the stairs, getting as far as the front room with its floor-to-ceiling windows that overlook the forest before it suddenly occurs to her what she's forgotten. Chucking the bag onto the floor, she places her phone on top of it and jogs back up the stairs to the first floor. It's already dark in the children's room. She rummages feverishly underneath the duvets and the beds, but it isn't until she glances at the windowsill that she finds the two small, indispensable panda bears. Grateful to have located them so quickly, she speeds back down the stairs, reminding herself that all she has to do now is remember her wallet and car keys. Both are in the kitchen, waiting for her on the big, rustic table made of Chinese timber. Then she reaches the front room and stiffens.

In the middle of the floor, where the black holdall had been a moment earlier, there is nothing. No bag, no mobile phone. Only the bluish light from the bulbs in the garden, which shines through the terrace doors onto the varnished wooden flooring—and a little doll made of chestnuts. For a moment, she's nonplussed. Maybe it's just a chestnut man one of the girls has made with the au pair, and maybe Anne has just put the holdall somewhere else; but a split second later she knows that isn't the case.

"Hello . . . ? Erik, is that you?"

The house is silent. No answer comes, and when she looks at the dog, which has begun to growl, its eyes are fixed on something in the darkness behind her.

40

Kragh is in the middle of summarizing the history of the internet from Tim Berners-Lee to Bill Gates and Steve Jobs when the classroom door opens. Glancing across from her spot by the window, Mathilde sees to her surprise that it's Kristine's father peering through the doorway. He sounds confused as he apologizes for barging in, as though only just realizing he's forgotten to knock.

"I need to speak to Mathilde. Only for a second."

Mathilde rises before the teacher can reply. She can sense he doesn't appreciate the interruption, and she knows why, but she doesn't care.

Once she's standing in the common area and the door has shut behind her, she can tell from Steen's face that something is wrong. She has vivid memories of the day one year earlier when he came to her house to ask if she knew where Kristine was. She tried to be helpful, but she could see her answers were only making him more ill at ease, although he'd tried to convince himself Kristine had probably just gone home with some other friend.

It's still difficult for Mathilde to get her head around Kristine not being there. Sometimes when she thinks of her, she feels as though it were all one long dream. That Kristine has just moved and is living somewhere else—that of course Mathilde will end up laughing with her again one day. But whenever she happens to walk past Gustav at school or she catches a rare glimpse of Rosa or Steen, she knows then that it isn't a dream. She knew them so well. She loved being at their house, and it makes her sorry to see what grief has done to them. She is eager to help if she can, but now that she's alone with Steen outside the classroom, she feels a little afraid—it is obvious he's not himself. He seems perplexed and hunted, and his breath smells sharp as he begins to apologize and explain that he needs her to tell him about making chestnut men with Kristine last autumn.

"Chestnut men?"

Mathilde isn't sure what she was expecting, but the question puts her even more on edge, and at first she doesn't even understand what he means.

"You mean, how we made them?"

"No. When you made the dolls, was it you or her that actually made them?"

For a moment, Mathilde can't dig up the memory, and he watches her agitatedly.

"I need to know."

"We both did, I think."

"You *think*?"

"No, we definitely did. Why?"

"So *she* made them too? Are you certain?"

"Yes. We made them together."

She can tell from his face that it isn't the answer he'd hoped for, and for some obscure reason she feels guilty.

"We always went to your place and made them, and—"

"Yeah, I know. Then what did you do with them?"

"Then we went down to the roadside and sold them. With cakes and—"

"To whom?"

"I don't know. To anybody who wanted to buy them. Why is—"

"But did you only sell them to people you knew, or were there others?"

"I don't know . . ."

"You must be able to remember whether there were others."

"But I didn't know them . . ."

"They were strangers, though? Or someone she knew, or what?"

"I don't know—"

"Mathilde, this might be important—"

"Steen, what's going on?"

Kragh appears in the doorway, but Kristine's father shoots him only a curt glance.

"Nothing. It'll only take—"

"Steen, come with me."

Kragh steps between him and Mathilde and tries to guide him away, but Steen stands his ground.

"If you have something important to say to Mathilde, you need to go about it the right way. This has been a difficult time for everybody, especially for your family, but for her classmates too."

"It's just a couple of questions. It'll only take a minute."

"I'd like to know what it's about. Otherwise I'll have to ask you to leave."

It's as though all the air has trickled out of Kristine's father as Kragh stands and gazes inquiringly at him. He looks confusedly at Mathilde, and then at the other students, who are gaping at them through the open door.

"Sorry. I didn't mean to . . ."

Steen hesitates and turns around. Mathilde sees him realize with a jolt that Gustav is watching him from the other end of the common area. He says nothing, merely stares at his father, but then he swivels on his heel and leaves. Steen begins to follow him, and he's nearly reached the corner before Mathilde reacts.

"Wait!"

Steen turns around slowly, and she walks up to him.

"I'm sorry I can't remember everything."

"It doesn't matter. Sorry."

"But now I think about it, I remember we didn't actually *make* chestnut men last year at all."

His gaze has been fixed on the floor, his whole body stooped and heavy with an invisible weight. But as her words sink in, he looks up and meets her eye.

41

Her seventh press interview of the day has just finished, and Rosa is pacing swiftly down the corridor with Engells when her mobile rings. She sees her husband's name on the display as she puts on her coat, but she doesn't have the time to talk—her chief of staff still has to run through the numbers from the latest ministry report with her.

All the interviews have gone well. She talked about the necessity of all their initiatives, and emphasized that she was very optimistic about working with the supporting party. All told, it was calculated to bring Bukke back into line. She tolerated the intrusive questions, although it had sapped her strength. *What's it like being back? How has this changed your life?* and *How do you get through something so terrible?* The strange thing is that the young journalist who asked Rosa that last question was assuming she was over the loss of her daughter purely because she had returned to her ministerial post.

"Hurry up! If the minister is going to make it, we'll have to do it on the way."

Liu is standing impatiently by the elevator and takes the report from Engells, who wishes Rosa luck with a pat on the shoulder.

"Where's Vogel?" asks Rosa.

"He's meeting us later outside the DR building."

They'd said yes to two live interviews on the television news—the first with DR and the next with TV2. The schedule is tight. They step into the elevator that leads down to the rear of the building, where it's easier for the driver to pick them up than at the traffic-choked main entrance. Liu presses the button for the ground floor.

"The prime minister is aware of the development, but Vogel said they still don't want you to fall out with Bukke."

"We're not going to fall out with Bukke, but we need to be the ones in the driver's seat—not him."

"I'm just repeating what Vogel said. And it's important how you come across now. The papers are one thing—"

"I know what I'm doing, Liu."

"I know that, but this is live, and they're going to ask about stuff besides politics. Vogel asked me to prepare you for them wanting to discuss your comeback. In other words, they're going to be asking you some rather prying questions, and Vogel couldn't get any guarantees."

"I'll just have to cope. If I back out now, there's no point. Where's the car?"

Rosa has stepped out of the elevator and passed the security guards by the rear entrance, Liu following. Now they are standing in windswept Admiralgade, but the ministerial car isn't in its usual spot. Rosa can tell Liu is surprised, but as always she pretends everything's in hand.

"Hang on, I'll find the driver. He often parks in a side street when he takes a break."

Liu takes off across the cobbles, scanning back and forth and taking her phone out of her bag. Rosa's mobile rings again. She picks up as she strolls after Liu. The wind feels cold, and as they pass Boldhusgade she can see across to Christiansborg on the other side of the canal.

"Hi, sweetie. I don't have much time. I'm on my way to DR, and I need to get ready in the car."

The line is so bad she can barely hear him. His voice sounds shaken and befuddled, and at first she only catches the words *important* and *Mathilde*. She repeats what she said, trying to explain she can't hear a thing, but he's desperate to tell her something. In the arch leading toward a small courtyard, she sees Liu halt and begin to talk animatedly with the new driver, who for some reason hasn't driven the car up to meet them.

"Steen, this isn't a good time. I need to hang up."

"Listen!"

The connection suddenly strengthens, and Steen's voice is clear and unambiguous.

"You told the police they made chestnut men. Could you have misremembered?"

"Steen, I can't talk now."

"I've just spoken to Mathilde. She says they *didn't* make chestnut men last year. They made animals and spiders and all sorts of other stuff last year, but no chestnut men. So how did the fingerprint get there? Do you understand what I'm saying?"

Rosa pauses; Steen's voice is cutting out again.

"Hello? Steen?"

She feels a knot in her belly, but the line is bad, and soon there's a little beep to indicate that it has gone dead. She begins walking toward Liu, who is staring at something inside the courtyard. Liu only looks up when the driver taps her arm and nods in Rosa's direction.

"Come on, we'll take a taxi instead."

"I just need to phone Steen. Why can't we take the car?"

"I'll tell you on the way. Come on."

"No, what's happened?"

"Come on, we need to hurry!"

But it's too late. Rosa can see the ministerial car. The windshield is shattered. Big, misshapen red letters are scrawled across the hood. They appear to be written in blood, and she stiffens with shock when she realizes what word the letters spell: MURDERER.

Liu takes her arm and leads her away.

"I told him to ring the security people. We need to go."

42

The silhouette of the forest looms in the darkness before them, and Thulin scarcely has time to slow down as Hess points out the street number. She swings into the driveway of the palatial house in Klampenborg at such speed that the car skids on the gravel. She drives straight up to the front door, but before the car comes to a halt Hess flings open the door and leaps out. To her relief, she sees that the local patrol unit she called is already parked outside, and as she runs up the stone steps and into the hall, one of the officers is coming down the stairs from the first floor.

"We've been through the house. Something happened in the front room."

"Thulin!"

Thulin races into the front room, where the first things she sees are the bloodstains on the wall and the dog, which lies lifeless on the floor with its head caved in. Some of the furniture has been overturned, one of the windows is smashed, and there is blood on the door frame and on the floor, where two stuffed panda bears have been dropped. A black holdall is hidden behind a door, and a mobile phone lies on the floor beside it.

"Get some officers and dogs into the forest, right now!"

Hess is tugging at the terrace door as he gives the orders to the officer, who nods, flustered, and gropes for his phone. A garden chair has toppled against the door, but Hess kicks it loose and Thulin dashes after him as he sprints across the lawn and into the woods.

43

Anne Sejer-Lassen is running for her life in the gloom, branches slapping against her face. She feels pine needles and roots cut into her bare feet, but she keeps running, keeps forcing herself onward, as her legs fill with lactic acid and cramps begin to set in. Every moment she hopes to recognize some detail in the forest she knows so well, but there is nothing but darkness and the sound of her breath, and the twigs snapping and betraying where she is.

She pauses by a tall tree. She flattens herself against the cold, damp bark and tries to stifle her breathing, listening to the forest. Her heart is about to burst, and she is close to tears. Very far away she thinks she can hear voices, but she can't get her bearings, and if she yells her pursuer might hear her. She knows she's been running a long time, and she tries to work out whether her pursuer could have kept up with her. She's lost, but when she looks back there's no flicker of a flashlight, no noise or movement in the darkness, and that *has* to mean she's gotten away.

Ahead of her, far away between the trees, she suddenly sees a light. It's moving in a slow arc, and soon she thinks she can hear a distant engine; all at once she knows where she is. The beam has to be from the headlights on a car driving down the lane that starts at the roundabout and leads down to the water. She tenses her muscles, screws up her courage, and begins to run. It's about a hundred and fifty yards to the lane, but she knows exactly where there is a sharp bend, and that she will come out in front of the car. Only fifty yards more, and then she'll begin to shout. Only thirty yards now, and even though the car is moving, the driver will be able to hear her voice, and her pursuer will have to give up.

The blow strikes her from the front. Something bores into her cheek, something that jabs, and she realizes immediately that he must have been standing in front of her, waiting for her to react to the beam. She senses the forest floor beneath her and tastes iron spreading in her mouth. She scrambles frantically to her knees, but at that moment she's struck in the face again, and she collapses onto all fours and begins to sob.

"Are you okay, Anne?"

The voice is whispering close to her ear, but before she can answer the blows begin to hail down. In the seconds between them, she hears herself whimpering and asking why. Why her, what has she done? And when the voice finally tells her, her strength gives out. A boot forces her arm to the ground, and she feels a sharp blade against her wrist. She begs and pleads for her life, not for her own sake but for the children's. For a moment, the figure seems to be deliberating, and Anne feels something stroke her cheek.

44

The light from Thulin's flashlight dances around the wet trees, leaping over stumps and branches as she calls for the woman in the dark. Ahead of her and far to her left, Thulin can hear Hess doing the same, and she sees the glinting beam of his flashlight moving constantly forward. They have run a long way now, several kilometers, and Thulin is about to call out again when she feels a searing pain in her foot. It's gotten caught in a root, and she's pitched to the ground. Blackness engulfs her, and she gropes desperately for her flashlight, which must have gotten switched off. Getting to her knees, she begins digging her hands into the wet undergrowth, searching the area around her. Then, abruptly, she notices the figure and freezes. It's standing quite still and observing her from the other side of a clearing, only twenty yards away and nearly indiscernible from the darkness.

"Hess!"

Her shout echoes through the forest, and she fumbles her gun out of its holster while Hess runs toward her with the flashlight. By the time he reaches her, she's aiming her gun at the figure, and he shines the cone of light in the same direction, panting.

Anne Sejer-Lassen is hanging in a little copse of trees. Two branches are wedged beneath her arms, holding up her battered body. Her bare feet dangle above the earth, and her head is slumped against her chest so that her long, fluttering hair covers her face. As Thulin approaches, she realizes what it is that struck her as off: Anne Sejer-Lassen's arms are too short. Both her hands are missing. And then she sees it. The little chestnut man protruding from the flesh of Anne Sejer-Lassen's left shoulder. To Thulin it seems to be grinning.

Tuesday, October 13th

45

The rain comes down in sheets. Long chains of dark-clothed officers are combing the woods, their flashlights fixed on the ground, while a helicopter floats restlessly above the treetops, raking them with its searchlight. Hess and his colleagues have been working for nearly seven hours, and it's past midnight. Three operations managers have mapped out the area, splitting up the forest into five different zones, each of which will be searched by a team equipped with Maglite flashlights and canine units.

All entrances and exits were closed off as soon as Anne Sejer-Lassen's corpse was found, and they set up roadblocks on several exit roads. Cars have been stopped and people questioned, but Hess is afraid it will all be pointless. They got there too late, and are still lagging behind. The rain started shortly after their arrival in the woods, and whatever evidence there must be—footprints, tire tracks, whatever—has been washed away, leaving them grasping at a phantom who has the weather gods on his side. Hess thinks about the corpse of Anne Sejer-Lassen, he thinks about the little doll stuck into her shoulder, and he feels like an unwilling theatergoer searching for an exit while some bizarre performance is being acted out before his eyes. His clothes drenched, he trudges back from the northern end of the woods down one of the main paths, which the operations managers have drawn on his map. A younger officer has stepped out of formation to take a piss behind a tree, and Hess snaps at him: he's supposed to leave the area being searched for evidence first. The officer hurries back into line, and Hess regrets his outburst. He knows he's rusty. His body is out of shape, his thoughts twitching and foggy. It's far too long since he's been on a case like this; in fact, he's never been on a case like this, and right now he ought to be watching football on a flat-screen TV in his shitty little apartment in the Hague, or on his way to yet another irrelevant assignment somewhere in Europe, but instead he's traipsing around in the woods somewhere north of Copenhagen, where the rain falls like bolts of iron and pins everything to the ground.

Hess finds his way back to the site where the body was found, to the heavy floodlights illuminating the copse and throwing long shadows behind the Forensics techs milling among the trees. Anne Sejer-Lassen's body was taken down several hours earlier and driven to the coroner for examination, but he's looking for Thulin. He sees her coming back from the western edge of the woods, her hair tousled and damp, wiping smears of mud from her face as she finishes a phone call. Noticing Hess, she shakes her head, indicating that nothing has been found to the west.

"But I did just speak to Genz."

When Genz appeared in the woods after the discovery of Anne Sejer-Lassen, Hess drew him aside and asked him to take the chestnut man straight back to the lab. Hess looks at Thulin through the rain, and he knows the result of Genz's examination before she says a word.

46

I t's midmorning. From the window in the task-force command center on the second floor of the police station, Nylander can just make out the free-speech vultures with their phones, cameras, and microphones hovering by the entrance to the main courtyard. Despite management's repeated admonitions to everybody on the force, it's often brought home to him that the system is about as watertight as a sieve, and today is no exception. Only twelve hours after the body was discovered in the woods, the press has started speculating about a connection between this murder and the killing of Laura Kjær in Husum, apparently on the basis of anonymous "sources in the police." Then, as if being besieged by the media weren't enough, Nylander's also had the deputy commissioner on the phone, although he temporarily dodged that bullet by saying crisply that he'd call back soon. What matters right now is the investigation, and he turns impatiently to Thulin, who is in the middle of updating the group of detectives on the case.

Most have worked all night long with only a few hours' sleep, but given the seriousness of the situation they have no trouble paying attention to Thulin's summary.

It has been a long night for Nylander too. The call about Anne Sejer-Lassen came during a dinner with the Management Society at a restaurant in Bredgade. The meeting had been full of bigwigs, and it was a great networking opportunity, but when the call came in he abandoned the meal mid-tiramisu. He isn't technically required to visit crime scenes in person. He has officers for that, but he's made it a principle to do so anyway. It's important to show a good example—and to run a tight ship. Once you start letting things slide, you leave your flank open to attack later on, and Nylander is too canny for that. He's seen countless bosses and civil servants get caught with their pants down and botch up their careers because power has made them arrogant. In the case of Laura Kjær, however, he skipped going to the crime scene because of the budget meetings, so when he got Thulin's call about the fingerprint it had seemed like a judgment. Yesterday evening, then, Nylander had left the restaurant immediately without any annoyance at all. In any case, dessert always marked the point by which the worst of the suits were so plastered they started basking in their own achievements. Nylander knows he will probably outstrip the lot of them, but to do so he needs to keep a clear head and his finger on the pulse if the red light starts flashing, as it did last night. Since his trip to the crime scene in the forest, he's been running the various scenarios in his head, but he still hasn't come up with a strategy, for the simple reason that it's all too incomprehensible. He'd personally dropped in on Genz and the Forensics Department that morning in the hopes of having the fingerprints declared a mistake after all, but found himself out of luck. Genz had explained that there were enough points of comparison in both cases to justify a match with Kristine Hartung, and now the only thing Nylander knows for sure is that he has to navigate carefully if he wants to steer clear of the rocks.

"—and both victims were in their late thirties and were surprised in their homes. According to the coroner's preliminary examinations, the women were assaulted and killed with a weapon that was rammed through their eye sockets and into their brains. In the case of the first victim, the right hand was sawn off, while in the second case both hands were amputated—and both women were alive when the amputation occurred."

The assembled detectives stare at the photographs of the corpses that Thulin has passed around the tables, and some of the newer ones frown or turn away. Nylander has seen the pictures too, but they don't affect him. When he first started as a policeman, it disconcerted him that he was left unmoved by that sort of stuff, but now he merely sees it as an advantage.

"What do we have on the murder weapon?" He interrupts Thulin's summary tetchily.

"Nothing conclusive. Some sort of club fitted with a heavy metal ball with small spikes. Not a mace, but the same principle. If you're talking about the amputations, we're looking at a kind of battery-powered saw with a diamond blade or similar. The preliminary examinations indicate that it was the same tool used in both—"

"What about the text message sent to Laura Kjær's phone, then? The sender?"

"The text was sent using an old Nokia phone with an unregistered prepaid card that you could buy anywhere. The phone itself, which was taped to Laura Kjær's right hand, didn't give us anything. There's no other data on it besides the text, and the serial number has been burned off with a soldering iron, according to Genz."

"But the courier who delivered the package, the one you were tracing via the phone signal, presumably they've got information about who sent it?"

"They do, but the problem is that Laura Kjær is listed as the sender."

"What?"

"Their customer service department says that a person called around lunchtime yesterday and ordered a courier to pick up a package from Laura Kjær from the front steps at 7 Cedervænget in Husum. Which is Laura Kjær's address. The package was ready for pickup along with the shipping fee when the messenger arrived just after one p.m. He drove it to the department store and delivered it to the 7-Eleven on the ground floor, which Sejer-Lassen's company uses for deliveries. That was all the messenger could tell us, and we could only find his fingerprints on the package, as well as the 7-Eleven clerk's and Sejer-Lassen's."

"But the person who called them?"

"The customer service agent couldn't even remember whether it was a man or a woman who called."

"Cedervænget, then? Someone must have seen who left the package there?"

Thulin shakes her head. "Our first suspect was Laura Kjær's boyfriend, Hans Henrik Hauge, but

Hauge has an alibi. The coroner says Sejer-Lassen was killed sometime around six p.m., and according to his lawyer, she and Hauge were in the parking lot outside her office at that time, discussing whether to complain about us not letting him back in the house."

"So we've got fuck all? No witnesses, calls, nothing?"

"Not yet. And it doesn't seem like there's any connection between the victims. They live in completely different places, move in completely different social circles, and apparently have nothing in common besides the two chestnut men and the fingerprints, so we're going to start—"

"What fingerprints?"

Nylander glances at Jansen, who asked the question. As always, he's seated beside his faithful companion, Martin Ricks. Nylander senses Thulin's eyes on him: he told her beforehand that he wanted to break that particular news himself.

"Someone had placed a chestnut man in the vicinity of both victims. In both cases there was a fingerprint on the doll, and according to the dactyloscopic analysis they're most likely identical with Kristine Hartung's."

Nylander's voice is deliberately dry and undramatic, and for a moment nobody speaks. Then Tim Jansen and a couple of the others burst into animated conversation. Their astonishment spreads, turning into baffled incredulity, until Nylander wades in again.

"Listen up. Forensics is still conducting various tests, so I don't want anyone jumping to conclusions until we know more. Right now we don't know anything. Maybe the prints aren't relevant at all, so if anybody makes so much as a peep about this outside these four walls, I will personally make sure that person never works again. Is that understood?"

Nylander has been considering how to handle the situation. Two unsolved murders is plenty to be getting on with. They might even have been committed by the same person—although Nylander has trouble accepting that bit too. And so long as there is still a trace of uncertainty about the identity of the fingerprint, he doesn't want it muddying the waters. The Hartung case was one of Nylander's finest achievements. At one point he'd thought it was going to scupper his career, but then came the breakthrough and the arrest of Linus Bekker.

"But you need to reopen the Hartung case."

Nylander and the others look around for the source of the voice, and their eyes land on the man from Europol. Until now he's been mute and invisible, engrossed in the photographs being passed around. He's still wearing the same clothes as in the woods, and his hair is matted and dirty, but although he looks like something that has been lying on the forest floor for a week he is quick and composed.

"One print could be a coincidence. Two prints can't be. And if they *are* Kristine Hartung's fingerprints, the previous investigation into her disappearance could have reached the wrong conclusion."

"What the hell are you talking about?"

Tim Jansen has turned around and is eyeing Hess warily, as though he's just been asked to hand over a month's salary.

"Jansen, I'll take this."

Nylander can tell which way the wind is blowing, and this is precisely what he wanted to avoid, but Hess speaks up before he can continue.

"I know no more than you do. But Kristine Hartung's body was never found, and the forensic tests they conducted back then were clearly not enough to establish her death beyond any doubt. Now these fingerprints have turned up, and all I'm saying is that it raises some questions."

"No, that's not what you're saying, Hess. You're saying maybe we didn't do our jobs well enough."

"It's not personal. But two women have been killed, and if we want to stop it happening again, we need to—"

"I'm not taking it personally. And I'm sure the three hundred other officers who helped solve the case won't either. But it's kind of funny getting aggro from someone who's only here because he was kicked out of the Hague, don't you think?"

A few of Jansen's colleagues snigger. But Nylander looks at Hess without expression. He registered what Hess said, and hasn't listened to the rest.

"What the hell do you mean, 'if we want to stop it happening again'?"

47

The station's female communications consultant is eager to help him plot a course of action, but Nylander cuts her off and says he'll manage by himself. Normally, he'd have taken the time, because he's been attracted to her ever since she turned up for work and started waltzing in and out of his department dispensing good advice. But right now, as he heads down the stairs to the courtyard, he wants to use the rest of the walk to clear his head before meeting with the press, and her media studies degree—probably three years of caffe lattes and casual sex—isn't going to help him there. Certainly not after the disconcerting meeting he's just had with Hess and Thulin in his office.

Before Nylander steps out into the porticoed courtyard, he's informed that Minister Rosa Hartung has found a gap in her calendar and is on her way to the station. He gives strict instructions that she and her husband should be brought in through the rear entrance and are not to be interviewed except by him personally.

It was Hess who suggested that he, Nylander, and Thulin take a moment in Nylander's office after the briefing so that they could continue their conversation in private. Hess had placed the crime-scene photos of Laura Kjær and Anne Sejer-Lassen on Nylander's desk.

"The first victim is missing a hand. The next one's missing two. It's possible the killer would have mutilated Anne Sejer-Lassen even more if we hadn't disturbed him, but what if he intentionally arranged the victims exactly as we found them?"

"I don't understand. Spell it out, I don't have all day," Nylander had said.

Thulin, who had evidently been taken into Hess's confidence before the meeting, had shown him two close-up photos of the chestnut men, which Nylander was already fed up of looking at.

"A chestnut man consists of a head and a body. The head has eyes, which are made with an awl or some other sharp implement, and the body has four matchsticks, which are supposed to be its arms and legs. But a chestnut man doesn't have any hands. Nor does it have any feet."

Nylander had fallen silent, staring at the chestnut men and their truncated arms. For a second he'd felt as though he were being read to at a kindergarten, and he didn't know whether to laugh or cry.

"You're not saying what I think you're saying."

It was a sick thought. You'd almost have to be sick yourself to come up with it, but suddenly Nylander grasped just what Hess had meant during the briefing about trying to prevent it happening again. Neither of them replied, but the notion that the killer could be making his own chestnut man of flesh and blood had been difficult to shake off.

Hess had insisted again on the necessity of reopening the Hartung case. He'd kept saying *you* when referring to the investigation—"you need to" and "you've got to consider the possibility that"—until Nylander had given him to understand two things. One, Hess was now a member of the department on exactly the same footing as the other investigators, and as far as Nylander knew nobody was agitating to get him back to the Hague. Quite the opposite. Two, reopening the Hartung case was flat-out unthinkable. No matter what the fingerprints signified, the Hartung case was closed. They had a confession, they had a conviction, and no power on God's green earth was going to start all that up again. For the same reason, Nylander had decided that he would conduct the interview with the Hartung parents personally and inform them of the new fingerprint himself. The discovery shouldn't be overdramatized, and anyway, the intelligence services had just told him that the minister had already had a rough week—one or more unknown persons had been harassing her, most recently smashing the window of her ministerial car and smearing the hood with animal's blood.

Nylander didn't deem it necessary to get Hess and Thulin involved in that side of things, and he'd kicked Hess out of his office so he could speak to Thulin alone. He asked her straight out whether Hess was sharp enough to be on the case. From an old personnel file he already knew the tragic reason Hess had originally left the department, and although the man had plenty of experience at Europol, he also had a serious problem with authority, which on the face of things made it seem like his best days were behind him.

Although it was clear Thulin didn't like the man, she'd answered in the affirmative, so Nylander had told her he wanted her and Hess to stay on the case—on the condition that if there was any hint of trouble from

Hess he wanted to know about it immediately. Of course, Nylander had added a remark about how the NC3 recommendation would have to wait until things had calmed back down, and he knew Thulin would interpret this exactly as it was meant—that loyalty was a condition of the recommendation.

Turning out of the station, Nylander approaches the vultures, who are hovering in the hopes of someone falling out of the window. It was Nylander's own idea to meet them head-on here instead of holding a press conference, because outside the building it's easier to wrap things up and withdraw into his hidey-hole again. Yet as the flashes begin to go off, he finds his face settling back into its familiar expression, and it strikes him that he's missed the attention. This is what he does best. True, his ass is on the line, but there is also plenty to be gained. Over the next few days, he will be the one everybody wants to talk to, and given the notoriety of the case it might just prove to be the opportunity Nylander is looking for. If it all goes to hell, it might even be useful to have Mark Hess up his sleeve.

48

The sound of the two girls crying upstairs filters into every corner of the vast house. Even into the kitchen, where Erik Sejer-Lassen is sitting at the imposing table made of Chinese timber, still in the suit he was wearing when Laura Kjær's hand was found at his office the day before. It's clear to Hess, who is sitting beside him, that the man hasn't even gone to bed. His eyes are bloodshot and swollen, his shirt grubby and crumpled, toys are scattered across the floor, and the stove behind him is stacked with dirty pots and pans. Hess can see Thulin trying to catch the man's eye from her chair on the other side of the table, but without success.

"Please take another look at the photograph. Are you sure your wife didn't know this woman?"

Sejer-Lassen looks down at the photo of Laura Kjær, but his eyes are absent.

"What about her? The minister for social affairs, Rosa Hartung. Is she someone your wife knew or spoke about, or someone you both met, or . . ."

But Sejer-Lassen shakes his head apathetically at the picture of Rosa Hartung that Thulin has slid across the table. Hess can see she's trying to suppress her irritation, and he understands. It's the second time inside a week she's sat face-to-face with a widower who seems completely blank when confronted with her questions.

"Mr. Sejer-Lassen, we need your help. You must be able to think of something. Did she have any enemies, was there anyone she was afraid of, or was there—"

"But I don't know anything else. She didn't have any enemies. She was only interested in the house and the kids . . ."

Thulin takes a deep breath and continues asking questions, but Hess senses Sejer-Lassen is telling the truth. He tries to ignore the sound of the children crying, and regrets not simply telling Nylander it wasn't his problem when the chance presented itself at the station earlier that day. But there's no way back now: he woke up that morning after three hours' sleep with the image of chestnut men and severed limbs burned into his retinas. The caretaker showed up moments later with a reprimand—he'd left painting tools and a floor polisher in the middle of the walkway—but Hess didn't have the time to deal with it. On his way to the station he'd phoned the Hague and done his best to apologize for missing the telephone meeting with Freimann, which had slipped his mind the previous afternoon. The secretary's coldness was unmistakable. Hess had given up trying to explain the reason for his oversight and instead jostled his way hurriedly through the busy morning rush at the train station so he'd have time to look in more detail at the photographs of Anne Sejer-Lassen's body. He'd decided in advance that he would stop worrying if he could find cut marks elsewhere besides her wrists. If there were several other concrete amputation marks left by the tool used to amputate her hands, then there was probably no reason to pursue the sick thought he'd woken up with. But there had been no indication that the killer had tried to amputate any other parts of Anne Sejer-Lassen. Hess had even rung the coroner's office to be sure: in both the first and second killing, the tool had been used solely to amputate the hands, confirming Hess's fears and making him seriously uneasy. He couldn't know whether he was right in predicting further victims, but his concern was growing. Ideally, he would have liked to press pause and immerse himself in the Kristine Hartung case before committing himself to a new direction, but Nylander had put his foot down, and so he and Thulin had gone to the Sejer-Lassens', where they still hadn't gotten anywhere.

Two hours they'd spent searching the mansion-like property and its grounds. First of all they'd discovered that the CCTV cameras facing the woods on the north side of the house had been deactivated. From the moment Anne Sejer-Lassen returned from her run and switched off the alarm, anybody could have climbed over the fence and forced their way into the house unseen. The neighbors had seen nothing, which was entirely believable, since the lavish homes along the street were spaced so far apart that real estate agents could legitimately describe them, without the customary exaggeration, as "secluded."

While Genz and the Forensics techs had focused on combing the garden, front room, and hall for potential evidence, Thulin and Hess had gone upstairs to check the bedrooms, drawers, and wardrobes, hoping to glean some information about Anne Sejer-Lassen's life. There were nine rooms on the first floor, if you counted the spa and walk-in closet. Hess was no specialist in material luxury, but the Bang & Olufsen screen in the bedroom alone looked like it might be equivalent to a deposit on a few apartments at Odin. Tastefully, there were no curtains or blinds obscuring the tall, magnificent windows, but standing in the room he couldn't help wondering whether the killer had used them to spy on Anne Sejer-Lassen and her evening routine from the dim garden, where the rain was once more bucketing down.

In the other rooms on the first floor too, the interiors and materials were carefully considered: Anne Sejer-Lassen's walk-in closet was neatly organized, with rows of high-heeled shoes, dresses, and freshly ironed pants on identical wooden hangers, while her socks and lingerie were arrayed in equally immaculate drawers. The en suite bathroom was like something out of a five-star hotel, with two sinks, a large sunken bathtub featuring Italian tiles, and a separate spa room and sauna. In the children's room, meanwhile, there were big, colorful wall paintings of Hans Scherfig's jungle animals encircling the two small beds, which looked up to a starry sky on the ceiling, complete with painted planets and stray space rockets.

Yet no matter where they searched, there was nothing to explain why anybody would have surprised Anne Sejer-Lassen in her home, chased her into a forest, and sawn off both her hands.

Instead they'd focused on questioning Erik Sejer-Lassen, who had told them how he and Anne met at Ordrup High School. As soon as the two of them had finished their studies at Copenhagen Business School, they'd celebrated by getting married, then set off on a round-the-world trip before settling down first in New Zealand and later in Singapore. Erik had made some lucky investments in various biotech companies, while Anne's greatest wish had been to have children and a family. They'd had two girls, and once the eldest reached school age they'd returned home to Denmark, initially to a rental property in one of the new buildings on Islands Brygge, where they'd lived until they could purchase the house in Klampenborg, close to the neighborhood where Erik had grown up. Hess got the impression the family's standard of living relied on Erik's income, and although Anne had trained as an interior designer several years earlier, she seemed mainly to have taken pride in being a mother, looking after the house, and arranging get-togethers for their circle of friends, most of whom were really Erik's. A detective had also been dispatched to Helsingør, where Anne Sejer-Lassen's mother lived, and from her summary of the conversation Hess had learned that she'd grown up poor, lost her father early, and from childhood onward was focused on building a family. Her mother, in a voice choked with tears, had explained that she hadn't seen as much of her daughter and grandchildren after they got home from Asia as she'd hoped, which she put down to Erik disliking her. Not that he or Anne had ever said so, but she'd usually only seen her daughter and grandchildren when Erik was at work, or on the rare occasions when her daughter drove up with the kids to say hello. The mother's impression was that the balance of power between Anne and Erik was much too uneven, but Anne had always defended her husband and refused to leave him; it had been clear to her mother that she needed to keep that sort of opinion to herself if she wanted to keep seeing her. Which, after the events of yesterday, she never would again.

The digital clock on one of the kitchen's two big Smeg ovens shifts another minute forward, and Hess forces himself to listen to Thulin's questions rather than the crying upstairs.

"But your wife packed a bag. She was on her way out the door, and she told the au pair she'd pick up the children herself, so where was she going?"

"I told you. She was going to visit her mother. They were going to stay the night."

"That's not what it looks like. She'd packed a bag with their passports and enough clothes for more than a week, so what was she going to do? Why did she want to leave?"

"She didn't want to leave."

"I think she did, and people don't run off like that without good reason. So either tell me what that reason was, or I'll get a warrant to go through your phone and internet traffic to see if I can find one."

Erik Sejer-Lassen looks like he's reaching the end of his rope.

"My wife and I had a great relationship. But we—or I—have also had some problems."

"What kind of problems?"

"I've had affairs. Nothing that meant anything. But . . . maybe she found out about that."

"Affairs, you say. With whom?"

"Different people."

"Who? How? Women, men?"

"Women. Casual stuff. Just people I met or messaged online somewhere. It didn't mean anything."

"So why did you do it?"

Sejer-Lassen hesitates.

"I don't know. Sometimes life just doesn't work out the way you'd hoped."

"What do you mean?"

Sejer-Lassen is staring vacantly into space. Hess couldn't have agreed more with his last sentence, yet he still can't help wondering what a guy like Sejer-Lassen had hoped for out of life if it wasn't a trophy wife, a family, and a house worth over thirty-five million kroner.

"When and how could your wife have found out about this?" continues Thulin snappishly.

"I don't know, but you asked whether—"

"Mr. Sejer-Lassen, we've examined your wife's phone, emails, and social media accounts. If she found out about what you've told us, it makes sense she would have spoken to someone about your infidelity—either you, her mother, or a friend—but she made no mention of it."

"Well . . ."

"Ergo, that probably wasn't why she was running off. So I'm going to ask you again: Why did your wife want to leave you? Why had she packed a bag and—"

"I *don't know*! You asked me for a reason, and that's the only reason I can come up with, for fuck's sake!"

Erik Sejer-Lassen's outburst of rage seems to Hess for a moment like an overreaction. On the other hand, the man is probably barely keeping it together. It's been a long day, and Hess sees no reason to continue the interview, so he interrupts. "Thanks, we'll leave it there. If you think of anything else, you let us know immediately, okay?"

Sejer-Lassen nods gratefully, and although Hess has turned his back to find his jacket, he can tell Thulin isn't pleased about the interruption. Luckily a voice forestalls any further comment.

"Can I take the girls out for ice cream?"

The au pair has come downstairs with the two girls, who are now wearing outdoor clothes. Hess and Thulin have already interviewed her. She hadn't seen Anne since yesterday morning, having had lunch at the Filipino Free Church and then getting a call from Anne that afternoon saying that she would pick up the girls herself. It's clear she has great respect for the Sejer-Lassen family and especially the police, and Hess guesses her residency permit isn't quite in order. The youngest of the girls is in her arms, the older holding her hand. They are red-eyed and tearstained, and Erik Sejer-Lassen, who has risen to his feet, is walking toward them.

"Yes. Good idea, Judith. Thank you."

Sejer-Lassen strokes one of his daughter's hair and gives the other one a forced smile, while all four walk toward the kitchen passage.

"When I'm finished with an interview, I'll say so myself."

Thulin has walked up to Hess, positioning herself so he can't avoid looking into her brown eyes.

"Look, we were with the man yesterday afternoon, when Anne Sejer-Lassen was being attacked, so there's no way he did it."

"We're looking for a common factor between these two killings. One victim changed the locks; the other one was trying to do a runner—"

"I'm not looking for a common factor. I'm looking for a murderer."

Hess tries to head into the front room to hear the Forensics techs' report, but Thulin blocks his path.

"Let's deal with this right now. Do you have a problem with this? Us two working together, coordinating?"

"No, I don't have a problem. But let's split things up so we're not getting into a tug-of-war like two idiots."

"Am I interrupting?"

The cream-colored sliding door into the hall glides open, and Genz appears in his white space suit, a flight case in his hand.

"We're packing up now. I don't want to disappoint anybody in advance, but on the face of it there doesn't seem to be any more to go on than with Laura Kjær. The most interesting thing is the traces of blood in the cracks in the hall floor. But they're old, and they don't match Anne Sejer-Lassen's blood type, so I'm assuming they're not relevant."

On the floor in the hallway behind Genz they can see traces of luminol glowing green under the phosphorescent lights, while a tech snaps photographs with a camera.

"Why are there traces of old blood on the hall floor?"

Thulin shoots the question at Sejer-Lassen, who has returned from the kitchen passage and begun somewhat apathetically to clear away the toys.

"If it's by the stairs, it might be from Sofia, our eldest. She fell and broke her nose and collarbone a couple of months back, spent some time in the hospital."

"Could be that. By the way, Hess, our office party committee told me to say hello and thanks for the pig."

Genz goes back to the other white-clad spacemen and shuts the sliding door behind him. A thought strikes Hess, and he gazes at Erik Sejer-Lassen with renewed interest, but Thulin beats him to the punch.

"Which hospital was Sofia staying at?"

"The Rigshospital. Just a couple of days."

"Which department at the Rigshospital?"

This time Hess is the one asking. The fact that both detectives are suddenly showing interest in the subject evidently bewilders Sejer-Lassen, who pauses in the middle of the room with a tricycle in his hand.

"Pediatrics. I think. But it was mainly Anne who took care of things and went to the clinic. Why?"

Neither of them answers. Thulin strides across to the front door, and Hess knows she won't let him drive this time either.

49

No one visiting the pediatric ward at the Rigs-hospital on Blegdamsvej can help pausing to admire the wall of innumerable colorful children's drawings, large and small, that decorate the corridor. Hess is no exception. So much pain and zest for life gathered in one place, and Hess can't stop staring at the wall, while Thulin goes up to the desk to announce their arrival.

Sejer-Lassen's mention of his daughter's stay at the Rigshospital prompted both of them to recall the re-minder letter pinned to the noticeboard in Laura Kjær's kitchen. On their way back into town, Hess phoned the department and confirmed that both Laura Kjær's boy and Anne Sejer-Lassen's eldest girl had been patients there, but the nurse he spoke to hadn't been able to provide any more usable information, let alone whether the children's stays had overlapped. Now they're at the hospital, mostly because it's the only common factor they have to go on, and because the Rigshospital is on their route back to the station anyway. As yet the day has produced no useful result, and they've also learned from Nylander that Rosa Hartung and her husband were able to contribute nothing new about Anne Sejer-Lassen, which didn't do much for the atmosphere.

Hess watches Thulin return from the desk, but she avoids his eye and makes for the thermos of coffee provided for visitors. "They're trying to get hold of the senior consultant. According to the files, he dealt with both children."

"So we'll speak to him now?"

"I don't know. If you want to do something else, that's fine with me."

Hess doesn't reply, glancing around impatiently instead. There are sick and ailing children everywhere. Children with scratched faces, with arms in slings and legs in plaster. Children without hair on their heads, children in wheelchairs, and children moving around attached to drip stands. In the middle is the activity room, with big panes of glass and a blue door covered in balloons and autumn twigs. The sound of children's voices singing coaxes Hess nearer to the door, which stands ajar. Inside, a few bigger children are drawing at one end, while a semicircle of smaller kids sit on brightly colored plastic stools at the other. They are singing, their faces turned toward a woman holding up a picture with a cute drawing of a red apple.

"Apple man, do come in. Apple man, do come in. Have you any apples that you've brought for me today? Thank you kindly, won't you staaaaay . . ."

The woman nods encouragingly at the children, and after they've trilled the final word long and loud, she puts down the poster of the apple and picks up one of a chestnut.

"Let's take it from the top!"

"Chestnut man, do come in. Chestnut man, do come in. Have you any chestnuts . . ."

The words are like a cold finger running down Hess's spine. As he recoils from the door, he realizes Thulin is watching him.

"Are you Oskar's parents, here for the X-rays?"

A nurse approaches them. Thulin, sipping coffee from a plastic cup, chokes, and starts to cough.

"No, that's not us," replies Hess. "We're police officers. We're waiting for the senior consultant."

"The consultant is still doing his rounds, I'm afraid."

The nurse is pretty. Sparkling dark eyes and long brown hair gathered into a ponytail. She's thirty-ish, but there is something serious about her face that makes her appear older.

"He'll have to cut them short. Please tell him we're in a hurry."

50

Senior consultant Hussein Majid asks them to take a seat in the staff room, among white coffee cups, greasy iPads, sweeteners, stained morning newspapers, and coats slung over the backs of chairs. He's the same height as Hess, in his early forties, well-groomed, wearing his white coat unbuttoned, with a stethoscope around his neck and angular black glasses. A gold wedding ring indicates that he's married, but that isn't the impression he gives when he shakes Thulin's hand. The hurriedness that accompanied the consultant's handshake with Hess quickly transforms into a smile and sustained eye contact when he turns to Thulin. For a moment, it catches Hess off guard that the doctor finds Thulin attractive, because he's never looked at her that way himself. So far he's mostly found her annoying, but grudgingly he has to admit that he can understand why the doctor's discreet gaze follows her slender waist and shapely backside as she turns away to find a chair. For a second, Hess wonders whether Majid also looked at Laura Kjær and Anne Sejer-Lassen that way when they appeared on the ward with their sick children.

"I'm afraid I'm in the middle of my rounds, but if we can get this done quickly I'd be glad to help you, of course."

"That's very kind. Thank you," replies Thulin.

Majid places two medical files and his mobile phone on the table as he offers to pour her a coffee, which she accepts coquettishly. It seems to Hess as though she's forgotten why they are there, but he swallows his irritation and leans forward in his chair.

"As we said, we have a few questions about Magnus Kjær and Sofia Sejer-Lassen, and we'd like you to tell us exactly what you know."

Throwing a glance at Hess, Hussein Majid replies with a natural authority and friendliness that is presumably mainly for Thulin's benefit.

"Of course. You're correct that both children were treated here—though for different reasons. May I first ask the reason for your questions?"

"No."

"Okay. Never mind."

The doctor shoots an expressive glance at Thulin, who shrugs as though to excuse Hess's lack of manners. Hess moves swiftly on.

"How were they treated?"

Majid puts his hand on the children's case files without making any move to consult them.

"Magnus Kjær came here in connection with a longer course of treatment that started approximately one year ago. The pediatric department and the associated team function as a sluice, directing patients to the relevant departments, so he was observed and diagnosed with autism by our specialists in neurology. Sofia Sejer-Lassen, on the other hand, was simply hospitalized with a minor bone break after an accident at home some months ago. She was quickly discharged. A relatively uncomplicated case, although she did need some rehab afterward, which was carried out mainly at our department of physiotherapy."

"So both children were on the pediatric ward," Hess persists. "Do you know whether they met? Or whether the parents did?"

"Obviously, I can't be sure, but it's unlikely they interacted, given their different diagnoses."

"Who brought them in?"

"As I recall, in both cases it was mainly the mothers, but if you want to know for sure you'd better ask them directly."

"But I'm asking you."

"Yes, and I've just answered the question."

Majid gives a pleasant smile. Hess judges he is of above average intelligence, and wonders whether the man knows perfectly well that Hess can't ask the mothers.

"But it was you who had contact with the mothers while they were here?"

It is Thulin who asks this innocent question, and the consultant seems pleased to be addressing himself to her instead.

"I have contact with many parents, but yes, them included. It's an important part of the job to make mothers—or fathers—feel like they're in safe hands. It can be crucial, building up trust and confidence during treatment. It benefits all concerned. Especially the patient."

The doctor smiles at Thulin and gives a jaunty wink, as though he's selling her a romantic holiday for two to the Maldives. Thulin smiles back.

"So it wouldn't be incorrect to say that you knew the mothers very well."

"Very well?" Majid looks a little baffled, but he is

still smiling at Thulin. The words take Hess by surprise too, but Thulin has only just gotten started.

"Yes. Did you see them in private? Did you fall in love with them, or did you just go to bed with them?"

Majid keeps smiling, but hesitates. "Sorry, come again?"

"You heard me. Answer the question."

"Why are you asking that? What's this about?"

"Right now it's just a question, and it's important you tell us the truth."

"I can do that very quickly. We're operating about ten percent above capacity on this ward. That means I have precious few minutes available for each child on my rounds. So I spend that time not on mothers, nor on fathers, nor on police officers, but on the children."

"But you just said it was important to have a close relationship with the mothers."

"No, that wasn't what I said, and I don't appreciate what your questions are implying."

"I'm not implying anything. Implying is what you just did when you winked at me and talked about confidence, but my question, without any implications, is whether you went to bed with them."

Majid smiles incredulously and shakes his head.

"Then tell us your impression of the mothers."

"They were worried about their children, as parents usually are when they come here. But if this is the sort of question you have for me, I have other things to do with my time."

Hussein Majid makes to stand up, but Hess, who has enjoyed the scuffle, slides a coffee-stained newspaper across to the consultant.

"You're not leaving. We're here for reasons of which you may already be aware. For the time being, you're the only common factor in our investigation."

The consultant looks at the press photo from the woods and at the headline, which links the two murders, and he seems a little shaken.

"But I don't *have* anything more to tell. I remember Magnus Kjær's mother best because his treatment was more drawn-out. They tried various diagnoses down in neurology, and the mother got very frustrated because it wasn't helping, then suddenly she just stopped bringing him in. That's all I know."

"She stopped coming because you made a pass at her, or—"

"I didn't make a pass at her! She phoned up and said she'd been contacted by the local council about the boy, so she wanted to concentrate on that. I thought she'd be back, but she never was."

"But Laura Kjær devoted all her time to her son's treatment, so she must have had an excellent reason for not wanting to see you anymore?"

"It wasn't *me* she didn't want to see—it had nothing to do with *me*! Like I told you, it was something about a notification from the council."

"What notification?" Hess's tone is insistent, but at that moment the young nurse pokes her head through the door and looks at the consultant.

"Sorry to disturb you, but we need an answer for room nine—they're waiting for the patient in the operating theater."

"I'm coming. We're done here."

"I asked you what notification?"

Hussein Majid has risen to his feet and is hastily gathering his things from the table. "I don't know anything. I only heard it from the mother—apparently somebody contacted the council and accused her of not taking proper care of the boy."

"What do you mean? Accused her of what?"

"No idea. She sounded shocked, and a caseworker phoned us a while later to get a statement about the boy, which we gave them. About his treatment, I mean, and how we'd tried to solve his problem. Goodbye now, thank you so much."

"And you're sure you didn't drop in, try to comfort her a little?" Thulin tries again as she rises from the chair and blocks his path.

"Yes, I'm sure! Now excuse me, please."

Hess too gets to his feet. "Did Laura Kjær say who'd reported her?"

"No. As far as I recall, it was anonymous."

Hussein Majid edges passed Thulin with his case files, and as he disappears around the corner, Hess can hear the children singing once more.

51

Social worker Henning Loeb has just finished a late lunch in the nearly empty basement cafeteria at city hall when he gets the call. The morning has been a trial. He got caught in the rain as he cycled to work, and by the time he finally reached the bike sheds at the back of the building his clothes and shoes were soaking wet. Despite that, his boss—the departmental head of Children's and Young Adult Services—had asked him to attend an emergency meeting with an Afghan family and their lawyer, who were trying to reverse the local authority's decision to take their child into care.

Henning Loeb knew the case inside out and had himself recommended the child be removed, but yet again he'd been required to waste an hour and a half sitting and listening to them driveling and bickering.

These days, most care orders were issued to immigrant families, and in this case it had been necessary to bring an interpreter to the meeting. Which, of course, had dragged the whole thing out. Frankly, the whole meeting had been a waste of time. The case was already settled: the immigrant father had repeatedly been violent toward his thirteen-year-old daughter because she had a Danish boyfriend. In a democratic society, however, even thugs like that had rights; they were allowed to be heard, and as the arguments flew back and forth across the table, Henning—still damp and chilly—had watched life pass by outside the windows of city hall.

Afterward, although Henning was still clammy all over with rain, he'd had to knuckle down and focus on his own cases, the clock ticking at the back of his mind, since by then he was behind on the day's work. He was only one interview away from a job at the better-organized and more pleasant-smelling Administration for Technology and the Environment on the second floor, which was supposed to take place that afternoon. If he could catch up on the backlog, then he'd have time to prepare, and if the interview went well, he'd soon be able to jump ship before it sank under the weight of all the violent, incestuous, and/or psychotic passengers hopping aboard from the social fringe. It seemed only fair that he be allowed instead to come up with suggestions for urban renewal and improvements to the municipal parks in an office with a decent view of the red-haired intern, an architecture student who wore miniskirts and a brazen smile all year round, rain or shine. She deserved a real man. Wouldn't necessarily be Henning who did the honors, of course, but the sight of her and the accompanying fantasies—those nobody could take away from him.

Within seconds, Henning regrets having answered the phone call, because he can't shake the detective guy off again. He talks in the way Henning hates most: with authority and in the imperative, and he quickly makes it clear to Henning that he needs the information *right now.* Not in a minute, and definitely not later that afternoon. So Henning has to drop what's in his hands and scurry back to the computer in his office.

"I need everything you've got on a case about a boy called Magnus Kjær."

The detective guy has the boy's national ID number, and Henning switches on the computer as he explains that he is responsible for literally hundreds of cases, so obviously he can't remember them all offhand, should the investigator be in any doubt.

"Just tell me what it says."

Henning skims the case notes on the screen, stalling for a moment. It turns out to be one of his own cases—luckily, one that can be swiftly and easily summarized.

"You're right, that was one of ours. There was a report—an anonymous email, actually—about the boy's mother, Laura Kjær, who according to the report was unfit to look after her son. We investigated and found the claim to be groundless, so there's not really much more I can—"

"I'd like to hear everything about the case. Right now."

Henning stifles a sigh. That could take awhile, so he picks up the pace and gives the detective bloke the shortest version he possibly can as he skims the file.

"The report came in via email around three months ago to the department's whistle-blower scheme, which was set up by the minister for social affairs at local authorities across the country so that people could call in or email anonymously with tips about children who were being abused. So we don't know who sent this particular one in. Basically, it said the boy ought to be removed from his mother's care ASAP because she was—and I'm quoting here—'a selfish whore.' End quote. There was also some stuff about her only thinking about spreading her legs while shutting her eyes to the kid's problems, even though she—and I'm quoting again—'ought to know better.' End quote. According to the email, we'd find proof at the house."

"What did you find there?"

"Nothing. We stuck to protocol and went to a lot of trouble to follow up on the claims about neglect, so we spoke to the introverted boy and the shocked parents— the mother plus a stepfather, I think. But there was nothing suspicious, and sadly that sort of spiteful prank isn't uncommon."

"I'd like to see the email. Can you send me a copy?"

It is the question Henning has been waiting for.

"I can do. Just as soon as you show me a court order. So, if there's nothing else—"

"But there was no information on the sender?"

"No, that's what 'anonymous' means. As I said—"

"What makes you call it spiteful?"

"Well, because we found nothing, and because it's mainly spiteful pranks that people use the whistle-blower scheme for. Just ask Tax and Customs. It's the politicians who've encouraged it. People tattle on each other over nothing at all, even if there's no justification. They never stop to think that somebody actually has to sit and spend time and resources investigating the shit they write down and send in. Anyway, as I said, if there's nothing more—"

"There is. Now that I've got you, I'd like you to

check whether you've also received a report about two other children."

The detective gives Henning two more ID numbers, this time for two girls, Lina and Sofia Sejer-Lassen. The family is now resident in Klampenborg, but the man knows they lived in Islands Brygge—under the purview of Copenhagen Council—until recently, and that's the period he wants to ask about. Irritably, Henning consults his computer again, shooting a glance at his watch. He can still make time to prepare if he just speeds things up a bit. The computer finally responds, and as Henning scans the case notes he hears the detective repeat the numbers. He's about to say he remembers the case, because it too was his, but then he catches sight of something on the screen that he hasn't noticed before. Quickly scrolling through, he flicks back to the Magnus Kjær case to check his hunch—and to check the wording of the anonymous email. Henning Loeb sees something he doesn't fully grasp, and that makes him wary.

"No, sorry. Nothing on them. Not as far as I can see, anyway."

"You're sure?"

"The system doesn't recognize the ID numbers. Was there anything else? I'm quite busy."

Henning Loeb is left with a bad taste in his mouth. To be on the safe side, he sends an email to the IT department explaining that the system has gone down, and that he's been unable to help the police with a particular request. Not that he thinks it will be relevant, but you never know. Henning is only one interview away from climbing up the ladder, up and away from all this bullshit. Far, far away. All the way up onto the second floor with Technology and Environment—maybe, if he plays his cards right, all the way up inside the redhead.

52

Darkness has settled across the residential neigh-borhood in Husum. The streetlamps have been lit along the small, child-friendly roads with their speed limits and sleeping policemen, and the garden paths glow in the cozy light of busy kitchens, where families are making dinner and chatting about another dull day on the treadmill. As Thulin steps out of the squad car on Cedervænget, she smells the aroma of frying meat-balls drifting out of an extractor fan from one of the Kjær family's neighbors. Only the white, modernist house with its sheet-metal garage and the number seven on the mailbox lies in darkness, looking abandoned and forlorn.

Thulin listens to Nylander's final grouchy remarks over the phone before running after Hess through the rain to the front door.

"Do you have the key?"

Hess holds out his hand. They've reached the entry-way with its distinctive yellow-and-black barrier tape, which seals the front door and marks the crime scene. Thulin fishes the key out of her jacket pocket.

"You say the council investigated the case after an anonymous tip about Laura Kjær, but they found no reason to believe the accusations held water?"

"Correct. Move—you're standing in the light."

Hess has taken the key out of her hands and is trying to fit it into the lock under the faint light of a streetlamp.

"Then what are we doing here?"

"I told you. I just want to see the house."

"I've seen the house. Several times."

When Thulin spoke to Nylander moments earlier, he was dissatisfied with the day's results—or the lack thereof—and didn't understand why they were headed back to Cedervænget. Nor did Thulin. Hans Henrik Hauge's alibi for the time of Anne Sejer-Lassen's murder was a setback, but Thulin accepted it; yet now here she is again, staring at the gloomy house where it all began.

Hess told her about the conversation with the case-worker at city hall, whom he'd called on his way to the parking lot after interviewing the doctor. Sitting in the car outside the Rigshospital, the rain splashing against the windshield, she'd heard all about the anonymous email accusing Laura Kjær of being such a bad mother that the boy ought to be taken into care. The council had investigated the case, and the report had proved groundless. It had been dismissed as a hoax, and Thulin's interest ended there. It was surprising that Laura Kjær had apparently only told the doctor at the Rigshospital about the report, but on the other hand it was understandable: Laura Kjær's son suffered from autism, according to the doctors, and the boy's behavior—as described by the school, for instance—could easily have led to the misunderstanding that the mother wasn't capable of looking after him. Which might easily have induced someone to write to the council. Moreover, of course, Laura Kjær couldn't have known whether the anonymous tipster was one of her friends, either at school or at work, so all in all it wasn't so strange she'd kept it quiet. Whichever way you looked at it, Laura Kjær seemed to have done everything a mother could possibly do to help her son, and although Thulin didn't like Hans Henrik Hauge, she had to admit that he seemed to have been a rock. So what were they supposed to do with the information about the tip-off? The caseworker also denied there being a corresponding report for Anne Sejer-Lassen; hence there was no common factor to investigate.

Still, Hess wanted to visit Laura Kjær's house, and on the way there Thulin regretted not getting the man taken off the case while she had the chance. She wasn't blind and deaf to Hess's prediction that the killer had only just begun, and she had instinctively felt the threat as they stood in the woods beside Anne Sejer-Lassen's body. But they were too dissimilar in their approaches to investigation. Nor was she keen on the idea of playing informant and telling Nylander if Hess strayed in the wrong direction and began poking his nose into the Hartung case. Not even if it was a condition for getting a recommendation to NC3.

"We're looking for a double murderer, and you said yourself there might be more on the way, so why are we wasting time rooting around in a house that's already been gone over with a fine-tooth comb!"

"You don't need to come in. Actually, it would be a big help if you could ask the neighbors whether they knew anything about the report, or who might have sent it. It'll be quicker that way, don't you think?"

"Why are we asking them in the first place?"

The barrier tape snaps as Hess opens the door and slips into the dry house. He shuts the door behind him, while the now-pounding rain sends Thulin dashing for the first house.

53

The silence is the first thing Hess notices once he's shut the front door behind him. His eyes try to adjust to the dark. Once he's flicked three different light switches with no result, he realizes the electricity company must have shut off the supply. The house is in Laura Kjær's name, her death has been registered, and the legal dismantling of a human life has taken its course.

Hess takes out his flashlight, walking down the corridor and farther into the house. His phone call with the caseworker is still niggling. The truth is that Hess doesn't know what it means. Or whether it means anything at all. He just knows he has to see the house again. Otherwise their interview of the consultant at the Rigshospital went well. For a while, he'd thought they might have found the right place and the right person. Both victims had interacted with the doctor, and his instinct that the children were the common factor had felt right. But then the doctor mentioned the report.

It's a shot in the dark, searching the place again. The whole thing has been gone over several times by various teams of investigators and techs. On top of that, the report is three months old, so if there has ever been something to find it's most likely gone by now. But somebody reported Laura Kjær—somebody had been interested enough to write a hate-filled email recommending her child be taken from her—and Hess can't help hoping the house will give him some answers. As he moves down the corridor, he notices it still bears evidence of the forensics team's work. Traces of white fingerprinting powder cling to the handles and door frames, and there are still numbered markers placed on various objects—objects that might or might not be used if and when charges are brought in connection with the murder of Laura Kjær. Hess wanders from room to room, finding himself at last in a small guest bedroom that evidently served as an office. It's eerily empty now; the desk has been cleared of its computer, which is still in police possession. He opens cupboards and drawers, reads random notes and scraps of paper, then drifts into the bathroom and kitchen. He repeats the process, but finds nothing of interest. As the rain drums against the roof, Hess picks his way back along the unlit corridor and into the master bedroom, where the bed is still unmade and a lamp is lying on the carpet. He's just pulled open Laura Kjær's underwear drawer when there comes a noise from the front door and Thulin reappears.

"None of the neighbors know anything. Or heard about the report. They just said, again, that the mom and stepdad were kind to the boy."

Hess opens a new cupboard and keeps rummaging.

"I'm heading off now. We've still got to check out the doctor, plus what Sejer-Lassen said about the affairs. Bring the key back when you're done."

"Fine. Bye."

54

Thulin deliberately slams the front door to 7 Cedervænget with a little more force than strictly necessary. Jogging through the rain, she has to dodge a dark-clad cyclist before she reaches her car and clambers inside. Her clothes are sodden after traipsing to the neighbors' houses. Hess will have to walk to the station if he wants to get back into town, but that's his problem. The day has been a bust. Still no leads, and it seems like the heavy rain is rinsing everything away while they run around in circles and accomplish nothing.

Thulin turns the key, puts the car in gear, and drives swiftly down the road. She has to go through all the feedback from the group that day, but all she wants really is to get back to the station and read through the case files. Start fresh. Go through them again. Find a connection. Maybe contact Hans Henrik Hauge and Erik Sejer-Lassen and question them about Hussein Majid, who knew both victims. Thulin is turning off Cedervænget and heading for the main road when something in the rearview mirror catches her eye and makes her brake.

She can only just make out the car parked fifty yards behind her. It's underneath the large spruce trees at the blind end of the road that joins Cedervænget, almost indistinguishable from the trees and the hedge, beyond which is the area with the playground. Thulin reverses until she is parallel with the vehicle. It's a black estate car. No distinctive features, inside or out. But the faint mist rising from the hood in the rain tells her the engine is still warm: the car can't have been parked more than a few moments ago. Thulin glances around. Anyone with an errand on a residential street pulls up outside the house they want, but this car is tucked away in the little niche just before the dead end. For a fleeting moment, she considers running the plates. But then her mobile rings, and she sees on the display that it's Le. It dawns on her that she's completely forgotten she was supposed to pick her up from her granddad's, and Thulin takes the call and drives away.

55

Magnus Kjær's bedroom is plain in comparison to the luxury of the girls' room at the Sejer-Lassens', but even in the weak glow of the flashlight Hess can tell it's cozy. Thick carpet, green curtains, a paper lantern dangling from the ceiling. Posters of Donald Duck and Mickey Mouse on the walls, and hordes of plastic figurines on the white shelving, creatures from fairy-tale worlds where good does battle with evil. On the desk is a cup of pencils and colorful felt-tip pens, and it is clear from the small bookcase next to it that Magnus Kjær is also interested in chess. Hess takes out a few books and leafs through them, without really knowing why. It feels like a safe room, maybe the best one in the house.

His eye falls on the bed, and an old habit makes him kneel down and shine the flashlight underneath it, although he knows his colleagues have already checked there. There's something wedged between the bedpost and the wall, but once he's managed to extricate it he sees it's only a handbook for League of Legends. It pricks his conscience; he hasn't kept his promise to go back to the hospital.

Hess puts down the handbook and begins to regret not getting a lift with Thulin while he had the chance. For a while, the news about the anonymous tipster had seemed like it was going to shed new light on the case, but now he feels like an idiot, not least because he'll have to trudge back through the rain into the city center, or at least to the nearest station, or until he can hail a taxi. Fatigue washes over him, and for a few seconds Hess wonders whether he can allow himself a nap on the boy's bed, where it feels soothing and comfortable, or whether he should head straight back to the police station and spin Nylander some bullshit story about needing to return to the Hague tonight. Or he could just tell the truth, of course. That he isn't up to the task. That Kristine Hartung and the fingerprints and all that crap has nothing to do with him. That it's probably only lack of sleep sparking all those nightmarish theories about severed limbs and chestnut dolls. With a little luck, Hess might still make the last flight to the Hague at eight forty-five p.m. and be genuflecting before Freimann by tomorrow morning at the latest—right now the idea sounds pretty appealing.

Hess throws a final glance out of the window into the garden and the playground where Laura Kjær was found, and that's when he sees them. Half-concealed behind the green curtain hangs a sheaf of children's drawings on A4 paper. They've been pinned to the wall. The first is a drawing of a house, a drawing Magnus Kjær must have done a few years earlier. Hess walks across and shines his flashlight onto them. The strokes are primitive. Nine or ten lines depict a house with a front door, above which the sun is shining. Some impulse makes Hess turn to the next page, but all it shows is another drawing of a house, this time painted white, and a little more exact and detailed. The house on Cedervænget, he realizes. The third drawing shows the same subject: the white house, the sun, and a garage. So do the fourth and fifth, and with each drawing Magnus is clearly growing older and better at drawing. For some reason Hess is impressed, and he smiles to himself. Until he comes to the last one. The subject is the same. House, sun, garage. But this time there is something wrong. The garage is disproportionally huge, much larger than the house itself. It towers above the rooftop, its walls thick and black, its symmetry unwieldy.

56

Hess slams the terrace door behind him. The air is chilly, and he can see his breath in the rain as he lights his way across the paving stones in the garden behind the house. As he rounds the corner, he finds himself at the entrance to the garage. The aroma of meatballs hangs in the air, vanishing only when he opens the garage door. He's about to walk inside when he realizes that although the door was sealed, he didn't hear the usual sound of the tape snapping as he opened it. Shrugging off the thought, Hess closes the door behind him.

The garage is spacious and high-ceilinged, about six yards long and four across. Built out of new materials, with a steel frame and sheet-metal walls. Hess remembers seeing this model in sales catalogs at the

DIY store; it's big enough to fit more than just a car. Dozens of transparent plastic storage containers take up virtually every inch of the concrete floor. Some of the containers have wheels, while others are stacked into tall towers. He's reminded of his own earthly possessions, still heaped higgledy-piggledy in cardboard boxes and plastic bags at a self-storage place in Amager, now for the fifth year running. As the rain beats against the roof, Hess edges past the plastic towers and farther into the garage, but as far as he can see in the flashlight's beam there is nothing remarkable in the containers. Just clothes, blankets, old toys, kitchen utensils, plates, and bowls, all neatly organized. Along one wall an impressive and equally neat array of gardening tools hang from large aluminum hooks, interrupted by a tall steel shelf lined with rows of paint cans, implements, and gardening supplies. But nothing else. Just a garage. Magnus's drawing had been eye-catching, but now that Hess is standing in the garage he realizes it was simply further evidence that Magnus Kjær is a dysfunctional child with serious medical issues.

Hess swivels irritably on his heel and is about to edge back toward the door when he suddenly notices he's stepped on something yielding and dimpled, raised a fraction above the concrete floor. Not much, maybe a few millimeters. Shining the light at the ground, Hess sees he's put his foot on a rectangular black rubber mat roughly one meter by half a meter. It lies on the floor in front of the steel shelves, as though intended to provide a comfortable working surface. You wouldn't think twice about it—unless, like Hess, you're looking for a needle in a haystack. He takes a step backward, and some instinct makes him bend down and pull the mat aside. But the mat won't budge. Hess can only get his fingertips two or three centimeters underneath it, and as he gropes along the edge he feels a thin crack running parallel in the concrete floor. Grabbing a screwdriver from the steel shelves, he holds the flashlight between his teeth, shoves the screwdriver underneath the mat and into the crack, then pushes down on the handle. The section of concrete floor and the glued-down mat lift slightly, enough for Hess to stick his fingers underneath and heave open what turns out to be a hatch.

Hess stares incredulously at the hatch and the black rectangle in the concrete floor. On the underside of the hatch is a handle, allowing it to be shut from the inside, and Hess takes the flashlight out of his mouth and directs it into the hole. It shines a few meters down, but all he can see is some kind of flooring at the bottom of the ladder mounted to the internal wall. Hess sits down on the concrete floor, puts the flashlight back in his mouth, places his foot on the top rung of the ladder and begins to climb down. He has no idea what he's going to find, but his sense of disquiet intensifies with every step he takes toward the bottom. The smell is distinctive, a strange blend of building materials and something perfumed. Only when he feels solid ground beneath one foot does he let go of the ladder and shine the beam around.

The room isn't large, but it's bigger than Hess expected. The space is approximately four meters by three, and he can just stand upright without having to duck his head. There are electricity sockets along the skirting board, whitewashed concrete walls, and a checkered laminate floor. Spick-and-span. At first glance there's nothing frightening about the room, apart from the sheer fact that it exists. Somebody measured up and dug it out. Bought materials, mounted and installed them, and finished the whole thing with a heavy, noise-insulating hatch. Although Hess left it open, the sound of the rain and of reality above is already long gone. He realizes part of his brain was afraid of finding Kristine Hartung's limbs down here, but to his relief the room is virtually empty. A nice white coffee table is positioned in the middle of the floor, on it a strangely shaped three-legged black lamp. A tall white wardrobe stands against one wall, a towel hanging from its handle. At the far end of the room, a reddish wall hanging has been placed over a bed neatly made up with white linen. The flashlight begins to flicker. Hess has to shake it to get the light back on. As he approaches the bed, he notices the lamps pointing toward it, but it's the cardboard box that catches his attention. Hess kneels down and shines the flashlight inside. Everything inside is jumbled up, as though flung inside in hurried disarray. Moisturizers and scented candles. A thermos flask and a dirty cup and padlock. Cables and Wi-Fi equipment. *Lots* of Wi-Fi equipment. And a portable MacBook Air, still attached to its cable, which leads across the laminate flooring to the lamp on the coffee table. Only then does Hess realize it isn't a lamp at all. It's a camera. A camera mounted on a tripod, the lens pointed, like the lamps, toward the bed.

Hess feels a wave of nausea and makes to stand up. He wants to leave, to escape the hole and come out into the rain. But his eye is caught. Suddenly it has registered the faint, damp footprints on the other side of the coffee table. It could have been him who'd left them, but it isn't. Something hurtles out of the wardrobe behind him with great speed and force. He's struck across the back of the head, one blow quickly becoming several. The flashlight falls from his hand, and he glimpses kaleidoscopic streaks of light chase across the ceiling as the blows hammer against his skull and his mouth fills with blood.

57

Hess falls onto the coffee table, half twisting around. He's still groggy as he mule-kicks backward in the dark, connecting with his attacker before staggering onto the bed and smacking his jawbone against the frame. Pain races through his skull. There's a ringing in one of his ears, and he sways clumsily on the mattress, trying to regain his balance. The sound of someone rummaging in the cardboard box then feet running toward the ladder tells him he needs to get back on solid ground. He stands up but can see nothing. Reeling through the blackness, his hands outstretched as he tries to recall where the ladder is, he skins his knuckles on the rough concrete wall—but then he feels a rung in his left hand. He senses the presence of his attacker by the hasty movements in the air above him, and his hands and feet remember the climb back up. Nearly at the top, he thrusts his arm into the dark and grabs an ankle, sending his attacker flying into a tower of plastic containers. The man begins to kick, but Hess clings on. He's dragging himself farther up when he notices a MacBook lying on the concrete floor. Then a heel strikes him twice in the face. He feels the man's weight; with surprising speed his attacker rams a knee into Hess's neck, pressing his face into the ground. Hess thrashes, his lower body still in the hole, and gasps for air. His feet twitch as though he's strung up from a gallows, and he senses the attacker reaching for the screwdriver Hess had been stupid enough to leave on the concrete floor. He knows he's seconds from blacking out—his vision is already dimming—but then he hears a voice. Thulin's voice. She's shouting his name, maybe from the road or inside the house, yet no matter how hard he tries he can't respond. He's pinioned against a cold garage floor somewhere in fucking Husum with one hundred kilograms on top of his windpipe, and the weight isn't budging. His arms flail, when suddenly he feels something in his right hand. Something cold—something made of steel. He can't tug it loose and use it as a weapon, so instead he pulls with all his strength. The steel gives way. There's a deafening crash as the rack of paint tins keels over and comes tumbling down around his ears.

58

Thulin stands in the terrace doorway, staring through the rain into the dark and silent garden. She's already called Hess several times—first inside the house itself and now outside—and every time there's no reply she feels like more of an idiot. It doesn't matter that she turned around and drove back as soon as she realized who might own that black estate car—what's annoying her now is that Hess didn't even remember to lock the front door when he left.

Thulin's about to slam the door again when suddenly she hears a crash from the garage. She takes a step and calls to Hess. For a moment, she thinks it must be him nosing aimlessly around, but then she sees a dark figure bolt out of the far end of the garage and disappear through the rain toward the back garden. In less than three strides she's in the garden, gun drawn. The figure barrels through the trees at the bottom of the garden and into the playground, and though she runs as fast as she can it's out of sight by the time she reaches the playhouse. She wheels around, already soaked and breathless, when the sound of an approaching freight train makes her turn. The figure has leapt down the embankment and is running along the tracks; Thulin sprints after it, the freight train looming behind her.

Horn blaring, the train shoots past at full speed, bowling her into the grass. The figure glances swiftly over its shoulder, then just before the train catches up it darts ninety degrees to the left and crosses the tracks. Thulin whirls around. She runs in the opposite direction, toward the end of the train, hoping to cross the tracks and continue her pursuit. But the string of carriages is endless, and at last she has to stop. In the gaps between them, she glimpses Hans Henrik Hauge's frantic face peering back at her before he vanishes between the trees.

59

Police cars, blue lights flashing, have blocked off the small close at both ends, and the first few eager crime reporters are already converging on the scene. Some have brought photographers and OB vans, recording material for use in the next news broadcast, even though they'll get no information from the police beyond what they can see from the cordon. A group of residents have gathered too, and for the second time in under a week they are gawping in shock at number seven. *Not much goes on in this neighborhood besides block parties and garbage sorting*, thinks Thulin, *and she guesses it will be many years before the events of that week are forgotten.*

Thulin is standing in the road outside the house to call and say good night to Le, who has cheerily accepted another overnight stay with her granddad. But she's struggling to concentrate on the conversation, and while Le chatters away about a new app and a playdate with Ramazan, she runs through the events of the evening in her mind. Driving down the ring road back into town, it struck her that the black car might be Hans Henrik Hauge's Mazda6. That's why she went back. But Hauge had escaped, and after the chase she found Hess on the concrete floor in the garage. He was still shaken and bruised, but not so much so that he didn't immediately focus his attention on the MacBook, which Hauge had evidently tried to take. She called Forensics, updated Nylander, and issued a warrant for Hans Henrik Hauge's arrest—so far without result.

By now the property is swarming with white-clad techs, this time in and outside the garage. They've brought their own power supply, setting up crisp-beamed floodlights. A white tent has been erected in the driveway, and most of the plastic containers in the garage have been carried outside to allow easier access to the underground bunker. Thulin finishes her conversation with her daughter and enters the garage just as Genz is emerging through the hatch with his camera. He looks weary, pulling down his mask and giving his report.

"The materials used for the room indicate that it was built around the same time as the new garage. It wouldn't have needed much digging out, so Hauge could have used a Bobcat if he rented one to do the garage foundation. It wouldn't necessarily have taken him more than a couple of days, so he could have made sure he was left in peace to work. The room was sound-proof, of course, once the hatch was closed—which I think we can assume Hauge preferred."

Thulin listens silently as Genz continues. A few of Magnus Kjær's toys had been found in the room, along with creams, soda bottles, scented candles, and other paraphernalia. The room had been connected to the electricity supply and set up with Wi-Fi. So far the ex-amination has revealed no fingerprints besides the boy's and Hans Henrik Hauge's. To Thulin, the whole thing is incomprehensible. Previously, she's only read about this sort of case or seen reports about them in the news— Josef Fritzl, Marc Dutroux, whatever those psychopaths were called—and it strikes her that until today they seemed unreal.

"Why was there Wi-Fi?"

"We don't know yet. It looks like Hauge came to get rid of a few things, but obviously we don't know what. On the other hand, we've found some pass-words in a notebook in the cardboard box. Seems he was using an anonymous peer-to-peer system. Maybe for streaming."

"Streaming what?"

"Hess and the IT techs are trying to open the Mac, but the password's tricky, so it looks like we'll have to bring it back to the department to crack it."

Thulin takes a pair of disposable gloves out of Genz's hands and makes to walk past him, but Genz puts a hand on her shoulder.

"Maybe you should just let the IT lot take it. They'll call ASAP and let you know what's on there."

Thulin can see in his dark eyes that it's kindly meant. He wants to spare her, but she continues down into the hole.

60

Thulin lets go of the rung above her. She sets both feet on the laminate flooring and turns to face the subterranean room, which is now lit at each end by powerful lamps. Two techs are having a muttered conversation with Hess around the MacBook and Wi-Fi gear, which are set up on the coffee table.

"Have you tried starting it in recovery mode?"

Hess turns sharply. One eye is swollen, his knuckles are wrapped in gauze, and he holds a clump of bloody paper towels to the back of his head with one hand.

"Yeah, but they say he's used FileVault, so they can't get it open here."

"Go away. I'll do it."

"They say it's better if they—"

"If you guys do something wrong, you might end up deleting some of the material in the program."

Hess looks at her, steps back from the MacBook, and nods to the IT techs, signaling that they should do the same.

It doesn't take long. Thulin is familiar with every operating system, and it takes her less than two minutes of typing in the latex gloves to reset Hauge's access code. The computer lets her in, and on the desktop they see a large picture of various Disney characters. Goofy, Donald Duck, Mickey Mouse. On the left-hand side of the screen are twelve or thirteen folders, each named after a month.

"Try the most recent one."

Thulin has already double clicked on the most recent folder, "September." A new window opens, and they are offered a choice of five icons, each marked with a play sign. Thulin double clicks on one at random and watches the video that appears. After thirty seconds, she realizes she should have done as Genz advised, as a wave of nausea sets her stomach churning.

61

So far the news on the car radio is reporting nothing but conjecture and repetition, as well as announcing the search for Hans Henrik Hauge. When the pop song that follows turns out to be a cheery paean to anal sex, Thulin decides to switch it off. She's in no mood to talk, so it suits her just fine that Hess is engrossed in his phone.

From Husum they drove to the ward at Glostrup Hospital, where Magnus Kjær is still a patient. In the staff room, they explained the situation to a female doctor, and Thulin found it reassuring that she seemed genuinely shocked and concerned for the boy. She gave instructions that Hans Henrik Hauge must under no circumstances be allowed to approach Magnus Kjær, should he decide to appear. Which was highly unlikely, given that he was on the run and wanted by the police. Luckily the doctor told them the boy was doing well, under the circumstances, but Thulin and Hess stopped outside his room on the way out anyway. The boy was asleep in his bed, and they paused for a moment to look through the rectangular window in the door.

For nearly fourteen or fifteen months, the boy had been repeatedly tortured, all while various doctors ascribed his difficulties with human contact to autism. As far as Thulin could gather, he'd been as well adjusted as any other child his age until his father passed away and his mother got together with Hauge. Hauge must have picked her out on the dating site precisely because her profile revealed she had a young son. What might have made her damaged goods in some men's eyes had been the very reason Hauge zeroed in. Thulin already knew from Hauge's dating history that he'd primarily messaged single women with children, but she hadn't given it a second thought until now; it had merely looked as though Hauge wanted to find a partner approximately the same age as himself.

From the clip Thulin saw on Hauge's MacBook, it was clear how he'd coerced the boy into silence. Sitting on the mattress in the underground room with the surrealistic red wall hanging in the background, he'd admonished Magnus in a didactic tone that surely he wanted to see his mother happy rather than sad, like she'd been when his father died, didn't he? Then, in a voice just as light and natural, he'd added that, of course, Magnus wouldn't want him to hurt her at all, would he?

Magnus hadn't resisted the rape that followed, and Thulin hadn't wanted to watch. But it had happened, and she knew from Hauge's I2P log that the session must have been shared or streamed online. Minus the initial conversation, of course, or the images in which Hauge's face could be seen. Not just once either. Far from it.

Laura Kjær couldn't have known about the abuse, but the anonymous tip to the council must have set alarm bells ringing. She had rejected the accusations of maltreatment, but they must have made her uneasy. Perhaps a suspicion had begun to take root, because the timing of the tip coincided with her increasing reluctance to leave the house unless the boy was with her or at school. Maybe she'd also been afraid of Hauge—after all, she'd changed the locks while he was away at a trade fair. Not that it had made much difference, sadly.

"Thanks, bye." Hess hangs up. "Doesn't look like we can get hold of the caseworker or anyone else at city hall who can tell us more until tomorrow morning."

"You think it's the anonymous tipster we're after."

"Could be. It's worth checking."

"Why couldn't it be Hauge who killed them?" Thulin already knows the answer to that, but she can't resist asking the question, and Hess takes his time.

"There's significant evidence to indicate that a single killer committed both murders. Hauge could be said to have a motive for the killing of Laura Kjær, but not for the killing of Anne Sejer-Lassen. For which, incidentally, he has an alibi. From the material we saw on the computer in the bunker, we know that Hauge is a pedophile. He derives pleasure from the sexual abuse of children. Not necessarily violence, amputations, or the murder of women."

Thulin doesn't reply. All her rage is directed at Hauge, and right now she wishes she could spend her time finding *him*.

"Are you okay?"

She senses Hess scrutinizing her face, but she doesn't feel like talking about Hauge and the images on his MacBook anymore.

"I should be asking *you* that."

Hess stares at her, a little perplexed, and although Thulin keeps her eyes on the road she points at a line of blood dribbling from his ear. Hess wipes it with the clump of paper towel as Thulin turns the car toward her building. A thought occurs to her.

"But how could the tipster have known Magnus was being abused when nobody else did?"

"I don't know."

"And if the tipster did know about it, maybe even knew that the mother didn't realize what was going on, why kill her and not Hauge?"

"I don't know that either. But if you're going to frame it like that, then maybe this is why: maybe because, in the tipster's eyes, she ought to have known. Maybe because she didn't react to the report. Not quickly enough, at any rate."

"That's a lot of maybes."

"Oh yeah, it's rock solid. Especially considering that the caseworker denied there was a similar report about Anne Sejer-Lassen. It all hangs together perfectly."

Hess accompanies his irony by rejecting a call on his mobile after having checked the display. Thulin pulls up and switches off the engine.

"On the other hand, Anne Sejer-Lassen was on her way out the door with a bag and her kids. Now we know what really happened to Magnus Kjær, it might be a good idea to check whether her older daughter's accident was random or a symptom of something else entirely."

Hess looks at her. She can tell he understands. He doesn't reply immediately, and she senses her words have already sent his mind spiraling in new directions.

"I thought you said it was too many maybes?"

"Maybe not."

After what they found in Laura Kjær's garage it feels wrong to smile, but Thulin can't help it. Humor puts some distance between her and the incomprehensible, and at the same time she's gripped by the sudden feeling that they might be on to something. The hard rap of knuckles against the pane makes her glance outside, and she realizes Sebastian is standing by the car door, his face all smiles. He's wearing a suit and a black trench coat. In one hand, he holds a bouquet of flowers wrapped in cellophane and ribbon, and in the other a bottle of wine.

62

Thulin opens her laptop at the table in the living room and begins to peruse the material gathered by the other investigators on the team that day, focusing on that pertaining to Erik Sejer-Lassen. Sebastian has left, which is what she wanted, but their encounter could have gone better.

"That's what happens when you don't return my calls—you risk me showing up out of the blue," he teased as they reached the apartment. Switching on the kitchen light, she was struck by how neglected it looked. The damp clothes she'd worn during the search of the woods at Klampenborg were still lying in a heap in the corner, and on the kitchen table was a bowl encrusted with that morning's dried yogurt.

"How did you know I was coming home now?"

"I took a chance, and I was lucky."

The situation on the street was awkward, and she's still annoyed that she didn't notice Sebastian's dark gray Mercedes in the row of parked cars outside her front door before he knocked on the glass. She had gotten out and Hess had done the same, crossing to the driver's side: they'd agreed he could use the car to get home. For a moment, he and Sebastian stood looking at each other and exchanged a nod—Sebastian energetically and Hess more reservedly—before Thulin walked toward her front door. It was a trivial thing, yet it irritated her that Hess had met Sebastian and glimpsed a fragment of her private life. Or was it Sebastian that irritated her? It had been like meeting a creature from another planet, but normally that was what she liked about him.

"Look, I really need to get stuck into work."

"Was that your new partner? The one they chucked out of Europol?"

"How do you know he's from Europol?"

"Oh, I had lunch with a guy from the prosecution service today. He just mentioned someone who'd got into a mess at the Hague and ended up being punted back onto the murder squad. So I put two and two together, because you were telling me about some twit who'd just started and couldn't be bothered to actually do anything. How's it going with the case?"

Thulin regretted saying anything about Hess when Sebastian phoned a couple of times during the past week. She had no time to meet because of the case, and she mentioned to him that she was busier than usual because her new partner was no help. Which no longer seemed a fair assessment.

"I saw on the news this evening that something happened at the first crime scene. Is that why his face looks like such a car crash?"

Sebastian came close to her, and she pulled away.

"You need to go. I've got a lot to read through."

Sebastian tried to caress her, and she rebuffed him. Then he tried again, saying he missed her and wanted her, even reminded her that her daughter wasn't home, so they could do it wherever they pleased. The kitchen table, for example.

"Why not? Is it about Le? How is she doing?"

But Thulin was in no mood to discuss Le, and instead she asked him again to leave.

"So that's how it is, then? You decide when and how, and I've got no say?"

"That's how it's always been. If you can't live with it, we can call an end to it."

"Because you've found someone else who's more fun?"

"No. But if I do, I'll let you know. Thanks for the flowers."

Sebastian laughed, but it was difficult to get him out the door, and she assumed it was rare for anyone to give him his marching orders once he'd shown up with flowers and wine. And maybe it was strange that *she* had done so, so she promised herself she'd call him tomorrow.

Thulin eats half an apple at the laptop before her mobile rings. It's Hess. After their conversation in the car, they agreed he would check up on the Sejer-Lassen girl's accident, so it isn't odd that he's calling. The odd thing is that he inquires politely whether he's disturbing her.

"No, it's fine. What do you want?"

"You were right. I've just spoken to someone at the Rigshospital A&E. Apart from the episode with the nose and the broken collarbone, which the older girl was hospitalized for, both Sejer-Lassen girls have been treated for accidents at home when they lived on Islands Brygge and at Klampenborg. There's nothing to indicate sexual assault, but it's possible the girls were abused. Maybe just in a different way from Magnus Kjær."

"How many accidents?"

"Haven't got a count yet. *Too* many."

Thulin listens to his research. Once he's finished describing the medical reports, she feels as though the nausea from the bunker has returned. She's barely listening when he suggests they begin the next day with a visit to the local authority at Gentofte.

"Sejer-Lassen's house in Klampenborg falls under the oversight of Gentofte Council, and if it turns out that there's an anonymous denunciation of Anne Sejer-Lassen in their inbox, then we'll know we've got the right end of the stick."

He ends the conversation on a surprising note: "By the way, thanks for showing up at the house, if I didn't say so before," and she hears herself say, "That's fine, see you," before she hangs up.

Afterward, she has trouble regaining her composure. She decides to opt for another distraction, this time fetching a Red Bull from the fridge so that she doesn't risk dozing off. As she stands up, she happens to glance out the window.

From the fourth floor, Thulin can usually see clear across the roofs and towers of the city, almost as far as the lakes. But the scaffolding on the building opposite, which was erected the month before, blocks most of the view. When the wind is blustery, as it is tonight, it sets all the tarpaulins fluttering, and the scaffolding creaks and grates at its metallic seams as though threatening to collapse. But it is the figure that catches Thulin's eye. Or is it a figure? Behind the tarpaulin on the gangway directly across from her apartment she thinks she can make out a silhouette. For a moment, it seems as though it's staring directly back at her. Suddenly the memory of a figure observing her through traffic as she dropped her daughter off at school flashes into Thulin's mind. Instantly, she is alert; her instincts tell her it's the same one. But as the wind jerks again at the tarpaulin, distending it into an enormous sail, the shape vanishes. When it falls back into place, the silhouette has gone. Thulin switches off the light and shuts the laptop. For several minutes, she stands in the darkened living room and stares at the scaffolding, reminding herself to breathe.

Friday, October 16th

63

It's early morning, but Erik Sejer-Lassen doesn't know the time. His forty-five-thousand-euro TAG Heuer watch has been locked inside a box on the second floor of the police station since late last night, accompanied by his belt and shoelaces. Erik himself is sitting in an underground cell, and when the heavy metal door opens an officer informs him that he is going to be interviewed again. He gets to his feet, walks through the basement and up the spiral staircase toward daylight and civilization, and prepares to vent his rage.

The police showed up unannounced at his home last night. He'd been talking to the crying children in their beds when the au pair called him to the front door, where two officers were waiting to take him in for questioning. He'd objected that he couldn't possibly leave home just then, but the officers had given him no choice, and it had wrong-footed him that they'd brought his mother-in-law to look after the kids. Erik hadn't spoken to her since Anne's death. He'd known she would ask worried questions about her grandchildren and offer help that Erik didn't want. But then she'd been standing on the stone step behind the officers, almost like a coconspirator, staring at him with timid eyes as though *he* were the one who'd killed her daughter. As Erik had been led to the waiting squad car, she'd crossed the threshold into his house, and the girls had rushed to meet her. They'd clung to her legs.

At the police station, he had been questioned, without explanation, about the reason for the girls' frequent accidents and injuries. He had understood nothing. Certainly not the relevance of it, and he'd yelled that he wanted to speak to their superior or be driven home immediately. Instead he'd been kept in custody for "withholding information pertaining to the murder of Anne Sejer-Lassen" and had had to put up with being caged inside a basement cell like some common delinquent.

The first time Erik Sejer-Lassen hit his wife was their wedding night. They had barely gotten through the door to the suite at the d'Angleterre before he'd grabbed his bride's arms and dragged her through the rooms as he shook her, hissing hatred through his gritted teeth. The wedding had been lavish. Erik's family had footed the bill, paying for the world-renowned chef, the twelve exotic courses, the rooms at Havreholm Castle, and all the other trappings, because Anne's family were as poor as church mice. But how had Anne thanked him? By talking too long and too intimately with one of his old boarding-school chums. It had humiliated Erik so much that he'd been seething with pent-up fury until the moment they'd left and driven to the d'Angleterre, where they were alone. Anne, in tears, had protested that she'd only talked to the man to be friendly, but in a fit of violent temper he tore her dress to shreds, hit her repeatedly, and raped her. The next day he apologized for his behavior, insisting that he loved her deeply. At the breakfast table, the guests ascribed her flushed red cheek to the passion of their wedding night. That exact moment was probably where it began, his hatred of her—because she'd taken it; because she still looked at him adoringly as she batted those long lashes.

Their years in Singapore were the happiest. He was a rising star, making a few smart investments in bio-tech firms, and he and Anne were rapidly accepted into the jet set among the English and American expats. He only lost his temper with her occasionally, usually because she didn't meet the standards he'd set for loyalty, which included telling him everything she did. In return, he sweetened the deal with trips to the Maldives and mountain treks in Nepal. With the arrival of the children, however, life changed. At first he'd opposed Anne's greatest wish, but gradually he'd come to see something patriarchally appealing about reproduction, which he'd spoken about so often himself and heard discussed at various management meetings at biotech companies. It had upset him that his sperm was such low quality they'd had to consult a fertility clinic—Anne's suggestion; in fact, he'd smacked her around in their penthouse for bringing it up at all. Nine months later, he felt no joy at the birth of their little girl at Raffles Hospital, but he assumed it would come. Only, it didn't. Nor did it when kid number two was born. *Definitely* not when number two was born. The doctors had had to cut Lina out, and Anne was so badly damaged that it put the kibosh on any hope of having a boy, as Erik wanted—as well as on their sex life.

During their remaining years in Singapore, he comforted himself with numerous affairs and the fact that his business instincts were still intact, but because Anne wanted the kids to go to school in Denmark, they'd moved back from Asia and into the large, luxurious apartment on Islands Brygge, where they lived for a year until the house in Klampenborg was ready. The hobbity social world of Copenhagen was restrictive and claustrophobic and obviously a radical adjustment from the international atmosphere and freedom he was used to in Singapore. He was soon bumping into old friends in Bredgade, which he despised as the chickenshit little backwater it actually was—all those petty status symbols and trophy wives jibber-jabbering about their homes and kids. Adding to his disappointment was the realization that his daughters were turning more and more into carbon copies of Anne: coarse, ungainly clones whose naïve drivel aped their mother's slushy, sentimental cast of mind. Worse still, they displayed the same lack of backbone as the woman he'd married.

One evening at bedtime, they'd been crying hysterically over some trivial nonsense, and because both Anne and the au pair girl were out, he was the one stuck with the two little millstones. At last he gave them a slap, and the crying had stopped. A few weeks afterward, the older girl had been unable to keep the food on her plate, despite being asked several times *and* shown how, so he hit her hard enough that she flew out of her chair. At A&E, where she was treated for concussion, he'd made it clear to Judith that she'd better keep her mouth shut unless she wanted to end up on the first flight back to the paddy fields. When Anne rushed back from visiting her mother, it surprised him how easy it was to invent some story about the little girl's clumsiness, and despite her limited intelligence the child knew enough not to tell her mother the truth.

There were many accidents at Islands Brygge, maybe *too* many, but they helped. Occasionally, Anne eyed him with suspicion, but she never asked—at least, not until the caseworker from the local council suddenly turned up just before they were due to move. The council had received an anonymous tip that the girls were being abused, and for a while Erik had to put up with the caseworker nosing around. With his lawyers' help, however, he sent the man packing, making it clear he'd better not come back, and Erik promised himself he'd show more self-control in the future. At least until he figured out who had dared send in the tip.

Afterward, Anne asked him for the first time outright whether he was responsible for the accidents. He denied it, of course, but after the move to Klampenborg and the episode on the hall stairs, she stopped believing him. She cried and blamed herself and said she wanted a divorce. Naturally, he was prepared for that. If she initiated a divorce, he'd set his lawyers on her and make sure she never saw her kids again. Ages ago, she'd signed a postnuptial agreement that guaranteed he would keep everything he'd earned, so she could look forward to a life of government handouts on her mother's sofa if she wasn't satisfied with her gilded cage in Klampenborg.

The atmosphere had never been good again, but he'd thought Anne had given up until the police told him she hadn't actually been going to visit her mother—she'd been running away instead. She'd been planning to leave him, leave *him* looking like the asshole, but then, as if by magic, she was taken out of commission. That part was still incomprehensible, but it gave Erik a feeling of justice. The relationship with the kids, which was now entirely his, would probably also be easier from this point on. He wouldn't have to take anyone else's opinion into account.

Erik Sejer-Lassen enters the interrogation room at the Major Crimes Division full of self-confidence. The two detectives present are the ones from before. The guy with the mixed-up irises and the little piece with the doe eyes. In a different context, he'd have given her a ride she'd never forget. They both look like shit. Tired and worn-out, especially the man, whose face is blue and yellow as though from a recent beating. Erik knows instantly he can ride roughshod over them. He'll be let go straightaway. They don't have shit on him.

"Erik Sejer-Lassen, we've spoken to your au pair

again, and this time she has explained to us in detail how she saw you hit your children on at least four occasions."

"I've got no idea what you're talking about. If Judith is saying I laid a hand on the girls, it's because she's lying."

Erik imagines they'll argue back and forth a little, but the two idiots take no notice of what he's said.

"We *know* she's telling the truth. Not least because we've spoken on the phone to the two Filipina au pairs you employed when you lived in Singapore. All three of them are telling the same story, independently of each other. The prosecution service has therefore decided to charge you with assault and battery against your children for the incidents described in the seven hospital reports from your time in Denmark."

The guy keeps talking, as Sejer-Lassen feels the doe-eyed girl's cold stare.

"For the time being, we have requested a forty-eight-hour extension of your custody. You have the right to a lawyer, and if you cannot afford one then one will be assigned to you by the court. Until a judgment has been passed, the social authorities will look after your children's interests in close conjunction with their grandmother, who has already offered to be their guardian. If you are found guilty and sentenced, a decision will be made as to whether you may retain parental rights and whether you will be allowed to see the children during supervised visits."

All sound vanishes. For a moment, Erik Sejer-Lassen gazes into empty space. Then he looks down. Spread out on the table in front of him are the hospital reports with doctors' descriptions, images, and X-rays of the girls' injuries, and suddenly he thinks it looks bad. Far away, he hears Doe Eyes telling him that Judith also said they'd received a visit from a local-authority caseworker after an anonymous tip-off shortly before the move from Islands Brygge. That's all they want to discuss with Sejer-Lassen on this occasion, before his case is passed to someone else.

"Do you know who sent it in?"

"Do you have any idea who it could have been?"

"Who besides the au pair could have known you were hitting your children?"

The detective with the blue-and-yellow swelling emphasizes how important it is that he answer, but Erik Sejer-Lassen can't get out a word. He merely stares at the images. A moment later, he is led out, and as his cell door slams shut behind him he crumples, missing his girls for the first time in his life.

64

Hess feels like his head's about to explode, and he regrets not staying in the cold wind outside the walls of city hall. The acute numbness in his skull after his fight with Hans Henrik Hauge has in the course of the week been replaced by an insistent headache. It doesn't help that Hauge still hasn't been found, or that this morning he's had to sit in on the interrogation of Erik Sejer-Lassen at the station before rushing over to city hall and interviewing the caseworker, Henning Loeb, and his boss, with whom he's now sitting in an overly warm office at Children's and Young Adult Services. The stiff atmosphere and mahogany paneling aren't exactly kid-friendly.

The caseworker is busily defending himself, probably mostly for the benefit of his departmental head, who's fidgeting nervously in his chair.

"Like I said, the system went down. That's why I couldn't help you."

"That isn't what you said when we spoke on Tuesday. You told me there was no report about Anne Sejer-Lassen's children, when in fact there was."

"I think maybe I said the system couldn't show me right then."

"No, that's not what you said. I gave you the girls' ID numbers, and you said—"

"Okay, look. I don't quite remember how the words—"

"Why the hell didn't you tell me the truth?"

"Well, it wasn't my intention to hide anything . . ."

Henning Loeb keeps squirming, casting apprehensive glances at his boss out of the corner of his eye, and Hess curses himself for not having gone to see the man several days earlier, as he'd first thought to.

Their suspicions about the anonymous tipster in the Laura Kjær case were dismissed for a while after the discovery of the basement room in the garage, because there was apparently no corresponding report for Anne Sejer-Lassen. Hess already had the caseworker's statement that no such tip had been received by city hall while the family lived on Islands Brygge, so he and Thulin focused instead on Gentofte Council, which was responsible for the Klampenborg area. At

Gentofte, they claimed no knowledge of a report about Anne Sejer-Lassen, so the theory that the two killings might be connected by child abuse began to fizzle out; nobody in the Sejer-Lassen family's circle thought the girls' injuries were anything but accidents. The au pair's answers were the most hesitant, but it wasn't until late yesterday afternoon—when Hess and Thulin assured her that they would protect her from Erik Sejer-Lassen's wrath—that she broke down in tears and got the whole thing off her chest. She took the opportunity to add that a caseworker from Copenhagen Council had shown up a while back at their old Islands Brygge address—he'd started asking questions because an anonymous tipster had accused Anne of not taking proper care of her children. Hess swore to himself, realizing they'd wasted precious time.

Hess's impression of the caseworker wasn't exactly stellar after their phone conversation on Tuesday, and nor has it improved during the interview. He's conducting it alone because Thulin and the IT techs have started scouring the department's computers for digital evidence of the tipster. The caseworker has defended his lie as a "technical error," but on reading through the two anonymous reports against Laura Kjær and Anne Sejer-Lassen, Hess has formed another theory about why Loeb was so evasive on the phone.

The tip about Anne Sejer-Lassen was received by the whistle-blower scheme approximately two weeks after the one about Laura Kjær, and shortly before the Sejer-Lassen family moved to Klampenborg. It's unusually verbose, taking up nearly a whole side of A4. In essence, it demands that Anne Sejer-Lassen's two girls, Lina and Sofia, be removed from her care, on the grounds that the girls are being abused. But the letter is rambling, almost devoid of commas, written like one long stream of consciousness, in sharp contrast to the succinct missive about Laura Kjær, which is chilly and matter-of-fact. Anne Sejer-Lassen is described as an upper-class airhead who is more concerned with herself than with her girls. She's obsessed with money and luxury, and it will be obvious to anybody who bothers to check the injury reports from various hospitals that the children need to be taken into care. The font and size of the two messages are also dramatically dissimilar, but if you read them one after the other, it's impossible not to notice that in both cases the sender uses the phrases "selfish whore" and "ought to know better"—several times, in fact, when it comes to Anne Sejer-Lassen. It suggests that the senders are one and the same person, and that the differences might have been feigned. Hess surmises that this is what made Henning Loeb uneasy, prompting him to lie about the Sejer-Lassen girls.

Loeb is hiding behind the rules, defending his handling of the cases: everything has been done by the book, and the parents have denied all knowledge of abuse. He says so repeatedly, as though it's to be expected that the parents will show all their cards as soon as the council comes knocking.

"But the police investigation sheds new light on these cases. Naturally, I'll be recommending an immediate and thorough internal review," interjects the departmental head.

The caseworker falls silent at this remark, while his boss continues to babble assurances. Hess feels the skin tighten again across his skull. He realizes he ought to have gotten checked out himself when they visited the A&E on Tuesday evening, but instead he returned to Odin and the self-inflicted mess of painting supplies. He fell asleep thinking about the man waiting for Thulin with a bouquet and a bottle of wine, and for some reason it irritated him that he was surprised—of course she has someone waiting for her when she clocks out. Not that it's any of his business.

The next day he woke up with the world's most excruciating headache, and just then his mobile began to ring. It was François, who didn't understand why Hess hadn't done more to speak to Freimann after their abortive telephone meeting. Didn't he want his job back after all? What the hell was he thinking? Hess said he'd call him back, then hung up. It was as though the officious Pakistani man from 34C had heard him wake up, because he was soon standing in the doorway and eyeing the shambles inside while he informed Hess that the real estate agent had made a fruitless visit the day before.

"What about those paint pots and the floor polisher in the walkway there? You've got to think of the other residents, you know."

Hess made every promise under the sun, but he didn't keep them; he and Thulin were too busy cooking Sejer-Lassen's goose.

"But what can you tell me about the tipster? Did you find out anything when you went to visit the families you claim you visited?" Hess tries again.

"We *did* go and investigate. It's not a *claim*. But as I said—"

"Just stop it. The boy was being raped in a basement room, and the two girls had been patched up so many times the whole thing stank to high heaven, but you clearly have a damn good reason why that wasn't discovered. All I'm trying to establish is whether you know anything about the person who sent in the tip."

"I don't know anything else. And I don't appreciate your tone. As I said—"

"That's fine. Take a break."

Nylander has arrived. He's standing in the door of the office, and with a nod he makes it clear to Hess that he wants a word. Hess is glad to escape the hot room for the stairwell, where staff bustle past, glancing at them curiously.

"It's not your job to evaluate how the council is doing."

"I'll try and give it a rest, then."

"Where's Thulin?"

"Next door, in there. She and the IT guys are trying to trace who sent the two tip-offs."

"We're thinking it's the killer?"

Hess tries to ignore the stab of irritation at his boss's use of *we*. Freimann talks in the same way, and Hess wonders whether he and Nylander have taken the same management course.

"That's the idea. When can we interview Rosa Hartung?"

"Interview her about what?"

"Well, about—"

"The minister has already been interviewed. She has no knowledge of either Laura Kjær or Anne Sejer-Lassen."

"But the fact that we're standing here means she has to be interviewed again. Both victims were anonymously reported with the aim of having their children taken into care. Or maybe that wasn't the killer's aim at all. Maybe he was just pointing the finger at a system that doesn't work, but either way you've got to be an idiot not to see that it could have something to do with Rosa Hartung. She's the minister for social affairs, after all, and the more you think about it, the more remarkable it is that the killing that started all of this happened more or less the same time as her comeback as a minister."

"Hess, you're doing a good job. And I'm not normally one to go after somebody because his reputation is slightly against him. But it sounds like you're calling me an idiot."

"Then you've misunderstood, of course. But when you add to that the fact that the fingerprints on the two chestnut men found at the crime scenes belonged to Rosa Hartung's daughter—"

"Now you listen to me. Your boss at the Hague has asked me for an evaluation of your professional competence, and naturally I want to help you get back in the saddle. But that means you need to focus on what's important. Rosa Hartung is not to be interviewed again, because it isn't relevant. Agreed?"

The information about his boss at the Hague catches Hess off guard. For a moment, he's too surprised to answer. Nylander shoots a look at Thulin, who's emerged from the room with the department's desktop computers.

"Well?"

"Both tip-offs were sent via the same server in Ukraine, but the people running it aren't known for their cooperation with the authorities. Quite the opposite. We may be able to get an IP address in a few weeks' time, but by then it won't matter."

"Will it help if I ask whether the justice minister would be willing to get in touch with his colleague in Ukraine?"

"I doubt it. Even if they want to help, it will take time we don't have."

"You're telling me. There were only seven days between the first killing and the second. If the killer is as sick in the head as you say, then we can't just sit here twiddling our thumbs."

"Maybe we don't have to. Both tip-offs were sent to the council via the whistle-blower scheme. The first one three months ago, the second two weeks later. If we assume both came from the killer, and if we assume he's going to try again—"

"—then he's already sent an anonymous message about the next victim."

"Exactly. There's only one problem. I've just been told that the whistle-blower scheme gets an average of five anonymous tip-offs per week addressed to Children's and Young Adult Services alone. That's a yearly total of two hundred and sixty. Not all of them are about having children taken into care, but there's no system, so we don't know how many we're actually dealing with."

Nylander nods.

"I'll speak to the head of the department. They've got good cause to help us out. What do you need?"

"Hess?"

His head's throbbing, and the news about an alliance between Freimann and Nylander isn't helping matters. Hess tries to think clearly so he can answer Thulin.

"Anonymous reports of neglect and abuse of children within the last six months. Especially against mothers between twenty and fifty, and demanding that their children be removed from their care. Cases that *have* been handled, but where no reason was found to intervene."

The head of the department has emerged through the door in the background and is watching the little group expectantly. Nylander takes the opportunity to explain what they need.

"But those cases aren't filed in any one place. It'll take time to find them," replies the departmental head.

Nylander looks at Hess, who's begun to walk back toward the hot room.

"Then you'd better get your whole department on it. We've got fuck all else to do, so we'll need them within the hour."

65

Anonymous reports to Copenhagen Council about women with children have turned out to be rather popular. Certainly there are quite a number of them, and as the staff are assigned to bring in the case files and add them to the growing stack on the table, Hess begins to worry whether their plan is the right one. But after the conversation with Nylander, there isn't much else to do besides pick a spot and make a start. While Thulin prefers to read through the cases on an Acer laptop in the large open-plan office, Hess settles down in the meeting room, where he sits turning pages, some of them still warm from the printer.

His method is simple. He opens the relevant case file and scans only the anonymous message. If it doesn't seem relevant, the file is chucked onto a pile to his left.

If it does—if it demands closer attention—the file goes onto a pile to the right.

Very quickly it becomes apparent that this rough sorting process is more difficult than he'd reckoned with. All of the files simmer with the same rage against the mothers that he recognizes from the accusations against Laura Kjær and Anne Sejer-Lassen. They're often written in a fury, some with such obvious give-aways that it's relatively easy to guess they've come from an ex-husband, an aunt, or a grandmother who felt compelled to send in an anonymous message listing the mother's deficiencies. But Hess can't be sure, and the pile to his right is growing. The emails themselves make for appalling reading. Most are evidence of the civil war in which the children are caught up—in which they might still be caught up, because all the cases Hess has requested are ones where the accusations have been dismissed. The department was, however, obliged to investigate, and although it doesn't absolve Henning Loeb of responsibility, Hess now has more understanding for the caseworker's cynicism. Often the tip-offs are motivated by far more than the children's well-being.

By the time Hess has gotten through the forty-odd reports from the last six months anonymously suggesting intervention, he's fed up to the back teeth. It's been altogether more time-consuming than he'd imagined, taking nearly two hours, partly because he kept having to flip through the original case file in order to compare. Worse still, the killer could in principle have written most of them. And not a single one used the phrases "selfish whore" or "ought to know better."

An employee explains that there are no more cases matching the criteria Hess has given them, so he begins going through the stack again. By the time he's finished the second go-round, darkness has fallen outside the flag-adorned windows of city hall. It's barely half past four, but the streetlamps have been lit on H.C. Andersens Boulevard, and motley bulbs glow among the dark, skinny trees along the gardens of Tivoli. This time Hess has, with difficulty, selected seven reports—but he's far from certain the right one is among them. In all seven cases, the tipster urges the council to remove one or several of the woman's children. They're all vastly different. Some short, some long. In one case, on further reflection he realizes the letter has to have come from a family member, while another seems to be from a teacher, because it contains internal information from a meeting that took place at an after-school club.

The last five, however, he can't decipher. He discards one because it uses old-fashioned language, as though written by a grandparent, and another because it's littered with spelling errors. That leaves three: a Gambian woman whom the writer has accused of exploiting her kids as child labor. A handicapped mother accused of neglecting her children because she's on the needle. A welfare mother accused of having sex with her own child.

All three are appalling claims, and it strikes Hess that if one of the reports is genuinely from the killer, then the accusation is probably true. It had been in the cases of Laura Kjær and Anne Sejer-Lassen, at any rate.

"You getting anywhere?" asks Thulin, walking into the room with the Acer laptop under her arm.

"Not really."

"There are three that stick out. The Gambian mother, the handicapped mother, and the retired mother."

"Yeah, maybe." Unsurprising that Thulin has nosed out the same ones he has. In fact, he's begun to wonder whether she might not be able to solve the case better if she were single-handed.

"I think we should take a closer look. Maybe at all three."

Thulin gazes at him impatiently. Hess's head is aching. Something about this whole exercise feels pointless, but he can't work out what it is. It's getting dark outside, and he knows they have to reach a decision if they're going to get anything done that day.

"The killer must be assuming that at some point we'll figure out that the victims were reported to the council. Right or wrong?" asks Hess.

"Right. It might even be part of his objective, us figuring it out. But he can't tell how *quickly* we'll figure it out."

"So the killer also knows that at some point we'll read the two tip-offs about Laura Kjær and Anne Sejer-Lassen. Right or wrong?"

"This isn't Twenty Questions. If we don't get a move on, we might as well go and interview the neighbors again."

But Hess continues, trying to hold on to his train of thought. "So if you were the killer and you'd written the first two messages—and you knew we'd find them and feel tremendously clever—how would you write the third one?"

Hess can tell she understands. Her eyes leap from him and back to the screen in her arms.

"Generally speaking, the readability score isn't high. But if we play with the idea that we're being deliberately thrown off track, then there are two that stand out. The one with all the spelling mistakes and the one written in old-fashioned Danish."

"Which one is the stupidest?" asks Hess.

Thulin's eyes skim the screen while Hess fumbles for the two folders on the table and flips them open. This time, when he reads the report with all the spelling mistakes, his instincts are roused. Maybe it's his imagination. Maybe not. Thulin turns her screen toward Hess, and he nods. It's the same one he's selected. The tip-off about Jessie Kvium. Twenty-five years old. Resident at the Urbanplan Housing Estate.

66

Jessie Kvium marches off with her six-year-old daughter, but the young Paki teacher with the kindly eyes catches her in the hallway before she rounds the corner.

"Jessie, can I speak with you for a moment?"

Even before she can finish saying that, oh, unfortunately she and Olivia are just rushing off to dance practice, she can tell from his determined face that she isn't going to escape. She's always trying to dodge him—he's so reliably good at pricking her conscience—but now she has to try and charm her way out. She bats her eyes coyly and brushes the hair from her face with her long, freshly painted nails so that he can see how good she looks today. She's been at the hairdresser's for two hours. Only the Paki one on Amager Boulevard, mind you, but they're cheap and they do makeup and nails if you wait awhile, like she did that day. Tight around her hips is her new yellow skirt, a recent purchase from H&M in town for only seventy-nine kroner—partly because it's a thin summer thing that was on its way off the shelves and partly because she was able to show the sales assistant it was coming apart at the seams. Which doesn't make a blind bit of difference to what she needs it for.

But her smile and batting eyelashes bounce off the teacher. At first she thinks she's going to get another earful about picking up her child dangerously close to the after-school-club closing time at five, so she's ready with a quick answer about how people are still allowed to get something for their taxes. Today, however, Ali— probably what he's called—asks about Olivia's lack of raincoat and boots.

"The shoes she has are absolutely fine, of course, but she says she's cold when they get wet, and they may not be so practical for autumn."

The teacher glances discreetly at Olivia's hole-riddled trainers, and Jessie feels like screaming at him to shut his mouth. She doesn't have five hundred kroner for that kind of stuff right now, and if she did have that kind of money she'd rather whisk her daughter far away from a classroom where fifty percent of the kids speak Arabic and every single word has to be translated by three different interpreters at parents' evenings. Not that she attends them herself, but that's what she's heard.

Unfortunately there are a few other teachers hovering in the background, so Jessie chooses plan B.

"Oh, but we *have* bought raincoats and boots. We just forgot them at the holiday cottage, but we'll remember them next time."

Total bullshit, of course, from start to finish. There are no rain clothes, no boots, and certainly no holiday cottage, but the half bottle of white wine she downed back at Urbanplan before she got dressed and drove over helps the words on their way, as it always does.

"Right, that's fine, then. And how would you say things are going with Olivia at home?"

Jessie senses the eyes of the passing teachers as she explains how swimmingly things are going. Ali lowers his voice and says he's a bit concerned, because there hasn't been much improvement in Olivia's relationship with the other children. He's afraid she seems very isolated, so he thinks it might be good for them to have another little chat soon, and Jessie hastens to accept with the same friendliness as though he's offered them a trip to the theme park with all expenses paid.

Afterward, she sits in the little Toyota Aygo while her daughter changes into her dance gear in the backseat and she smokes a cigarette out of the open window. She tells Olivia that the teacher was quite right about what he'd said, and that they'll buy that rain gear for her soon.

"But it's also important that you pull yourself together and play more with the others, okay?"

"My foot hurts."

"It'll stop once you've warmed up. It's important to go every time, sweetheart."

The dance studio is on the top floor of Amager Shopping Center, and they arrive barely two minutes before the beginning of class. They have to run up the stairs from the parking level, and of course the other little princesses are all standing ready on the varnished wooden floor in their expensive, trendy outfits. Olivia's wearing her supermarket-bought lilac dress, the one she had last year too, and despite being a tad tight across the shoulders it's still a passable fit. Jessie tugs off her daughter's coat and sends her out onto the floor, where the teacher greets her with a kind smile. All the mothers are lined up along one wall, a row of stuck-up bitches deep in conversation about wellness, autumn getaways to Gran Canaria, and how their kids are doing in school. She greets them politely and smiles, although she wishes they'd all go to hell.

As the girls begin to dance she glances impatiently around, adjusting her skirt, but he still hasn't come, and for a moment she stands exposed beside the mothers, feeling let down. She had been sure he'd come, and the fact that he isn't there makes her unsure of the relationship she thought they had. She feels embarrassed in the other women's company, and although she'd planned to keep quiet, she begins to prattle nervously.

"Gosh, don't they look lovely today, the little princesses. I can't believe they've only been dancing for a year!"

With every word she feels herself more engulfed in their pitying glances. Then, finally, the door opens and he comes into the studio. Also with his daughter, who scurries over to the others and joins the dance. He looks at her and the mothers, gives a friendly nod and an effortless grin, and she feels her heart begin to pound. His movements are confident, and he's casually swinging the keys to the Audi she has come to know so well. As he exchanges a few words with the other mothers and makes them laugh, she realizes he hasn't even properly looked her way. He's ignoring her, even though she's standing beside him like a fawning dog, and it prompts her to blurt out that, oh, by the way, there's something she'd like to discuss with him. Something important about the "classroom culture" at the school—a word she's just picked up from one of the other women. He looks surprised, but before he can answer, she starts walking toward the exit. Shooting a glance over her shoulder, she notes with satisfaction that it was too odd for him to refuse her invitation to talk about something so important, so he has to excuse himself to the other mothers and follow.

As she comes down the stairs and pushes through the heavy door into the corridor beneath the studio, she can hear his footsteps behind her. She pauses and waits, but as soon as she sees his face, she can tell he's angry.

"What the hell is wrong with you? Don't you get that this is over? You've got to leave me be, for Christ's sake!"

She grabs him, grabs his pants and unzips them, sticks down her hand, and immediately finds what she's seeking. He tries to push her away, but she holds on, and soon she's drawn it out and taken him in her mouth, and his resistance turns to suppressed moans. As he's about to come, she turns around and bends forward across the recycling bin. Her hand fumbles to pull up her skirt, but he gets there first, tearing the new yellow skirt aside. She hears the fabric rip. Feeling him inside her, she thrusts her hips backward so he can't help himself, and within a few seconds he's finished. Stiffening, he gasps for breath. She turns and kisses his lifeless lips, holding his damp member, but he takes a step back as though she's given him an electric shock, then slaps her across the face.

Jessie's too stunned to speak. She feels the heat spread across her face as he zips up his fly.

"That was the last time. I feel nothing for you. Not a fucking thing, and I will never leave my family. You got that?"

She hears his steps and the heavy door slamming behind him. Left alone, her cheek burning. She can still feel him between her legs, but now in a way that makes her feel ashamed. In a sheet of metal on the wall she sees her distorted reflection, and she adjusts her clothes, but the skirt has been torn. The rip is visible from the front, and she has to button her coat so it can't be seen. Wiping away her tears, she hears the distant, happy music from the studio above, and pulls herself together. Jessie goes back the way she came, but now the door to the stairs is locked. She tugs at it in vain, and when she tries to call for help, all she hears is the faint sound of the music.

She decides to take the other route, down a long corridor lined with heating pipes, where she's never been before. But a little farther down, the corridor splits, and the first direction she chooses is a dead end. Jessie tries a new door: it too is locked. She retreats, walking back along the corridor with the heating pipes, but she hasn't gone twenty yards before she hears a noise behind her.

"Hello? Is someone there?"

For a moment she tries to tell herself it's him, that he's come back to apologize, but the silence tells her something else. Disconcerted, she walks on. Soon she begins to jog. One corridor follows another, and Jessie thinks she can hear footsteps behind her. This time she doesn't call out. She tugs at every single door she passes, and when one finally opens she flies into the stairwell and up the steps. She thinks she can hear the door opening below her, and when she reaches the next landing she shoves the door leading to the main shopping center so hard that it bangs into the wall.

Jessie Kvium bolts up to the top floor, where families are milling around with their shopping carts to the sound of autumn offers. Turning to face the entrance to the dance studio, she sees a woman and a tall man with a bruised face questioning one of the mothers, who is pointing in her direction.

67

"But is it her or isn't it?"

"We don't know. She did feel like she was being followed at the shopping center. Problem is, she's not exactly keen to help us. Or maybe she just doesn't know anything."

It's Thulin who answers Nylander, while Hess stands staring into the interview room through the one-way mirror. It's coated on one side so that he can see Jessie Kvium, but Jessie Kvium can't see him. Hess can't be sure, but his gut tells him she might be keeping the kind of secrets that interest the killer. That said, she's markedly different from the previous victims. Hess's impression is that Laura Kjær and Anne Sejer-Lassen were more bourgeois and concerned with appearances, while Jessie Kvium seems unrulier, more belligerent.

On the other hand, that's precisely what made her a glaring target. You'd take note of Jessie Kvium among a hundred other women, feeling both attracted and intimidated as a man. Right now the young woman is conducting a furious argument with the poor officer standing guard by the door, doing her best to talk her way past him, and Hess is grateful that the volume of the loudspeaker on the wall is turned down to a minimum. Outside the sky has blackened, and for a second Hess reflects that it would be nice to turn down Nylander's volume too.

"But if she can't help, then maybe you're looking at the wrong woman?"

"Or maybe she's just rattled, in which case we need more time."

"More time?"

Nylander chews over Thulin's words, and a lifetime's experience with police chiefs tells Hess what's coming next.

Thulin and Hess had driven straight from city hall to Urbanplan, where they rang Jessie Kvium's doorbell. The door had remained unopened. Nor had the woman been picking up her phone. The case file had mentioned no relatives, only the number of the social worker who was in weekly contact—they were checkups, strictly speaking—with mother and daughter. The social worker had explained over the phone that they'd agreed the daughter would go to dance lessons every Friday at five fifteen p.m. on the top floor of Amager Shopping Center.

As soon as they found Jessie Kvium, they could tell something was wrong. The young woman said she'd felt someone was following her when she went down to put the parking receipt in her car. They immediately checked the stairs, corridors, and basement area, but found nothing suspicious. There were no CCTV cameras in the corridors, and the parking lot itself was too busy with people doing their weekend shopping.

During her interview at the police station, Jessie Kvium became increasingly aggressive. She smelled of wine, and when she was asked to remove her coat they noticed that her skirt was torn to pieces. The woman said she'd caught it on the car door, and demanded to know what the hell she was doing at the police station. They tried to explain the situation, but Jessie had no useful information. She hadn't otherwise felt like she was being followed, and as far as she was concerned there was no doubt who'd sent in the anonymous tip-off to the council two months earlier, in which she was accused of beating and neglecting Olivia.

"One of those busybodies at the school. Always so fucking judgmental, because they're scared to death their dirty old husbands will think the grass is greener on the other side of the fence. But she couldn't even spell."

"Jessie, we don't believe the report came from one of the mothers at school. Who else could it have been?"

But Jessie was unbending: that was what had happened. To her satisfaction, the council had ended up believing her version, although obviously it had been "a pain in the fucking ass to have them poking about all that time."

"Jessie, it's extremely important that you tell us the truth now. For your own sake. We're not trying to accuse you of anything, but if there's any truth to the email, then the person who wrote it may be planning to harm you."

"Who the hell do you think you are?"

Jessie Kvium went ballistic. Nobody had the right to call her a bad mother. She looked after the girl herself without any help from the dad, who'd never paid a krone—the last few years with the excuse that he was in jail in Nyborg for dealing drugs.

"If you have any doubt about that, you can ask Olivia how she's doing!"

Hess and Thulin hadn't been planning to do that. The little six-year-old girl, still in her dance outfit, was sitting in the cafeteria with a fizzy drink and a few pieces of crispbread, watching a cartoon with a female officer in the belief that her mother was getting her car checked out. Her clothes were threadbare and full of holes, she was maybe a bit scrawny and untidy, but it was impossible to say whether the girl was being abused. Given the circumstances, it was hardly surprising she was quiet, and it would have seemed like bullying if they'd started asking pushy questions about how her mother treated her.

From the interview room, they hear Jessie Kvium spit another string of obscenities, telling the guard that she wants permission to leave, but she's drowned out by Nylander. "There *is* no more time. You said this was the right move, so now you'd better make use of it or pick another direction."

"Maybe this would be quicker if we could do the interviews we believe are actually necessary," said Hess.

"You're not referring to Rosa Hartung again."

"I'm just saying we weren't allowed to talk to her."

"How many times do I have to spell it out for you?"

"I don't know. I've stopped counting, but it doesn't seem to be having any effect."

"Listen! There's another option."

Hess and Nylander stop bickering and look at Thulin.

"If we agree that Jessie Kvium could be the next intended victim, then in principle all we have to do is let her get on with her life while we keep a watch on her and wait for the killer to show up."

Nylander stares at her, shaking his head.

"Out of the question. After two murders, I'm damn well not sending Jessie Kvium back out onto the street while we sit on our hands waiting for a psychopath."

"I'm not talking about Jessie Kvium. I'm talking about myself."

Hess gazes at Thulin in surprise. She's five foot six at the most. A nimble little thing who appears like a gust of wind could bowl her over, but one look into her eyes and you found yourself doubting your own strength.

"I'm the same height, same hair color, and roughly the same build as Jessie Kvium. If we can find a doll to serve as her daughter, then I think we can fool the killer."

Nylander is staring at her with interest.

"When did you have in mind?"

"As soon as possible. So the killer doesn't start wondering where she is. If Jessie Kvium is the target, then he knows her routine. Hess, what's your take?"

Thulin's suggestion is a simple solution. He is usually in favor of simple solutions, but he doesn't like this one. There's too much they don't know. So far the killer has been one step ahead of them, and now all of a sudden they think they can turn the tables?

"Let's question Jessie Kvium again. Maybe—"

The door opens. Tim Jansen appears, drawing an exasperated glance from Nylander.

"Not now, Jansen!"

"It's got to be now. Or you could just switch on the news."

"Why?"

Jansen's eyes land on Hess.

"Because somebody hasn't kept their mouth shut about Kristine Hartung's fingerprints. It's on all the channels. They're saying maybe the Hartung case wasn't cleared up after all."

68

The pans are simmering on the little gas stove in her Vesterbro apartment, and Thulin has to turn up the news to drown out the extractor fan and doorbell.

"Go and open the door for Granddad."

"You can do it yourself."

"Just help me out. I'm busy with the food."

Le walks reluctantly into the front hall, the ever-present iPad in her hands. They've had an argument, but Thulin doesn't have the energy to deal with it right now. The media has indeed gotten their hands on the information about Kristine Hartung's fingerprints on the two chestnut men found near Laura Kjær's and Anne Sejer-Lassen's bodies. As far as Thulin could glean from a quick skim online, the initial report came from one of the two major tabloids late that afternoon, but the rival paper followed up so quickly it was hard to tell whether it came from a separate source or was simply a rewrite of the first article. The headline—SHOCK: IS KRISTINE HARTUNG ALIVE?—spread like a forest fire to more or less every media outlet, all of which referenced the tabloids as a source and repeated the same content. "Anonymous sources in the police" had hinted there might be a connection between the two murders and the Kristine Hartung case after mysterious fingerprints found on two chestnut dolls cast doubt on the girl's death. A boiled-down version of the truth, essentially, although Nylander and other senior officers had denied all such speculation. The twist was so sensational that it was the top story everywhere, and if Thulin had forgotten how surprised she'd been the first time she heard about the fingerprints, then it was certainly brought home to her now. All kinds of theories and conjectures were being floated, and one online paper had even taken to using "the Chestnut Man" to refer to the killer; plainly, this was only the beginning of an avalanche of news reports. Thulin understood very well why Nylander had instantly abandoned them to focus on strategy meetings and contend with the press.

Meanwhile, she had flung herself into preparations for that evening's operation at Urbanplan. Their attempt to ambush the killer had been approved by Nylander, although Hess had been against it. Jessie Kvium had taken the news that she and her daughter weren't going to be allowed to return to their apartment with incredulous frustration, but her arguments had been swept aside. Toothbrushes and other necessities would be provided, and they'd have to prepare for a few nights under close watch at a cabin in Valby, which was offered by the council to low-income families. Jessie Kvium and her daughter were already familiar with it, having spent a week's holiday there during the summer.

Jessie had been willing to answer questions about her routine, and as the questions grew more detailed and insistent, it had dawned on her that all their talk of threats had to be serious. It was Thulin herself who, along with Hess, had questioned her, absorbing all the information so that she knew exactly how Jessie would behave from the moment she arrived at the housing complex in her car, which the police were also using as part of the operation.

Thulin had been ready to set off for Urbanplan immediately, but as it turned out Jessie's routine was different. Every Friday evening after her daughter's dance class, she had to go straight to the Alcoholics Anonymous meeting at Christianshavns Torv, which the council had stipulated that Jessie must attend from seven p.m. to nine p.m. if she wanted to continue receiving family allowance as part of her welfare payments. Her daughter usually dozed in a chair in the corridor until Jessie was finished and took her back to the car. But since by that time it was already past seven, it was decided that Thulin would start living as Jessie Kvium only once the single mother was supposed to have left the AA meeting.

While the task force and its leader spent the wait studying floor plans and the routes to and from Urbanplan, Thulin had picked up Le from her playdate with Ramazan and gone home to make pasta before Granddad showed up and took over. Le had taken the news with frustration, because it meant Thulin wouldn't have time that evening to help her reach the next level in League of Legends, the game to which her life was apparently dedicated, and Thulin had to admit once again that she spent too much time away from home.

"Come on, time to eat! If Granddad hasn't had dinner, you can eat together."

Her daughter reemerges from the front hall, and there is something triumphant about her expression.

"It isn't Granddad. It's someone from your job with bruises on his head and two different eyes. He says he'd *love* to show me how to get to the next level."

69

Thulin hadn't planned to waste time eating dinner herself, but Hess appearing under the lamp in the front hall changes things.

"I came early because I've been given some drawings of Urbanplan and the apartments. You need to get up to speed before we go."

"But first you've got to help *me*," pipes up Le, before Thulin can answer. "What's your name?"

"Mark. But as I said, I'm afraid I don't have time to help you with the game right now—another time I'd love to, though."

"You've got to eat now, Le," adds Thulin swiftly.

"Then Mark can eat with us. Come on, Mark, then you can explain it to me. Mom's boyfriend isn't allowed to eat with us, but you're not Mom's boyfriend, so *you* can."

Le vanishes into the kitchen. It feels too strange to overrule her child, so Thulin shifts hesitatingly aside and gestures Hess into the apartment.

In the kitchen, he sits down beside Le, who swaps her iPad for a laptop while Thulin fetches three plates. With the charm and magnanimity worthy of a princess, Le preoccupies her guest's attention. At first, her friendliness is probably a display to spite Thulin, but as Hess explains more about the game—the source of his knowledge is still mysterious—the girl becomes increasingly engrossed in his advice about getting to the promised land of level six.

"Do you know Park Su? He's world-famous!"

"Park Su?" asks Hess.

Soon a poster and a little plastic figurine of the Korean teenager are set out on the table. They start eating, and the conversation turns to other games Thulin didn't realize her daughter had heard of, but it turns out that Hess only knows that one game and has never tried any others. For her daughter, it's like having a visiting apprentice. She expands his knowledge in a rapid stream of words, and when the topic is exhausted she fetches the cage with her parakeet—

which is soon going to have a playmate, so that they can add more names to the family tree.

"Ramazan has fifteen on his family tree, but I've only got three. Five, if I count the parakeet and the hamster. Mom doesn't want her boyfriends on there, so that's why I haven't got any more—otherwise I'd have loads."

At that point Thulin interjects that it's about time her daughter starts work on level six, and after a few more bits of advice from Hess, Le finally sits down on the sofa and goes to war.

"Smart girl."

Thulin nods curtly, bracing herself for the usual peppering of questions about the girl's father, family, and the general situation, which she doesn't feel like getting into. But instead, Hess turns to his jacket, which is flung over the back of a chair, and removes a sheaf of papers, spreading them out on the table.

"Here, let's have a quick look at these. Run through the plan."

Hess is thorough, and Thulin listens earnestly as she follows his fingers, which trace the floor plans, stairwells, and areas outside the buildings.

"The whole complex will be under surveillance, but at a suitable distance, of course, so the task force doesn't scare off the killer. If he shows up at all."

He also mentions the doll, which is going to be swaddled in a duvet so that Thulin can pretend she's carrying the sleeping child inside. Thulin only has a few remarks about the surveillance team, which she's worried might rouse the killer's suspicions, but Hess insists it's necessary.

"We can't take chances. If Jessie Kvium is the next intended victim, then the killer's probably highly familiar with Urbanplan, and we've got to be on the scene so we can intervene quickly. If there's any danger, you need to let us know immediately. And you can always pull out now, if you'd prefer someone else to take over."

"Why would I pull out now?"

"Because it's not exactly un-dangerous."

Thulin looks into the blue and green eyes, and if she didn't know better, she'd have guessed the man is worried about her.

"It's fine. I've got no problem with that."

"Is she the one you're trying to find?"

Le has left the front room without them noticing, coming into the kitchen for a glass of water. She's staring at Thulin's iPad, which is propped against the wall on the kitchen table showing the beginning of yet another news broadcast. This one also with Kristine Hartung as the top story, the newsreader reveling in the past and present of the case.

"You shouldn't be watching that. It's not for children."

Thulin rises, and in a quick movement she reaches the screen and switches it off. She explained to Le that she needed to work later, and when her daughter petulantly insisted on knowing why, Thulin said it was because they were going to find someone. She didn't mention it was the killer they were after, so Le assumed it was Kristine Hartung.

"What happened to her?"

"Le, just go back in and play your game."

"Is the girl dead?"

The question is put with straightforward innocence, as though she's asked whether there are still dinosaurs living on Bornholm Island. Yet beneath the curiosity is concern, which makes Thulin promise herself that in future she'll remember to switch off any news feeds when Le is around.

"I don't know, Le. I mean . . ."

Thulin doesn't know what to say. There are pitfalls on every side, no matter what her reply.

"Nobody really knows. Maybe she just got lost. Sometimes you can get lost and struggle to find your way back home. But if she is lost, then we'll find her."

It's Hess who replies. It's a good answer, and the brightness comes back into her daughter's eyes.

"I've never got lost. Have your children ever got lost?"

"I don't have any children."

"Why not?"

Thulin sees Hess smile at the girl, but this time he says nothing. Then the doorbell rings in the front hall, and the wait is over.

70

Urbanplan is a public housing complex in West Amager, just three kilometers from city hall in central Copenhagen. The blocks had been thrown up in the 1960s to meet the general lack of apartments, but something went wrong, and for several years in the early 2000s, the area slipped onto the government's list of ghettos. The council still hasn't fixed the problems, and as in the case of Odin, the presence of pale Danish police officers attracts a lot of attention even if they appear in casual civilian clothes. It's therefore the officers more ethnic in appearance who've been assigned the most exposed posts—including in some of the vehicles in the dark parking lot to the left of the block where Hess is positioned.

It's nearly one by the clock on the oven in the empty ground-floor apartment. It's vacant, up for sale, so the police decided to use it for the operation. The lights are off, and from the window in the small kitchen Hess can see clear across the pitch-black estate, with its virtually bare trees, its play area and benches, to the illuminated entryway that leads up to the stairs and elevator in Jessie Kvium's block. Although the surveillance teams seem to be in the right place, Hess is nervous. There are four access points to Jessie Kvium's block, one for each point of the compass, and all are in sight of either him or the officers positioned around the building, so they can keep constant watch over the people coming and going. Snipers are posted on the roofs, skilled enough to hit a single krone piece at two hundred yards, and only two minutes away, the bus carrying the task force is poised to intervene if they are called over the walkie-talkie. Yet Hess still feels it isn't enough.

Thulin's arrival went without a hitch. Hess recognized the little Toyota Aygo at once as it turned off the road and into the lot, where it parked in the agreed-upon bay, vacated moments earlier by an unmarked police vehicle.

Thulin was dressed in Jessie Kvium's hat, clothes, and coat; only her skirt had been swapped for a similar

yellow one, and at a distance there was nothing to indicate she wasn't the woman she was pretending to be.
Thulin had taken the doll in its duvet out of the backseat, locked the car with a struggle—supporting herself
and the child against the car door—then headed toward
the entryway, carrying the girl in the same slightly
exasperated way Jessie Kvium would have done. Hess
watched her figure disappear into the stairwell, where
the light came on. What they hadn't foreseen was that
the elevator was being used and took ages to appear,
but luckily Thulin simply walked up the stairs to the
third floor, even making it look as though the child felt
heavier and heavier each time she reached a landing.

Some other residents passed her in the opposite direction, but apparently without taking any notice. At
last she vanished from sight, and Hess held his breath
until the light in the apartment with the small balcony
was switched on.

By now three hours have passed, and nothing has
happened. Earlier in the evening the estate was busy—
people coming home late from work, or mulling over
the state of world affairs as shriveled leaves whirled
around their heads—and in the block to the right, a
small party had begun in the community rooms in
the basement. The sound of Indian sitar music drifted
among the blocks for several hours, but gradually the

party died down, while more and more of the lights in the apartments were put out. It grew late.

The light at Jessie Kvium's place is still on, but Hess knows it will soon be switched off; it's part of Jessie's routine to go to bed at this time, at least on the rare occasions when she stays home on Friday nights.

"Eleven-seven here. Have I told you the one about the nun and the seven little officers from Europol, over?"

"No. Come on, then, Eleven-seven. We're listening."

It's Tim Jansen, entertaining his colleagues via walkie-talkie while taking a barely concealed jab at Hess. Hess can't see him from his post by the kitchen window, but he knows he is sitting in a car not far from the entryway to the west, with one of the younger officers of ethnic-minority origin. Although he doesn't approve of radio contact being used for jokes, he lets it go. At the team meeting at the station, before Hess had gone to see Thulin, Jansen had already expressed his doubts about the operation, because Hess had been unable to say for sure that Jessie Kvium was definitely in danger. It was clear he suspected Hess of being the one who'd squealed to the press, and that sort of thing didn't go unpunished. For several days, Hess had sensed Jansen's eyes on the back of his neck whenever he was at the station, but after the media explosion earlier that night, several other colleagues were now shooting him dubious looks. It was utterly ridiculous. When the press started scribbling about murder cases, it rarely boded well, so Hess was accustomed to keeping journalists at arm's length. In fact, the leak had irritated him—if there *was* a leak. The killer obviously knew about the fingerprints, and it had occurred to Hess that he would probably be amused to watch the department being turned into a public laughingstock. He reminds himself that they still need to investigate the newspapers' sources, and reaches tetchily for the walkie-talkie as Jansen launches into yet another joke.

"Eleven-seven, suspend radio contact not pertaining to the operation."

"Or what, Seven-three? You'll call the tabloids?"

There's the sound of scattered laughter, until the task-force leader intervenes and orders silence. Hess peers out of the window. The light in Jessie Kvium's place is out.

71

Thulin keeps away from the large, dark windows, but she potters occasionally from room to room in order to let the killer know that she—or rather, Jessie Kvium—is home. Assuming the killer is out there watching, of course.

The playacting in the parking lot had worked. The doll was a good match, and the black artificial hair had mostly been concealed beneath the duvet. The issue with the elevator had been a snag, but she'd judged that Jessie Kvium was so naturally impatient that she'd rather clump up the stairs than wait. On the way up she'd passed a young couple, but they barely gave her a glance, and she unlocked the apartment with Jessie's key then locked it behind her as soon as she stepped into the hall.

Although Thulin had never been in the apartment before, she was familiar with its layout, and had carried the doll straight into the bedroom, where she laid it on the bed. The room included both her and her daughter's beds. The windows were curtainless, with a view over yet another concrete block. She knew that Hess was somewhere beyond the dark windows on the ground floor, but she wasn't sure who might be able to see in from the upper stories, so she undressed the doll and tucked it up in the sheets as though putting Le to bed at home. It had struck her as paradoxical that she was saying good night to a doll in her capacity as an officer instead of tucking in her own daughter, but now wasn't the time for thoughts like that. Next she had gone into the front room and switched on the flat-screen TV, following Jessie's routine, before settling in the armchair with her back to the window and scanning the apartment.

The last person who'd been inside it was Jessie Kvium herself, and she clearly hadn't bothered to tidy up. The place was a mess. Dozens of empty wine bottles, food-encrusted plates, pizza boxes, and dirty dishes. Not many toys. Although she couldn't be sure Jessie Kvium was actually neglecting her child, it didn't seem like an appetizing place to grow up. Which reminded Thulin of her own childhood, and since she didn't feel like thinking about that, she focused on the flat-screen.

The Kristine Hartung case was still the high priority, and everything was being rehashed on the grounds that the case might not have been solved after all. The news said Rosa Hartung had refused to give a statement, and Thulin was feeling sorry for the minister and her family, once more being confronted with a past they so wanted to put behind them, when the avalanche reached another climax:

"Keep watching in a moment, when Steen Hartung—Kristine Hartung's father—is a guest on the *Nightly News.*"

Steen Hartung was a guest on the last news broadcast of the night, and in a lengthy interview he made it clear he believed his daughter might still be alive somewhere. He implored people to come forward to the police if they knew anything, and also made a direct appeal to "the person who has taken Kristine," pleading with them to return her unharmed.

"We miss her . . . she's still only a child, and she needs her mom and dad."

Thulin understood why he was doing it, but she wasn't sure how much good it would do the investigation. The justice minister and Nylander, also interviewed, had taken up the challenge and distanced themselves sharply from all such speculation. Nylander, in particular, had appeared steely, almost angry with the media, but he also spoke with such relish that it made her suspect he was enjoying the attention. In the middle of it all, Thulin had received a text from Genz, who asked what the hell was going on—the reporters had now started calling *him*. She replied that it was vital he didn't give a statement. He'd joked back that he promised not to if she agreed to a fifteen-kilometer run with him next morning, but she hadn't answered that one.

The media hullaballoo had finally come to an end around midnight, followed by tedious reruns of various TV shows. The optimism and tension she felt as she drove from Christianshavn has gradually given way to doubt. How sure can they be that Jessie Kvium is the right one? How sure can they be that the killer will try something? When she hears Tim Jansen start killing time with silly jokes via walkie-talkie, she partly understands. The man is an idiot, of course, but if they've made a mistake then it leaves them way behind with the investigation. Thulin checks the time on her phone, then rises to switch off the light in the front room as agreed. Before she can sit back down, Hess calls her.

"Everything okay?"

"Yep."

She can sense him calming down. They chat a little about the situation, and although he doesn't say so she can tell he's still on high alert. More than she is, at least.

"You shouldn't take any notice of Jansen," she suddenly hears herself say.

"Thanks. I don't."

"He's been preening about the Hartung case ever since I first started. When you—and now the press too—started questioning the investigation it was like you shot him in the gut with a sawed-off shotgun."

"Sounds like you'd fancy doing that yourself."

Thulin grins. She's about to reply when Hess's voice changes.

"Something's happening. Switch to the radio."

"What's going on?"

"Do it. Right now."

The connection is cut.

As Thulin sets down her phone, she's suddenly aware of how alone she is.

72

Hess stiffens at the window. He knows he can't be seen from outside, but still he doesn't move a muscle. Approximately a hundred yards away, by the entryway at the end of Kvium's concrete block, he has just seen a young couple with a baby carriage unlock the door to the bike room in the basement and vanish inside. The hydraulic door swings very slowly shut behind them, and Hess notices a movement in the shadow of the adjoining building. For a second, he thinks it might be the wind in the trees, but then he sees it again. A figure breaks into a jog and disappears inside just before the door closes. Hess picks up the walkie-talkie.

"Our guest may have arrived. East-side door, over."

"We saw it, over."

Hess knows what's at that end, although he's never been there himself. The entryway leads down to the bike storage room in the basement, and from there underneath the block and up to the stairs and elevator, which offers access to the upper floors.

He leaves the ground-floor apartment and goes into the stairwell, shutting the door behind him. Instead of heading for the main exit and the open space outside, he takes the stairs down to the basement. He leaves the lights off but carries his flashlight. On reaching the basement level, he knows from his prep work which way he should take. Holding out the flashlight in front of him, he races down the corridor that leads underneath the area outside and into Kvium's block. It's roughly fifty yards, and as he approaches the heavy metal door to Kvium's complex he hears over the walkie-talkie that the elevator is being used by the couple with the baby carriage.

"The unidentified person must be on the stairs, but the light hasn't been switched on, so we can't be sure. Over."

"We're doing a search from the bottom upward, and we're starting now," answers Hess.

"But we don't even know if—"

"We're starting now. No more chat."

Hess switches off the walkie-talkie. Something is wrong. The figure must have arrived on foot over the unlit lawn, and that doesn't seem thought through. It occurs to Hess that he wouldn't be surprised if the killer made his entrance by lowering himself from the roof or jumping out of a manhole cover. Anything but a main lobby. He turns the safety off on his gun, and by the time the metal door glides shut behind him he's already on the first landing.

73

Thulin is looking out of the window. It's been eight or nine minutes since the guest was announced. She can see nothing in the forecourt, and it strikes her how silent it is in the complex. The sound of music has stopped; only the wind can be heard. She hadn't objected to staying in the apartment when they had agreed on the details of the operation, but now it seems like a dumb idea. She's never been any good at waiting. Plus there's no back door to the apartment—nowhere to run, if it came to that. So when she hears a knock on the door in the front hall, she's relieved. It has to be Hess or one of the others, come to help her.

Peering through the spy hole, however, she finds the corridor dark and unoccupied. No one in sight, only the fire cupboard in the recess opposite the door. For a moment, she wonders whether she could have misheard. But there *had* been a knock. She switches the safety off her weapon and prepares herself. Sliding back the bolt, she twists the latch to the left and steps out into the corridor, gun at the ready.

A few switches glow faintly, but she doesn't touch them. The darkness feels like protection. All the apartment doors seem to be shut along the wide linoleum-floored corridor, and as her eyes grow accustomed to the low light she can see all the way to the far wall on the left. She looks the other way, toward the stairs and elevator on the right, but that too is empty. There's no one in the corridor.

From inside the apartment, she hears a crackle over the walkie-talkie. Someone is calling her name impatiently, and she begins to retreat toward the door. But just as she turns her back on the corridor, the figure lunges out of the recess beside the fire cupboard. It had been crouched in a huddle, waiting for exactly that moment, and she feels its weight hurl her through the doorway and onto the ground. Chilly hands coil around her throat, and she hears the voice whisper into her ear.

"Fucking slut. Give me the pictures or I'll kill you."

Before the man can say another word, Thulin has broken his nose with two crisp jabs of her elbow. For a second, he sits there in the dark, dazed. He barely knows what's hit him before Thulin strikes him for a third time, and he collapses onto the floor.

74

By the time Hess reaches Kvium's apartment, the door is open, and as he dashes inside with two officers behind him he can hear the man shrieking in pain. He flicks on the light. The apartment is a mess. On the floor, amid laundry and pizza boxes, a man with a bloodied nose is lying with both arms twisted behind his back. Thulin is sitting on top of him, gripping his wrists between his shoulder blades with one hand while the other is busy frisking him.

"What the hell are you doing? Fucking let me go!"

When she's finished the two officers haul the man upright, still with his hands between his shoulder blades, making him shriek even louder.

He's roughly forty. Muscular, a salesman type with slicked-back hair and a wedding ring. He's wearing nothing but a T-shirt and a pair of sweatpants underneath his coat, as though he's just stepped out of bed. His nose is crooked and swollen, and his roll-around on the floor has smeared the blood all over his face.

"Nikolaj Møller. Mantuavej 75, Copenhagen S."

Thulin reads aloud from the man's health-insurance card, which is tucked alongside credit cards and family photos in the wallet she's found in his inside pocket, as well as a mobile phone and a car key stamped with the Audi logo.

"What's going on? I haven't done anything!"

"What are you doing here? I asked you what you're *doing* here?"

Thulin steps directly up to the man and forces his bloodied face upward so that she can see his eyes. He's still shocked, and clearly amazed to see a strange woman dressed as Jessie Kvium.

"I just wanted to talk to Jessie. She texted me to say I should come over!"

"That's a lie. What are you doing here? Eh?"

"I haven't done anything, for fuck's sake! She's the one taking *me* for a ride!"

"Show me the text. Right now."

Hess takes the phone from Thulin and holds it out to the man. The officers let him go, and with his bloodied fingers he begins, sniveling, to input the screen-lock password on his phone.

"Come on, hurry up!" Hess is impatient. He knows instinctively that this is the answer to his misgivings, but not how or why.

"Show me—come *on!*"

Hess tears the phone out of the man's hand before he can pass it back, and stares at the display.

There's no number for the sender—it reads only "unknown"—and the text is short and sweet:

"Come over now. Or I'm sending the pictures to your wife."

Hess sees that an image is attached to the text, and he taps the screen to enlarge it. The photo has been taken at four or five yards' distance from its subject, and Hess recognizes the recycling bins from the corridor underneath the dance studio at the shopping center where they found Jessie Kvium. Two people are pressed close together, and it's obvious what they're doing. The one in front is Jessie Kvium, wearing the same clothes Thulin now has on, and behind her is Nikolaj Møller with his pants around his ankles.

A thousand thoughts explode inside Hess's mind. "When did you receive this text?"

"Let me go. I haven't done anything!"

"*When?!*"

"Half an hour ago. Now what the fuck is going on?!"

For a moment, Hess stares at the man. Then he releases his grip and bolts toward the door.

75

Hammock Gardens in Valby, comprising just over a hundred plots and cabins, is closed for the winter. In the summertime, it is one of the town's liveliest oases, but when autumn bites, the small wooden houses and gardens are locked up and left to their own devices until the next spring. Only in one cabin, in the heart of the darkened gardens, is there a light—in the cabin belonging to Copenhagen Council.

It is late, but Jessie Kvium is still awake. Outside, the wind is rattling at the trees and bushes, and sometimes it sounds almost as though the roof of the little two-room cabin is being torn off. The smell in the house is different from in the summer, and from the bed in the dark room where she is lying with her small, sleeping daughter she can see the light from the main room through the crack under the door. She can still hardly comprehend that there are really two police officers sitting on the other side, protecting her and Olivia. Jessie strokes her daughter's cheek. She rarely does so, and although she is close to tears, although in a moment of clarity she's realized her daughter is the only meaningful thing in her whole shitty life, she also understands that she has to give her up if things are ever going to get better.

The day has been dramatic. First the scene with Nikolaj, who humiliated her at the shopping center. Then her flight through the corridors, the interrogation at the police station, and finally being brought to the deserted community gardens. Although Jessie stoutly protested her innocence, she's been shaken by the accusations during the interview. The accusations that she hit and neglected her daughter, as the council's anonymous tipster claimed. Or maybe it isn't the accusations that have shaken her. She's heard them before, of course; it's more that she was shocked by the seriousness that accompanied them. The two detectives are different from the council lot. It's like they know what has happened. She threw a fit and screamed and shouted, the way she imagined a wronged mother would do, but no matter how convincingly she lied they didn't believe her. And although she doesn't understand why she and her daughter have to be kept under guard in a damp and chilly hut, she does know it is her own damn fault. Like so much else.

Once they were alone in the bedroom, Jessie thought at first she could pull herself together. Change overnight. Stop partying and drinking, stop degrading herself in an eternal attempt to make somebody take the bait, make herself feel loved. She's already deleted Nikolaj's info from her phone, so she won't end up contacting him again. But will it last? Won't there just be others? There have been others before him, guys and girls, and now her crap life has become Olivia's too, left to cope with all this stuff. With long days at institutions, with solitude in playgrounds, with crazy evenings at bars, even mornings with total strangers Jessie drags home and lets do whatever they please, if only they'll add a little sweetness to her life. She hated her daughter, and she hit her. At times, only the child-benefit allowance from the council kept her from giving Olivia away.

But no matter how much she regrets it, and no matter how much she wants to turn things around, Jessie also knows she won't be able to do it by herself.

Gingerly, she slips out from under the duvet, careful not to wake Olivia. The floor feels icy beneath her bare feet, but she takes the time to tuck the covers around her daughter before she goes to the door.

76

Detective Martin Ricks's belly growls noisily as he scrolls through the pages of naked women on Pornhub. He's been on the job for twelve years, and it is always tedious as fuck whenever he is assigned a task like tonight's, but Pornhub, bet365, and sushi are among the few things that perk up the wait. He continues to flick through the endless rows of pornographic images, but this time no number of plastic tits, high heels, and bondage ropes can get rid of his frustration about that asshole Hess and the media explosion around the Hartung case.

Martin Ricks has been Tim Jansen's right-hand man ever since he transferred to the murder squad from Bellahøj Station six years ago. At first he didn't much take to the tall, arrogant man with the intense, probing gaze.

Jansen is always ready with a quip and a put-down, and Ricks, who's never been very sharp with words, lumped him in with all the other idiots ever since his school days who've thought he was stupid. Until he got the chance to beat them to a pulp, anyway. But it wasn't like that with Jansen. The more experienced detective saw something in his doggedness and general mistrust of people and the world. In Ricks's first six months they spent time together in cars, interview rooms, operation rooms, changing rooms, and canteens, and when Ricks's official mentorship period was over they told the boss they wanted to keep working as a duo. After six years, they know each other inside and out, and it's no exaggeration to say that despite the revolving door of bosses, they've achieved a status nobody dare challenge. At least, not until that asshole showed up a few weeks ago.

Hess is a broken reed. He might have been decent once, long ago, when he was in the department, but now he is cut from the same elitist, arrogant cloth as the rest of Europol. Ricks remembers him as a loner, quiet and snooty, and it was a relief to get rid of him. But now Europol has apparently had enough, and instead of making himself useful Hess has started questioning the investigation that is Ricks's and Jansen's greatest feat to date.

Ricks still has detailed memories of those days in October last year. The pressure was huge. He and Jansen slogged day and night, and it was they who interviewed and arrested Linus Bekker off the back of the anonymous tip—they who initiated the search. Sitting with Bekker during yet another interrogation several days afterward, Ricks sensed this one would be special. They were holding good cards. Evidence they could rub the guy's face in. Obviously, in the end, he had no option but to come clean. The relief was tremendous, and they celebrated the confession by drinking themselves senseless and playing billiards at a dive bar in Vesterbro until well into the morning hours. True, they never found the kid's body, but that was only a minor detail.

And now Ricks is freezing his balls off in a cottage in Valby, babysitting some alkie single mom—all because of Hess and that cunt Thulin. While the rest of the team, including Jansen, is bustling around in Urbanplan, where all the exciting stuff is happening, he's stuck here. Best-case scenario, he'll be relieved at half past six tomorrow morning.

Suddenly the bedroom door opens. It is the woman he is supposed to be guarding, wearing nothing but a T-shirt. Ricks puts down his phone, screen down. For a moment she peers around in surprise.

"Where's the other officer?"

"Not officer. Detective."

"Where's the other detective?"

Although it isn't actually any of her business, Ricks explains that he's gone down to fetch sushi on Valby Langgade.

"Why do you ask?"

"No reason. I just wanted to speak to the two detectives who interviewed me today."

"About what? You can talk to me."

Although alco-mom is standing behind the sofa, Ricks can see she has a decent ass. For a moment, he wonders whether he has a chance—whether there's time for a quickie on the sofa before his partner comes back with the sushi. It is one of Ricks's many fantasies. Sex with a witness under his protection. But that particular fantasy has gone unfulfilled.

"I'd like to tell them the truth. And I'd like to speak to someone about having my daughter placed with a good family until I can get my act together."

The answer disappoints Martin Ricks. He replies dryly that she'll have to wait. The social welfare office isn't open yet. "The truth," on the other hand, he would like to hear, but before the woman can open her mouth his phone rings.

"It's Hess. All okay?"

Hess is out of breath, and it sounds like he is slamming a car door while someone starts an engine. Martin Ricks makes an effort to sound arrogant.

"Why shouldn't it be okay? What about you lot?"

But Ricks never hears the answer, because at that moment a car alarm goes off. In the community gardens.

The loud siren wails in an infuriating loop, and Ricks turns to look at his car, which is parked outside. The lights are flashing in the autumn dark like a merry-go-round at Tivoli.

Martin Ricks is baffled. As far as he can tell, there is no one in the vicinity of the vehicle. He still has the phone to his ear, and when he tells that asshole Hess that the car alarm has gone off he can hear Hess's voice grow alert.

"Stay in the house. We're on our way."

"Why are you on your way? What's happening?"

"Stay in the house and protect Jessie Kvium! You hear what I'm saying?"

Martin Ricks hesitates a moment. Then he breaks the connection, so that the only sound is the alarm. If Hess thinks Ricks is going to take orders from him, he has another think coming.

"What's going on?"

Now alco-mom is staring worriedly at him.

"Nothing. Go inside and sleep."

The answer doesn't convince her, but before she can protest they hear the sound of a child crying from the bedroom, and she hurries inside.

Ricks stuffs his mobile in his pocket and undoes the strap on his gun holster. He isn't stupid, and he's realized from the conversation that the situation has flipped. This might be his only chance to shut all their mouths. Hess's and Thulin's and especially the Chestnut Man's, as the media has started calling the killer. Soon the task force will come bursting through the gate, but right now the stage is empty, ready for the taking.

Ricks draws his car keys from his jacket and unlocks the door. With his gun in his hand, he walks down the garden path as though down a red carpet.

77

Olivia isn't fully awake, although she's sitting up in bed against the wooden wall.

"What's going on, Mommy?"

"Nothing, love. Just lie back down."

Jessie Kvium hurries over and sits down on the bed, stroking her daughter's hair.

"But I can't sleep when it's noisy," whispers her daughter, leaning against Jessie's shoulder just as the alarm falls silent.

"There, it's stopped now. You can go back to sleep, sweetie."

A moment later Olivia has dropped off again, and while Jessie watches her she thinks it helped saying something to the officer. It wasn't enough, of course, and she wishes she could have told him more, got it all properly off her chest. But the car alarm abruptly changed the mood. She felt a fear she's never known before, but now the siren has stopped, and when she hears the familiar sound of the officer's mobile phone ringing somewhere in the garden, she feels silly. Until it strikes her that he isn't picking up. She listens and waits, but the ringtone ceases. Then it starts afresh, but no one answers this time either.

Outside, the wind seizes Jessie's hair. She is wearing shoes, but it is bitingly cold, and she regrets not putting a blanket around her legs before walking through the door. She can hear the phone ringing somewhere by the vehicle, but she still can't see the officer.

"Hey? Where are you?"

No answer. Hesitantly, Jessie approaches the hedge and the car, which is parked on the gravel outside the gate. If she takes one more step, all the way onto the gravel, she'll be able to see the whole car and probably also the phone, which is ringing somewhere very nearby. But then she remembers what the detectives said during her interview, and the danger they were talking about comes creeping up on her. Out of the garden's bent trees and stripped bushes it prowls, the threat, snatching at her bare legs, and Jessie turns and runs back into the house, up the wooden steps, and in through the open door, which she slams behind her.

From the officer's phone conversation a moment ago she knows help is on its way, and she tells herself she mustn't panic. She turns the key in the lock and heaves a chest of drawers up against the door. Then she runs into the kitchen and the small bathroom to make sure the doors and windows are still locked. In a kitchen drawer, she finds a long knife, which she picks up. She can see nothing out of the windows into the back garden, but suddenly it strikes her that she is bathed in light. If anyone is out there—and she no longer doubts that there is someone—they will be able to see every single move she makes. In a few steps she is back in the living room, and after several feverish attempts to find the right switch she manages to get all the lights turned off.

Jessie stands quietly, her eyes fixed on the front garden. Nothing. Only the wind, trying to knock the cabin over. She is standing close to the electric radiator, and realizes she accidentally turned it off when she was looking for the light switch. Jessie bends down and turns it back on. The radiator begins to hum, and in the weak reddish light from its display she can suddenly see the little figurine on the chair where the officer had been sitting.

For a few seconds she doesn't know what it is. But then it dawns on her. And although the little chestnut man is quite innocent, reaching its matchstick arms despairingly toward the sky, it fills her with dread: she knows instantly that it wasn't there a moment ago, when she went out to find the officer. When she looks back up, it's as though something in the gloom has come alive in front of her, and gathering every ounce of strength she slashes the knife through the air.

78

The squad car crashes through the main gate to the community gardens and continues down the gravel path. It is pitch-black in the little huddle of small houses and garden plots, and only the long beam of the headlights gives them a glimpse of a reflective number plate farther inside. Thulin races all the way up to the unmarked police vehicle, and Hess leaps out.

A couple of sushi boxes lie discarded on the gravel, and a young officer is bent over a figure. He sees Hess and screams for help, trying frantically with both hands to stem the flow of blood that is pumping from a deep gash in Martin Ricks's throat. Ricks is convulsing, his eyes fixed rigidly on the black trees above him, and Hess speeds onward toward the cabin. The door is locked. He kicks it in, shoving a chest of drawers out of the way. It is dark in the front room, but as he brandishes his gun he can gradually see that the chairs and tables are overturned as though there's been a fight. In the bedroom, Jessie Kvium's daughter is clinging to the duvet, confused and tearful. Jessie isn't there, and it is Thulin who points out to Hess that the kitchen door is wide open.

The rear garden angles steeply down, and in three steps they are on the grass at the back. Hess and Thulin run past the tall apple tree in the middle of the lawn, but there's no one in sight when they reach the thin fence adjoining the neighbor's plot. The row of windswept gardens continues as far as the high-rise blocks on the boulevard, and it isn't until they turn back toward the house that they discover her. The lowest branches on the apple tree aren't branches. They are Jessie Kvium's bare legs. Her body has been arranged in a seated position where the trunk splits in two, crammed astride the thickest limb, so that her legs are sticking out unnaturally in both directions. Her head is tilted, her lifeless arms supported by branches that point them toward the sky.

"Mommy?"

Through the wind they hear the confused voice, and by the kitchen door they can see the faint outline of the girl, who has stepped out into the cold. But Hess can't move, and it is Thulin who flies up the slope and scoops the girl inside while Hess remains by the tree. Although it is dark, he can see that both arms are unnaturally short. So is one leg. And when he treads closer still, he can just make out a chestnut man with outstretched matchstick arms, the doll jammed upright inside Jessie's open mouth.

Tuesday, October 20th

79

Thulin jogs through the rain between the blocks, searching for signposts. Water seeps into her shoes, and when she finally sees the sign for 37C it is pointing in the opposite direction from the way she is headed.

It is early morning, and she's just dropped her daughter off at school. Only a few days have passed since she was standing among the squat blocks at Urbanplan; she didn't realize then that Hess also lives in social housing, but for some reason it doesn't surprise her. Friendly but vigilant glances from women in niqabs and head scarves make it clear she is drawing attention, and as she searches for the right route it irks her again that Hess is impossible to get hold of now all hell has broken loose.

For nearly four days the media circus has been in full swing, endlessly featuring live coverage and reportage from the crime scenes, Christiansborg, the police station, and the coroner's office. There have been portraits of the three female victims and Martin Ricks, who died in the gravel at the community gardens. There have been interviews with witnesses, neighbors, relatives—there have been opinions from experts and the experts' critics, and there have been statements by the police, especially from Nylander, who has been repeatedly called to stand in front of banks of microphones, often cross-cut with co-ordinated statements from the justice minister. On top of that there has been the story about Rosa Hartung, who lost her daughter and now has to suffer the indignity of knowing that the case might not have been solved after all. Then, when the news editors begin to realize they are repeating themselves, they have started guessing when the next hideous thing is going to happen.

Hess and Thulin haven't gotten much sleep since Friday. The shock of the killings at the community gardens has given way to grunt work: endless questioning and phone calls, collecting data about Urbanplan and the garden owners' association, disentangling Jessie Kvium's familial and romantic situation. Her six-year-old daughter—who thankfully didn't see her dead mother—has been sent for a medical examination, and the doctors have found numerous signs of neglect, malnourishment, and physical abuse. A psychologist has spoken to her, focusing solely on her grief over her mother's death, and afterward he was genuinely impressed by the little girl's ability to put her loss into words. It bodes well, despite everything, that she has been picked up by her grandparents from Esbjerg, who are only too happy to look after her, although they'll have to wait and see whether they are allowed to keep her long-term. Thulin, stepping in, has managed to keep the girl and her grandparents out of the media, who in any case are far more interested in reporting the latest news about the Chestnut Man.

Thulin hates it when the press mythologizes killers in this way. Especially because she is certain that in this instance the killer *wants* to generate fear, is perhaps even spurred on by all the publicity. But it is hard to stem the tide, given that the forensic examinations and countless interviews have produced no breakthrough. Genz and his people have been working night and day, but thus far with no viable result. Nor have they been able to trace the text message to Nikolaj Møller's phone, and there are no witness statements to suggest who might have been watching Jessie Kvium—not at Urbanplan or that day at the shopping center, even though they returned a second time to pore over the CCTV footage. Just as in the cases of Laura Kjær and Anne Sejer-Lassen, all trace of the killer has vanished into thin air.

According to the coroner, it is clear that Jessie Kvium died at approximately 1:20 a.m. The amputations were carried out with the same implement as in the other two cases, and she was alive at the time. Certainly during the amputation of the hands, at least. It also seems that the fingerprint on the little chestnut man, which this time was found in the victim's mouth, belongs to Kristine Hartung. There is general agreement, of course, that the anonymous tip-offs about the three dead women must have been written by the same person. But the council and various caseworkers are no real help, and the three emails and their labyrinthine server connections offer no clue as to the true sender. The situation is so desperate that Nylander has posted officers to guard a short list of women who have been anonymously reported through the council's whistle-blowing scheme, and he has put the department on the highest level of alert.

The atmosphere at the station has been deeply affected by the situation. Martin Ricks may not have been the brightest bulb, but after six years' service on the squad with only a few days' absence here and there, he was as permanent a fixture at the station as the golden star above the main entrance. He had also been engaged, which came as a surprise to most of his colleagues. At noon the previous day, they held a minute's silence at the station, and the stillness was noisy. Colleagues cried, and the investigation took on the grim ferocity that always results from an officer being killed in the line of duty.

For Hess and Thulin, the biggest unanswered question is how the killer could have outmaneuvered them on the night of the murder. They lay in wait at Urbanplan, but the killer found out. How, exactly, Thulin doesn't know, but that *has* to be what happened. Then he went to the community gardens, which only makes sense if he knew in advance that Jessie Kvium and her daughter had spent a week there over the summer and so might have been taken there. The text to Nikolaj Møller was sent before the killings—at precisely 12:37 a.m.—using a phone with a prepaid card from somewhere in the gardens, and that part is almost more frightening still. The killer had the presence of mind to lure a bewildered, unfaithful husband to Urbanplan and into the arms of the police, and that tells Thulin he wants to make them feel bested and ridiculous. Just like when he sent a text to Laura Kjær's phone after her death. That, on top of the arduous yet fruitless investigative slog, means it's small wonder things exploded into a confrontation with Nylander the night before.

"What the hell are you afraid of?! Why can't we interview Rosa Hartung?"

Hess was insisting once again that the killings were somehow connected with Rosa Hartung and her daughter's case.

"It makes no sense to investigate one and not the other. Three fingerprints on three chestnut dolls are about as clear as it gets. And it won't stop here: first there was a hand missing, then two, then two hands and a foot. What do you think the killer is planning for the next round? It couldn't be any more blatantly obvious! Rosa Hartung is either the key or she's the target!"

But Nylander kept his cool and persevered. The minister had already been questioned once, and she has had more than enough to deal with.

"Enough of what? Surely there's nothing more important than this?"

"Cool it, Hess."

"I'm just asking."

"According to the intelligence services, some unknown person has been harassing and threatening her for the last couple of weeks."

"What?"

"And you didn't think we ought to know that?" Thulin interjected.

"No. It can't have anything to do with the killings! According to Intelligence, the most recent threat was smeared on the hood of her ministerial car on Monday, October 12th—the same time period when the killer must have been busy attacking Anne Sejer-Lassen."

The meeting ended in acrimony. Both Hess and Nylander stalked off, and Thulin tried to ignore the feeling that the cracks emerging in the department were all too symptomatic of the state of the investigation.

At last she is out of the rain and on the covered walkway, reaching number 37C at the far end. A jumble of paint tins, varnish, and cleaning fluid are stacked up on both sides of the door, and in the middle of the mess is a bulky machine Thulin assumes is a floor sander. She knocks impatiently, but of course there is no answer.

"Are you the one he phoned about the floors?"

Thulin looks at the short Pakistani man who has just stepped out onto the walkway, a little brown-eyed boy at his legs. The man is wearing a bright orange rain cape, but his gardening gloves and rubbish bags indicate that he's probably just clearing the complex of dead leaves.

"That's fine, as long as you're a professional. The man's all thumbs, but he thinks he's Bob the Builder. And he isn't. You know Bob the Builder?"

"Yeah . . ."

"It's a good thing he's selling up. This isn't the place for him. But if he wants to be rid of that apartment he's got to spruce it up a bit. I mean, I didn't mind giving the walls and the ceiling a fresh lick of paint—the man can't tell a spade from a paintbrush—but I'm not about to polish his floors. And I don't want him messing about with it himself."

"I'm not planning to mess about with it either." Thulin flashes her police badge to get rid of the man, but he stays put, watching as she knocks again.

"You're not taking over the apartment? Back to square one, then."

"No, I'm not. Do you know if Bob the Builder is home?"

"See for yourself. He never locks the door."

The Pakistani man elbows Thulin aside and gives the door, which is sticking, a little shove.

"That's a problem too. Who decides to leave their door unlocked on this estate? I told him as much, but he says he's got nothing to steal, so it doesn't matter, but—Allahu Akbar!"

The short Pakistani man is struck dumb. Thulin can see why. There isn't much to look at in the room, which reeks of fresh paint. A table, a few chairs, a packet of cigarettes, a mobile phone, some takeout boxes, and a few brushes and tins of paint on the newspaper-covered floor. Evidently not a place Hess spends much time at a stretch. For some reason or other it crosses Thulin's mind that the man's apartment in the Hague, or wherever he is living, probably isn't much more lavishly furnished than this one. Yet it isn't the interior that has caught their attention—it's the walls.

Small, torn-off notes, photos, and newspaper clippings hang everywhere, and between them words and letters are scrawled directly onto the walls. Like a huge, snarled cobweb, the material spreads across the two newly painted surfaces, and an insistent red pen connects the various items with intricate strokes and markings. It evidently started in one corner with the murder of Laura Kjær, then expanded to include the subsequent killings, including that of Martin Ricks. Along the way various lines in pen and drawings of chestnut men have been added, as well as the names of people and crime scenes, which are either illustrated with photographs or written in pen directly onto the wall. The scraps on the wall include crumpled receipts or cardboard torn from pizza boxes, but the material has evidently run out. At the bottom is a torn-out piece of newspaper featuring Rosa Hartung and the date of her comeback, to which Hess has added a line that leads to the murder of Laura Kjær, and from there myriad lines multiply into incalculable connections, reaching all the way across to a separate column, in which is written "Christiansborg: threats, harassment, intelligence." At the very top is an old newspaper photo of twelve-year-old Kristine Hartung, next to a panel drawn in pen: inside it is written, in capital letters, LINUS BEKKER, and here too, there are notes scribbled on the wall. Most of them are illegible, and Hess must have struggled to get up there, even using the small stepladder on the floor.

Thulin gapes at the gigantic spider's web, her feelings mixed. When Hess took off the night before, he was withdrawn and taciturn, and when she wasn't able to get hold of him this morning she didn't know what to think. Judging from the walls, the man hasn't given up. On the other hand, there is something crazy about what he's done. Possibly he started out trying to get a coherent overview, but it hasn't ended up that way. Even a gifted cryptographer or a Nobel Prize–winning mathematician would have a tough time deciphering anything beyond that the web's creator is in the grip of an obsession, or even a mental disorder.

A torrent of Pakistani curses erupt from the little man when he catches sight of the walls, and matters are not improved by Hess's sudden appearance in the doorway. He is out of breath and completely soaked from the rain, clad only in a black T-shirt, shorts, and running shoes. His breath and body are steaming in the cold air. He looks surprisingly muscular and sinewy, but he is clearly not in good shape.

"What were you thinking? We just painted all this!"

"I'll paint it again. It needs two coats, you said."

Thulin looks at Hess, who is supporting himself on the doorway with his left hand, and notices that he is holding a rolled-up plastic sleeve in the other.

"It *had* two coats. It had three!"

The brown-eyed boy has gotten sick of waiting for his dad, and the Pakistani man is reluctantly drawn back out onto the walkway. Thulin glances briefly at Hess before following suit.

"I'll wait in the car. Nylander wants to meet. We're interviewing Rosa Hartung at her offices in an hour."

80

"Am I interrupting?"

Tim Jansen stands in the doorway. He has rings under his eyes and a distant gaze, and Nylander notes the day-old reek of spirits.

"No, come in."

Behind Jansen the department hums busily, and Nylander has already refused his pleas to remain on the case after the memorial service the day before, so that isn't why he's sparing the time. But Hess and Thulin have just left the office, and Jansen didn't return their greeting: he stared straight ahead as though he hadn't heard them, and that, among other reasons, makes it seem like a good idea to invite him in.

Nylander had wasted no time delivering his message to Thulin and Hess. He'd been in touch with the Min-

istry for Social Affairs that morning, and Minister Rosa
Hartung had communicated via her advisor Frederik
Vogel that she was happy to help with whatever infor-
mation she could.

"But the minister is not under suspicion and her
credibility is in no way being called into question, so a
precondition is that we call this a conversation and not
an interview."

Nylander guessed that Vogel didn't approve of the
situation and had advised his minister to avoid the
"conversation" entirely, so she must have insisted personally on helping. Despite the news, Hess, whom
Nylander was increasingly coming to dislike, remained
planted in the office.

"Does this mean you're reopening the case of Kristine Hartung's disappearance?"

Nylander didn't fail to catch that Hess said "Kristine
Hartung's disappearance" and not "Kristine Hartung's
death."

"No, that's not up for discussion. If you can't get
that through your head, you're welcome to head back
out to Urbanplan and keep ringing doorbells."

Late last night, Nylander had been inclined to postpone the interview with Rosa Hartung once again, but
by now the pressure on the department was enormous.
The sight that greeted him at the community gardens

had been out of a nightmare, and Ricks's murder had made the investigation personal for many of his officers. A life was a life, and there ought to be no difference between the killing of a policeman and that of anybody else, but the cold-blooded attack on the thirty-nine-year-old detective—who according to the coroner had been grabbed from behind, his carotid artery slit—reverberated deep inside the DNA of anyone who'd ever sworn allegiance to the force.

At seven that morning, Nylander had been asked to give an update at an emergency management meeting. In principle, it was easy to tell them about the upgrade to high alert and the various investigatory boats they'd launched, many of which seemed promising. But although he didn't once mention her name, Kristine Hartung cast a shadow across his whole explanation. It was as though they were just waiting for him to finish so they could get to the real point of the meeting: those stupid fingerprints on the chestnut men.

"In light of what's happened, have there been any doubts raised about the outcome of the Kristine Hartung case at all?"

The deputy commissioner had phrased his question diplomatically, but it was still an insult. At least that was how Nylander took it. It was a crucial point in the conversation, and Nylander felt the eyes of the others on him. None of the bosses in the room would have wanted to be in his shoes—the question was as riddled with mines as a supply road in the Middle East—but Nylander answered. Taken on its own, there was nothing about the Hartung case to suggest it hadn't been solved. The investigation had been extremely thorough, all possibilities explored, until eventually the evidence had been brought before the court and the guilty man had been sentenced.

On the other hand, it was true that three slightly smudged fingerprints belonging to Kristine Hartung had been identified on the three chestnut dolls found in connection with the murders of three women. That could mean almost anything, though. It could be a kind of signature, a way of criticizing the minister and the social welfare authorities, and for that reason the minister should of course be kept under close guard. And the chestnuts *could* have come from Kristine Hartung's stall before her death. Thus far it was all up in the air—except that there was no indication the girl was still alive. To keep his bosses quiet, Nylander even suggested that it might be the killer's intention to sow the seeds of doubt and uncertainty, so as professionals they ought to focus on facts and reality.

"But from what I've heard through the grapevine, not all your detectives share that opinion."

"Then you've heard wrong. There might be one person getting a little creative, but that's not so odd, given that the individual in question wasn't part of the massive investigation we conducted last year."

"Who the hell are we talking about?" a senior police inspector had asked.

Nylander's deputy explained loyally that they were talking about Mark Hess, the liaison officer who'd had problems in the Hague and had recently been put out to grass until his future was decided. Nylander sensed from the others' disapproval that they didn't think much of a liaison officer souring the relationship with Europol still further. He'd thought the discussion was over, but then the deputy commissioner had butted in, saying that he remembered Hess very well and knew for a fact the man was no fool. Hess might be a tad unorthodox, but in his day he'd been one of the best detectives ever to set foot in the department.

"But I'm hearing you say he's got the wrong end of the stick. That's reassuring to know, especially considering that I heard the justice minister on the radio less than an hour ago, denying once again there was any reason to start digging back into the Kristine Hartung case. On the other hand, we've got four murders and a cop killer to deal with, so it's crucial we act *now*. We're only shooting ourselves in the foot if there are things

THE CHESTNUT MAN · 417

not being checked because we're trying to look after our own skins."

Nylander had denied trying to look after anything, but doubt had lingered in the air above the mahogany table in the parade hall. Luckily he'd been quick-witted enough to add that he was about to order a more detailed interview of Minister Rosa Hartung that very day. Just to double-check whether she and her office might have any further information that could lead to the killer's apprehension.

Nylander had left the parade hall with his head held high, and without revealing that somewhere deep down a worry had begun to niggle: perhaps they *had* made a mistake in the Hartung case.

He's run through it in his mind countless times, but he still can't see what the mistake could possibly be. At the same time, he knows he can kiss goodbye to all hope of a high-flying career at the station or anywhere else in the city unless they reach a breakthrough soon.

"You need to let me back on the case."

"Jansen, we've talked about this. You're not getting back on the case. Go home. Take a week off."

"I'm not going home. I want to help."

"No way. I know what Ricks meant to you."

Tim Jansen hasn't sat down on the Eames chair Nylander has offered him. Instead he remains standing, his eyes fixed on the columned courtyard outside the window.

"What's happening right now?"

"A lot of hard goddamn work. I'll let you know when we have something."

"So they've still got fuck all, then? Hess and that cunt?"

"Jansen, go home. You're not thinking clearly. Go home and sleep."

"It was Hess's fault, this. You do realize that?"

"Ricks's death was no one's fault but the killer's. I was the one who gave the operation the green light, not Hess, so if you're going to be angry with anyone it should be me."

"Ricks never would have left that house by himself if it hadn't been for Hess. It was Hess who pushed him to do it."

"I don't understand what you mean."

At first Jansen doesn't respond.

"We barely slept for three weeks . . . we gave everything we had, until finally we had proof and we got that confession . . . but then that asshole comes waltzing in from the Hague and starts spreading rumors about how we fucked it up . . ."

The words come slowly, and Jansen's eyes are far away.

"But you didn't. The case was solved. So you didn't fuck it up. Did you?"

Again Jansen doesn't reply, but then his phone rings and he leaves to take the call. Nylander watches him go. Suddenly he hopes more than anything that Hess and Thulin will get something out of their visit to the minister.

81

The minister for social affairs' civil servants are carrying in boxes and placing them on the white oval meeting table in the middle of the high-ceilinged room.

"This should be the lot. Let me know if you need anything else," the chief of staff adds helpfully before making for the door. "Good luck."

For a moment the boxes stand bathed in sunlight, particles of dust dancing above them, before the clouds gather outside the windows once more and leave the light to the Poul Henningsen lamps. The detectives get started on the folders in the boxes, but for Hess the déjà vu is paralyzing. Only a few days before he'd been in another meeting room with another stack of cases, and now it is as though the killer has thrust him into yet another Kafka-esque nightmare of new cases to read through. The more folders Hess counts in the boxes, the more clearly he realizes that he needs to do something completely different. Break the mold, do the unpredictable. But he doesn't know how.

He'd put his hope in the interview with Rosa Hartung. After some irrelevant chitchat with her advisor, Vogel, who emphasized to Thulin and Hess that this wasn't an interview but a *conversation*, the three of them went into her office, where the minister was waiting. She professed to know nothing about the murdered women, although they'd gone through them laboriously, victim by victim. To Hess it was obvious the minister was genuinely trying to recall whether she'd ever come across the victims or their family members before, but it didn't seem that she had. He even had to fight back a feeling of sympathy. Rosa Hartung, a beautiful, talented woman who'd lost her daughter, had in the brief time he'd known her become haggard and drawn. Her eyes were confused, vulnerable, like a hunted animal's, and as she pored through the photographs and papers Hess could see her slender hands trembling, even as she fought to stop them.

Still, he kept the tone brisk; he was certain Rosa Hartung was the key. The murdered women had something in common. In all three cases, their children had been appallingly abused or maltreated at home. In all cases, the killer had sent an anonymous tip recommending they be taken into care, and in all cases, the system had mistakenly cleared the families of suspicion and neglected to intervene. Since the victims had each been left with a chestnut doll marked with Rosa Hartung's daughter's fingerprint, the likelihood was that the killer wanted to call her to account. So the cases *had* to mean something to the minister.

"But they don't. I'm sorry, but I don't know anything."

"What about the threats you've had recently? I understand you received an unpleasant email, and somebody wrote 'murderer' on your ministerial car. Do you have any idea who might have done that? Or why?"

"The intelligence people have been asking me the same thing, but I can't think of anyone . . ."

Hess had deliberately avoided linking the threats with the murders, because if the car had been vandalized at the same time as Anne Sejer-Lassen was attacked, then the two things had to be independent. Unless they were dealing with *two* people, but so far there was nothing to suggest that. Thulin lost her patience.

"But surely you must know what this is about? Obviously, you're not popular in all quarters, and you must know whether you've done something to make someone want revenge?"

The minister's advisor, Vogel, protested at her harsh tone, but Rosa Hartung insisted on trying to help. She just didn't know how. It was widely known that she'd always done her best for children, and had always recommended removal if they were being abused; that was part of the reason why she'd asked the councils to set up whistle-blower schemes like the one at city hall. Children's needs were her key issue, and the first thing she'd done when selected as minister was to encourage the councils to be more proactive on that front. After some unusually unpleasant cases of neglect among certain Jutland councils, the need had been made obvious—but it was clear that she might have opponents, not least among the councils and the families that had felt the effects of her clampdown.

"But there could well be somebody who thinks you've let children down, couldn't there?" Thulin had pursued.

"No, I can't imagine that."

"Why not? As a minister, it must be easy to get distracted by—"

"Because I'm not like that. Not that it's any of your business, but I was a foster child myself, so I know what's at stake, and I *don't* let children down."

Rage blazed in her eyes as Rosa Hartung set Thulin straight, and although Hess was glad she'd asked, he suddenly understood why Hartung was so popular. After a few rough years as a minister, she still possessed the sincerity that all politicians tried to conjure while the cameras were rolling, but in Hartung's case was instinctive.

"What about the chestnut men? Can you think of any reason why anybody would want to confront you with chestnut men or chestnuts in general?"

The killer's signature was unusual, and if Hess was right that Hartung was the key, he hoped she might be able to come up with something.

"No, sorry. Only that Kristine had a stall in the autumn. When they sat at the table, she and Mathilde, and . . . but I've already told you that."

The minister had been fighting back tears, and Vogel tried to cut short the interview, but Thulin objected that they still needed her help: since the minister had encouraged more children to be taken into care by the councils, Thulin and Hess would like to see all the cases that had been handled during her tenure. The killer might be someone involved, perhaps eager for revenge on the minister and the system she represented, and with a nod Rosa Hartung sent Vogel out to have a word with the chief of staff, who would see to their request. Hess and Thulin had risen and thanked Rosa Hartung for her time, when suddenly she surprised them with a question.

"Before we leave, I'd like to know whether there's a chance my daughter is alive."

Neither of them knew what to say. It was an obvious question, yet they were unprepared. At last, Hess heard himself reply.

"Your daughter's case has been solved. A man confessed, and he was sentenced."

"But the fingerprints . . . three times?"

"If the killer doesn't like you for reasons of his own, it would be the cruelest thing he could make you and your family believe."

"But you don't know that. You can't know that."

"As I said—"

"I'll do anything you say. But you need to find her."

"We can't do that. As I said . . ."

Rosa Hartung hadn't said another word, merely looked at them with shining eyes until she came to herself and Vogel arrived to fetch her. Hess and Thulin had then been given the meeting room, and Nylander had hastily instructed ten detectives to help them screen the case files.

Thulin enters with yet another box, which she sets down on the table.

"There was one more. I'm reading on a laptop next door. Let's get going!"

The optimism Hess had felt when they were given permission to speak with the minister has dissipated. Yet again they are sitting and reading. Reams of awful childhoods, wounded feelings, council interventions, and failure; probably the killer wants to confront the police and the authorities with it all. Hess realizes he's had too little sleep. His mind is leaping around, racing too quickly, and he's struggling to focus. Is the killer to be found among the injured parties in the case files on the table? It seems logical, but is the killer logical? He must have foreseen well in advance that they would pore over precisely these files, so why risk drawing them in his direction? And why make chestnut men? Why cut off the hands and feet, why hate the mothers instead of the fathers? And where was Kristine Hartung?

Hess reassures himself that the plastic sleeve is still in his inside pocket, then makes for the door.

"Thulin, we're leaving. Tell your people to ring if they find anything."

"Why? Where are we going?"

"Back to the beginning."

Hess disappears through the doorway without waiting to see whether Thulin is behind him. On the way out, he catches a glimpse of Frederik Vogel, who nods a goodbye and shuts the door to the minister's office.

82

"**B**ut why are we talking about the Hartung case when Nylander says it's not relevant?"

"No clue. If it's about machetes and pig dismemberment, I'm out, but you can ask *him*."

Thulin is standing across from Genz in his lab. She nods irritably at Hess, who shuts the door so that nobody can hear what they are saying. They have driven straight from the minister's office and through the city to Genz's angular building, with its glass cages and white coats. On the way over, Hess asked Thulin to make sure Genz was there, while he himself had been engrossed in a conversation on his mobile. Genz sounded pleased to get Thulin's call, perhaps especially so because it was unexpected, but maybe also a tad disappointed when she said Hess wanted to go over a few things with him. Thulin had hoped Genz would be too busy, but apparently a canceled meeting had given him some free time, and by now Thulin is regretting having tagged along. They are standing by the desk where they were shown the first of Kristine Hartung's thumbprints, but that feels like a long time ago. A welder and various paraphernalia over a heat source in the background tells Thulin that Genz has been warming plastic to test its flexibility, but now his pleasant if wary eyes are glued to Hess, who approaches the desk.

"Because I believe the Hartung case *is* relevant. But neither I nor Thulin were around during the investigation, so I need help, and you're the only one I trust. If you're worried about getting into hot water, just say so now and we'll leave."

Genz grins. "I'm curious. As long as you're not asking me to carve up another pig, it's all right with me. What's this about?"

"The evidence against Linus Bekker."

"I knew it."

Thulin rises from the chair where she's just sat down, but Hess catches her hand.

"Hear me out. Until now, we've only been doing what the killer expects. We need to find a shortcut somehow. If it's a waste of time digging around in the old case, then we'll establish that once and for all right now, and then I'll keep my mouth shut. About Kristine Hartung too."

Hess lets go of her hand. Thulin stands there for a moment before returning to her seat. She can tell Genz noticed Hess reach out and grab her hand, and for some reason it embarrasses her that she didn't simply tear it back. Hess opens a thick case file.

"In the afternoon of October 18th last year, Kristine Hartung went missing on her way home from handball practice. Her disappearance was quickly reported to the police, and the investigation began in earnest when her bike and bag were found dumped in the woods a few hours later. They searched for three weeks, but it was like she'd vanished into thin air. Then they got a tip, an anonymous tip, recommending they search the home of a particular man, Linus Bekker, twenty-three, who lived in a ground-floor apartment at a complex in Bispebjerg. Sound about right so far?"

"Yep. I was present at the search myself, and it turned out to be a solid tip."

Hess doesn't address this remark, continuing instead to flip through the file. "They went to Linus Bekker's, interviewed him about Kristine Hartung, and did a search, as you say. The man appeared suspicious. No job, no education, no social network. Living alone, spending his days in front of the computer, most of his income from online poker. More significant still, he'd done three years in prison for raping a mother and her teenage daughter at a house in Vanløse, which he'd broken into at the age of eighteen. Bekker also had a few minor convictions for indecent behavior and was being treated for psychological problems at the local clinic, but from the very first he denied all knowledge of any crime against Kristine Hartung."

"I think he even said he was normal again. But then we opened his laptop, of course. Or the tech guys did, I should say."

"Exactly. As I understand it, Linus Bekker turned out to be a first-rate hacker. Self-taught, but persistent. Ironically, his interest in computers had been sparked by an IT course in prison, and they discovered that for at least six months he'd been able to break into the police's digital archive of crime-scene photographs and look at pictures of dead bodies."

Thulin had intended to keep quiet to save time, but on this point she has to correct Hess.

"Technically speaking, he hadn't broken in. He'd intercepted a login cookie from one of the computers logged in to the system, and because the system was old and insecure he'd been able to trick it by resending the cookie. It's a disgrace the system wasn't replaced ages ago."

"Fine. Either way, Bekker'd had access to hundreds of photographs from crime scenes going back years, and it must have been a shock when it was discovered."

"Not just a shock. It was a nuclear bomb," interjects Genz. "The guy had managed to access something nobody is supposed to access apart from us. It also emerged from his user data that he'd used it to access some of the worst killings he could possibly have found."

"That was my understanding too. Mainly sexually motivated murders of women. Women who'd been stripped and mutilated were apparently among his favorites, but he also went in for crimes against children, especially underage girls. Bekker confessed to having sadistic urges and was sexually aroused by looking at the pictures. But he still denied having laid a finger on Kristine Hartung, and at that point there was nothing to suggest he had. Correct?"

"Correct. Until we analyzed a pair of his shoes."

"Tell me about the shoes."

"It's fairly simple. We checked everything in the apartment, including his old white sneakers, which had been placed on newspaper in a wardrobe. Analysis of the soil in the treads revealed a one hundred percent match with the type of soil in the area of woodland where Kristine Hartung's bike and bag had been found. No doubt about it. But then he began to lie, of course."

"By 'lie,' you mean his explanation of when he'd visited that spot in the woods?"

"Absolutely. As I understand, he said he was drawn to crime scenes—like with the pictures in the archive—and when he heard the news about Kristine Hartung's disappearance he drove out into the woods. You'd have to ask Tim Jansen or one of the others, but I believe he claimed he'd been standing behind the police cordon along with the other curious onlookers and felt sexually excited by being at the scene."

"I'll get back to that. But the fact is that the man still maintained he hadn't killed Kristine Hartung. He had more general difficulties accounting for his behavior, and he acknowledged he had blackouts—part of his diagnosis as a paranoid schizophrenic—but he continued to deny the murder, even after you found the weapon with Kristine Hartung's blood on it. The machete, I mean, which was discovered on a shelf in the garage, next to his car."

Hess finds a spot in the case file.

"It wasn't until he was interrogated by Jansen and Ricks and confronted with images of the weapon that he finally confessed. Is that roughly accurate?"

"I'm not aware of what happened during the inter-rogations, but the rest seems correct."

"Fine. Can we go now?" Thulin is looking sharply at Hess. "I can't see the point of all this. Isn't it all to-tally fucking irrelevant? The man was clearly sick in the head, so it makes no sense wasting time on him while another killer is getting away."

"It's not that I think Linus Bekker seems healthy. The problem is simply that I believe he was telling the truth right up until the day he suddenly confessed."

"Oh, come on."

"What do you mean?"

Genz's curiosity has been piqued, and Hess taps the case file.

"Twice in the year prior to the Hartung case, Linus Bekker was picked up for indecent behavior. The first time in a rear courtyard at a student resi-dence in Odense, where a young woman had been raped and murdered by her boyfriend a few years before. The second time on Amager Common, where ten years earlier a woman had been killed by a taxi driver and dumped in the bushes. In both cases, Bekker was seen masturbating at the old crime scenes, and he was subsequently arrested and given a minor sentence."

"That tells you all you need to know?"

"No. That simply tells us it's possible Linus Bekker decided to visit the site of Kristine Hartung's disappearance in the woods as soon as he heard about it on the news. It might be incomprehensible to other people, but for a man with his inclinations it would make sense."

"Yeah, but surely the point is that he didn't say so straight off the bat. An innocent person would have. But funnily enough it wasn't until we analyzed the sneakers that he offered up that explanation."

"I'm not sure that's so strange. Maybe he was hoping initially that you wouldn't find the traces of soil. It had been three weeks, after all, and without knowing Linus Bekker personally I can imagine he gambled on not having to say anything about his urge to visit crime scenes. But then he was confronted with the soil analysis, so he had to tell the truth."

Thulin gets to her feet. "We're going in circles. I don't see why we're suddenly assuming the desperate excuses of a convicted psychopath were the truth, so I'm going back to the ministry now."

"Because Linus Bekker *was* in the woods. At exactly the time he said."

Hess draws a plastic sleeve from his inside pocket and takes out a stack of crumpled prints. Before he slides them across to Thulin, she notices it's the wallet she'd glimpsed in Hess's hand at Odin that morning, when he appeared after his run.

"The Royal Library keeps articles and photographs in their digital archive, and among the photos taken at the site that evening in the woods I found this one. The top print shows the picture as part of an article in a morning newspaper the day after the girl went missing. The others are close-ups."

Thulin eyes the little collection of prints. The top one is a photo she's seen before. It's almost iconic, because it's a 1:1 reproduction of one of the first photos she remembers from the press coverage of the case. The image shows a section of the woods, floodlit, teeming with officers and canine units—presumably coordinating the search. They look grim, giving the viewer a sense of the situation's import. Far in the background, journalists, photographers, and other curious onlookers are gathered behind a police cordon, and Thulin is about to protest once more that they are wasting time. Then, in the next print, she sees him. The image is grainy and pixelated. It's a close-up of a section of faces, and Thulin realizes instantly that it must be from the crowd behind the cordon. At the very back, almost hidden behind the shoulders of the others, in the third or fourth row, she makes out Linus Bekker's face. The enlargement has made his eyes look like black, blurry holes, but the shape of his features and the sparse light hair leave no doubt.

"The question, of course, is how he could be standing there when he later claimed to be driving north with Kristine Hartung's corpse at that very moment, looking for a place to bury her."

"Christ . . ."

Genz has taken the sheaf of prints from Thulin, who still doesn't know what to say.

"Why didn't you say something before? Why didn't you say something to Nylander?"

"I had to double-check the time it was taken with the photographer who took it. Make sure it was *definitely* taken that evening, and I only got confirmation in the car on the way over here. As for Nylander, I thought it was best if the two of us discussed it first."

"But this still doesn't exonerate Bekker. In theory he could have killed Kristine Hartung, hidden the body in the car, then driven back to the woods to watch the police's activities before heading north."

"Yes. We've seen that kind of behavior before. But as I said, it's also striking that the machete was completely devoid of bone dust, if he really did dismember her. So the mystery begins to—"

"But why would Linus Bekker confess to something he didn't do? It makes no sense."

"Could be any number of reasons. But I think we should ask him ourselves. Frankly, it's my view that the killer in the Kristine Hartung case is the same one we're after right now. And with any luck, Linus Bekker can help."

83

It's approximately a hundred kilometers to the town of Slagelse, and the GPS calculates the journey time as nearly an hour and fifteen minutes. But when Thulin turns off toward the old fairground near Grønningen, where the psychiatric hospital and the secure ward are located, barely an hour has passed.

It was nice to escape the city limits and watch the fields and forests of the autumn landscape flit by in shades of red, yellow, and brown. Soon the colors would vanish and the part of autumn that was only gray would set in. Thulin tried to enjoy the view, although her mind was still stuck in the lab at Forensics.

Hess expanded on his theory as they turned it over with Genz. If Linus Bekker was innocent of any crime against Kristine Hartung, then somebody else had deliberately tried to throw suspicion on him. In many ways he was an ideal scapegoat, with a rap sheet and psychological constitution bound to attract the attention of the police as soon as he entered the spotlight. But the killer—and here Hess didn't mean Linus Bekker— must therefore have planned all this long ago, probably with the specific purpose of making it look like Kristine Hartung was dead and buried. The anonymous tip about Linus Bekker that had led to the case being wrapped up now seemed suspicious.

First Hess questioned Genz about the investigation into the phone call that had led the police to Bekker. Genz rushed straight to the keyboard to check the details in the tech report. The anonymous tip had been phoned in to a landline early one Monday morning, but unfortunately not to 112, the emergency line, which recorded all calls automatically. The odd thing was that the call had come via a direct line to Nylander's administrative offices. In itself, this wasn't necessarily suspicious; after all, Nylander had been splashed all over the media at the time, so it might make sense for someone following the case to send their tip to him. The call had apparently originated from a mobile phone with an unregistered prepaid card, so it had been impossible to trace the informant. There the trail went cold. According to the report, the secretary who'd taken the call had been unable to give any account beyond that a "Danish-speaking man" had briefly stated they ought to check out Linus Bekker and search his residence in connection with the Hartung case. Linus Bekker's name was repeated, and then the line went dead.

Hess then asked Genz to run through the forensic evidence again as soon as possible. The moment the investigation had zeroed in on Bekker, other apparently irrelevant leads may well have been dumped—and those were the leads that interested Hess now. It would take time, but Genz was willing to give it a shot. He did, however, ask what he was supposed to say if anybody noticed him poking around in the Hartung reports on physical and trace evidence.

"Say I asked you to do it, so you don't get into trouble yourself."

For a moment, Thulin wondered what *she* was supposed to say. There was no doubt in her mind that the present development fell under the general umbrella of things Nylander wouldn't like, and if they were caught then it might affect her chances of getting into NC3. Yet she couldn't bring herself to call Nylander. Instead she phoned one of the detectives reading through the files at the minister's office, looking for potential enemies of Rosa Hartung. Nothing new on that score, apart from the fact that most of the cases involved strong emotions and antipathy toward the authorities. So when Hess suggested they try and arrange a conversation with Linus Bekker, she assented. He then phoned the secure ward where Bekker was being held. The consultant psychiatrist was in a meeting, but Hess gave the gist of the matter to his second-in-command, explaining that they were on their way down and expected to arrive within the hour.

"You okay to come along? You don't need to, if you feel it's going to compromise you."

"It's all right."

Thulin still had a hard time believing the visit would prove useful. It seemed most likely that Linus Bekker had been telling the truth when he confessed to the crime. He could still have shown up behind the police cordon in the woods. From what she knew of Tim Jansen, and also of Martin Ricks, they certainly weren't afraid to get a little rough—or worse—if a suspect needed encouragement confessing, but no matter how much they'd leaned on Linus Bekker he'd had many chances later to withdraw his confession. So why should it be false? Despite his purported blackouts, Bekker had remembered enough that the whole series of events had been pieced together. He'd agreed to a reconstruction in which his actions had been mapped out, from the afternoon when he'd been meandering around in his car and caught sight of a girl with a sports bag until later that same night, when he'd found himself with a corpse in the woods up north. He'd described the sexual assault and strangulation, described driving around with the body and not knowing what to do. In his statement in court, he'd even apologized to the girl's parents.

It *had* to be true; anything else was unrealistic. This is Thulin's last thought before she pulls up outside the gates of the secure facility.

84

The recently constructed secure unit, which is situated in its own square-shaped plot near the psychiatric hospital, is bordered on all four sides by two walls six meters high, with a deep trench between them. The only point of access is from the south, where the system of gates abuts the parking lot, and Hess and Thulin stand in front of the dome camera and speaker beside the heavy gate.

Unlike Hess, Thulin has never been to a secure ward before, but obviously she's heard of this place. The facility is the country's largest forensic psychiatric institution, home to the most dangerous criminals. Its thirty-odd inmates have been convicted by special decree, a measure the courts can use in the rare cases where there is reason to suppose that the individual is a persistent danger to others. Because this danger is judged to be the result of mental illness, the individual is taken to the secure psychiatric unit—a hybrid psychiatric ward and maximum-security prison—and contained there for the duration of their indeterminate sentence. The inmates, referred to as patients, include murderers, pedophiles, serial rapists, and arsonists, and some of them, the intractably ill, will never be considered for reintegration into society.

The electronic gate opens, and Thulin follows Hess into a kind of empty garage, where a guard sits waiting for them behind bulletproof glass. Behind him they can see another guard in front of a bank of surveillance monitors. Of which there are many. As requested, Thulin hands over her phone, belt, and shoelaces. In her case and Hess's, they are also required to hand over their guns, but it's the phone that hurts the most, because Thulin is now deprived of the opportunity to contact her colleagues at the ministry, which she hadn't foreseen. A body scanner exempts her from any extra searches, then she and Hess wait in the garage for another gate to open. They pass through, deeper into the system of gates, and only once one has shut completely is the next one unlocked. A solid metal door is opened electronically at the end of the room by a heavyset male nurse with a name badge that reads HANSEN.

"Welcome. Follow me, please."

With its bright corridors and pleasant view over the courtyard, the ward looks at first glance like a modern training center. Only until you realize most of the furniture is bolted to the floor or the walls, of course. The sound of rattling keys is ever-present, and the interlocking system of gates continues, just as in an ordinary prison, as they move deeper into the facility, glimpsing a few patients on sofas and at Ping-Pong tables along the way. Unshaven men, some of them clearly medicated, most shuffling around in slip-on sandals. The patients Thulin sees wear grieved expressions. They remind her most of all of residents at a nursing home, but Thulin recognizes a few of them from press photographs, and although their faces look old and dull, she knows they have human lives on their consciences.

"This is most disruptive. I don't know why I wasn't brought into the loop before."

Consultant psychiatrist Weiland is none too pleased to see them. Although Hess had explained their visit to his second-in-command, he now has to start from the beginning.

"I'm very sorry, but we do need to speak to him."

"Linus Bekker is making progress. He cannot be confronted with news about death and violence—it's *precisely* the kind of thing that could set him back. Linus Bekker is one of our patients who is forbidden access to all forms of media apart from a one-hour nature program per day."

"We only want to ask him about things he's talked about before. It's crucial we speak with him. If you won't allow us access, I'll have to get a warrant, but any delay could cost lives."

Thulin can tell the consultant was unprepared for this answer. For a second, he hesitates, evidently not fond of backing down.

"Wait here. If he says yes, then it's fine, but I'm not forcing him to do anything."

Moments later, the consultant returns. He gives Hansen a nod and tells them Linus Bekker has agreed, before he disappears. Hansen glances after him, then begins telling them about the security measures.

"No physical contact whatsoever. If it looks like Bekker is getting even remotely agitated, you need to pull the emergency cord in the visitors' room. We'll be right outside the door if a situation arises, but ideally it shouldn't. Clear?"

85

The visitors' room measures roughly five meters by three. The thick, reinforced windows render bars unnecessary, offering an unobstructed view over the green courtyard and the six-meter-high wall beyond. Four hard plastic chairs are meticulously arranged around a small, angular table, bolted to the floor. Linus Bekker is already sitting in one when Hess and Thulin are ushered in.

He is surprisingly short, perhaps five foot five. A young man with virtually no hair. A childlike face, but powerfully built. A little like a gymnast, which is what he resembles in his gray sweatpants and white T-shirt.

"May I sit by the window? I like sitting by the window best."

Bekker has risen and is standing staring at them like a nervous schoolboy.

"Absolutely fine. Your decision."

Hess introduces himself and Thulin, and she notices he takes pains to come across as friendly and trusting. He ends the introductions by thanking Bekker for his time.

"Time is one thing I'm not short of here."

Bekker speaks without irony or a smile. It's a simple statement, and his eyes blink at them uneasily. As Thulin sits down on one of the bolted-down chairs opposite the young man, Hess begins to explain that they have come because they need his help.

"But I don't know where the body is. I'm terribly sorry, but I really can't remember anything beyond what I've already told you."

"Don't you worry about that. It's about something else."

"Were you two on the case? I don't remember you."

Bekker seems a little frightened. Guileless, blinking eyes. Sitting straight-backed in his chair, picking apprehensively at his nail beds, which are frayed and red.

"No, we weren't on the case."

Hess launches into the lie they've settled on. He flashes his Europol badge and explains that he is a profiler based at the Hague. By mapping out the personalities and behaviors of individuals like Linus Bekker, profilers can help solve similar crimes. Hess has come to Denmark to help his Danish colleagues, including Thulin, set up an equivalent department. They are conducting conversations with selected inmates to learn about their reaction patterns in the lead-up to their crimes, and are hoping Bekker will take part.

"But nobody told me you were coming."

"No, there's been a mistake. You should have been informed much earlier so that you could prepare, but I'm afraid there was a misunderstanding. It's completely up to you whether you want to help. If you prefer, we can go."

Bekker looks out the window and starts picking at his nail beds again, and for a moment Thulin is sure he will say no.

"I'd like to. It's important, if I can help other people, isn't it?"

"Yes, exactly. Thank you, that's kind of you."

Hess spends the next few minutes checking various facts with Linus Bekker. Age. Residence. Family situation. School. Right-handedness. Previous hospitalizations. All harmless, irrelevant questions to which they already know the answers, intended solely to build trust and make Bekker feel safe. Thulin has to admit Hess is adept at this, and her skepticism about their cover story proves groundless. But the performance takes time, and she feels as though they are sitting in the eye of the tornado, driveling on about pointless crap while a storm rages outside. At last, Hess reaches the day before the murder.

"You said the day was vague to you. You remember it only in flashes."

"Yeah, I had blackouts. My illness made me dizzy, and I hadn't slept in a couple of days. I'd spent too much time with the pictures in the archive."

"Tell me how it started with the archive."

"It was sort of a boyhood dream. If I can put it like that. I mean, I had those urges . . ."

Bekker pauses, and Thulin guesses that part of his psychological treatment involves him no longer yielding to his sadism and passion for death.

". . . and from documentaries about crimes I knew there were pictures taken at crime scenes. I just didn't know where they were kept. Not until I got into the server at the Forensics Department. And then the rest was so easy."

Thulin can attest to this. The only defense for the lack of security is that it had seemed unthinkable anybody would break into the digital archive of victim and crime-scene photographs. Right up until Linus Bekker had broken down the barrier and done it.

"Did you tell anyone what you had accessed?"

"No. I knew I wasn't allowed. But . . . like I said . . ."

"What did the pictures do for you?"

"I actually thought the pictures . . . that they were good for me. Because that way I controlled my . . . urges. But today I realize they weren't. They excited me. Made me think of only one thing. I remember feeling like I needed fresh air. So I took a drive. But after that, it's difficult remembering."

Bekker's apologetic gaze sweeps across Thulin's, and although he looks childlike and guileless, she gets goose bumps.

"Did anybody around you know you had these blackouts? Or did you tell anyone about them?"

"No. I didn't see anybody back then. I was home, mostly. If I went out anywhere, it was to see the scenes."

"What scenes?"

"The crime scenes. New, old. In Odense, for example, and on Amager Common, where I was arrested. But other places too."

"Did you have blackouts on those occasions as well?"

"Maybe. I don't remember. I mean, that's how it is with blackouts."

"How much do you remember of the rest of the day of the murder?"

"Not much. It's hard to say, because I get it mixed up with what I found out later on."

"Can you remember, for example, whether you followed Kristine Hartung into the woods?"

"No. Not exactly. But I do remember the woods."

"But if you don't remember her, how do you know you were the one who attacked and killed her?"

For a moment Bekker registers surprise. It seems to catch him off guard, as though he's long ago accepted his guilt.

"Because . . . they told me so. And they helped me remember the other things."

"Who?"

"Well, the officers who interrogated me. They'd found things, you know. Soil under my shoes. Blood on the machete I'd used to . . ."

"But at that point you still said you hadn't done it. Did you remember the machete yourself?"

"No, not at first. But then things began to point in that direction."

"Originally, when the machete was found, you said you'd never seen it before. That somebody must have put it on the shelf in the garage next to your car. It wasn't until a later interview that you confessed and said it was yours."

"Yes, that's right. But the doctors have explained that that's how my illness works. If you're a paranoid schizophrenic, your mind plays tricks with reality."

"So you can't think who might have put it there, if indeed it was put there?"

"But it wasn't . . . it was me who did it. I don't think I'm doing very well with all these questions . . ."

Linus Bekker looks uncertainly toward the door, but Hess leans toward him and tries to catch his eye.

"Linus, you're doing just fine. I need to know whether anybody was close to you during that period. Somebody who knew how things stood with you. Somebody you confided in—somebody you suddenly met or wrote to online, or—"

"But there wasn't. I don't understand what you want. I think I'd like to go back to my room now."

"Don't be nervous, Linus. If you give me a hand, I think we can figure out what happened that day. And what exactly happened to Kristine Hartung."

Bekker, who had been on the verge of standing up, stares skeptically at Hess.

"You think so?"

"Yeah, I think so. Definitely. You just have to tell me who you had contact with."

Hess is looking trustingly at Linus Bekker. For a moment, it seems from the expression on Linus Bekker's timid, childlike face that Hess has talked him around. But then it splits into a laugh.

Linus Bekker splutters with laughter. Thulin and Hess stare in disbelief at the little man, who is trying in vain to hold his laughter back. When he finally begins to speak it is as though he's taken off a mask, and there is no longer any trace of uncertainty or nerves.

"Why don't you just ask me what you'd really like to know? Skip all this bullshit and get to the point."

"What do you mean?"

"What do you mean?"

Bekker mimicks Hess's voice, rolling his eyes with a teasing grin.

"You're gagging to know why I confessed to a crime if I didn't commit it."

Thulin stares at Linus Bekker. The transformation is stunning. The man is insane. Stark raving mad, and for a moment Thulin feels like calling in the consultant so that he can see Bekker's progress for himself. Hess tries to maintain his composure.

"Okay. Why did you confess, then?"

"Piss off. That's what they pay you to find out. Did they really bring you home from Europol to drag this shit out of me, or was that just a cardboard badge you showed me earlier?"

"Linus, I don't understand what you're saying. But if you had nothing to do with Kristine Hartung, it's not too late to say so. We could help you bring your case back to court."

"But I don't *need* help. Assuming we're still living in a law-abiding society, I'll probably be home again by Christmas at the latest. Or as soon as the Chestnut Man's done with his harvest."

The words strike Thulin like a hammer. Hess too, who sits like a pillar of stone. Bekker knows. He smirks, and while Thulin tries to act like nothing has happened it's as though night has suddenly fallen in the room.

"The Chestnut Man . . . ?"

"Yeah, the Chestnut Man. The reason you're here. Sweet little Hansen, the bulky one, he forgets we still have teletext on the flat-screen in the common room. Only thirty-eight characters per line, but you can still make something out of it. Why didn't you show up before now? The boss didn't want you fiddling around with his nice, tidy case, eh?"

"What do you know about the Chestnut Man?"

"*Chestnut man, do come in. Chestnut man . . .*"

Bekker hums the tune derisively. Hess is losing patience.

"I asked what you know."

"It's too late. He's way ahead. That's why you're here, pleading with me. Because he's taken you for a ride. Because you have no idea what to do."

"You know who he is?"

"I know *what* he is. He's the master. And he's made me part of his plan. Otherwise I'd never have confessed."

"Tell us who he is, Linus."

"Tell us who he is, Linus."

Linus Bekker is aping Hess again.

"What about the girl?"

"What about the girl?"

"What do you know? Where is she? What happened to her?!"

"Does it matter? She must have had fun . . ."

Linus Bekker is watching them innocently, an obscene leer spreading across his face. Thulin has no time to react when Hess rises and lunges at him. But Bekker is prepared, and at that very moment he pulls the cord. The alarm goes off with a deafening howl. Almost the exact second the metal door flies open and the broadshouldered men barge in, Linus Bekker transforms back into the tentative schoolboy with the timorous expression.

86

The gate is opening slowly, but Hess can't wait. While Thulin is taking their belongings back from the guard behind the bulletproof glass, she sees him squeeze his way through the partially opened gate and continue into the parking lot. As she follows, the cold, wet wind feels liberating, and she sucks fresh air into her lungs to get rid of Linus Bekker.

They were chucked headlong out of the facility. Consultant Weiland had demanded an explanation of the incident in the visitors' room. Bekker had been convincing. Fearful and anxious, he'd flinched away from Hess and Thulin as though he'd suffered physical or psychological damage. To the consultant he'd complained that Hess had "grabbed him" and asked "strange questions about death and murder," and the consultant had taken his side. It was pointless to argue against his claims; neither Hess nor Thulin had thought it would be necessary to record their conversation with Bekker, and of course their phones had been in the guard's possession in any case. Driving down here was a catastrophe, and listening to her voicemail as she crosses the parking lot does not improve Thulin's mood. In the time they've been inside, her phone has rung seven times, and when she hears the first message she begins running through the rain toward the car.

"We've got to get back to the ministry. They've found cases we need to check out."

Thulin reaches the car and unlocks it, but Hess remains standing in the rain. "The ministry doesn't matter. The killer won't be in any case file he led us to himself. Didn't you hear what Bekker said?"

"I heard a psychopath rambling and you going nuts. Nothing else."

Thulin opens the door, climbs in, and tosses Hess's gun and belongings onto the seat beside her. Checking the clock on the dashboard, she calculates they won't reach the city before dark, and she knows she will have to ask Le's granddad to look after her once again. Hess has barely placed one foot on the passenger-side floor before she starts the engine and swings out onto the road.

"Bekker knew we would come. He's been expecting it ever since he was convicted. He knows who we're looking for," Hess says as he slams the door.

"No, he knows fuck all. Linus Bekker is a perverted sex offender who's read a little teletext. He wanted to provoke us and mess us around, and you swallowed it hook, line, and sinker. What the hell were you thinking?!"

"He knows who took her."

"Like hell he does. He took her himself. The whole world knows the girl's dead and buried. You're the only one who hasn't got it yet. Why the hell would he confess to a crime he didn't commit?"

"Because he suddenly realized who *had* committed it. Someone he'd gladly take the blame for, because in his sick head he sensed it was all part of a grander plan. Someone he admired—someone he looked up to. And who would Linus Bekker look up to?"

"Nobody! The man's nuts. All he's interested in is death and destruction."

"Exactly. Somebody expert in what Bekker values most. Something he must have seen in the archive of crime-scene photos he hacked into."

The words slowly sink in. Thulin slams on the brakes, narrowly avoiding a collision with the massive truck plowing through the rain along the main road.

A long row of cars whizz past in the truck's wake, and Thulin feels Hess looking at her.

"I'm sorry I crossed the line. That was wrong. But if Linus Bekker is lying, that means nobody knows what happened to Kristine Hartung. Not even if she's dead."

Thulin doesn't reply. She speeds up again, dialing a number on her phone. Hess has a point. Infuriatingly. It takes a moment, but then Genz picks up. The connection is bad, and it sounds as though he too is in a car.

"Hey, why couldn't I get hold of you? How did it go with Bekker?"

"That's why I'm calling. Do you have access to all the crime-scene photos he got his hands on? The photos he hacked into?"

Genz sounds surprised.

"I assume so, but I'll have to check. Why?"

"I'll explain later. But we need to know which specific photos Bekker was most interested in. It must be possible to trace which ones were his favorites. Draw up a list of the images he clicked on most. Plus the ones he downloaded, if there are any of those. We think there might be an important clue in them, so we need them ASAP. Just make sure Nylander doesn't get wind of this, okay?"

"Yeah, okay. I can get hold of the tech guys when I get back. But shouldn't I wait until we know whether Jansen is right?"

"Jansen?"

"He didn't call you?"

Thulin feels a stab of disquiet. She'd forgotten all about Jansen since their curt encounter with him that morning as they left Nylander's office. He'd looked like a dead man. Withdrawn and mute. She'd felt reassured to see Nylander bringing him in for a chat, and hoped it would end with him being sent home. Something tells her that wasn't the case.

"Why would Jansen have called?"

"About the address in Sydhavnen. I heard him over the police radio a little while ago, asking for backup because he had a hunch the suspects might be inside."

"The suspects? What suspects? Jansen isn't even on the case."

"Oh, right. Doesn't seem like he knows that. Right now he's raiding an address where he thinks the killers are holed up."

87

I n the front seat of his police vehicle, Tim Jansen checks the cartridges in his magazine and slides it with a click back into his Heckler & Koch. It will be at least ten minutes before backup arrives, but that's not a problem. He isn't planning to wait for them anyway. Ricks's killer might be inside the building, and Jansen would rather conduct the first confrontation or interrogation alone. At least now people know where he is, if he does get into trouble, and when they ask him to explain why he went in he can always claim he had no choice, that the situation demanded it before backup arrived.

Jansen feels the dank wind on his face as he emerges from the car. The old manufacturing district in Sydhavnen is a hodgepodge of tall warehouses, new self-storage buildings, scrap yards, and a handful of dwellings squeezed between the industrial plots. Sand and trash whip through the air, and there are no vehicles on the street as he strides toward the building.

The building facing the street is two stories, easily confused with an ordinary residential block, but as he approaches he sees the remnants of a sign on the dilapidated wall, announcing that the building once served as a slaughterhouse. The shop window by the main door is covered on the inside with a piece of black material, blocking the view onto the street, so instead Jansen walks down the driveway and into the courtyard. The big, oblong building set back slightly from the one fronting onto the road has to be the old slaughterhouse: running alongside the building are platforms underneath the big gates used for loading and unloading. Farther away, the slaughterhouse is bordered by a garden with a broken-down fence and three or four fruit trees, which look as though they are being torn up by the wind. Jansen turns back toward the front building and notices a back door; there is no sign, but there is a doormat and a pot planted with a shriveled spruce tree. He raises his hand and knocks, while with the other he switches the safety off the Heckler & Koch in his coat pocket.

For Jansen, the days since Martin Ricks's death have been unreal. Unreality descended at the sight of his partner's lifeless figure, amid the flashing lights of the ambulances and the barking of the police dogs as they strained from nook to cranny in the community gardens. Arriving from Urbanplan, he knew nothing of his friend's fate, and then out of the blue he found himself staring at something incomprehensible. At first he didn't think the deathly pale creature could possibly be his colleague. That death could have reduced Ricks to the inert holster at his feet. Yet so it had. And although for several hours afterward, Jansen had almost expected Ricks to show up and rake someone over the coals for leaving him on the gravel so long, that hadn't happened.

They'd partnered up almost by accident, but as Jansen recalled they'd been on the same wavelength from day one. Ricks had possessed exactly the qualities that made him a bearable partner. Neither particularly clever nor quick with repartee—in fact, he rarely spoke for long at any one stretch—he was, however, immensely dogged and loyal once you'd gotten him on your side. Moreover, Ricks had possessed a healthy mistrust of nearly everything and everyone, most likely because he'd been picked on for most of his childhood, and

Jansen had understood instantly how the man's potential could be realized. If he was the head, then Ricks was the body, and they'd soon come to share a natural aversion to bosses and lawyers, none of whom knew a single fucking thing about policework. Together they'd locked up so many bikers, Pakis, wife-beaters, rapists, and killers they ought to have been showered with raises and medals all the way up to retirement. But society didn't work like that. The blessings of the world were unequally distributed. They'd often talked about that, celebrating by themselves in bars and clubs until they were fall-down drunk or had swung by the little brothel in Outer Østerbro.

All that is over. The only thanks Ricks will get is his name engraved beside all the other names on the memorial wall at the station. Jansen isn't sentimentally inclined, but when he came to work yesterday morning it affected him to walk through the columned courtyard with that knowledge. For two days, he'd stayed at home. On the night of the killing, he'd been too shocked to make any contribution besides informing Ricks's better half of what had happened, and later that night his own wife had woken to find him sitting apathetically in the unlit conservatory in Vanløse. The next day, his family had gone to a birthday party while he'd begun putting together the IKEA bookcase waiting in a box in the boys' room. But the instructions were incomprehensible, and around half past ten he'd started on the white wine. By the time his wife got home with the kids that afternoon, he'd staggered out into the shed in the back garden, moving on to vodka and Red Bull, and when he woke up later on the floor he knew he needed to get back to work pretty quick.

Monday was his first day back. The station was a hive of activity and purpose, and people nodded sympathetically at him. Nylander refused to let him back on the case, of course, so instead he gathered together a handful of colleagues in the changing room and made it clear that as soon as anything important came up in the hunt for the killer he wanted to be told. Some seemed to disapprove of the idea, but others shared his view: that Ricks had died because Hess and Thulin weren't up to the task. On top of that, it must have been one of them, probably Hess, who'd talked to the press, and his continuing doubts about the Hartung case were an even bigger slap in the face now that Ricks had been murdered.

Unfortunately things were still stalled when his colleagues were dispatched to the minister's office that morning. Jansen's own assignments were unimportant, so instead he drove out to the suburb of Greve, bought a six-pack at a kiosk on the way, and drank a few before knocking at the little ground-floor apartment by the subway station, where Ricks had lived. His girlfriend had been in floods of tears. He'd been invited in and had just accepted a cup of tea when one of the detectives called from the ministry. They'd come up with a few possibilities—people with good reason to loathe the state, the system, the Ministry for Social Affairs, and the world at large. Jansen listened to the options, and one of the cases seemed to promise a stronger motive than the others. After making sure Hess and Thulin hadn't yet been informed, he hung up, made his excuses to Ricks's girlfriend, and drove straight to the address in Sydhavnen.

"Who is it?" comes a voice from behind the door.

"Police! Open up!"

Jansen knocks impatiently, his hand gripping the gun in his pocket. The door opens, and a furrowed face peeps anxiously out. Jansen suppresses his astonishment. It's an old woman, and behind her he can smell cigarettes and spoiled food.

"I need to speak to Benedikte Skans and Asger Neergaard."

Jansen had been given the names by his colleague at the ministry, but the old woman shakes her head.

"They don't live here anymore. They moved out six months ago."

"Moved out? Where to?"

"I don't know. They didn't say. What's this about?"

"Live here alone, do you?"

"Yes. But I don't recall saying you could take that familiar tone with me."

Jansen hesitates a moment. He hadn't been expecting this. The old lady coughs and draws her cardigan more tightly around her against the chill.

"Is there something I can help with?"

"Forget it. Sorry to disturb you. Goodbye."

"Goodbye, goodbye."

Jansen steps away from the door, and the old lady shuts it. For a few seconds, he isn't sure what to do. The woman's response has caught him off guard. He's about to return to the warmth of his car and ring his colleague at the ministry when his eye suddenly comes to rest on a first-floor window. It dawns on him that he's looking at a mobile hanging from a ceiling. A mobile with small birds, the kind that usually hang above a crib, and Jansen knows instantly that it shouldn't be there if the old lady is right that Benedikte Skans and Asger Neergaard have moved.

He knocks again, harder this time. When at last the old lady opens the door, he pushes past her, drawing his gun. The woman shouts in protest. He walks purposefully down the narrow corridor, into the kitchen, and through to the front room, which once served as the shop floor. Assuring himself that it's empty, he makes for the stairs, which the old witch is now blocking.

"Move!"

"There's nothing there! You can't just—"

"Shut up and move!"

He pushes her aside, bounding up the stairs with the woman still whining behind him. Gun at the ready, his finger rigid on the trigger, he shoves open door after door. The first two are bedrooms, but the last is a child's room.

The mobile hangs peacefully above the crib, but otherwise it's empty, and for a heartbeat Jansen thinks he's made a mistake. Then he notices the wall behind the door, and immediately he knows he's solved the case that killed Martin Ricks.

88

Darkness has come, and by this time the last vehicles are usually departing Sydhavnen, leaving the streets deserted. But not today. Outside the ramshackle buildings that were once one of Copenhagen's major slaughterhouses, the street is writhing with officers and Forensics techs, milling around with their flight cases. The vehicles have formed a queue, and sharp floodlights glare from every single window in the front-facing building. From the room on the first floor, Hess can hear the old lady crying every now and then as she is interviewed, and the sound intermingles with rapid instructions, footsteps, crackly radio messages— but mostly with Thulin and Jansen's conversation by the door.

"But who tipped you off to come out here?"

"Who says I got a tip? Maybe I was just out for a drive."

"Why the hell didn't you call?"

"You and Hess? What the fuck good's that supposed to do?"

The photo has to be roughly two years old. The glass is dusty, but it's nicely framed with black edges, lying on the pillow in the white crib beside a dummy and a lock of thin white hair. The young mother in the picture is standing beside an incubator and holding a child swaddled in a blanket, smiling for the camera. It's a forced expression, bespeaking tiredness and great exertion, and because the young woman is still wearing a crumpled hospital gown Hess thinks the picture must have been taken at the hospital shortly after the birth. The woman's eyes are unsmiling. There is something fragile, something divorced from reality about her expression, as though she's just been handed the child and is trying to play a role for which she hasn't prepared.

There is no doubt that the Benedikte Skans in the photograph is the same pretty, grave-faced nurse he and Thulin met at the Rigshospital's pediatric ward when they interviewed Hussein Majid about Magnus Kjær and Sofia Sejer-Lassen. Since the photo was taken, her hair has grown longer, her features older, and her smile is gone. But it *is* her, and Hess struggles to understand the connection.

Ever since he and Thulin left the secure psychiatric ward, the conversation with Linus Bekker had been thickening inside him like a malignant tumor. All his energy and attention had been riveted on the possibility of tracing the killer through the images in the archive Bekker had hacked, but then the news began to trickle in. First from Genz, then from one of the detectives they'd left at the ministry, who had rushed out to Sydhavnen after Jansen's call for backup. It didn't take much imagination to figure out that Jansen must have been tipped off by one of the detectives going through the files at the ministry, but right now that detail seems trivial in comparison to the breakthrough about Benedikte Skans and her boyfriend.

"How far have you got?"

Nylander has just arrived, and Jansen appears relieved at the interruption.

"The lease is in the name of Benedikte Skans. Twenty-eight, nurse at the Rigshospital. She and her boyfriend had their child removed by Copenhagen Council eighteen months ago. The child was sent to a foster family, and Benedikte Skans took legal action. She also went to the press and attacked the minister for social affairs for encouraging the councils to take more children into care."

"Rosa Hartung."

"Yup. The media lapped it up, until they suddenly realized that the council had removed the child for good reason, and the case was forgotten. But not by Benedikte Skans and her boyfriend, because shortly afterward the child died. Skans was packed off to a locked ward, and she wasn't let back out until spring this year. She got her old job back and moved here with her boyfriend, but as you can see from the wall, they never forgot what happened."

Hess is busy scanning the wall, and isn't listening. He knows most of the information already from copies of the case file from Copenhagen Council, which a detective had brought from the ministry. Benedikte Skans's youth in Tingbjerg was frittered on hash, nightlife, and an unfinished traineeship at a clothing boutique, until at the age of twenty-one she was accepted into nursing school in Copenhagen. She completed the course with solid marks, and it was around the same time that she met her boyfriend, Asger Neergaard, who'd been a few years above her at high school in Tingbjerg. In the meantime, Neergaard had been a soldier at the barracks in Slagelse, later deployed to Afghanistan, and together they'd set up home at the dilapidated slaughterhouse.

Benedikte Skans got a job as a nurse on the Rigshospital's pediatric ward, and meanwhile she and her
boyfriend were trying to become parents themselves.
According to the caseworker's notes, when Benedikte
did get pregnant, she began to exhibit anxiety and
issues with self-esteem. At the age of twenty-six, she
delivered a baby boy two months premature, which
triggered puerperal psychosis. It didn't seem like the
child's father had been much of a help. The caseworker
found the then-twenty-eight-year-old soldier immature
and withdrawn, occasionally even aggressive, if Benedikte Skans egged him on. The council had done its best
to provide support through various programs, but after
six months Benedikte Skans's psychological problems
had grown worse, and she was diagnosed with bipolar
disorder. When they'd been unable to get hold of the
family for a few weeks, the council turned to the police,
who conducted a raid—which turned out to be the right
decision. The seven-month-old boy had been lying unconscious in his crib, sticky with feces and vomit, and
there were worrying signs of malnourishment. At the
hospital, it emerged that the boy had chronic asthma, as
well as food allergies that made it dangerous to eat the
squares of nutty chocolate they had given him.

Although the intervention had probably saved the
child's life, it left Benedikte Skans furious. She'd been

interviewed several times, expressing her outrage at the way her family had been treated: "If I'm a bad mother, then there are plenty of them" read one of the headlines reproduced in the case file. Because the council didn't make the child's neglect public, it must have seemed like Skans had a good case—but only until Rosa Hartung came forward and reminded both the press and the councils that it was in the children's best interests to interpret paragraph forty-two of the relevant legislation as strictly as possible. The media went quiet. Then came the boy's tragic death from acute pulmonary disease, only two months after being taken into care. Benedikte Skans responded violently to the caseworker who gave her the news, and her visits to the outpatient psychiatrist turned into a lengthy stay at Sankt Hans in Roskilde. She was discharged in the spring and took up her old job at the Rigshospital, on a probationary footing.

Hess shivers at the thought, because the wall behind the door makes it clear the young woman is anything but healthy.

"My view is that she and the boyfriend are in it together," Jansen continues to Nylander. "They obviously felt they were unfairly treated, so they cooked up this plan in their sick little heads to mock the minister and make her look ridiculous, to expose the system and punish women who weren't looking after their kids. As you can see, there's no question who the crowning glory is supposed to be."

Jansen isn't wrong about that part. While one side of the room serves as a mausoleum for the dead child, the other side reveals a pathological obsession with Rosa Hartung. From left to right, there are clippings of newspaper photographs and headlines about her daughter's disappearance, including paparazzi snaps of the grieving minister. Words like DISMEMBERED AND BURIED or RAPED BEFORE SHE WAS CUT UP are pasted mockingly next to a photo of Rosa Hartung dressed in black, breaking down at a memorial service. There are several featuring such headlines as ROSA HARTUNG CRUSHED or SICK WITH GRIEF, but then the clippings jump forward in time, and toward the right side of the wall are newer images, probably three or four months old, beneath the headline HARTUNG RETURNS. In one article pinned to the wall, there is a hand-drawn circle around the minister's return to parliament on the first Tuesday in October, and beside it hangs an A4 page with various selfies of her daughter as well as the words "Welcome back. You're going to die, slut."

Far more concerning, however, is the fact that the clippings give way to another series of images. Not from newspapers this time: photographs developed from film, evidently shot at some point after the end of September, before autumn had set in fully. Photographs of the minister's house from various angles, of her husband, of her son, a sports hall, her ministerial car, her ministerial office, and Christiansborg, as well as a profusion of Google Maps printouts showing routes into the center of town.

The material is overwhelming. It torpedoes the frail house of cards Hess was on the verge of forming as he left the secure unit. Had the visit to Linus Bekker been pointless? Try as he might, he can't rebuild it—but this isn't the only thing nagging at him. There is clearly another threat. Something close at hand, something that demands their attention *right now*, just when they think they have the case under control, so Hess continues to scan the wall while Nylander questions Jansen.

"And where is the couple now?"

"They haven't seen hide nor hair of the woman at the Rigshospital since she called in sick a few days ago, and we don't know where the boyfriend's staying either. He's the one we know the least about. They're not married, so everything's in Benedikte Skans's name, but we're getting his papers from the military. Have Intelligence been informed of what we've found?"

"Oh yes. The minister is safe. Who's the woman downstairs?"

"Asger Neergaard's mom. Apparently, she lives here too. She says she doesn't know where they are, but we're not finished with her yet."

"But we believe this young couple are responsible for the killings?"

Hess hears Thulin interrupt before Jansen can answer, when suddenly he becomes aware of several pins in the wall. A few scraps of paper remain caught beneath one or two of them, as though a photo has been torn down in a hurry.

"We don't know that yet. Before we jump to any conclusions, we need to—"

"What else do we need to know? Christ, we've all got eyes in our heads," exclaims Jansen.

"Exactly! There's all this material about Rosa Hartung, but nothing about the murdered women. If this couple is responsible for the murders, then there ought to be some hint of them here, but there isn't!"

"But the woman worked as a nurse on a ward where she could have met at least two of the victims and their children. That's irrelevant, is it?"

"No, it's not irrelevant. Obviously, we need to arrest and interrogate them, but it will be a fucking nightmare now that you've ridden in all guns blazing and told the whole world we're waiting for them!"

Hess still can't find the photo that must have been pinned to the wall, and in the background he hears Nylander's voice chime in coolly.

"As I see it, Jansen was well within his rights to act, Thulin. According to the consultant psychiatrist at Bekker's unit—who was kind enough to ring me a few minutes ago—you and Hess have been busy harassing Linus Bekker . . . despite the fact that I specifically ordered you not to. Any explanation for me?"

Hess knows the moment has come to defend Thulin, but instead he turns toward Jansen.

"Jansen, could the woman have removed something from up here before you came in?"

"What the hell did you two want with Linus Bekker?!"

The argument continues behind him as he tries to figure out where he'd hide something if the police were knocking at the door. When he shifts a chest of drawers away from the wall, a crumpled photograph drops to the floor, and he hurries to pick it up and unfold it.

The young man, whom Hess guesses must be Asger Neergaard, is tall and straight-backed, standing beside a car with a set of keys in his hand. He's wearing a smart dark suit, and the black car shines in the weak sunlight as though it has just been washed and polished. The suit and the expensive German car are in stark contrast with the crumbling slaughterhouse behind them. At first Hess doesn't understand why Asger Neergaard's mother would have chosen this particular photo to get rid of, but then his eye is drawn back to the car, and when he dashes back to the wall and compares it with the photo of Rosa Hartung's ministerial vehicle, all doubt is dispelled: her car is identical to the one in the image of Asger Neergaard. Yet before Hess can say a word, Genz sticks his head around the door, clad in his usual white overalls.

"Sorry to interrupt. We've just started searching the old slaughterhouse building and there's something you need to see. It looks like one of the rooms has been kitted out to keep someone prisoner for a good long while."

89

It's late afternoon, and the E20 motorway southwest of Copenhagen is dense with traffic. Asger honks the horn to clear the outside lane, but the row of idiots in front of him insist on driving cautiously because of the rain, and he edges impatiently along the inside. The minister's car is an Audi A8 3.0, and it's the first time he's properly let the engine loose. He doesn't care about attracting attention; what matters now is getting away. The whole thing has gone to hell, and Asger knows it's only a question of time before the police realize it's him and Benedikte they are after—if they don't know already.

Everything ran like clockwork until thirty-five minutes ago. He'd created an alibi by following the little bastard into the tennis hall and saying a quick hello to the manager, who was always fussing around before training, checking the nets. Then he'd said goodbye and driven around to the back of the hall, parking between the fir trees before entering through the side door, which he'd left ajar when he followed the boy inside. The hall was largely empty at that point, so it had been easy to sneak into the changing rooms unseen. The boy had been busy getting changed and didn't hear a thing, but just as Asger was standing there like a clown in gloves and a balaclava, getting out the chloroform, he heard approaching footsteps. The manager was coming in, and although Asger managed to rip off his mask, it was awkward when Gustav realized that Asger was standing in the room. The manager, on the other hand, seemed relieved.

"Oh, there you are. I've got the intelligence services on the phone. They asked me to find Gustav because they couldn't get hold of you, but now you can speak to them yourself."

He handed the phone to Asger. One of Hartung's arrogant bodyguards ordered him to drive Gustav to his mother at the ministry, where an emergency had arisen: the police had found the address where the murder suspects were staying—some abandoned slaughterhouse in Sydhavnen. Asger felt his throat constrict. Then, however, it occurred to him that the police had no idea yet it was *him* they were looking for. He was reprimanded for not answering his phone, and then he left the hall again with the little bastard. The manager followed them with his eyes, so he had to usher Gustav into the car, although none of that mattered now. The ministry was the last place Asger was about to go.

"Why are we going this way? This isn't the way to my—"

"Shut your fucking mouth and give me your phone."

The boy in the backseat is too astonished to react.

"Give me your phone! Are you deaf?!"

Gustav obeys, and once Asger has the phone in his hand, he throws it out of the open window, hearing it clunking and clattering over the wet asphalt behind them. Asger realizes the boy is scared, but he doesn't care. The only thing worrying him now is where the hell he and Benedikte should go, because at no point did they plan a concrete escape route. Asger had imagined they'd be long gone before the police suspected a thing, but it hasn't panned out like that. His head is abuzz with panicky thoughts, but he knows Benedikte would forgive him. It isn't his fault the plan has fallen through. She'll understand, and as long as they're together it will all be fine.

Asger had felt like that from the moment he'd looked into her dark eyes. They met at the shabby old high school in Tingbjerg with its tied-back curtains, where he'd been a few years above her, and he'd been in love with her ever since. They'd skived off, and drank, smoked, and said fuck you to the entire world as they lay on their backs in the grass beside the ring-road crash barrier, and Benedikte had been the first girl he'd slept with. But then he'd gotten chucked out of school because of all the fist fights, and when he'd ended up at a juvenile institution in South Jutland, the relationship had fizzled out. Almost ten years later, he'd bumped into her again at the hippie commune at Christiania, where she'd been with one of her nurse friends from the hospital, and the very next day they'd discussed moving in together.

Asger loved it when she nestled up to him and felt protected by him, although deep down he knew she was infinitely stronger than he was. His time in the military had suited him fine, but after two deployments to Afghanistan driving patrol vehicles and supply trucks, he'd quit; he was beginning to suffer from panic attacks, and often woke up at night bathed in sweat, feeling fragile. But Benedikte took his hand, held it fast in hers, and calmed him down. Until the next time, at least. When she came home from her shift, she always told him about the kids she'd treated on the ward, and one day she said she wanted a family of her own. Asger saw in her face how much it meant to her. They soon found a cheap, roomy place in the former slaughterhouse— nobody else fancied living there—and when Benedikte got pregnant they made sure Asger was registered at the address of an old soldier friend. That way she'd be eligible for the single-parent benefits they needed.

Asger didn't understand what happened to her after the birth, and he started thinking it must be the kid's fault. Having it taken into care was a shock, of course, but on the other hand he'd never really gotten attached to the boy. After the delivery, he worked tough hours as a scaffolder to bring in cash, and in his eyes Bene-dikte was a good mom—certainly much better than his, who was always crashing at their place or whee-dling money out of him for booze. Benedikte contacted lawyers, newspapers, and TV channels, railing against that stupid whore Rosa Hartung, but then it all came to nothing, and she explained, tears in her eyes, that the journalists didn't want to help them anymore. Shortly afterward, the boy passed away from some lung disease or other, and that changed everything. Benedikte was forcibly committed because of a bust-up with one of the fuckheads from the welfare office, and every day after work Asger drove to Roskilde to visit her at the psychi-atric ward. At first she was too medicated even to make facial expressions, and he was given long, incomprehensible explanations by a female doctor he felt like slamming into the wall. Although Asger was painfully slow at it, he started reading newspapers and magazines out loud to Benedikte. Going home and letting himself into the slaughterhouse at night, he felt alone and powerless. Often he had to drink himself to sleep in front of the TV, but when the minister's daughter went missing last autumn, they started making progress.

The minister losing a child had been a great comfort to Benedikte, and one afternoon when he'd driven down after work, she'd actually put the newspaper out for him on the chair so that he could read it aloud. That was the day the investigation was wrapped up and the case was closed. Gradually, the articles had petered out, but Benedikte had begun to smile again, and when the snow came and the ice froze on the lake behind the hospital, they started taking long walks. In early spring, just as Asger thought they'd put the whole episode behind them, the papers announced that Hartung would be back to work after the summer holiday. It said she was looking forward to it. Benedikte took Asger's hand and clasped it, and Asger knew he would do anything she said as long as her hand was in his.

They started planning as soon as Benedikte was discharged. Their first thought was to threaten Hartung with anonymous emails and texts, break into her house and smash shit up, maybe even run her down and leave her by the roadside. But when Benedikte visited her website looking for an email address, an ad popped up saying that the ministry was looking for a new driver, and the plan grew more concrete.

Benedikte wrote Asger's application, and not long afterward he was called for an interview with some deputy at the ministry. It was obvious the idiots had no clue about his connection to Benedikte and the media dispute with the minister, presumably because he was still registered at a different address. In the interview, they emphasized that Asger had a strong military record, was flexible, without family obligations, and afterward he had a casual chat with an intelligence agent who was supposed to screen the various candidates. When, later, he was told he'd gotten the job, he and Benedikte had celebrated by collaging together Facebook photos of the Hartung girl to make the email, ready to welcome the minister back on her first day at work.

The day Asger started at his new job, he met Rosa Hartung for the first time. He picked her up outside her big luxury villa in Østerbro and was ordered around by her advisor, Vogel, the kind of arrogant asshole Asger couldn't help but want to punch. Not long after that, they scrawled on the minister's car using the blood of a few rats from the old slaughterhouse. They'd come up with several other spiteful pranks as well, when suddenly all these weird murder cases and chestnut men with mysterious fingerprints started popping up, and Rosa Hartung got dragged into them. That part had been fine by him—by Benedikte as well—but then the bomb had dropped: Rosa Hartung's daughter, whom the whole world thought was dead and gone, might not be dead after all.

The notion had spurred them on, but now Rosa Hartung was protected by intelligence agents. Even for Asger, it was impossible to get to her, so instead Benedikte asked him about the little bastard. Shifting his focus, he accepted it would be more worthwhile to snatch the boy. Asger also thought the police might believe it was the murderer who'd kidnapped Gustav, and now, as he signals and turns off the highway, he can't help but appreciate the irony that he and Benedikte are wanted for crimes they know fuck all about.

The rain hammers against the windshield, and the last light of day has vanished by the time he reaches the emergency lane. At the end, he can see the van they picked up from Hertz that morning, but he deliberately parks twenty meters away and switches off the engine. Asger takes his things out of the glove compartment and turns briefly toward the boy.

"You stay there until somebody comes and finds you. You stay there. Got that?!"

The boy nods timidly. Asger climbs out, slams the door, and runs across to Benedikte, who has leapt out of the van and is waiting for him in the rain, although she's wearing only a thin gilet and red hoodie.

She does not look pleased. She must be able to tell that things have not gone according to plan, and Asger explains breathlessly what has happened.

"There are only two options left, baby. Either we get the hell out of here or we drive straight to a police station and explain the whole fucking thing before it gets worse. What do you reckon?"

But Benedikte doesn't respond. Nor when he flings open the door of the rented van and stretches out his hand for the keys. She's standing in the rain, staring somewhere behind him with the silent, serious gaze that has muted her smile and laughter far too long. When Asger glances over his shoulder, he realizes it's the little bastard's anxious face, resting against the tinted window of the ministerial car, that she's focused on. All at once, Asger knows she isn't about to change her mind.

90

As Rosa follows the intelligence agent down the stairs from the prime minister's office, she tries in vain to get hold of Steen on his mobile. She can hardly wait to speak to him—she knows he'll share the feelings whirring inside her right now. Moments earlier, the agent had interrupted her meeting to inform her that the police had just conducted a raid and found what was assumed to be the killers' hideout. Rosa had tried to suppress her emotions for so long, but after Steen made her see that Kristine's fingerprints on the chestnuts had to mean something, she began to yield to longing. The police's discovery might be the breakthrough they've been waiting for, and yet there's still something making her anxious and uneasy.

When Rosa reaches the door to Prins Jørgens Gård, which is normally reserved for the prime minister's office, several agents are waiting for her. They shield her as they guide her toward a dark car, and after the car has traversed the hundred-yard stretch to the Ministry for Social Affairs, they repeat the precaution while she climbs out and walks toward the main entrance.

Rosa ignores the questions from the journalists who've set up camp by the doors, and when she gets inside and passes the security guards she finds Liu standing by the elevator, waiting to accompany her upstairs. Ever since the media got hold of the sensational news about Kristine, they'd made countless approaches, although she had no intention of making any comment. At first, she was exasperated and angry with Steen when he started raving about Kristine's stall, her friend Mathilde, chestnut men, and chestnut animals. She knew he drank, and she knew he made an effort every single day to show that he was strong, but in reality he was perhaps even more frayed than she was. They'd argued about the significance of the fingerprints on the chestnuts at the first two murder scenes—whether they were important, whether Mathilde and Kristine had actually made chestnut men the year before—but she realized it didn't matter what she said, because Steen couldn't be held back.

Maybe no one else was on his side, either at home or in the police, but at last he'd talked her around. Not because she believed his reasoning, but because she believed *him*, because she wanted to believe. Steen was no longer the shadow of himself he'd been for so many months, and when she'd asked him in a quivering voice whether he really believed their girl might still be alive, he'd nodded and taken her hands, and she'd burst into tears. They had made love for the first time in more than six months, and Steen had told her about his plan. She'd supported him without knowing whether she could actually go through with it, but then on Friday evening he'd announced on the news that he believed Kristine was still alive. Just as he'd done a year earlier, he'd encouraged people to come forward with information, and asked the kidnapper to let Kristine go. Rosa had tried to watch the feature with Gustav, preparing the ground as well as she could. But Gustav had been angry, he hadn't understood, and Rosa had sympathized with his confusion and reluctance. She'd almost regretted their decision. Later that same night, Rosa and Steen had been informed that yet another chestnut doll marked with a fingerprint had been found at a crime scene—the third one—and the news had bolstered their spirits, even though the head of Homicide and the two detectives who'd interviewed her today had insisted they shouldn't get their hopes up.

All the well-meaning messages from people who'd seen Steen on the news had proven useless, however, and nor had Steen's self-initiated investigation into Kristine's activities on the day she disappeared produced any result. Over the weekend, he'd begun reconstructing the various routes Kristine might have taken from the sports hall, hoping to find new possibilities or witnesses that could help solve the riddle. As an architect, he had access to plans of sewer systems, tunnels, and electrical substations, which might have been used to stow Kristine quickly out of sight. It was like looking for a needle in a haystack, but Rosa had been moved to see how dedicated he was to the task. So she was looking forward to telling him the news that interrupted her meeting moments earlier, an unpleasant meeting, which had begun when the prime minister greeted her at the door.

"Come in, Rosa. How are you doing?"

He gave her a hug.

"Not brilliant, thanks. I've reached out to Gert Bukke several times for another meeting, but I've heard nothing back, so I think we should start negotiating with the other side ASAP."

"It wasn't Bukke I meant—right now it's clear why he doesn't want to sit down with us. I meant you and Steen."

Rosa had thought she was supposed to report on the stalled-out budgetary negotiations, but the justice minister was there too, and the agenda was clearly quite different.

"Please don't misunderstand me. We appreciate your position, but as you know, the government has already taken a few scratches to the paintwork this year, and the current situation certainly isn't helping matters. Steen's appearances in the media are an implied criticism of the justice minister's work. The minister has explained several times that Kristine's tragic case was thoroughly investigated—that no stone was left unturned, that everything was done to help you, and you yourself expressed gratitude for that—but now there are serious doubts being raised about his credibility."

"I'd say the credibility of the whole *government*," the justice minister had interjected. "My office has been inundated with calls, day and night. Journalists are putting in freedom of information requests left right and center, the opposition wants the case reopened, and there've even been a few calls to drag me into an official meeting to discuss it. Fine by me, but this morning the prime minister himself was asked to comment on the case."

"I have no intention of doing so, of course, but the pressure is unmistakable."

"What do you want me to do?"

"I'm asking you to toe the justice minister's official line. Distance yourself from what Steen is saying. I understand that will be difficult, but I need you to live up to the confidence I showed in you by allowing you to return as minister."

Rosa was incensed. She insisted that there *were* uncertainties about the case. The prime minister tried to find a compromise, but the justice minister was only getting more frustrated before they were interrupted. Rosa didn't care. As far as she was concerned, they could both shove it, and she leaves a hasty message on Steen's voicemail as she and Liu enter the office.

"How did it go with the PM?" asks Vogel.

"Doesn't matter. What do you know?"

Vogel, two intelligence agents, Engells, and a few other colleagues are gathered around the table, and she sits down while they summarize the situation. Ten minutes ago, Intelligence gave the ministry the name of the individual renting the property in Sydhavnen, and Engells had immediately located the case file on Benedikte Skans. They go through it for her, although

Rosa remembers it now, and Engells and Vogel outdo each other in speculation about what might be going on. One of the agents gets a phone call, and he steps out of the room to answer it. Rosa hears the other agent ask her whether she recalls any recent contact with Benedikte Skans—or her boyfriend, for that matter. They still haven't managed to get a picture of him, but there are lots of old press photos of Benedikte Skans.

"This is her."

Rosa recognizes the young woman with dark, furious eyes. It's the girl who bumped into her just over a week ago in the lobby. She wore a gilet and a red hoodie, and they collided the same day someone scrawled in blood on her car.

"I can confirm that. I saw her too."

The agent jots down what Vogel has said, and Engells continues reading from the case file: Benedikte Skans's son was taken into care, but tragically the boy died with his foster family, and suddenly it occurs to Rosa why she's so uneasy.

"Why hasn't Gustav arrived?"

Vogel takes her hand. "The driver is bringing him now. Everything's okay, Rosa."

"What else do you remember about Benedikte Skans? Was she with anybody that day at Christiansborg?" the agent persists.

But the sense of unease has snagged. For some reason, it crosses Rosa's mind that the driver had asked yesterday whether he or Steen was driving Gustav to tennis. But it's the sound of Engells's voice that makes her stiffen.

"Apparently, we don't know as much about the boyfriend, the child's father, except that he was deployed to Afghanistan as a driver and is called Asger Neergaard . . ."

Vogel goes rigid too, and they exchange a glance.

"Asger Neergaard?"

"Yeah . . ."

Instantly, Rosa checks an app on her phone, while Vogel leaps so violently from his chair that it overturns behind him. It's a security app, Find My Child, which she and Steen installed last year to keep track of where Gustav's phone is located. But the GPS map is blank. Gustav's mobile isn't broadcasting a signal. Before Rosa can say that out loud, the intelligence agent strides back through the door, lowering his phone from his ear. The moment she sees his face, she feels the floor evaporate beneath her—just like the day Kristine disappeared.

91

It dawns on Hess that he's not been listening for several minutes. He's sitting to Thulin's left at the long table in the operation room, his eyes fixed apathetically on the windows overlooking the courtyard, which now are shrouded in darkness. Around him is a thrum of busy, stressed voices, reminding everybody of the situation's gravity. He's been here before. No matter where in the world you are, it's always the same story when a kidnapping comes in. Except that it is significantly more intense when the victim is the child of a prominent politician.

Hartung's ministerial car was found abandoned nearly five hours earlier on the shoulder of a highway southwest of Copenhagen. No trace of the boy, Benedikte Skans, or Asger Neergaard. No demands from the kidnappers either. The discovery of the empty car has launched one of the biggest searches in Danish history. Borders, airports, train stations, bridges, ferry terminals, and coastlines are being guarded or patrolled, and Hess feels as though the entire fleet of squad cars has been dispatched onto the streets to keep a lookout. Control of the operation is being shared between Intelligence and the Copenhagen Police, and even members of the Civil Defense Force have been yanked away from their dinner plates and sent out into the autumn gloom. Colleagues in Norway, Sweden, and Germany have been apprised, as have Interpol and Europol, but Hess hopes they will play no part in the search. If the international authorities contact them, it will be because there are indications the kidnappers have crossed several borders, in which case any chances of finding Gustav Hartung are dramatically reduced. Of finding him alive, especially. The rule of thumb in kidnapping cases is that the chances are best in the first twenty-four hours, when the trail is still warm. Yet with every passing day the likelihood decreases, and Hess knows from the statistics at the Hague that the estimate is based on actual cases of missing children. He tries to think of something other than the kidnapping case he'd been involved in a few years earlier, which had required the collaboration of the German and French police. A two-year-old boy from Karlsruhe had disappeared, and the French-speaking kidnapper demanded two million euros' ransom from his father, a German bank manager. Hess was present at the exchange, but the money was never picked up at the appointed place, and one month later they found the boy's body in a drain, just five hundred yards from the bank manager's house. The medical examination revealed that the boy's skull had been cracked, probably because the kidnapper had dropped him onto the asphalt near the manhole cover as he fled the area, the same day as the kidnapping. They never found the killer.

The circumstances of Gustav Hartung's disappearance are different, luckily, and there are still grounds for optimism. Detectives are currently interviewing Asger Neergaard's colleagues at the ministry and at Christiansborg, while others are doing the same for Benedikte Skans at the Rigshospital. So far nobody can say where the couple might have fled with the boy, but it is too soon to rule out the possibility. The news is filled with images of Gustav Hartung, which will make it harder for the kidnappers to travel with him in public. That's both good and bad. Good because most citizens will soon be able to recognize Gustav Hartung and inform the authorities if they catch sight of him. Bad because it will put intense pressure on the kidnappers, and there is always a chance that might lead to a fatal decision made in the heat of the moment. The issue was a matter of fierce discussion among senior officers and intelligence agents, but in the end it proved moot: the Hartung family insisted on putting out an alert for the boy, silencing all debate. Hess understands their decision perfectly. One year ago, the family had gone through a nightmare from which they've barely woken up, and now a fresh one has begun. No avenue can be left unexplored. Beside him, he hears Thulin's impatient voice addressing Genz, who is in the middle of updating them from his post at the Forensics Department via the loudspeaker on Nylander's mobile phone, which is lying on the table.

"But there's no news on tracing their phones?"

"Nope. Neither Benedikte Skans nor Asger Neergaard have had their phones switched on since 4:17 this afternoon, which I think we can assume was the time of the kidnapping. It's possible they have other unregistered phones, but we can't—"

"What about iPads or laptops from their home? There was at least one iPad and a Lenovo laptop, and there might be digital receipts for flights, ferries, trains. Or any credit card charges?"

"As I say, we haven't found anything useful yet. It'll take a little while to access the deleted files on the Lenovo, because it's been damaged and—"

"So you haven't checked shit. Genz, we don't have time for this! If there are deleted files on the Lenovo, all you need to do is run them through a recovery program. I mean, for Christ's sake—"

"Thulin, Genz knows what he's doing. Genz, tell me as soon as you find something."

"Of course. Back to the grindstone."

Nylander hangs up and puts the phone back in his pocket. Thulin is standing like a boxer who's just been told she isn't allowed into the ring.

"Anything else? We're moving on," continues Nylander.

Jansen slides his notepad forward on the table.

"I've spoken to the psych hospital in Roskilde. Nothing we can use here and now, but there's no doubt Benedikte Skans has had a screw loose for a while since the child's death. One of the consultants insists the woman made a full recovery during her stay, but she can't rule out the possibility of violent behavior. Great, thanks. That's so reassuring when you bear in mind that Skans works on a pediatric ward."

"So no idea where she is. What about Asger Neergaard?"

"Ex-soldier, thirty years old, deployed to Afghanistan as a driver twice with Battle Groups Seven and Eleven. Decent record, but when you start asking former comrades at the barracks, you hear that some of them thought he left the military for reasons beyond simply getting sick of it."

"Spell it out."

"Some of them said he was getting shaky hands and avoiding contact with others. Developed a temper, got aggressive, plus a few other signs of PTSD, although he was certainly never treated for it. How Intelligence could have approved him as a ministerial driver is beyond me, and I imagine a head or two will roll."

"But nobody you spoke to knows where he might be?"

"Nope. Nor the mother. At least, she's not saying so."

"Then we call a halt to the meeting here and keep going. We've got bugger all, and that's not good enough. There's no doubt about the motive in the Hartung case, so we need to focus all our energies on finding the boy. For the time being, we'll divert resources from the inquiry into the four murders they committed, just until the boy is safe and sound."

"*If* they committed the murders."

It's the first time Hess has spoken during the meeting, and Nylander looks at him as though he were a stranger at the door, wanting to come inside. Hess continues before the door slams shut.

"So far there's nothing concrete at the couple's property to indicate they're responsible for the killings. They sent Rosa Hartung death threats, and they planned and carried out the kidnapping of her son. But there's nothing there about the three female victims, and Asger Neergaard has an alibi for at least one of the murders—according to Intelligence, while Anne Sejer-Lassen was being murdered he was standing with Rosa Hartung and her secretary in a courtyard near the ministry."

"But Benedikte Skans wasn't."

"No, but that doesn't necessarily mean she killed Anne Sejer-Lassen. Anyway, what would their motive have been?"

"I don't want to hear any more rambling defenses of your visit to Linus Bekker. Benedikte Skans and Asger Neergaard are our prime suspects, and we'll discuss your little excursion later."

"But I'm not trying to defend—"

"Hess, if you and Thulin had spent your time sensibly on the case files at the ministry you might have got to Skans and Neergaard sooner, in which case Gustav Hartung wouldn't have been abducted! Do you get what I'm saying here?"

Hess goes quiet. He's been thinking the same thing himself, and for a moment he feels guilty, even though he knows it isn't justified. Nylander leaves the room, Jansen and the rest of them at his heels, while Thulin picks up her coat from the chair behind her.

"Right now what matters is finding the boy. If they didn't commit the murders, we'll figure out who did."

She doesn't wait for an answer. Hess watches her walk down the corridor, then he peers through the panes of glass at the detectives scuttling diligently around with the energy and purpose that take hold when a case is nearing its conclusion. Yet Hess can't share that feeling. He feels as though the puppets' strings are still hanging from the ceiling, and when he stands up it is to go outside and get some fresh air.

92

Asger isn't normally bothered by the dark. His eyes adjust rapidly, and he usually feels calm and in control, even when driving at high speed in the pouring rain, as he is now.

In Afghanistan, he really came to enjoy night driving. When troops or supplies had to be transported from one camp to the next, it sometimes happened after sundown, and although Asger's fellow drivers associated those trips with danger, it had always struck him differently. Anyway, he loved being behind the wheel. It was like his mind grew hushed and his field of vision transformed with the rhythm of the new surroundings. But in Afghanistan, he learned he liked night driving best. Even though there was less to look at. The darkness felt protective, bringing a calm and a balance he otherwise lacked—but it doesn't feel like that now. The inky road is surrounded by dense forest on both sides, and although he can barely see it, he feels as though danger might lurch out of the blackness at any moment and swallow him whole. He feels his skin prickle and the pressure in his ears increase, and as he steps on the accelerator it's as if he's trying to escape his own shadow.

There have been police blockades everywhere, and they've had to change direction constantly. First they made for the port at Gedser, then the Swedish ferry at Helsingør, but both times they'd been overtaken by police cars with sirens blaring, and it wasn't hard to guess their destination. Right now, Asger has set a course for Sjællands Odde, where ferries leave from the tip of the peninsula. The Great Belt Bridge seems too obvious and thus out of the question, but Asger hopes the ferry to Jutland might be unguarded, although he knows it's unlikely. His head whirrs with thoughts about what they should do if that road too is blocked, but he has no next step, and Benedikte is sitting taciturn and gloomy in the passenger seat.

Asger wasn't in favor of bringing the little shit along, but it wasn't up for discussion. He understands. If they just gave up, then the whole thing was a farce; then the minister bitch would never understand what it was she'd done. It's only right that she should go through hell too, and Asger has no moral qualms about kidnapping the boy, who has only his mother to thank for the fact that he's now being flung about in the back of the van.

Asger slams on the brakes. For a moment, he feels the van skid out of control on the slippery asphalt, until he eases off and straightens the vehicle. Farther down the road, he can see the glare of blue lights among the dripping trees, and although he can't see the squad cars, he knows they'll be waiting by yet another blockade after the next bend. Pulling over, he slows down until the car rolls to a stop.

"What the hell are we doing?"

Benedikte doesn't respond. Asger turns around and begins racing back toward the road, talking loudly through their options.

When she finally speaks, it isn't what he's been expecting. "Go into the forest. Next turn."

"Why? What're we doing in there?"

"Turn off into the forest, I said."

When they reach the next exit, Asger turns off into the forest, and soon they are driving down a smaller, bumpy gravel road. Then he understands what she wants. Benedikte has realized, of course, that they are surrounded, so now they are doing the only sensible thing: retreating as far as possible into the woods so they can wait for the storm to pass. Asger had been the soldier, so it should've been him to think of it, but as ever it's Benedikte who has a way out. After they've been driving for three or four minutes, before the forest is quite thick enough for Asger's liking, she asks him abruptly to stop the car.

"No, not yet. We need to get farther in. They'll see us if they—"

"Stop the car. Stop the car now!"

Asger brakes, and the vehicle jars to a halt. He switches off the engine but leaves the headlights on. Benedikte sits still for a moment. He can't see her face, only hear her breathing and the rain on the roof. She opens the glove compartment and takes something out before opening the van door.

"What are you doing? We don't have time to stop here!"

Benedikte's door slams, and for a moment Asger sits in the van, listening to the echo of his own voice. In the beam of the headlights, he sees her walk around the front of the van, and as she turns to pass his door, he opens it instinctively and climbs out.

"What are you doing?"

Benedikte slips past him, reaching determinedly for the sliding door to the inside of the van. Asger catches a glimmer of the sharp object in her right hand, and remembers he left his military knife in the glove compartment that morning when he picked up the van from Hertz. It dawns on him what she wants, and although it surprises him that he has feelings for the little bastard after all, he grabs Benedikte. He feels how strong she is, how much she wants this.

"Let me go! Let me go, I told you!"

They grapple in the dark, and Asger feels the knife cut him somewhere in the groin as she tries to rip herself free.

"He's just a boy! He's not the one who did anything to us!"

Gradually, he manages to pull her close. Her arms go limp, and she begins to sob. The tears overpower her, and Asger doesn't know how long they stand there in the forest, but it feels like an eternity. It's the best moment in a long time. He knows Benedikte has realized the same thing as him. The forces arrayed against them are too great, but they still have each other. He can't see her face, but her tears ebb away, and he takes the knife from her hand and chucks it onto the ground.

"We'll let the boy out. It's easier if it's just us two, and as soon as he's found, the cops will ease off a bit. Okay?"

Asger is sure it will work out for them now, now he can feel her body so close to his. He strokes her face and kisses her tears away, feeling her nod and snivel. She's still clinging to his hand, and with the other he reaches to pull the sliding door aside. If the boy is told what direction to walk, he'll reach the police blockade in a few hours, and that will give Asger and Benedikte the time they need.

It's the noise that makes Asger pause and glance around watchfully in the dark. The distant sound of an approaching engine. He looks back down the way they've come, still holding Benedikte's hand. Approximately fifty yards away, a set of car headlights are reflected in the puddles on the road, and soon he and Benedikte are bathed in light, blinking. The car stops, and after the driver has observed them for a moment, the engine and then the headlights are switched off.

It's now utterly dark on the road. A thousand thoughts explode inside Asger's head. First he thinks it's an unmarked police car, but the police wouldn't be so calm in a situation like this, and for an instant he thinks it might be a farmer or a forestry official. Then it strikes him that the only reason anybody would be driving up the gravel road at this hour is to find *them*. But nobody can have seen them turn into the woods, and he made sure ages ago that their phones couldn't be traced.

Asger feels Benedikte's hand tense in his, and when he hears a car door open, he asks a question in the dark that goes unanswered.

"Who is it?" repeats Asger. From the approaching footsteps, he realizes he'll find out soon enough, and immediately he bends to pick up the knife from the grass.

93

Thulin empties the garbage onto two newspaper inserts on the kitchen floor, then takes a fork from the drawer and begins to root through it. She wears latex gloves, and the smell of rotten food, cigarette butts, and tinned goods is acrid in her nostrils as she unfolds the soiled receipts, hoping they'll reveal where the couple has fled. Genz and the Forensics techs had already gone through the whole place earlier that day, but Thulin prefers to do her own spot tests. Yet she finds nothing. Only everyday items bought at the supermarket, as well as dry-cleaning receipts, presumably from the clothes Asger Neergaard wore when he drove Rosa Hartung. Thulin leaves the garbage on the inserts. She's in the habitable part of the old slaughterhouse, and apart from her and a few patrol units watching the buildings from a slight distance, the place is empty. So far she has to admit Genz and his people have done their jobs flawlessly. There is nothing here to indicate that the young couple has any other place to stay, nor any sign they'd planned escape routes or alternative hideouts. Earlier that day they'd confirmed that one of the cold stores in the old slaughterhouse had been outfitted with a mattress on the floor, a quilt, a portable toilet, and a few Donald Duck magazines—it seems clear that this is where they intended to keep Gustav Hartung.

Thulin shivers at the thought; still, from what she's observed in the house there's no hint they are dealing with cold-blooded killers. Not the way she imagines them, anyway. It's obvious that Asger Neergaard lived here and not in the room he'd supposedly been renting from a former comrade, and he clearly had a fondness for Japanese manga featuring naked women. But that's the most radical thing she's found among his possessions. On the face of it, it seems to say more about his character that he liked seventies sitcoms and old Danish movies starring Dirch Passer and Ove Sprogøe; the best you could say about those was that they were all set in a sun-drenched era of green fields and fluttering Danish flags. He had played them on a dusty DVD player and watched them on an old flat-screen TV, lying on a scruffy leather sofa, but that didn't scream psychopath or insanity to Thulin.

The traces they found of Benedikte's personality were more concerning: textbooks about the council's powers to take children into care, printouts of paragraphs from social-welfare legislation, which had been interpreted and combed through, as well as legal journals about child welfare and similar topics. Among her belongings in several drawers in the living room there were files and ring binders dedicated to the case about the couple's little boy, as well as to the correspondence she'd had with the authorities and her court-appointed lawyer. On almost every page she had added handwritten notes, some illegible, but all crowded with question and exclamation marks, and the rage and frustration behind them was palpable. Yet there were also albums from Benedikte's time at school, one with a photograph of her and Asger Neergaard in the grass outside an ugly crash barrier, as well as certificates and papers from her nursing training and various additional courses on pregnancy and birth.

The more Thulin saw, the more she struggled to accept that the couple could be the killers she and Hess were investigating. It was at least as difficult to imagine that they could have managed to get the better of a vast murder inquiry for several weeks, so she reached the conclusion that Hess was right to be skeptical.

Seeing the walls of his apartment at Nørrebro that morning, she'd started to think he was losing the plot. That he simply couldn't accept the Hartung girl was long dead. Nor had it done much to change her mind when he suggested those unorthodox visits to Genz and the secure unit. She'd reminded herself that she didn't really know a thing about Hess or his past, but their trip to see Bekker had left her with doubts, and now she could see herself and Hess trying to speak to him again, trying to find out what he knew about the murders and Kristine Hartung.

Right now, however, what mattered was Gustav Hartung, and when Thulin has finished rifling through the chests of drawers in the bedrooms she goes downstairs: if she drives to the Forensics Department, she can help Genz with the Lenovo laptop that seems to be proving tricky. She's rounded the corner at the bottom of the stairs and is walking down the hall when a faint sound makes her stop short. An alarm is going off somewhere outside the house. The sound is slower in rhythm than a car alarm, but just as insistent. Turning back and cutting through the kitchen, Thulin reaches the corridor that leads to the slaughterhouse itself. She opens the door, and the sound grows clearer. The vast oblong hall is unlit, and she pauses, unsure where to find the light switches. In a flash it strikes her that if the couple isn't behind the killings, the real murderer might be somewhere in the dark. She tries to shake off the thought—there's no reason to believe he'd come out here now. Even so, she takes out her gun and turns off the safety catch.

By the light of her mobile phone, Thulin edges her way through the old slaughterhouse. She moves toward the sound, passing one cold store after the next, including the one meant for Gustav Hartung. A few of them are completely empty apart from meat hooks hanging from the ceiling, but most are stacked with boxes and old junk.

She pauses by the door to the final storeroom. The sound is coming from inside, and she is barely two steps across the threshold before she realizes Neergaard must have been using it as a gym. In her phone's wan glow she can see battered old kettlebells, a barbell, a rickety bike, and a punching bag fighting with muddy military boots and a grubby camouflage uniform for the limited floor space. What catches her attention, however, is the stench. Although she is in a disused slaughterhouse, none of the other rooms smell like rotten meat—but this one does. Scarcely has the thought crossed her mind before she notices a movement in the corner. She whips the beam of light toward it, and although the animals are bathed in white light they don't react. Four or five rats are gnawing frenziedly at the bottom of a battered mini-fridge, which is standing in the corner next to some gardening tools and a folded ironing board. The display on the front of the fridge is flashing and beeping, presumably because the rats have bitten through the lower strip of rubber that seals the door, forcing it slightly ajar. Thulin approaches the fridge, but it isn't until she gives the rats a nudge with her foot that they scurry off between her legs. They pause a short distance away, darting to and fro, squeaking hysterically. When Thulin gingerly swings open the door and looks inside the fridge, she has to clap her hand to her mouth to stop herself throwing up.

94

"**B**ut you're *absolutely* sure? Benedikte Skans was on a night shift Friday, October 16th, to Saturday, October 17th?"

"Yup, hundred percent. It's just been confirmed by the head nurse on the ward. She worked the same shift herself."

Hess thanks the detective and hangs up, just as he's reaching the floor that houses Rosa Hartung's offices. It's nearly eleven at night, and the front office buzzes with suppressed nerves and ringing phones. A few detectives are still interviewing members of the staff, two red-eyed female employees are talking softly and sniffling, and there are white plastic bags of takeout sushi scattered across the tables, which no one has yet had the time to open.

"Is the minister in her office?"

The harassed-looking ministerial secretary shoots Hess a nod, and he makes for the mahogany doors as he memorizes the pass code to the iPad he borrowed moments earlier in the drivers' break room at Christiansborg.

Thulin was right to say the Hartung boy was more important than anything else just now, so Hess drove from the station straight to the ministry to help dig up information about the couple's likely behavior and hideouts by questioning the people who had daily dealings with Asger Neergaard. Very rapidly, however, it had become plain that no one knew anything. The detectives have already done their jobs, and Hess wasn't going to come up with anything new by talking to the same people himself. Neergaard wasn't on friendly terms with anybody, and certainly never brought up his private life, what he did in his free time, or anything else that might be of interest. Instead Hess has heard nothing but descriptions of his personality. Some people thought the driver had been a little off from the get-go—weird, quiet, maybe even a little dangerous—but for Hess such descriptions bore all the hallmarks of hindsight. For hours the TV channels had been carpet-bombing the nation with the search for Gustav Hartung, giving descriptions of the alleged kidnappers, one of whom—sensationally enough—had proven to be Rosa Hartung's very own driver. If anybody doubted the story's saleability, they'd only have to glance down at the army of OB vans and journalists gathered on the narrow square outside the ministry, but the downside was that any statements about Neergaard's character had long since been colored by the media. Hess did, however, trust the parts of those statements that made it clear Neergaard was introverted and slightly simple, kept to himself, and spent his breaks smoking and making phone calls by the canal—unlike his colleagues, who preferred the warmth of the drivers' break room at Christiansborg.

Hess made a visit there himself, and an older driver told him he'd repeatedly had to help Asger with the locking system in the garage where the ministerial cars were parked overnight. That alone made it seem rather improbable that he and his girlfriend had been capable of planning the meticulously contrived murders of Laura Kjær, Anne Sejer-Lassen, and Jessie Kvium.

It seemed more improbable still when Hess was introduced to the drivers' digital calendar by another of Asger Neergaard's colleagues—the energy minister's driver, if he remembered correctly. The various drivers' activities were closely tracked by the system, and it was every driver's responsibility to note in the digital log where they were at what time, as well as what they were doing. Hess's eye quickly fell on a particular date in Asger Neergaard's calendar, after which Hess returned to the ministry. On the way he phoned one of the detectives dispatched to Benedikte Skans's workplace, and that was what he wanted to discuss with Rosa Hartung.

When Hess enters the minister's office, it's obvious she is worried sick about her son. Her hands shake, her eyes are fearful and red, and her mascara is smeared as though she's tried to wipe it off. Her husband is there too, engrossed in a telephone conversation. He seems about to end it when he sees Hess, but Hess shakes his head, signaling that he hasn't brought any news. Rosa Hartung and her husband had chosen to stay at the ministry, partly because they needed to be questioned about Asger Neergaard and partly because the staff could help keep them abreast of the current situation. Hess guesses too that they prefer not to be alone. At home they'd be face-to-face with their fears, but here they can at least feel like they are doing something—questioning the detectives about the results of each interview as it happens.

While Steen Hartung continues his conversation, Hess looks at Rosa Hartung and points at the meeting table.

"Can we sit down for a moment? I have a few questions I hope you can answer. It would be a big help."

"Do you have any updates? What's happening right now?"

"I'm afraid there's no news. But we've got every officer mobilized, every vehicle out on the streets, and every border under surveillance."

He can see the fear in her eyes, and he knows she realizes her son is in mortal danger, but he has to turn the conversation toward his discovery, so in the moment it takes for her to accept that he hasn't brought any news, he places the iPad on the table.

"On Friday, October 16th, at 11:57 p.m., your driver, Asger Neergaard, wrote in his digital log that he arrived at the Royal Library to pick you up after a function. He noted in the log that he remained on standby in the foyer until 12:43 a.m., and then he wrote, 'Done for the day. Driving home.' Is that accurate? He waited in the foyer and didn't drive you home until that time?"

"I don't understand why this is important. What's it got to do with Gustav?"

Hess doesn't want to agitate her further by reminding her that it was the night of the third and fourth murders. If the information in the log is correct, Asger Neergaard can't possibly have made it out to the community gardens in time to kill both Jessie Kvium and Martin Ricks *and* amputate two hands and a foot before Hess and Thulin arrived. And now that Hess has learned Benedikte Skans was on shift at the pediatric ward that same night, it is a crucial question.

"I can't tell you why it's important right now. But it would be a great help if you could try to think back. Is it correct that he was waiting, and that you didn't drive home until quarter to one?"

"Well, I have no idea why it says that in his log. I cried off that night, so I wasn't there."

"You weren't there?"

Hess tries to hide his disappointment.

"No. Frederik—Frederik Vogel, my advisor—made my excuses."

"You're sure you weren't there? Asger Neergaard wrote—"

"I'm sure. We'd agreed that Frederik and I would walk because it's not far from the ministry. But then we had another chat about it a few hours beforehand. It was the same night my husband was going to be on TV, and Frederik didn't think canceling would be a problem, which was a relief, because I wanted to be with Gustav anyway . . ."

"But if Vogel canceled for you, why does the log say the driver—"

"I don't know. You'll have to ask Frederik."

"Where *is* Frederik?"

"There was something he had to do. I'm sure he'll be back soon. But right now I want to know what's being done to find Gustav."

Frederik Vogel's spacious office is dim and empty. Hess steps inside, shutting the door behind him. It's a nice room. Lounge-like and cozy, unlike the cold, impersonal offices of the ministry. He catches himself thinking this might be the kind of casually luxurious space women think is sexy. Verner Panton lamps, shaggy rya rugs, and low Italian sofas with plenty of soft cushions. All it needed was a little Marvin Gaye, and for an instant Hess considers whether he is jealous because he'll never have the energy to put something like that together.

It isn't the first time that evening Hess has wondered where the minister's advisor has gotten to. He knows that detectives questioned thirty-seven-year-old Frederik Vogel about Asger Neergaard around seven o'clock, and that Vogel had been able to offer up nothing but shock. Yet by the time Hess arrived at the ministry a few hours later the advisor was gone, apparently running an errand in town, according to the secretary.

Which strikes Hess as suggestive, given that his minister is in crisis and besieged by the press.

What Hess knows about Vogel isn't a lot. Rosa Hartung told him previously that he'd always been a great support to her. They'd studied political science together in Copenhagen for several years before going their separate ways after Vogel got into journalism school. They'd kept in touch, and gradually Vogel became a friend of the family. When she was selected as minister, he was the obvious choice as her advisor. He supported her and her family enormously during the difficult year since Kristine's disappearance, and he was a major factor in building up her courage to make a comeback.

"What's he said about your and your husband's hopes that your daughter might still be alive?" Hess had asked.

"Frederik is very protective, so at first he was probably very worried. About my situation as a minister. But now he's backing us to the hilt."

Hess noses around a little, trying to get an impression of the man whose desk is bulging with papers on the old Benedikte Skans case as well as handwritten notes about press strategies, but which otherwise contain nothing of interest. At least, not until Hess happens to nudge the mouse of the MacBook on the desk. The laptop's screen saver begins displaying images of Vogel in various professional contexts: Vogel outside the EU headquarters in Brussels, Vogel shaking hands with the German chancellor in the lobby at Christiansborg, Vogel in New York outside the World Trade Center memorial, Vogel and Rosa Hartung visiting a UN children's aid camp. But among the official photos there suddenly appear personal images of Frederik Vogel and the Hartung family: at children's birthday parties, handball games, and trips to Tivoli. Traditional family images, of which Vogel is a part.

At first Hess tries to tell himself it's nice that his prejudices about a heartless, Machiavellian snake aren't being borne out. But then he realizes abruptly what it is that strikes him as odd. Steen Hartung is missing. He isn't in a single photograph. Instead there are selfies of Vogel with Rosa and the children, or with Rosa by herself, as though they are a couple.

"The minister's secretary said you wanted to speak to me."

The door swings open, and Vogel's eyes come to rest on Hess, growing vigilant as he looks from Hess to the screen, which is still illuminating Hess's face. His coat is wet with rain and his brown hair is disheveled, until he runs a hand through it and strokes it back into place.

"What's the situation? Have you found the driver?"

"Not yet. We couldn't find you either."

"Meetings in town. I've been trying to minimize the amount of prying and exploitation those assholes in the media can do. What about the driver's girlfriend? Surely you've been doing something with your time?"

"We're working on it. Right now I need your help with something else."

"I've got no time for anything else. Make it quick, please."

Hess notices Vogel close the laptop with a discreet, natural-looking gesture as he throws his coat over the chair and takes out his phone.

"On Friday, October 16th, you withdrew the minister from an evening function at the Royal Library. You'd spoken a few hours earlier, and she told you her husband was going to be on TV. You said it would be fine to cancel."

"That's probably true. Except that the minister doesn't need my permission to cancel—she makes those decisions herself."

"But I assume the minister generally does as you advise?"

"I'm not sure how to answer that. Why do you ask?"

"No matter. But it was you who sent her excuses?"

"It was me who called the organizer and canceled on the minister's behalf."

"Did you also tell Asger Neergaard that the minister had canceled and wouldn't have to be driven home after the function?"

"Yes, I did that too."

"It says in his digital log that he was working that evening. That he was on standby in the foyer of the Royal Library from around midnight until nearly quarter to one, waiting for the function to be over so he could drive her home."

"Who the hell would trust something *he* wrote? Maybe he needed it as an alibi for something else he was off doing. I'm pretty sure I let him know. Anyway, isn't it a waste of time pissing around with this stuff when Gustav Hartung is missing?"

"Not quite. Did you tell Asger Neergaard that evening or didn't you?"

"Like I said, I'm pretty sure I did. Or maybe I got somebody else to."

"Who?"

"Why the hell is this important?"

"So it's possible you *didn't* tell him and he *was* waiting in the foyer?"

"If this is what our conversation's going to be about, then I really don't have the time."

"What were you doing that evening?"

Vogel is making for the door, but he stops short and looks at Hess.

"I assume you were supposed to accompany the minister to the Royal Library, but when you canceled that made time for other things?"

The hint of a mocking smile crosses Vogel's face.

"You're not saying what I think you're saying."

"What do you think I'm saying?"

"You're fishing for what I was up to at a particular moment when a crime was occurring instead of concentrating on the kidnapping of the minister's son, but I certainly hope that's not the case."

Hess merely eyes him.

"If you really want to know, I went back to my apartment, watched Steen Hartung's broadcast and prepared for the fallout. I was alone, no witnesses, and with plenty of time to commit a murder and fiddle around with chestnuts all night long. Is that what you want to hear?"

"What about the night of October 6th? Or October 12th around six?"

"I think I'd better tell you that during an official interview with my lawyer present. Until then I'd like to get on with my job. And I think you should get on with yours."

Vogel nods goodbye. Hess doesn't want to let the guy go, but at this moment his phone rings, and Vogel slips through the doorway. The display tells him it's Nylander. Hess has just decided to explain his discovery and his suspicions about Vogel when Nylander forestalls him.

"It's Nylander. Tell everybody to suspend the investigation at the ministry and Christiansborg."

"Why?"

"Because Genz has traced Skans and Neergaard. I'm headed up there now with the task force."

"Headed up where?"

"West of Holbæk, somewhere in the forest. Genz managed to open the Lenovo and found an invoice for a Hertz van in the guy's inbox. He called the company— apparently they rented the van at Vesterport Station this morning and Genz was able to track it. Seems they put tracking units in all their vehicles in case they're stolen. Let everybody know, then get back to the station and write your report."

"But what about—"

Nylander has already hung up. Frustrated, Hess thrusts his phone back into his pocket and hurries over to the door. After notifying a detective of Nylander's instructions he rushes farther down the corridor, and on his way out he catches a glimpse into the minister's office through the open door: Vogel, with a comforting arm around Rosa Hartung.

95

Despite the rain, the trip to northwest Zealand takes only forty minutes with the lights flashing, although it feels like an eternity. Reaching the murky road that runs through the forest, Hess can see the turn he needs. The empty task-force vehicles are parked at the edge of the road near a gravel track, a handful of squad cars beside them, and after showing his badge through the window to two soaking-wet officers, Hess is allowed to continue. The fact that they let him through must mean the operation is over. With what result, however, he can't tell, and he isn't keen to waste time asking a couple of officers who couldn't possibly be fully informed if they are posted out by the main road.

Hess has driven quickly, and he has to force himself to ease up as he races down the gravel road. He ignored

Nylander's orders to go to the station, and on the way there, he decided to check up on Frederik Vogel. Probably he should have done so much earlier.

Something tells him Asger Neergaard will confirm he was at work late on the evening of October 16th. At any rate, Hess has just spoken to Hartung's secretary, who claimed Neergaard had called and woken her up that night just past half twelve to ask where the minister had got to, having waited for her in the foyer at the Royal Library. She'd apologized that nobody had kept him in the loop, and if Neergaard genuinely had been in the foyer then other witnesses would probably be able to confirm that. If Benedikte Skans had been on a night shift at the Rigshospital during the same window, then the couple couldn't possibly have murdered Jessie Kvium and Martin Ricks, which makes Vogel look more interesting. He didn't seem to have an alibi for either of the community garden killings, and Hess is itching to question Asger Neergaard about Vogel's whereabouts at the time of the other two murders. He might even know something about the relationship between Vogel and Rosa Hartung. Maybe there is actually a motive Hess and Thulin haven't clocked before. Hess gets the urge to call Thulin again. He's already tried to get hold of her twice on the drive up from Copenhagen.

Headlights are approaching in the opposite direction along the narrow gravel road, and he has to jerk aside to let an ambulance pass. Its siren isn't going, but Hess can't tell whether that's good or bad. Behind it follows an unmarked police car, and he catches a fleeting glimpse of Nylander in the backseat, absorbed in a conversation on his phone. He keeps driving, now passing dribs and drabs of task-force officers heading back toward the main road, and in their earnest faces he senses the presence of death. When he reaches the cordon he realizes that the situation isn't what he hoped.

There are more police a little farther away, and an area roughly ten yards by ten is harshly lit by floodlights. In the center of the area is a van with the Hertz logo on its tailboard. One front door is open, as is the sliding door, and by its left front wheel lies a figure covered in a white sheet. Another one lies about ten meters distant.

Hess climbs out of the car, heeding neither the rain nor the wind. The only face he recognizes is Jansen's, and although they aren't exactly on good terms, it's Jansen he approaches.

"Where's the boy?"

"What are you doing here?"

"Where is he?"

"The boy's all right. He seems unharmed, but they're taking him to be examined as we speak."

Hess feels a surge of relief, but now he knows who's lying on the earth underneath the two white sheets.

"It was the task force who found him and let him out of the van. Everything went fine, so there's no use for you here, Hess."

"But what happened?"

"Bugger all. We found them like this."

Jansen lifts the sheet from the figure by the front of the van. The young man, whom Hess recognizes as Asger Neergaard, has died with his eyes open, and his torso is a pincushion of stab wounds.

"Our working assumption is that the woman went nuts. We're about six kilometers from one of our block-ades, so they probably drove in here to get out of sight, but she must have realized the jig was up. First she used the military knife on the boyfriend, and then she slit her carotid artery. The bodies were still warm when we arrived, so it happened within the last couple of hours. And no, I'm not rubbing my hands over this—I'd much rather have seen them rot for thirty years for what they did to Ricks."

Hess feels the rain dripping down his cheeks. Jansen lets the sheet fall, so that only Neergaard's lifeless hand is sticking out. For a moment it appears to Hess as though he were reaching toward Benedikte Skans's shrouded body, which lies in the mud less than thirty feet away.

96

"**B**ut what did they say? They must know something by now?"

Rosa knows Frederik Vogel doesn't have the answers, but the questions slip out anyway.

"They're checking and investigating, but the head of Homicide will contact us as soon—"

"It's not good enough. Ask them again, Frederik."

"Rosa—"

"We have a right to know what's going on!"

Vogel decides to humor her, although she can tell he thinks it's pointless ringing up the station again. Deep down she is grateful for his help, because she knows he will do whatever he can, even if he doesn't agree with her methods. He's always been like that, and Rosa can't wait any longer. It's 1:37 a.m., fifteen minutes since she,

Steen, and Vogel brought Gustav home from the Rigshospital. She's already pestered half to death the two
officers on guard outside their home, who are making
sure the army of journalists keep their distance, but the
officers know nothing. Only the head of the murder
squad can give them answers to the questions about
Kristine she is burning to ask.

Rosa began to cry the moment she and Steen entered the A&E at the Rigshospital, where Gustav, looking a bit scruffy after his ordeal, had been brought for
examination. She'd feared the worst, but he was unharmed, and she was allowed to give him a cuddle. He
had few apparent injuries, and now that he is sitting
in the kitchen at his usual spot in the corner, eating
the wholemeal rolls with liver pâté Steen has just made
for him, she can scarcely comprehend that he's been in
mortal danger. Walking up to him, she strokes his hair.

"Do you want anything else to eat? I can make pasta
for you, or—"

"No thanks. I'd rather play FIFA."

Rosa smiles. The answer is a healthy sign, but there
is still so much she doesn't know.

"Gustav, what happened, exactly? What else did
they say?"

"I told you."

"Tell me again."

"They took me with them and locked me in the van. Then they drove for ages, and then they stopped the van, and then they started fighting, but it was raining loads so I couldn't hear what they were saying. Then there was a really long silence, and then the policemen came and opened the door, and that's all I know."

"But what were they arguing about? Did they say anything about your sister? Where were they driving?"

"Mom—"

"Gustav, it's important!"

"Sweetheart, come with me."

Steen draws Rosa into the living room so that Gustav can't hear them, but she refuses to calm down.

"Why haven't the police found any sign of her where the kidnappers were living? Why haven't they made them say where she is? Why the hell aren't we being *told* anything?!"

"There could be all sorts of reasons. The most important thing is that they've got the kidnappers, and I'm sure they'll find her now. I don't doubt it for a minute."

Rosa wants so much for Steen to be right. She holds him close, until she realizes somebody is watching them. Turning, she sees Vogel in the doorway, and before she can ask he says there's no point phoning the station. The head of Homicide has just arrived.

97

Although Nylander knows he was inside this hall some nine months earlier, informing the Hartung family that their daughter's case was finally closed, he can't remember the room. He feels like the situation is repeating itself, and the fleeting thought crosses his mind that this is what Hell must be like: having to replay the same appalling scenes over and over again. But Nylander also knows this is a necessary visit, and that he will feel much more comfortable once he has stepped back outside. In his head he is already running through the press conference he's going to hold once he has gotten back to the station and updated the top brass. Unlike previous meetings over the last two weeks, this one will be tinged with triumph.

Such an outcome seemed dramatically unlikely only hours earlier, when he arrived in the forest with the task force and found Benedikte Skans and Asger Neergaard lifeless on the ground. He was relieved, of course, to find the minister's son unharmed in the van, but with the two kidnappers mute he knew he'd never get the explanations and confessions needed to wrap up the case once and for all. Yet just as he was sitting in the backseat of a car, eyeing the ambulance carrying the minister's son and wondering how the hell he was going to silence the doubters, Thulin called. Ironic, really, that she should be the one to tell him about the discovery in the mini-fridge at the old slaughterhouse, given that Hess seems to have rubbed off on her of late, making her even more exasperating than she usually is. But the news was an almost perfect coda to the day. Immediately he asked her to call Genz and get the evidence secured pronto, and by the time he hung up he was no longer afraid of the doubters at the press conference or at the station.

"Is Gustav okay?"

Nylander addresses Steen and Rosa Hartung, who have come out into the hall, and Steen Hartung nods.

"Yes. He seems to be doing well. He's eating right now."

"I'm glad to hear it. I won't disturb you for long. I simply came to let you know that as far as we're concerned the murder cases are now closed, and that we—"

"What have you found out about Kristine?"

Rosa Hartung interrupts Nylander's speech, but he is prepared, skipping straight to the bit where he explains, calmly and gravely, that unfortunately there is nothing new to report about their daughter.

"The circumstances around your daughter's death were cleared up last year, and the current case doesn't alter that fact. As I've been trying to tell you all along, these are two entirely different chains of events, and you will of course be given a full account of the current case once our investigations are complete."

Nylander can see frustration overwhelming both parents, as they begin talking over each other, demanding more details.

"But what about the fingerprints?"

"They must mean something, surely?"

"What did the kidnappers say?! Haven't you interviewed them?"

"I understand your frustration, but you must have faith in our investigation. My people have searched the vehicle where Gustav was found, as well as the kidnappers' residence and workplaces, but they've found no indication that Kristine is still alive. No indication, in fact, that the kidnappers had anything to do with her whatsoever. I'm afraid they had already taken their own lives when we found them. Presumably to avoid being arrested and punished, so they can't give us any answers. But, as I said, there's no sign that interrogating them would have given us anything new on your daughter."

Nylander can see neither of them wants to let go of the straw they are clutching, and Rosa Hartung's next outburst is fierce and aggressive.

"But you could be wrong! You don't know anything for sure! There were those chestnut men with her fingerprints, and if you haven't found any sign of Kristine then maybe it's because they're not the real killers!"

"We know for a fact that they are. With one hundred percent certainty."

Nylander describes the irrefutable proof they found in the old industrial slaughterhouse that evening. He was thinking of the evidence with a tingle of happiness in his belly, but when he finishes speaking he can see in Rosa Hartung's eyes that he has snuffed out her last hope. She looks at him without seeing him, and suddenly he finds it hard to imagine that this human being will ever heal. It throws him, makes him embarrassed.

Out of nowhere he is gripped by the urge to take her hands and tell her everything will be all right. They still have a son. They still have each other. They still have so much to live for. But instead Nylander hears himself mumbling something about how he can't really explain, sorry, how the chestnut men with Kristine's fingerprints came into the killers' possession, but that it doesn't change the upshot.

The minister hears nothing. Nylander takes his leave and shuffles backward through the hall until he feels he can allow himself to turn around. By the time he's outside the front door and has shut it behind him, there are still twenty minutes to go before his meeting with the top brass, but he gasps for breath and hurries toward his car.

98

Hess jogs over the wet tiles in the empty court-yard. He can hear the nightly broadcast on the flat-screen in the guardhouse by the police station entrance—they're reporting live from Rosa Hartung's residence in Outer Østerbro. But he ignores it. As he reaches the top of the stairs in the rotunda and paces down the corridor into the department, he catches a glimpse of beer cans being opened to celebrate the closure of the case. A long day is drawing to an end, but for Hess it isn't over.

"Where's Nylander?"

"Nylander's in a meeting."

"I need to speak to him. It's crucial. Right now!"

The secretary takes pity on him, disappearing through a meeting-room door while Hess waits outside. His shoes are muddy, his clothes sodden with rain. His hands are shaking, and he doesn't know whether it's agitation or the chill of the forest where he has spent the last few hours, stubbornly defying the coroner's entreaties to let him work in peace. It was not in vain.

"I don't have time right now. The press conference is starting in two ticks."

Nylander, emerging, has just bidden goodbye to a few bigwigs. Hess knows from experience that this is the moment every police chief looks forward to: being able to publicly declare the case closed so that the press will disperse. But he needs a word with Nylander before he meets the press, so he follows him down the corridor and explains that the case isn't solved.

"Hess, it doesn't surprise me that you're taking that line."

"For one thing, there's nothing to indicate that Benedikte Skans and Asger Neergaard knew the murdered women. There's nothing on their property that so much as hints they were anywhere *near* them."

"Not sure I quite agree with you there."

"For another thing, they had no motive to kill them. Nor any motive to cut off their hands and feet, for that matter. Their anger was directed against Rosa Hartung, not against women or mothers in general. In theory

Skans could have accessed the medical records about the victims' children through her work at the hospital, but if she and Neergaard really made those reports to the council, then why haven't we found evidence of that?"

"Because we're not done with the investigation, Hess."

"Thirdly, Skans and probably Neergaard both have an alibi for the murders of Jessie Kvium and Martin Ricks on the night of October 16th. If it turns out Neergaard *was* in the foyer at the Royal Library, then neither of them could have committed the murders that night, which means it's not likely they committed the other killings either."

"I've got no idea what you're babbling about, but if you've got proof then I'd love to hear it."

Nylander has reached the operations room and is ready to pick up his papers for the press conference, but Hess blocks his path.

"Plus I've just spoken to the coroner. Benedikte Skans appears to have cut her own carotid artery, but when you reconstruct the movement it's unnatural— and it *could* be interpreted as a sign that somebody tried to make it look like suicide."

"I've spoken to him as well. And he emphasized that it was just as conceivable she *did* do it herself."

"The stab wounds on Neergaard's torso are also slightly too high for Skans's height, and if she imagined that she and her boyfriend were going to die together, then why the hell were they lying ten meters from each other, as if she was trying to escape."

Nylander is about to say something, but Hess doesn't give him the chance.

"If they were capable of carrying out those murders, then they wouldn't have been stupid enough to abduct the boy in an easily traceable rented van!"

"So what do you think should be done, if it were up to you?"

Nylander's question catches Hess off guard, and he can feel himself getting carried away as he speaks. He can hear himself rambling about Linus Bekker and the archive of crime-scene photographs, which they need to check through ASAP. He has just reminded one of the IT techs about the material, which he asked Genz to provide earlier in the day.

"And Hartung's advisor, Frederik Vogel, we need to have him checked out, especially about whether he has an alibi for the times of the murders!"

"Hess, you haven't listened to the message I left on your phone . . ."

Hess turns toward Thulin's voice and realizes she has entered the room. She is staring at him and holding a little sheaf of photos in her hand.

"What message?"

"Thulin, bring him up to speed. I don't have time."

Nylander makes for the door, but Hess grabs his shoulder.

"What about the fingerprints on the chestnut men? You can't go in there and claim the case is solved before we figure that bit out! Three murdered women could still become four if you make a mistake now!"

"I'm not making a mistake! You're the only one who doesn't get that."

Tearing himself free, Nylander nods at Thulin and adjusts his clothes. Hess gazes inquiringly at her, and, hesitating, she passes him the photographs. He finds himself staring at the top one. A picture of four sawn-off human hands, lying higgledy-piggledy on a shelf in a fridge.

"I found them on Skans and Neergaard's property. In a mini-fridge in one of the cold stores in the old slaughterhouse . . ."

Hess leafs incredulously through the various images of the amputated female hands, pausing at a different photograph: a bluish female foot, sawn off at the ankle, lying in the crisper drawer like an installation by Damien Hirst.

Hess is nonplussed. He struggles to find words.

"But . . . why weren't these found by the techs earlier in the day? Was the place locked? Could anybody have put them there?"

"Hess, go home, for Christ's sake."

When he looks up, he is met by Nylander's gaze.

"But the fingerprints? The Hartung girl . . . if we stop looking, and if the girl's not dead . . ."

Nylander vanishes through the doorway, leaving Hess stupefied. When he glances at Thulin a moment later, seeking her agreement, he finds she is looking at him with compassion. Her eyes are somber and sympathetic, but not because of Kristine Hartung. Not because of a girl who went missing and was never found, not because of mysterious fingerprints on chestnut men, but because of him. He can see in her eyes that she believes he has lost his common sense and power of judgment, and it fills him with horror, because he isn't sure that she's wrong.

Hess staggers backward through the door and veers down the corridor, hearing her call his name. In the rain outside he dashes across the courtyard, and although he doesn't turn around he can feel her looking at him through the window. Just before the exit, he breaks into a run.

Friday, October 30th

Friday, October 10th

99

It's the earliest snow Hess can remember. It's only the penultimate day in October, but already there are two or three centimeters, and it is still snowing outside the tall panes in the international terminal at the airport, where Hess has just smoked a Camel that he hopes will let him get through the trip to Bucharest without going into withdrawal.

Hess first noticed the snow forty-five minutes earlier, as he slammed the door to his apartment one final time, went out into the clear, frosty air, and descended the stairs to the waiting taxi. The daylight had blinded him, and he felt relieved when his hands found the battered pair of sunglasses in his inside pocket—he hadn't been sure they'd be there. He wasn't sure of much in general, if it came to that, having woken with a nasty hangover, so the fact that the sunglasses were where they ought to be made him feel like it might be a good day after all. During the taxi ride he enjoyed watching the autumn be slowly interred, and the good vibes continue as he passes through security and moves deeper into the cosmopolitan atmosphere of the airport. Hess is surrounded by tourists and other foreigners, all gabbling away in their various languages, and he already feels as though he's put Copenhagen behind him. He checks the departures board and sees with satisfaction that his flight is boarding. The snow isn't affecting planes yet—another sign that luck is on his side. Picking up his bag, packed with the few possessions he has brought, Hess heads for the gate. As he catches a glimpse of himself in the window of a clothes store, it strikes him that his attire might be even less suitable for the climate in Bucharest than it was in Copenhagen. Was it warm in Bucharest, or was there snow and frost? Might be best to grab a parka and a pair of Timberland boots at the terminal, but the hangover and his yen to leave the country overpower him, so he contents himself with a croissant and a takeout Starbucks.

The green light from the Hague had come yesterday evening in the form of a call from Freimann's secretary and a one-way ticket to Romania. Ironically, Hess is in much worse shape now than when he fell out of favor and was dispatched to Copenhagen just over three weeks before. For the last ten days he'd been soaking himself in alcohol at the bars and pubs so plentiful in Copenhagen, and he was barely able to speak clearly when the call came through. After a moment he was put through to Freimann himself, and his boss informed him tersely that the evaluation had concluded in his favor.

"Understand, however, that if there's a whisper of neglect, insubordination, or the merest hint of a vanishing act, the hammer will fall so fast it'll make your head spin. Your superiors at Copenhagen have spoken positively about you and guaranteed that you're highly motivated, so it shouldn't be difficult for you to comply."

Hess steered clear of long sentences, merely answering in the affirmative. There was no reason to explain that Nylander's positive assessment was motivated solely by a desire to get Hess out of his hair, and once the message sank in, Hess rang François to thank him for his help. The prospect of retreating back into his comfortable shell at Europol is a tremendous relief. After a detour via Bucharest, of course—another faceless hotel room and another Euro case—but anywhere was better than here.

Things have panned out with the apartment too. The contract wasn't quite signed yet, true, but astonishingly the real estate agent has managed to find a buyer. Mainly, Hess assumes, because he agreed to lower the asking price by two hundred thousand kroner on one of his drunker days. Late last night, Hess dropped off his keys with the caretaker, who seemed every bit as relieved to get rid of him as Nylander and the crowd at the station. The man had even made a song and dance earlier in the week about being happy to polish the floors and touch up the apartment if it meant Hess could sell it. Hess had thanked him, but the truth was he couldn't give a toss about floors and asking prices so long as he got the piece of crap off his hands and never needed to return.

The only piece of unfinished business is the awkward situation with Naia Thulin, and that's so insignificant it can barely be called a business at all. The last time he saw her he got the distinct impression that she thought his theories about the Hartung girl were the product of an unbalanced mind. That she judged him incapable of assessing things as they really were, purely because he had his own shit to deal with. Most likely someone had told her ages ago about his past, and the reasons why one might think that—and perhaps she was right. At any rate, he'd spent no more time musing on chestnuts and fingerprints since that night. The case was solved—the amputated limbs discovered in the old slaughterhouse had made that plain—and now that he is queuing at his gate, his boarding pass ready on his phone, it feels weird to recall how strongly he disagreed. The only things that would haunt him from his time in Copenhagen are Thulin's clear, resolute eyes and the fact that he did not call to say goodbye. But that's all fixable—or at least, such is his frame of mind as he boards the aircraft and sits down in 12B.

A disapproving glance from the businessman beside him tells Hess he reeks of spirits, but he sinks deep into the seat for an hour or two's nap. He's just promised himself a restorative gin and tonic to guarantee some solid beauty sleep when a text, in English, arrives from François.

"I'll pick you up at the airport. We go straight to headquarters. Make sure you read the case before arrival!"

The latter had slipped Hess's mind, but no harm done—he can still read up on the case if he postpones his beauty sleep and starts now. Reluctantly he opens the inbox on his phone for the first time in more than a week, only to find he hasn't received the material. Another text exchange with François makes it clear the mistake is his.

"Check again. Emailed you the case at 10:37 p.m., you lazy Danish douche."

Hess discovers why he hasn't received François's email. A huge file attached to a different email has filled all the space in his inbox, blocking everything else. The email is from a digital forensics tech, and the file turns out to be the material Thulin asked Genz to procure after their visit to Linus Bekker, which Hess prodded the techs to send him later that same night. Specifically, it's the hit list of images from the crime-scene archive that had attracted most attention from Bekker before his arrest and confession.

Since the email is now irrelevant, Hess is about to delete it—but then his curiosity gets the better of him. Meeting Linus Bekker was not pleasant, but from a professional standpoint his psychology is interesting, and Hess has time: there are still passengers sidling down the aisles to find their seats. He double clicks on the file. It takes a moment, and then he has a full view of the images Linus Bekker had most enjoyed. Only on his phone's small screen, true, but that's plenty.

At first glance, Linus Bekker's hit list consists exclusively of images from crime scenes featuring murdered women. Mainly between the ages of twenty-five and forty-five, many of them probably mothers, at least judging by the objects scattered around them or visible in the background: plastic tractors, playpens, tricycles, and the like. Some of the images are in black and white, but the majority are in color, and overall they represent murders stretching over many years, all the way from the 1950s to the point of Bekker's arrest. Naked women, clothed women, dark-haired, fair-haired, big, and small. Shot, stabbed, strangled, drowned, or beaten to death. Some clearly after being raped. A grotesque, sadistic potpourri, and Hess struggles to get his head around the idea that Linus Bekker had been sexually excited by them. He feels the Starbucks croissant forcing its way back up, but as he scrolls hastily back to the top to get out of the file—an old habit—the volume of data proves too much for his phone and the screen freezes on an image he didn't notice first time around.

It's a photograph nearly thirty years old, taken in a bathroom, and the typewritten caption at the bottom reads MØN ISLAND, 31 OCT. 1989. A naked woman's body lies twisted and disfigured on a terrazzo floor, smeared with blood that is black and congealed. She is probably around forty, but it's difficult to say for sure, because her face has been battered beyond recognition. It's the amputation that catches Hess's attention. One arm and one leg have been chopped off, lying separate from the torso. It seems to have taken numerous attempts—as though done with an axe, heavy and unwieldy, that only gradually learned to obey its owner. The savagery of the attack attested to the killer's lust for blood, and although the scene resembles nothing Hess has seen before, he feels compelled by the photograph.

"All passengers please take your seats."

The cabin staff are busy stuffing the last pieces of hand luggage into place, and the steward puts the telephone back on the wall by the cockpit.

It turns out that the photo of the naked woman in the bathroom is the first in a short series of images of murders apparently committed in the same house and with the same caption: MØN ISLAND, 31 OCT. 1989. A teenage boy and a teenage girl lie murdered in the kitchen, the boy slumped against an oven, the girl sprawled across the table with her head in a bowl of porridge. Both had gunshot wounds. Hess scrolls on, finding to his surprise that the next victim in the series is an older police officer, who lies dead on a basement floor. Judging by the state of the man's face, he's been killed with the axe as well. The image is the last in the series, and Hess is about to return to the dismembered woman on the bathroom floor when his attention is suddenly caught by the number in brackets that accompanies the photo of the policeman. [37]. It dawns on Hess that the figure must be the tech's note of the number of times Linus Bekker had clicked on that specific image.

"All electronic devices should now be switched off, please."

Hess nods to signal that he's understood the steward, who continues past to deliver the message to the next row. It makes no sense that Bekker would have looked at a photo of a murdered policeman thirty-seven times. Not when he so obviously favored women. Hess swiftly checks a few of the other pictures, now looking for the small number accompanying every photo. But none of the other images has as high a count as the one of the murdered policeman. Not even the woman in the bathroom, whose number reads [16].

Hess feels his stomach knot. There has to be something important about the picture of the policeman on the basement floor, and he tries for a moment to repress the possibility that the tech has simply made a mistake. Out of the corner of his eye he sees the steward heading back through the plane, and he curses the tiny screen—he has to use his shaky, half-drunken fingers to zoom in on the photo and search for the details he's overlooked. The task is impossible. Soon his eyes are swimming with checkered pixels that offer no clue as to why Linus Bekker had focused on this particular image.

"Time to switch that off, please!"

This time the steward doesn't budge. Hess is about to give in when his fingers brush the screen, moving the image so that it focuses on some shelving above the policeman. Hess stiffens. At first his brain doesn't comprehend what it is looking at, but then he zooms out and time stands still.

On the basement wall above the policeman's body are three rickety wooden shelves. All are crammed with small, childish dolls: chestnut men, chestnut ladies, chestnut animals. Big and small, some unfinished, still missing limbs, others dusty and dirty. All stand there mute with empty eyes, like small soldiers, a mighty army of the outcast.

Without being able to explain why, he knows instantly that this is why Bekker viewed the image thirty-seven times. He senses the plane jolt into motion, and before the steward can stop him he is making for the cockpit.

100

The business lounge at Copenhagen Airport is nearly deserted, smelling of perfume, freshly brewed coffee, and newly baked bread, but it takes more than five minutes of arguing with the hostess at the entrance before Hess is allowed to go inside. Her young face is perfectly made-up, and although she smiles and nods pleasantly it is clear she finds it hard to connect his appearance and behavior with the European police badge with which he repeatedly tries to explain his important errand. It isn't until a young Somali security guard is called and verifies the badge that she shows mercy and permits Hess to enter the hallowed halls of the business lounge.

Hess makes a beeline for the three computers available to guests at the back of the lounge. The few people already in the room are absorbed in their smartphones and low-calorie brunch at the round tables, and it's doubtful whether the tall, empty chairs in front of the screens have ever been used except by children occasionally dragged along on business trips. Hess settles at a keyboard, inwardly cursing and fuming as he logs on and navigates through Europol's security system before reaching his inbox. He knows there are several departures to Bucharest that day, even if it means a stopover somewhere tedious in Germany, but the delay will irritate Freimann if it reaches his ears. Still, Hess doesn't feel he has a choice, and as soon as he opens Bekker's hit list again and sees the chestnut dolls, he forgets all about his boss.

On the bigger screen the silent dolls in the photograph, nearly thirty years old, seem even more uncanny, but Hess still isn't sure what his discovery means. Clearly Bekker has attached great value to the image. That much is obvious from the thirty-seven times he viewed it, as well as the fact that the victim isn't his preferred type. But *why* did he value it? The first time he saw it—about eighteen months ago, when he hacked into the archive—there had been nothing in the press or anywhere else about a mysterious killer who murdered women and left chestnut dolls at the scene of the crime. That killer didn't even exist at the time Bekker originally viewed the photograph, so from that perspective it makes no sense that he'd be so enthralled by the army of handmade chestnut dolls. Yet there is no doubt in Hess's mind that he was.

For a moment Hess wonders whether Bekker's interest might have been piqued by something he read in the case files about the crimes on Møn Island in 1989. A police report on the case could perhaps explain the appeal—he might, for example, have realized he knew the victims or the crime scene, or stumbled across some other relevant piece of information that had made him check and recheck the image of the murdered policeman and the dolls. But there *were* no case files in the material Bekker hacked. Not for the Møn case or any other. It was an archive of photographs taken at crime scenes, pure and simple. Nothing else. The reports were located in another digital archive, and if Hess's memory served, Bekker didn't access anything besides the specific archive that provided an outlet for his sexual proclivities.

Hess is none the wiser. His hangover is back, and he is starting to regret hammering on the door of the cockpit like a nutjob and forcing the German-speaking pilot to let him off the plane. It would have taken him to Bucharest. It was even leaving on time. His eyes flick to the departures board, but instead he sees Linus

Bekker's face and hears his laughter. Hess decides to run through the images again. Starting from the top, he scrolls back down through the hideous litany of gruesome crimes. One picture is followed by the next, each crueler than the last, without offering any explanation of why these specific images gave Bekker such immense enjoyment. Hess presumes it has to be something sick, something that only a pervert like Bekker would notice, and suddenly it strikes him what it might be. He understands it before he sees it—he understands it because it is the most terrifying thing he can imagine, and at the same time so inconceivable that it might make Linus Bekker excited.

He goes back to the start, skimming over the images he already knows, but this time scanning for one thing: he is no longer looking at the subject of the pictures, but at everything else—foreground, background, objects, anything that is apparently without significance. In the ninth picture he finds what he is seeking. It is from another crime scene, labeled RISSKOV, 22 SEPT. 2001. No different at first glance from the rest. A blond woman, approximately thirty-five years old, lies dead on a floor in something that looks like the front room of a house or apartment. She wears a dark brown skirt, a torn white camisole, and high-heeled shoes, one heel of which has snapped off. In the background he can make out toys and a playpen, while the table to the left is neatly laid for two—but the meal had never been eaten. The killing had been frenzied, uncontrolled, presumably committed on the right side of the image, where everything is overturned and spattered with blood. But it is the playpen that catches Hess's eye. The playpen, and the shy little chestnut man hanging from the rail beside a rattle.

The blood begins to whistle in Hess's ears. He continues the hunt, and it's as though his eyes adjust, drawn only to the pattern they are seeking. All else is extraneous; nothing exists in the world but the small doll, and at the twenty-third image he pauses again.

NYBORG, 2 OCT. 2015. This time a young woman in a little black car. Taken through the windshield. She sits in the driver's seat, her upper body resting against a child's car seat on the passenger's side. Smartly dressed, as though she were on her way to or from an appointment or a date. One eye is smashed in, but there is virtually no blood in the picture, and the killing seems more controlled than the one in Risskov. From the rearview mirror in the foreground hangs a little chestnut man. Only visible in silhouette, but it is there.

There are nearly forty images left, but Hess logs off and gets to his feet. On his way down the escalator to the ground floor, it crosses his mind that murders spread across nearly thirty years can't have the same killer. It's impossible. Somebody would have noticed. Somebody would have done something. There's nothing remarkable about chestnut men, necessarily, certainly not in autumn. Maybe Hess is simply seeing what he *wants* to see?

Even so, he can't stop picturing Linus Bekker's face as he fills out the paperwork at the car rental desk and waits to be handed the keys. This is the connection Bekker made. The chestnut doll is the signature of a murderer who's struck again and again. By the time he gets the keys and runs to the parking lot, the snow is falling more thickly than before.

101

Thulin avoids eye contact with the two detectives who look up from their screens as she empties her locker and slams the metal door a little too hard. She has deliberately avoided drawing attention to the fact that this is her last day at the department, and she doesn't want to change that now. Not that it would make a difference. There's nobody she will miss, and probably nobody will miss her. She'd preferred it that way from day one, and it suits her just fine to stay as invisible as possible until she's out of the building. She happened to bump into Nylander a few minutes ago, passing her in the corridor with his bevy of assistants as he made for the latest press conference, of which there have already been plenty. Today the excuse is that the results of the coroner's final examination and the DNA analyses are now available. Thulin wonders whether the real reason is simply that Nylander enjoys the spotlight. That's how it looks, anyhow, as he stands posing beside the justice minister in his slightly too shiny suit, or when, in an attempt at a generous gesture, he emphasizes his detectives' search in Sydhavnen as the crucial turning point in the investigation.

Nylander stopped to wish her good luck.

"Bye, Thulin. Say hello to Wenger for me."

He meant Isak Wenger, Thulin's new superior officer at NC3, and she took his comment to mean that Nylander now felt the balance of power between the departments had shifted, and that Thulin ought to be regretting her choice. She'd nearly forgotten the career change she herself had set in motion until the NC3 boss had called her personally that Monday and congratulated her on closing the murder case.

"But that's not why I'm ringing. I hope you're still interested in a job with us?"

Wenger had offered her the position, although in the end she'd neither applied nor been given a recommendation from Nylander. If she accepted the job, Wenger would sort out the practical side of things with Nylander, and she could start at NC3 after a late autumn holiday. That is now the prospect before Thulin: a whole week for Le and herself, and although in a way things had worked out like they were supposed to, irritatingly enough Thulin had spent the last few days reassuring herself that the case had been properly wrapped up.

The discovery of Anne Sejer-Lassen's and Jessie Kvium's severed hands as well as Jessie's foot in the mini-fridge at the former slaughterhouse had been so irrefutable that Thulin could see no logical option but to side with Nylander's interpretation. Hess had raised some unanswered questions, certainly, but the overwhelming likelihood remained that his personal issues had made him fixate on them.

That was Nylander's unsentimental view, in any case, and he'd confided to Thulin that Hess's original exit from the department and from Copenhagen had been motivated by a personal tragedy. Not that he knew much about it, because in those days Nylander hadn't been involved in the department himself, but the gist was that one May night just over five years earlier, Hess's twenty-nine-year-old wife had died in a fire that broke out in their Valby apartment.

The information had made an impression on Thulin. In the police report, which she'd looked up on the database, it said that the fire had started around three in the morning and had spread with astonishing speed. The building had been evacuated, but the fierceness of the flames made it impossible for the firefighters to reach the apartment on the top story. When the fire was put out, the young woman's charred body was found in the bedroom, and her husband, "a detective at the Major Crimes Division, Mark M. Hess," in Stockholm on a case, was informed by telephone. The cause of the fire remained undetermined. Faulty wiring, oil lamps, and arson had all been investigated, but no definitive conclusions reached. The woman had been seven months pregnant, and the couple had gotten married just one month earlier.

The report turned Thulin's stomach. Suddenly so much about Hess's character fell into place, yet on the other hand it was impossible to comprehend. In any case, it no longer made any sense to think about the questions Hess had raised, and perhaps that was why she felt relieved when she heard the deputy commissioner telling Nylander earlier that day that Hess had been restored to favor at the Hague and was on his way to an assignment in Bucharest. Hess was leaving the country, then, and it was definitely for the best. She tried to reach him several times that week, but he did not call back, and it disconcerted her when Le asked when "the guy with the eyes" was coming over to see how far she'd gotten in League of Legends. The same thing happened when she called to ask after Magnus

Kjær, who'd been transferred to a children's home while the authorities tried to find a suitable foster family. An administrator said the boy was improving, but also that he'd asked several times about "the policeman." Thulin wasn't sure how to respond to that. She decided to dismiss Hess from her mind, and usually she found it easy to disregard people like that. Sebastian, for instance: although he still left messages on her voicemail, she felt no urge to contact him again.

"Naia Thulin?"

Turning back to her empty desk, she finds a bike messenger looking at her, and in spite of what she's promised herself, Hess is the first person who enters her mind when she sees the bouquet. Yellow, orange, and red autumn flowers, the names of which she doesn't know. Flowers have never meant much to her. She signs for the delivery with the digital pen the courier hands her, and then he waddles swiftly out again in his cycling shoes. Thulin opens the card, counting herself lucky that her colleagues are gathered around the flat-screen in the cafeteria, where Nylander's press conference is being broadcast live.

"Thanks for the run. Good luck at NC3. Step away from that desk. "

Thulin smiles to herself for a moment, but throws Genz's card into the wastepaper basket. By the time she's vanished down the stairs, heading for freedom and Le's school Halloween party, she's left the bouquet on the desk in the admin office, where she knows it will be appreciated.

Outside the station, the snow is still falling, and Thulin is annoyed she didn't think to arrange for a car before she starts at NC3. Her sneakers are soon soaked through, and she hurries up Bernstorffsgade toward the main station, where she will take the metro to the Dybbølsbro stop.

The snow hadn't yet begun to fall when she met Genz that morning—she'd chosen to mark her last day on the murder squad by finally accepting his invitation to go for a run. Now that they were no longer going to be colleagues, it seemed like a nice way to conclude their relationship. Plus she had her own agenda. They'd agreed to run along Strandvejen, so at half six she met Genz outside his building at one of the attractive new complexes in Nordhavn. It surprised her that Genz had the money for a place like that, but on the other hand it made sense he'd be good with his finances, given how meticulous he was.

The first part of the run was a good experience, especially watching the sun rise above Øresund, and they spent some time discussing the investigation. How

Benedikte Skans and Asger Neergaard's desire for revenge must have developed in the aftermath of their tragedy; how the nurse must have gathered information on the abused children and the mothers they'd selected as victims; how the couple must have used an internet café with access to a Ukrainian email server to send the anonymous tip-offs instead of their own computers, and how the contents of the mini-fridge must have been overlooked during the preliminary forensic search. The bludgeon and saw used to kill and maim the victims still hadn't been found, but as a nurse Benedikte Skans had access to instruments from the operating theater, which were in the process of being examined and tested.

Genz didn't think there was any reason to doubt the conclusions of the investigation, although Thulin suspected he was more engrossed in the run than in their conversation. She regretted having told him about her love of long runs, because as it soon became clear he had to hold back so as not to outstrip her. After eight kilometers they turned around and she fell behind him like a Sunday jogger in the tow of a Kenyan athlete; only when he noticed she was several meters behind did he ease up and allow the conversation to continue. If she'd thought Genz's invitation was an excuse to get cozy with her, she was very much mistaken: he was as passionate about his running as he was about his lab work.

Thulin barely had enough breath to speak for the remainder of the run, but when they stopped at a red light at Charlottenlund Fort she'd aired her frustration that they were still unable to explain why chestnut men with the Hartung girl's fingerprints had been left at the crime scenes. There had been no sign of chestnut men at the young couple's property, and how Neergaard and Skans could have gotten hold of them was a mystery.

"Unless Nylander's right, and for some reason the couple bought them at the stall Kristine Hartung and her friend set up before she went missing," Genz had suggested.

"But how likely is that? Steen Hartung doesn't even think the girls *made* chestnut men that year."

"Maybe he's misremembering? Skans was a patient at Roskilde at that point, but Neergaard could easily have driven around the neighborhood and started laying the groundwork even then."

"And then he just so happened to be beaten to the punch by Linus Bekker, you think? Coincidentally at nearly the same moment?"

Genz shrugged and gave her a smile.

THE CHESTNUT MAN • 579

"It's not *my* theory. I'm just a tech."

They'd probably never get a conclusive answer, but there was something about the chestnut men that continued to niggle. Almost as though there were something they'd forgotten to check or forgotten to take into account. But then she and Genz finally reached Svanemøllen Station, the snow began to fall, and Thulin staggered into the shelter of the platform while Genz continued his run, taking a quick little detour around the park.

"I'm looking for 3A?"

"Try the classroom. Just follow the noise."

Shaking off the snow, Thulin walks past the two teachers in the common room, which is decorated for Halloween. She has arrived at the school, which is located on a side street not far from Dybbølsbro Station, precisely on time, and she promises herself that from now on it will always be that way. Far too many times she's arrived late or not at all to the various school get-togethers, and she can see a flash of surprise on a few of the parents' faces when she enters the classroom. They are standing by the row of carved pumpkins along the walls, while the children scamper merrily around in their Halloween costumes. It isn't Halloween until tomorrow, but because it's the weekend the school has decided to throw the party today. The girls are dressed up as witches and the boys as monsters, many of them in macabre masks. Each one is gorier than the last, and some of the parents ooh and ahh in mock terror as the kids race past. The teacher, a woman Thulin's age, is also dressed as a witch, in a low-cut black dress, black fishnet stockings, and black pumps, the whole thing crowned with chalk-white makeup, red lipstick, and a pointy black hat. She looks like a character from a Tim Burton film, and it isn't hard to imagine why the fathers, especially, are in a better mood than usual this Friday afternoon.

For a moment Thulin can't see Le or her grand-dad among the parents and small, blood-thirsty monsters, but then she notices the rubber zombie mask with its split skull and yellow brains spilling down its forehead. The rubber mask is from a game called Plants vs. Zombies, and it was the only costume Le wanted when she dragged Thulin to the comic-book store in Skindergade yesterday. Now she is standing with her granddad, who is adjusting the skull so the brains didn't slip down around her neck.

"Hi, Mom. Can you tell it's me?"

"No, where are you?"

She glances around, and when she turns back Le has lifted the rubber mask to reveal her sweaty, triumphant face.

"I'm the one carrying the pumpkin into the party ahead of everyone else."

"Cool. I'm looking forward to seeing that."

"Are you going to stay and watch?"

"Of course."

"Do you want me to hold the brain for a bit so you don't die of heatstroke?" asks Aksel, wiping Le's forehead.

"It doesn't matter, Granddad."

With the zombie mask hanging from her neck, Le tears across the room toward Ramazan, who is dressed as a skeleton.

"Everything all right?"

Aksel looks at her, and she knows he means her last day at the station.

"Yeah, fine. All done and dusted."

Aksel is about to say something, but then the teacher claps her hands to get everybody's attention. "Right, we're going to get started! Children, you come over here to me," she says in a brisk tone before turning to the parents.

"Before we head over to the common room for the party, we just need to wrap up the project week about autumn. The children have prepared three presentations they're looking forward to showing you!"

The decorations are still up, ready for the party, and so are the posters of the family trees. She was only once present at an event where the children performed—something about a circus, where one of the skits had involved the children crawling three times through a Hula-Hoop dressed as lions. The parents' hysterical applause made Thulin's toes curl.

This time isn't much different. The first group of kids present posters featuring twigs and reddish-yellow leaves from the forest, while the parents smile and watch the whole thing through the cameras on their phones. Thulin realizes it will be a long time before she stops associating red and yellow leaves with the eerie sight of Laura Kjær, Anne Sejer-Lassen, and Jessie Kvium, and the next group's presentation—the class collection of chestnut dolls—doesn't improve her mood.

Finally it is Le's turn. She, Ramazan, and a few other children are shepherded up to the teacher's desk, where they announce that chestnuts can be eaten too.

"But first you need to make a cut in them! Otherwise they'll explode in the oven! They need to be roasted at precisely two hundred twenty-five degrees, and then you eat them with butter and salt!"

Le's voice is clear and bright, and Thulin is nearly bowled over with astonishment: her warrior-like little girl has never shown any interest in anything kitchen-related before. A few bowls of roasted chestnuts are passed around the parents, while the teacher turns to Ramazan, who has obviously forgotten his response.

"And Ramazan, what should you remember if you roast and eat chestnuts?"

"You've got to choose the right kind. The ones called edible chestnuts."

"That's right. There are lots of different kinds of chestnut, but only some are edible."

Ramazan nods, takes a chestnut, and munches it noisily, as his mom and dad grin proudly and bask in the other parents' acknowledgment. The teacher launches into an anecdote about how the children themselves have prepared the chestnuts the parents are eating, but Thulin isn't listening.

"What do you mean there are lots of different kinds of chestnut?"

The question comes too late, and out of context. The teacher turns to Thulin in surprise, and so do a few of the parents, who've stopped laughing.

"I thought there were just two types of chestnut. Edible chestnuts, and then the ones you make chestnut men out of?"

"No, actually there are several different kinds. But now Ramazan is going to—"

"How sure are you?"

"Quite sure. But now we're going to—"

"How many?"

"How many what?"

"How many different types of chestnut are there?"

The room has gone quiet. The parents stare from Thulin to the teacher and back again, and even the children are silent. Thulin's last question has been sharp and inquisitorial, shorn of her initial politeness. The teacher hesitates, smiling uncertainly; she has no idea why she is suddenly being tested.

"I don't know all of them. But there are various kinds of edible chestnut, like for example European chestnuts and Japanese chestnuts, and there are different kinds of horse chestnut. So, for instance—"

"Which kind do you make chestnut animals from?"

"Well, all of them. But the most common ones around here are horse chestnuts . . ."

Nobody speaks. The parents are looking at Thulin, while she stares vacantly at the teacher. Somewhere in the corner of her eye she registers her daughter's face, which tells her this is possibly the most embarrassing moment of her life. But seconds later Thulin is already out the door. As she runs through the common area toward the exit, the Halloween party is in full swing.

102

"If you've come to challenge me to another run, I'll have to take you up on that next week."

Genz smiles at her. He is standing beside an oblong flight case and a small holdall, and is busy putting on an oilskin coat as Thulin enters the big laboratory. She already knows from the receptionist who met her that he's just returned from a crime scene but is now heading straight out the door for a conference held at the Herning Exhibition Center over the weekend. Still, she managed to talk her way in to see him. She already tried to get hold of him on the phone in the taxi ride over, but didn't get through, and she is relieved to find him at the department, although clearly she's come at a bad time.

"It's not that. I need your help."

"Can we discuss it on the way down to the car?"

"The chestnut dolls left with the victims, the ones with Kristine Hartung's fingerprints on them, what kind where they?"

"What kind?"

Genz has begun to switch off the halogen lamps, but pauses a moment and stares at her.

"What do you mean?"

Thulin had run up the stairs, and she realizes she is still out of breath.

"A chestnut isn't just a chestnut. There are several different kinds, so what kind were they?"

"I can't remember offhand—"

"Were they horse chestnuts?"

"Why do you ask? What's happened?"

"Maybe nothing. If you can't remember, it must be in one of your lab reports."

"I'm sure it is, but I'm just—"

"Genz, I wouldn't ask if it weren't important. Can you check right now?"

With a sigh Genz sinks into the seat in front of the big screen. A few seconds later he's in the system, and Thulin follows what he's doing on the screen mounted on the wall behind him. Genz accesses a folder and scrolls purposefully through various numbered reports before selecting one and double clicking. The volume of figures and analyses is enormous, but Genz scrolls rapidly through the report, clearly familiar with its contents, and pauses at a particular paragraph marked SPECIES AND ORIGIN.

"In the first instance, i.e., Laura Kjær, the fingerprint was on an edible chestnut. Specifically one called *Castanea sativa x crenata*. Satisfied?"

"What about the others?"

Genz lets his gaze rest on her for a moment, as if to tell her this isn't funny.

"Come on, it's important!"

Genz rummages around again on his digital desk, double clicking on another report, then repeats the procedure a third time. When he's done, Thulin knows the answer before he says it out loud.

"In the other cases the result was the same. *Castanea sativa x crenata*. Okay?"

"And you're sure. There's no doubt?"

"Thulin, this part of the analysis was done by my assistants, because I was concentrating on the fingerprint itself, so of course I can't guarantee—"

"But it's not likely your assistants got it wrong three times in a row?"

"No, it's not likely. Since none of them are experts in chestnuts, the usual procedure would be to find an expert to identify the species. I imagine that's what they did. Now, would you mind telling me what all this means?"

Thulin is silent. She had made two calls from the taxi: one to Genz and the other to Steen Hartung. Hartung had answered the call with a lifeless voice. With a stab of guilt, she'd apologized for disturbing him and explained that she was just finishing her report and needed to remind herself of the type of chestnut the family had at home, the type Kristine and her friend had used to make their chestnut dolls. Hartung didn't have the energy to be surprised, and when she added that it was just a formality he answered without further comment. The big chestnut tree in the garden was a horse chestnut tree.

"It means we've got a problem. We need to get hold of that expert. Immediately."

103

The ground between the red gate and the Peter Lieps Hus restaurant in the Deer Park is blanketed in fresh snow, and Rosa Hartung chooses to run on the gravel path instead of the asphalt road, which feels as slippery as soap. When she reaches the end of the road she glances at the amusement park, closed this time of year, its rides abandoned and spectral, then turns right, heading down one of the paths sheltered by the trees and thus almost untouched by the snow. Her legs don't want to continue, but the air is clear and cold, and she forces herself onward in the hope that the run will shake off her despondent mood.

For ten days she's barely left the house in Outer Østerbro. All the strength she mustered for her comeback at the ministry deserted her when it was brought home to her that her hopes of seeing Kristine again weren't anchored in reality. Everything turned gray and insignificant, just as it was most of the previous winter and spring, and although Vogel, Liu, and Engells were very kind, encouraging her to return to the ministry, it had no effect. She stayed home, and no matter what they said, Rosa knew her days as a minister were numbered. The prime minister and the justice minister both made public statements full of solicitude, but behind the scenes there was no doubt Rosa was finished in the party. Once a little more time had passed she'd be pushed down the ranks, either because she'd disobeyed the prime minister or because she was considered too unstable, and Rosa couldn't care less.

Her grief, however, she could not ignore, and that morning she visited her psychiatrist, who advised her to go back on antidepressants. So she forced herself into her running gear as soon as she got home—the way she used to do after lunch when she was working from home—but today it is mainly because she hopes the run might produce enough endorphins to raise her mood just a tiny bit, and give her the strength to resist another course of pills.

Another reason for the run, of course, is that the removal men are coming to pick up Kristine's things. After the session Rosa was despairing enough to follow her psychiatrist's advice to get rid of them once and for all; that way it would be easier to let go of the past. A symbolic act, he said, which would help her move on. So Rosa called a moving company and pointed out the things in Kristine's bedroom to the au pair: four big boxes of clothes and shoes, as well as her desk and bed, where Rosa had so often sat. The au pair had been given the number of a charity shop on Nordre Frihavnsgade so that she could ring and tell them a van would soon be arriving with the boxes and furniture, and then Rosa left and drove up to the Deer Park.

On the way she wondered whether she should ring Steen to tell him about the decision, but she couldn't face it. They barely spoke anymore. The man from Homicide was clear and unambiguous, but Steen still clung to his hopes, and it was more than Rosa could cope with. He refused to sign the papers declaring her dead, even though he was the one who asked the lawyer to send them, and although he never mentioned it she knew he was going door-to-door in neighborhoods Kristine might have passed through on the day she disappeared. It was his partner, Bjarke, who let her know. He talked anxiously about how Steen's office was still cluttered with plans of sewage systems, residential neighborhoods, and road networks, plans that had nothing to do with his job; how every morning he simply drove off without saying where. Yesterday Bjarke decided to follow him, and found him wandering restlessly through an area of houses near the sports complex. But Bjarke probably regretted making the call, because Rosa responded with nothing but resignation. Steen's search was pointless, but, then again, so much was. They ought to stick together, to think of Gustav, but right now they don't have the strength.

When at last Rosa reaches the red gate again, she's run herself to the point of exhaustion. Her sweat feels cold and unpleasant. Her breath rises like smoke from her mouth, and for a moment she has to support herself on the wooden gate before heading back to her car. On the way home, driving past the statue of Knud Rasmussen and Arne Jacobsen's gas station, she notices a tiny crack in the bank of clouds above. The weather has briefly cleared, and as the sun's rays break through the clouds, the snow lights up like a carpet of glimmering crystals, and she has to squint so as not to be blinded. When she turns onto her driveway, she realizes her breathing is different from when she left. Slightly calmer—as though it is reaching all the way down into her diaphragm and not merely getting stuck somewhere between her throat and her chest like a clogged sink. Climbing out, she sees the van's wide tracks in the snow, and feels slightly relieved that it's done. Out of habit she walks around to the rear of the house, to the utility-room door. It's the one she always uses when she's been out for a run, so she doesn't trail dirt and mud into the hall. She can't be bothered to stretch: all she wants to do is get inside and collapse on the sofa before the thought of Kristine's things being gone for good overpowers her. The fresh, untouched snow crunches underneath her feet, but as she rounds the corner of the back porch, she jerks to a halt.

Someone has left something on the mat in front of the door, but at first she can't tell what it is. As she takes a step closer she can see it's a delicate wreath or decoration of some kind, and her mind turns immediately to Christmas and Advent, perhaps because of the snow. It isn't until she bends down to pick it up that she realizes it's made of chestnut men. They are arranged in a garland, holding hands to form a circle.

Rosa flinches and glances around her warily. There is no one in sight. Everything in the garden, including the old chestnut tree, is covered in new, unblemished snow, and the only footprints are her own. She looks back at the wreath, picks it up cautiously, and goes inside. She's been asked about the chestnut men and their possible significance so many times she's lost count, and she can think of no connection apart from the dolls Kristine and Mathilde painstakingly made at the dinner table every year. Yet as she runs upstairs to the first floor, still in her wet running shoes, calling for the au pair, she feels altogether different and much more ill at ease, in a way she can't quite place.

Rosa finds the au pair in Kristine's empty room, vacuuming the carpet where the boxes and furniture had been. The girl looks up, startled, when Rosa switches off the vacuum cleaner and shows her the wreath.

"Alice, who left this outside? How did it get here?"

But the au pair knows nothing. She's never seen the wreath before, and she doesn't know when it was placed outside the utility-room door or who might have put it there.

"Alice, this is important!"

Rosa repeats her questions, insisting that the confused girl must have seen something, but apart from the removals men, she hadn't noticed anyone since Rosa went out. Not until there are tears in the au pair's eyes does Rosa realize she's started to shout, desperate for answers the girl doesn't have.

"Alice, I'm sorry. I'm so sorry . . ."

"I can call the police. Do you want me to call the police?"

Rosa looks at the wreath, which she'd set down on the floor to put her arms around the still-sniffling au pair. The small garland is made up of five chestnut dolls bound together with steel wire. They look like the dolls the police showed her, but now Rosa notices that two of them are taller than the other three. As though the tall dolls are the parents. Chestnut parents holding chestnut children's hands, like a family dancing in a ring.

Comprehension flashes into Rosa's mind. She recognizes the wreath, and instantly she understands why it has been placed outside her door of all doors, so that she of all people would find it. She remembers when she saw it first and who gave it to her—and why. All is clear, but her common sense still tries to tell her it can't be so. That can't be why. It was far too long ago.

"I'll call the police now, Rosa. It's better to call the police."

"No! No police. I'm okay."

Rosa lets Alice go. As she runs down to her car and drives away, she does so with the feeling that someone is watching—that someone has been watching for a very long time.

104

The drive into town feels long, with endless delays. She changes lanes when she can, and at the Triangle and later by the Castle Gardens she darts through the crossing even though the lights are red. Memories come flooding back. Some of them she can recall with certainty, while others are irresolute and porous, as if her brain has stitched them together afterward to give the whole thing meaning. Arriving at the ministry, she wonders where to park so as not to draw attention to herself, and after managing to find a spot she hurries toward the back entrance. It occurs to her she's forgotten her access card, but the guard waves her on.

"Liu, I need your help."

Inside her office she finds her secretary midmeeting with two young women Rosa recognizes as new members of the staff. Liu is clearly startled to see Rosa, and the conversation stalls.

"Yes, of course. We'll pick this up later."

Liu dismisses the two women, who shoot Rosa curious sidelong glances on their way out. It dawns on her that she is still in her running gear, still damp, and still has mud on her shoes.

"What's happened? Are you all right?"

She has no time to absorb Liu's concern.

"Where are Vogel and Engells?"

"Vogel never showed up today, and I think Engells is at a meeting somewhere in the building. Shall I get hold of them?"

"No, it doesn't matter. We can probably find it ourselves. The ministry has access to the council's register of foster families and children taken into care, correct?"

"Yes . . . why?"

"I need information about a foster family. The one I'm looking for is from Odsherred Council. Probably from 1986, but I'm not sure."

"1986? Well, then I'm not sure it will be digitali—"

"Just try! Okay?"

Liu is clearly unnerved, and Rosa feels contrite.

"Liu, you mustn't ask why. Please just help me."

"Okay . . ."

Liu sits down at her laptop, which is already on the table, and Rosa gives her a grateful look. She types in her login for the Odsherred Council register and is granted access, while Rosa takes a chair and moves it closer to the screen.

"The foster family was called the Petersens," she tells Liu. "They lived in Odsherred, at 35 Kirkevej. The father's name was Poul, a schoolteacher. The mother was Kirsten, a potter."

Liu's fingers fly across the keyboard as she types in the information.

"Nothing's coming up. Do you have their ID numbers?"

"No, I don't, but I do remember that they had a foster daughter. Rosa Petersen." Liu starts typing in the ID number Rosa gives her, but then she pauses and looks at Rosa.

"But that's you, isn't it . . . ?"

"Yes. Just search. I can't tell you what this is about. You've got to trust me."

Liu nods uncertainly and keeps searching, and a few seconds later she finds what they are looking for.

"Rosa, female infant. Born Juul Andersen. Adopted by foster parents Poul and Kirsten Petersen—"

"Now use their ID numbers and search for a case from 1986."

Liu does as Rosa says and searches again, but after a few minutes' typing she shakes her head.

"There's nothing from 1986. As I said, they haven't finished digitizing everything, so maybe—"

"Try '87 or '85. There was a boy joined our family, and his sister too."

"Do you have the boy's name, or—"

"No, I don't have anything. They weren't there long. A few weeks or months . . ."

Liu had kept typing during the conversation, but now she halts. Her eyes are fixed on the screen.

"Here's something, I think. 1987. Toke Bering . . . and his twin sister, Astrid."

Rosa can see Liu has reached a page with a file number and a block of text. The typeface is old-fashioned, revealing that the file was originally written on a typewriter. The names mean nothing to her. Nor does the fact that they were twins, but she knows it has to be them.

"Looks like they stayed with you for three months before they were transferred."

"Transferred where? I need to know what happened to them."

Liu lets Rosa closer to the screen, so that she can see the old file for herself. And Rosa reads. By the time she has finished reading the social worker's three typed pages, her whole body is quivering. Tears run down her cheeks, and she feels like throwing up.

"Rosa, what's happened? I don't like this. Should I call Steen, or . . ."

Rosa shakes her head. Her breath catching, she forces herself to read the text again. This time because she thinks there must be a message in it for her. Something the owner of the chestnut wreath wants her to pick up on. Or is it too late? Is the awful message simply that *this* is the reason for it all? Is the punishment that she'll have to live with that knowledge for the rest of her life?

This time Rosa takes in all the details, frantically scanning for clues about what to do next. And suddenly she understands. When her eyes fall on the name of the place the twins were taken, it is obvious, and she knows it can only be *there* she is supposed to go. It *has* to be there.

Rosa stands up, memorizing the address in the file.

"Rosa, could you please tell me what this is about?"

She doesn't answer Liu. She's just discovered a text from an unknown number on her phone, which she placed on the desk. It is an emoji with a finger placed in front of its mouth, and Rosa knows she has to be silent if she ever wants to know what has happened to Kristine.

105

The snow is coming down in dense flakes, and the part of the landscape Hess can view through the windshield is white and ill-defined. On the motorway it was bearable because the snowplows had been shuttling up and down, but now he's turned off the E47 and is driving down the country road toward Vordingborg, he keeps having to slow to a twenty-kilometer-per-hour crawl to avoid bumping into the cars in front.

On his way out of Copenhagen and through Zealand he called the local police at Risskov and Nyborg, but as he feared they weren't much help. Most limited had been the information about the 2001 killing in Risskov. Since the crime was seventeen years in the past, his inquiries were given short shrift by the Aarhus Police, and he was transferred three times before a female constable took pity on him and looked up the case: it was long ago marked unsolved and shelved. She wasn't familiar with it personally, but she was willing to read out fragments of the case report over the phone. None of which proved useful. The victim, a lab assistant, had been a single mother, and the evening of the murder she'd found someone to look after her one-year-old girl because she was expecting a friend for dinner. When the friend arrived, he found her stabbed to death on the living-room floor and called the police. Two years later, the investigation was deprioritized and the case shelved—they'd run out of suspects and had no more leads to follow.

When it came to the Nyborg case from 2015, the situation was different. The victim was the mother of a three-year-old boy, and the investigation was still active. The boy's father, an ex-boyfriend, was the main suspect, and there was a warrant out for his arrest, but he was believed to be hiding in Thailand. The motive, apparently, was a mixture of jealousy and money. The man had "biker-gang connections," and the local inspector's working theory was that he'd followed the victim in her car and observed her assignation with a married professional football player. On the way home he'd forced her onto the hard shoulder, then struck or stabbed her with an unidentified weapon, piercing her brain through her left eye. Since Hess didn't think it likely that the victim's ex-boyfriend, now presumed to be in Pattaya, could be responsible for the recent murders in the capital, he asked the inspector whether there had been any other suspects. Anybody who'd had a connection to the woman without being a close friend, ex-boyfriend, or relative. But the inspector didn't think so, and Hess sensed the man took the question as an indirect criticism of his work. He decided not to push. Instead he approached the issue of the doll hanging from the rearview mirror in the woman's car.

"When you were interviewing people and you showed them images from the crime scene, did anybody notice any objects that gave them pause, or that didn't belong?"

"How on earth did you know that? Why do you ask?"

"Could you let me know who it was?"

"The victim's mother was surprised to see a chestnut man hanging from the rearview mirror. She said the victim had had nut allergies since childhood, so it was a bit odd."

The inspector, who didn't like loose ends, had taken pains to solve the mystery. Questioning at the child's kindergarten had revealed that one of the classes had made chestnut men a couple of weeks back, so it wasn't inconceivable that the mother had put one of her child's creations in the car herself, despite her allergies. The information gave Hess chills. Although the inspector's theory sounded plausible, he didn't for a moment believe it was true. But who'd spend any time wondering about the presence of a chestnut man in September or October? Probably no one. For a moment Hess had sensed his question had opened the door to fresh doubt and self-examination for the inspector, so he hurried to shut it again. There was no reason to raise the alarm when he had nothing more than theories to go on.

Unable to dig further into those two cases for the time being, Hess turned south in hope of finding someone to discuss the case from Møn. Luckily Møn fell under the jurisdiction of Vordingborg, in Denmark's southernmost province, so at least he doesn't have to make the endless drive down there. But he was beginning to regret his decision. For the same reason he still hadn't contacted Thulin or Nylander, and as he walked up the slippery steps of Vordingborg police station he doubted whether he'd have to. Since his moment of clarity at the airport he'd realized how difficult a task he'd set himself. Even if it turned out that the same person had been killing and terrorizing women for decades, it might take just as long to prove as the murderer had spent committing the crimes. *If* it was true at all.

606 · SØREN SVEISTRUP

In the busy reception area at Vordingborg police station, Hess lies smoothly, explaining that he is with the Major Crimes Division in Copenhagen and would like to speak to the local chief of police. The station is busy. Apparently it's a mess out there, and people are continually driving into one another, but a friendly soul takes the time to point Hess down a corridor and tell him to ask for Brink.

Hess enters a grubby open-plan office where a pockmarked, red-haired man around sixty years old and a hundred kilograms in weight is shrugging on his coat and chatting on his phone.

"Then leave the piece of crap where it is, if it won't start. I'm on my way!"

The man hangs up and strides toward the entrance, showing no sign of stepping aside for Hess.

"I'm supposed to speak to Brink?"

"I'm on my way out. You'll have to wait until Monday."

Hess hurries to fish out his police badge, but the man is already past him and heading down the corridor, zipping up his parka.

"It's important. I have a few questions about a case, and—"

"I'm sure you do, but I'm off for the weekend. Ask at reception. I'm sure they'll be able help you. Goodbye!"

"I can't ask at reception. It's about a murder case on Møn back in 1989."

Brink's hefty figure comes to a standstill in the middle of the hallway. For a moment he remains with his back turned, but then he wheels around and looks at Hess as though he's seen a ghost.

106

Police Inspector Brink would never forget October 31st, 1989. Everything else in his experience as an officer paled in comparison to his memories of that day. Even now, many years later, sitting opposite Hess in the dimly lit office with the snow drifting down outside, the thickset man can't help but be moved.

When Detective Brink arrived at Ørum's farm the afternoon before his twenty-ninth birthday, he was responding to a call for assistance from Inspector Marius Larsen. Larsen, known in those days as "the sheriff," had driven out to see Ørum because a neighbor or two had been complaining that his animals were wandering around on their fields. It had happened before. Ørum, a father in his early forties, ran a small farm, but also worked part-time at the ferry terminal. He wasn't trained in farming, let alone experienced or dedicated, and people said he was simply trying to earn a bit of extra cash by keeping animals. He'd bought the farm for a song at a forced auction, and since the animals, stalls, and grazing areas had been part of the bargain he'd tried to capitalize on them. Which, unfortunately, hadn't gone so well. Generally speaking, "money," and maybe especially "short of money," were the words that came to mind most often when the conversation turned to Ørum. Some people thought it was lack of money that had made Ørum and his wife register as a foster family. Each time a child or a young person was sent to stay at Ørum's farm a check would follow, and over the years they'd added up. Others in the small community on Møn had probably sensed that the family wasn't one of the soft, socially minded brigade, but on the other hand it was felt that the children taken under the Ørum family's wing would benefit from the environment on offer. Plenty of fresh air, fields, and animals, and the children could learn to help out and earn their keep. The Ørum youngsters, both foster and biological, were easy to recognize in the local community because they were more shabbily dressed than their classmates, often in clothes inappropriate for the season. True, there was perhaps a tendency for the family to keep to itself, as well, but in the case of the foster children, especially, this shyness was put down to their unfortunate backgrounds. So although the Ørum family wasn't particularly well liked, it enjoyed a certain standing, because—money or no money—it was doing a good thing for children who didn't have much else in their lives. That Ørum knocked back more than his fair share of beer when he was working at the ferry terminal or sitting in his old, beat-up Opel by the harbor—well, that was his right.

It was with this limited knowledge that Brink and another colleague arrived at the farmyard about thirty years earlier, along with the ambulance the sheriff had requested. The dead pig behind the tractor had been an omen of the bloodbath that awaited them inside the house. Ørum's two teenage children had been shot at the breakfast table, the mother had been chopped to bits in the bathroom, and in the basement they found the still-warm body of Marius Larsen, who had been killed with several blows to the face from the same axe used on the mother.

Ørum wasn't there. His old Opel was in the barn, but the man himself had vanished. Since Larsen must have been murdered within the last hour, they knew he couldn't have gotten far, but they had searched high and low without result. Not until three years later was Ørum's corpse found quite by chance by a new owner, sunk in the fertilizer pit just behind the farm, where it seemed Ørum had taken his own life with a hunting rifle. He must have done it just before Brink and his colleague arrived. According to Forensics, the hunting rifle in the pit was the same one used on the teenagers in the kitchen and the pig in the yard, and with that things fell into place. The case was solved.

"What happened? Why did Ørum do it?"

Hess has been taking notes on a block of Post-its, and now he looks at the policeman on the other side of the desk.

"We couldn't be sure. Guilt, maybe. We assumed it was because of what they'd done to the foster children."

"What foster children?"

"The twins. The ones we found in the basement."

Initially Brink simply did a swift check that the twins, the girl and the boy, were alive. Then the ambulance people took care of them, while Brink and his colleague concentrated on getting the search for Ørum off the ground as more officers arrived on the scene. But when Brink went back into the basement, it dawned on him that the place was anything but ordinary.

"It looked like a dungeon. Fitted out with padlocks, bars on the windows, some clothes, a few schoolbooks, and a mattress—you didn't want to know what *that* had been used for. In an old cupboard we found a stack of VHS tapes, so we soon learned what had been going on."

"What had been going on?"

"Why is this important?"

"It just is."

Brink stares at him and takes a deep breath.

"The girl had been abused and raped. It started the day they arrived, and continued the whole time they were there. Different kinds of sex. With Ørum himself or with the teenagers—Ørum and his wife forced them to participate. On one of the tapes they even dragged the girl into the pigpen . . ."

Brink falls silent. The man rubs his ear and blinks, and Hess can see his eyes are shining.

"There's not much I can't take. But sometimes I can still hear that boy screaming at the mother, trying to get her to intervene . . ."

"What did the mother do?"

"Nothing. She was the one filming it."

Brink swallows.

"On another tape you could see her locking the boy into the basement and telling him to make his chestnut men until it was over. And he did. Every time, by the looks of it. The whole basement was filled with those damned dolls . . ."

Hess pictures the scene. The boy was locked into a basement room by his foster mother while his sister was being tormented on the other side of the wall, and for a moment Hess tries to imagine what that might do to a small human mind.

"I'd like to see the file."

"Why?"

"I can't give you the details, but I need to find out where the boy and girl are today. And I need to find out soon."

Hess gets to his feet to emphasize the rush, but Brink remains seated.

"Because you're doing a profile of an inmate in the secure unit in Slagelse?"

Brink raises an eyebrow as though to ask whether Hess takes him for an idiot. That was the explanation Hess gave him when he arrived. He'd judged it would be easier to expand on one lie than to start a new one, so he said he was helping the Danish police profile an inmate at a secure facility, Linus Bekker, whose brain, oddly enough, was obsessed with a particular photo from the 1989 Møn case. The less said about his true purpose the better.

"I think it's time to stop this. Give me the name of your superior officer on the murder squad."

"Brink, this is important."

"Why should I help you with a damn thing? I've already given you half an hour I should have used to help my sister out of the snow."

"Because I'm not sure it was Ørum who killed your colleague, Marius Larsen. Or any of the others, for that matter."

The policeman stares at him. For a moment Hess thinks he is about to break into an incredulous laugh. But when Brink answers it is without surprise, and he sounds mostly as though he were trying to convince himself.

"It *can't* have been the boy. We discussed it at the time, but it was impossible. He was only ten or eleven."

Hess doesn't reply.

107

The case files about the bloodbath on Møn are comprehensive. The process of digitization in the archive at the Vordingborg police station is advanced enough that Hess can read them on a screen instead of flipping through dusty reports like the ones around him, although actually he prefers that. As he listens impatiently to the hold music on his phone, his eyes sweep across the shelves, and it strikes him what an incredible amount of human suffering must be documented by the state, lying forgotten in archives, registers, and servers up and down the country.

"You are number . . . seven . . . in the queue."

Brink has followed him down to the basement and unlocked the archive, a primitive, dirty room with a long row of shelves carrying boxes and folders. There are no windows, only long old-fashioned fluorescent tubes, the kind Hess last saw at school, and the room reminds him how much he hates basements and underground rooms.

The extent of the case files was so massive, said Brink, that the case was one of the first to be digitized when they started the process a few years back; they'd wanted to save on space. And so Hess had to read the case on the buzzy old computer in the corner. Brink offered to help, almost insisting on staying, but Hess preferred to look through the material without interruption. His phone rang a few times, including several calls from François, and he guessed the Frenchman has realized he never arrived at Bucharest.

Hess knew what he was looking for in the material, but he still got bogged down in the details. The description of the officers' first encounter with the twins made for lurid reading. They'd been found hugging each other tightly in a corner of the basement, the boy with his arms around his sister, who had seemed apathetic, as though in a state of shock. The boy had fought being separated from her when they were led out to the ambulance, and his behavior was compared to "a wild animal's." A medical examination of the children had confirmed the abuse and violence already evidenced by the basement, but when they tried to interview the twins it proved impossible. The boy had been completely mute. He'd refused to say a word. His sister, on the other hand, answered unreservedly, apparently without understanding the questions. The psychologist present had declared the girl was living in a kind of parallel world—probably an attempt to repress her experiences. A judge excused the children from appearing in court, and by that point they'd already been sent to foster families in other parts of the country. The authorities had decided to split them up, hoping it would help the twins to put the past behind them and start afresh. To Hess it hadn't sounded like a particularly wise decision.

The first thing he'd jotted down on the block of Post-its beside the computer were the twins' names, Toke and Astrid Bering, as well as their ID numbers, but otherwise the report wasn't very informative about their background. A memo from a social worker said that they'd been found abandoned in a stairwell at a maternity hospital in Aarhus in 1979, no more than a few weeks old, and had been named by the midwives. Without going into detail, the memo noted that the twins had lived with other foster families before being transferred to Chestnut Farm—this being the name of Ørum's farm—two years before the bloodbath. With every line he read Hess felt as though he was coming closer to an explanation, but then he looked up the twins' ID numbers in the police register to find out where they were today.

"You are number . . . three . . . in the queue."

The extended police register, which cross-references various databases potentially relevant to policework, shows where a particular person has lived and when. Each entry includes a chronological list of a person's residences and moving dates, as well as information on whether the individual has been married, divorced, charged with a crime, convicted, deported, or in any other way been involved in activities of interest to the police.

But what should have been a routine search turned out to be a new mystery.

According to the database, after staying at a state institution for deprived children, twelve-year-old Toke Bering had been rehomed with a foster family in Langeland. Then one in Als, then another three foster families, before the trail went cold shortly after his seventeenth birthday. There were simply no other addresses or events connected to his ID number.

If Toke Bering was dead, it ought to say so, but he had merely ceased to be tracked in the system, so Hess phoned the national database for an explanation. The woman who answered the phone was able to glean no more than Hess, however, and her best guess was that Toke Bering has left the country.

He'd taken the opportunity to ask about the sister, but again she was able to offer no more information than what he'd already found. Astrid Bering was sent to several foster families after her stay at Chestnut Farm, but the social workers and child psychologists had obviously changed their strategy with the girl, because they'd transferred her out of the foster system and into various homes for mentally ill young people. From the age of eighteen to twenty-seven her address was unregistered, which could mean she'd been abroad, but after that one home for the mentally ill had followed another. Until just under a year ago, when, at the age of thirty-eight, she'd vanished into thin air. Hess had contacted her most recent address, but the place had gotten a new manager since then, and he had no idea where Astrid Bering might have gone after being discharged.

"You are number . . . two . . . in the queue."

So Hess had chosen the hard way: phoning all the twins' former foster families to find out whether they'd heard from either of them over the years, and whether they knew where to find them. Hess started

chronologically—*before* the stay at Chestnut Farm—
but two calls had gotten him nowhere. The foster parents had seemed obliging, but they'd had no contact
with the twins, so now Hess has moved on to foster
family number three.

"Odsherred Council, Department for Families, how
can I help you?"

The old landline for the Petersen foster family from
Odsherred was disconnected, so instead Hess is turning to the council. He explains who he is and that he is
looking for Poul and Kirsten Petersen, residents at 35
Kirkevej in Odsherred—he hopes they will be able to
give him some information about twins who were in
their care in 1987.

"Not unless you've got a direct line to the Lord. According to what it says on my screen, Poul and Kirsten
Petersen are both dead. The husband died seven years
ago, the wife two years later."

"How did they die?"

He inquires out of habit, but the tired voice on the
phone doesn't have that information on her screen.
Since the husband and wife were seventy-four and
seventy-nine, respectively, and died a few years apart,
it didn't seem of interest anyway.

"What about children? Did they have any children
living there at the time?"

Hess asks because it's possible siblings or foster siblings might have stayed in touch, even if the parents were no longer alive.

"Nope, not as far as I can see."

"Okay, thanks. Bye."

"Oh wait, hang on. They'd already fostered a child, and it looks like they adopted her. Rosa Petersen."

Hess is about to hang up when he registers what the voice has said. It could be a coincidence, and his instincts tell him there are thousands of people with that first name. But still.

"Do you have an ID number for Rosa Petersen?"

She gives him the number, and he asks her to hang on while he turns back to the computer. A moment later he's checked the database and found that Rosa Petersen married fifteen years ago, changing her name to her husband's, and he is no longer in any doubt: Rosa Petersen is Rosa Hartung. Hess fidgets in his seat.

"What exactly does it say about the twins' stay with the Petersen family?"

"Nothing. All I can see is that the Petersens fostered them for about three months."

"Why not longer?"

"Doesn't say. And it's about time I clocked off."

When the caseworker hangs up, Hess still has his phone to his ear. The twins had only spent three months in Odsherred with the Petersens and their adopted daughter, Rosa. Afterward they'd been sent to the Ørum family on Møn. Hess knows no more than that, but he is certain this is the connection: the Petersens, the boy in the basement at Chestnut Farm, the chestnut men left with the victims, the victims mutilated to look like the dolls—a killer making his own chestnut man out of human body parts.

Hess's fingers quiver as the images whirl around in his head, trying to fall into place. It has all been about Rosa Hartung, right from the start. Again and again the fingerprints have led them in her direction, even though he hadn't understood why, but *this* is what he's been looking for. The insight jolts him to his feet, but then everything darkens when it suddenly dawns on him what is going to happen next.

Immediately he phones Rosa Hartung. The dial tone is replaced by her voicemail, and Hess hangs up. He's about to try again when he receives a call from an unknown number.

"It's Brink. Sorry if I'm interrupting. I've asked around, but no one really knows what became of the twins."

"That's fine, Brink, I don't have time right now."

Brink had offered to help Hess call around the community, and Hess had only agreed to get him out of the way, so it's irritating that he is calling back to report.

"And there's a dearth of information in the system, particularly when it comes to the boy. I just asked my sister's youngest girl, who was at school with the twins, but she couldn't get hold of them when the class held a school reunion a few years back."

"Brink, I need to run!"

Hess hangs up and makes another call, standing impatiently by the computer, but Rosa Hartung still isn't picking up. He leaves a message and decides to call her husband, but then he receives a text. At first he thinks it's a notification that Rosa Hartung has returned his call, but it's a text from Brink.

"Class photo of 5A from 1989. Don't know if it's of use. My niece says the girl must have been sick the day the picture was taken, but the boy's the one on the far left."

Hess immediately clicks on the attached photo and surveys it. There are fewer than twenty students in the faded photograph, presumably because it's a rural school. One row of pupils are standing up, another sit on chairs in front. They wear pastel colors; some of the girls have permed hair and shoulder pads, while the boys are in Reebok shoes and Kappa or Lacoste sweaters. In the front row sits a girl with large earrings, a sunbed tan, and a small sign that reads "5A," and most of the students are smiling at the camera as though someone, maybe the photographer, has just said something hilarious.

But once you catch sight of him, it is the boy on the far left who grabs the viewer's attention. He isn't tall for his age. Not as developed as the other boys, in fact, and his clothes are scruffy and down-at-heel. But his eyes are piercing. He's staring straight into the camera with an expressionless face, and it's as though he's the only one who hasn't heard the joke.

Hess stares at him. Hair, cheekbones, nose, chin, lips. All the features that change so radically during adolescence. Hess recognizes him, yet at the same time he doesn't, and it is only when he zooms in and covers the boy's face so only his eyes are visible that he can see who it is. He can see it, but it is as impossible as it is obvious. When comprehension dawns, his first thought is that it is too late to fight back.

108

Her ankles are slender and delicate, perfectly suited to her high-heeled shoes, which he loves to watch at moments like this, when he lets her leave the press room first and walk ahead of him down the corridor. She turns and says something to him, and Nylander nods in acknowledgment, while in reality he is thinking how to begin the affair he's already decided to have with her. The kickoff could easily be later today. Maybe he'll offer her a coffee at one of the nearby hotel bars around the train station, so they can discuss the future. He'll thank her for her efforts and waffle about her options as a communications consultant with the police, but if he's taken the temperature correctly it won't take much foreplay to get her up to one of the rooms for an hour or two before he has to go home and mix drinks for the usual Friday get-together his wife has organized. Nylander long ago made up his mind that he still loved his wife—at least, loved the idea of family life—but that his wife had plenty to do with the kids, the school council, and the general façade, so he didn't see anything amiss with secretly enjoying his freedom. And today, in particular, he can't shake the feeling that he deserves a reward after the week he's had.

The final press conference is over, and they've at last finished presenting the case to the public—with the result Nylander wanted. Few people understand how fine a balancing act it is to come across as serious and credible in the media, but Nylander realized long ago how a well-judged public statement can be used to pave the way for other agendas, whether at the station, the prosecutor's office, or the justice ministry. He'd also sensed that his status internally grew with every passing minute he appeared on screens and media platforms. His critics have been put in their place, and he couldn't care less if people think he's pushed himself too far into the limelight. Personally he thinks he's been generous with his praise for his team, especially Tim Jansen, although it wasn't necessary to draw any attention to Hess or Thulin. Thulin found the severed limbs, of course, but on the other hand she'd defied him by going to see Linus Bekker, and this very morning he'd been thinking it would be nice to get her off his hands. Even to NC3. His department will soon be flooded with new resources, and he'll probably be up to his ears in types like her—even if the odd little thing does have something special about her.

Hess, on the other hand, he doesn't have a good word to say about. He's praised him to the skies, of course, in his conversation with some boss at Europol, but only to be rid of him. Hess hasn't shown up at the station even once since the case was solved, and Nylander has had to ask Thulin and the others to write reports that were strictly Hess's responsibility, so it's good news the man is on his way out of the country. It's a surprise, therefore, to find that Hess is calling his mobile phone.

His first thought, obviously, is to reject the call, but then he realizes why Hess is calling, and suddenly he finds himself looking forward to the conversation. A few minutes earlier, a colleague informed him that a Frenchman from Europol had called and asked whether anybody knew why Hess hadn't shown up as agreed, but Nylander was barely listening. He didn't care. Now, however, he imagines Hess explaining how he missed his flight to Bucharest, pleading with Nylander to call the Hague with some excuse and save his bacon. But Hess *deserves* to get the sack, and as Nylander picks up the phone he is merely wondering how he can make sure the guy doesn't end up getting knocked back into his court.

Three minutes and thirty-eight seconds later, the conversation is over. Its precise duration appears on the display, and Nylander stares at it apathetically. A yawning hole has opened beneath his feet. His brain is still protesting against the revelations Hess shared before he hung up, but deep down he knows they could be true. He becomes aware that the communications consultant with her sweet little mouth is still talking to him, but he breaks into a jog. Reaching the department, he grabs the nearest detective. *Get the task force together. Get hold of Rosa Hartung. Now!*

109

Steen Hartung is soaked with the snow that has again begun to fall in the suburban neighborhood he is canvassing. The alcohol in the little bottles is the only thing keeping him warm, but he's running out, and he reminds himself to stop by the gas station on Bernstorffsvej. He trudges up yet another snow-smothered garden path, past yet another parade of snow-smothered Halloween pumpkins, and rings yet another doorbell. As he waits, he casts a brief glance over his shoulder at his footprints in the snow, and at the heavy white flakes swirling around the neighborhood as though inside a snow globe. Some doors open, others don't; judging by the wait, this would be a door that stayed shut. Yet just as he has turned and is beginning to walk down the steps, he hears the door behind him open. The eyes that meet his are familiar. Though it's a stranger, Steen feels he recognizes the man. But he's tired, he's been trudging for hours without result, and exhaustion makes him doubt himself. Somewhere inside he has become aware the sole purpose of his search is to alleviate the pain he feels. He studies maps and plans and knocks on doors, but in his heart of hearts he's begun to grasp that it's all for nothing.

To the eyes in the doorway he begins to stammer out why he's come. First he outlines the situation, then explains his hope that the man might be able to remember anything, anything at all, from the afternoon of October 18th last year, when his daughter might have cycled through the neighborhood down exactly this street. Steen accompanies his words with a photo of his daughter, whose face by now is damp with snowflakes, her colors running like smeared mascara. Yet before Steen can finish, the man at the door shakes his head. Steen hesitates a moment and tries again, but the man shakes his head a second time, making to shut the door, and suddenly Steen loses control.

"I remember seeing you before. Who are you? I know I've seen you!"

There is mistrust in Steen's voice, almost as though he's recognized a suspect, and he puts his foot in the door so the man can't close it.

"I remember you too. It's not that strange. You rang my doorbell on Monday and asked exactly the same questions."

It takes Steen a moment to realize the man is right. Mortified, he hears himself apologizing as he backs away from the doorstep and toward the road. Behind him he hears the man asking if he's all right, but Steen doesn't reply. He runs through the white maelstrom of snow and doesn't stop until he reaches the car at the end of the street, where he slips and has to grab the hood so as not to fall. He wedges himself into the front seat and bursts into tears, sitting in the gloom of the blanketed car, sobbing like a child. His phone starts to vibrate in his inside pocket, but he ignores it. Only when it crosses his mind that it might be Gustav does he force his hand to find the phone and realize he has numerous missed calls. Instantly he is afraid. He picks up, but it isn't Gustav calling. It's the au pair, and Steen's first instinct is to hang up without a word. But Alice is saying something about needing to find Rosa straightaway—something is wrong. It isn't clear what she means, but the words *chestnut men* and *police* thrust him out of one nightmare on that suburban street and into another.

110

The three police vans, sirens blaring, clear the road of traffic. Nylander is sitting in the convoy of cars behind them, and the whole way out of the city he racks his brains for another connection besides the one Hess has put forward on the phone. He returns his gaze again and again to the picture of the school class Hess has texted him, and although he recognizes the childish face on the far left, he can't quite believe it.

Just before they arrive, the sirens are switched off to avoid alerting the suspect, and when the vans draw up outside the building of the Forensics Department, they split up as agreed. Within forty-five seconds the place is surrounded, and as the first curious people start watching from the windows in the cube-like building, Nylander wades through the snow toward the main entrance, where nothing appears out of the ordinary. There is soft Muzak playing in the reception area, and people are exchanging weekend plans with colleagues over the fruit basket on the desk. When the accommodating, lemon-perfumed receptionist tells them Genz is in a hurriedly arranged meeting in his lab, Nylander begins inwardly cursing himself for having listened to Hess and raised the alarm.

Ignoring the blue plastic overshoes on offer because of the weather, and as lab coat–wearing techs glance up curiously from their glass-walled workstations, Nylander and three detectives march toward the laboratory, which he so often visited whenever he wanted to reassure himself that evidence was in fact as described in reports or telephone conversations.

But the lab is empty. So is Genz's private office, which adjoins it. The state of normality in both rooms is comforting, however—everything is neat and tidy, and a plastic cup containing a few last drops of coffee stands peacefully on the desk in front of the big screen.

The receptionist, who has followed them into the lab, seems unfazed by her boss's absence, and announces she will find him. As soon as she's gone, Nylander begins plotting how to make Hess's life and career harder—payback for the gaffe he's been browbeaten into committing. When Genz arrives he'll explain. He might even laugh and point out that it isn't him in the picture. That he's never been called Toke Bering, that he hasn't spent years of his life preparing his revenge, that of course he isn't the psychopathic killer Hess claims he is.

But then he sees it. Standing in the lab, his eyes sweeping across the room, he glances into Genz's office and at the objects on the desk, which he hadn't noticed when he first peered inside. Genz's ID card, keys, work phone, and access card are laid out neatly on the bare surface, almost as if abandoned, never to be used again. Yet that isn't what horrifies him. It's the innocent little chestnut man enthroned on the box of matchsticks beside them.

111

Just as Hess gets through to Nylander, he joins the final stretch of motorway toward Copenhagen. He'd tried calling several times already, but only now is the idiot picking up—and he is clearly not in a chatty mood.

"What do you want? I'm busy!"

"Have you found them?"

The laboratory had been empty. No sign of Genz, apart from the signature he left to greet his pursuers. At first his staff had thought he must be at a conference in Jutland, but when they inquired it turned out Genz had been a no-show.

"What about his home address?"

"That's where we are right now. Some big pent-house apartment in a new complex in Nordhavn.

But it's empty, and I mean *empty*: no furniture, nothing left behind. Not so much as a fingerprint, I reckon."

Hess can see no more than twenty yards ahead on the motorway, but he puts his foot down a little harder on the accelerator.

"But you have got Rosa Hartung, correct? This whole thing is about her, and if Genz—"

"We've got bugger all. Apparently no one knows where she is, and her phone's off, so we can't trace it. Her husband doesn't know anything either, but it seems the au pair girl saw her drive off in her car after she found some sort of ornament made of chestnut men outside the back door."

"What kind of ornament?"

"I haven't seen it."

"Can't Genz be traced? His phone or his car—"

"Nope. He left his phone in his office, and there are no tracker units in the cars from Forensics. Any other handy suggestions?"

"What about the computer in his lab? Get Thulin to break the code so we can see what's on there."

"We've already got a team trying to access it."

"Get hold of Thulin! She'll have it sorted in no—"

"Thulin's gone."

There's something ominous about Nylander's words. Hess can hear him and the others walking down some steps in an echoing stairwell, and he guesses the search of Genz's empty apartment is over.

"What do you mean?"

"Apparently she went looking for Genz at the Forensics Department and met with him earlier today. A tech in the garage said he saw them coming down the back stairs, getting into Genz's car, and driving off a couple of hours ago. That's all I know."

"A couple of hours ago? Surely you've tried calling her, then?"

"No answer. I've just been told her phone was found in a trash can outside Forensics."

Hess brakes, veering toward the hard shoulder beside the snowy motorway. Several cars beep at him, and he avoids a truck in the inside lane by the skin of his teeth before he reaches the hard shoulder and stops the car.

"Genz has no use for her. He might have just dropped her off somewhere. Maybe she's at home, or with her—"

"Hess, we've *checked*. Thulin is missing. Do you have anything I can use? Any idea where he might be?"

Hess hears the question. Traffic thunders past. He tries to force himself out of his paralysis, but the only thing moving is the windshield wipers, which glide back and forth.

"Hess!"

"No. I don't know."

Hess hears a car door slam, and the line go dead. A few seconds pass before he lowers the phone from his ear. Cars plow past him in the snow, and the windshield wipers keep resolutely squeaking back and forth.

He should have called her. He should have called her from the airport the moment he realized something was wrong. If he'd called, she would be absorbed in Bekker's favorite crime-scene photos right now, and she'd never have gone to see Genz. But he hadn't, and the emotions sticking in his throat tell him there are more reasons for that than he wants to admit.

Hess tries to cling to a rational train of thought. It might not be too late. He has no idea why Thulin visited Genz, but if she got into a car with him willingly then it had to be because she didn't know who he was. Ergo, Genz has no reason to harm her, much less any interest in spending time with her. Unless Thulin discovered something, and sought out Genz as an ally she could talk to.

The thought is terrifying. But Thulin is at most a bump in the road for Genz, and he isn't going to shift focus on her account. This is about Rosa Hartung—it has been about Rosa all along. Rosa Hartung and the past.

Suddenly Hess knows what to do. It's a shot in the dark, maybe more a feeling than a rational thought, but the other possibilities are either too unlikely or already covered by Nylander and the detectives in Copenhagen. He glances over his shoulder and stares into the fog lights of the rows of cars whizzing past, sending black snow spraying. When there is a few seconds' respite—enough, at least, so that the next phalanx of cars has a chance to get out of the way—he slams the pedal to the floor and swings clear across the highway, aiming for a gap in the crash barrier. The wheels spin, and for a moment he thinks the car is going to whirl around like a stuck bowling pin. But then the wheels bite the tarmac, and he crosses the central divider onto the opposite lane. He hasn't even looked at those cars, so he simply leans on the horn and slips in between two vans, only righting himself when he reaches the slow lane.

Hess drives back the way he came. Seconds later, the speedometer reaches 140 kilometers per hour, and he has the whole outside lane to himself.

112

"It's a nice day for a trip to the woods, but as far as I can see there's nothing but ordinary beeches around here."

Genz's words make Thulin peer even more intently out of the windshield and side windows, but it looks like he is right. Even without the snow, it would probably have been difficult to identify the chestnut trees, and with Møn covered in white powder it's feeling more and more impossible.

They are driving down a narrow, winding country road, and Genz, who is sitting behind the wheel, glances at his watch.

"It was worth a shot. But let's head back to the bridge. I'll give you a lift to the train station at Vordingborg, then I'll drive on to Jutland. Okay?"

"Sure . . ."

Thulin realizes the trip has been pointless, and she falls back in her seat.

"Sorry I wasted your time."

"It's completely fine. Like you said, I was going this way anyway."

Thulin tries to return Genz's smile, although she is freezing cold and tired.

It didn't take long to track down the expert who helped Forensics determine the type of chestnut.

Ingrid Kalke, professor of botany at the Faculty of Natural Sciences, Copenhagen University, was exceptionally young for a professor, perhaps thirty-five years old, but the slender woman spoke with authority. Addressing them from her office via Skype, she confirmed that the chestnuts she'd been asked to identify were a different kind from the horse chestnuts predominantly found in Denmark.

"The kind of chestnut these dolls were made of is an edible variety. Normally the climate in this country is too cold for them, but you do find a few trees roundabout, near the Limfjord, for instance. To be precise, this is a hybrid of the European and Japanese chestnut, what's known as a *Castanea sativa x crenata*. At first glance they look to be Marigoules, which in itself is not unusual. The unusual thing is that these ones seem to have been crossed with Bouche de Betizacs. Most experts believe that precise combination is extinct in this country, and the last I heard about them was several years ago, when the last few trees were allegedly killed off by a particular fungus. But I've already told you all this."

The young professor had covered this ground with the assistant who had contacted her, and Thulin noticed Genz fall quiet when she reminded them of this. Clearly he felt it embarrassed his department that the information hadn't found its way to the police before now.

The investigation might have ended there, if Thulin hadn't asked one final question.

"Where in Denmark was the Marigoule-Betizac variety last sighted?"

Professor Ingrid Kalke double-checked with a colleague, and it turned out that the most recently registered chestnut trees of that type were from sites on Møn, but she repeated that the variety was now extinct. Even so, Thulin carefully noted down the different locations on the island before saying goodbye to the professor; then she had to spend some time convincing Genz, who didn't quite understand the significance of the discovery.

Thulin explained that if the chestnuts with Kristine Hartung's fingerprints weren't horse chestnuts then they couldn't come from her stall, which made their origin even more mysterious than first thought. It no longer seemed logically possible to explain how Benedikte Skans and Asger Neergaard could have gotten hold of them, certainly not ones with Kristine Hartung's fingerprints on them, and that cast doubt on Nylander's reading of the case. On the other hand, Thulin was glad that recent sightings of the variety could be traced back to relatively few places in Denmark—specifically, to a handful of sites on Møn. If the variety was as rare as the expert had claimed, those locations might open up a new avenue of investigation. Best-case scenario, they might even offer something new about the killer—or about Kristine Hartung.

By that point Genz had realized Thulin believed there was a chance the murders were still unsolved. That Hess could have been right. That somebody might have made it appear as though the young couple had committed the crimes.

"You don't believe that. You're kidding."

At first Genz laughed and refused to drive her to Møn to look for chestnut trees. Even after she tried telling him it was on his way, if he was driving to Jutland.

More or less, anyhow. But he shook his head—until he realized she was going to do it no matter what. Then he capitulated, and she was grateful. Partly because she didn't have a car of her own that day, and partly because she could use his help identifying the variety, assuming they actually found one.

Unfortunately things hadn't gone as she'd hoped. Genz had made good time on the journey—despite the snow they managed it in an hour and a half—but once they reached the locations the expert had given them, either there had been nothing but old snow-covered stumps or the trees had long since been cleared to make way for new housing developments. In one last-ditch attempt, Thulin had Genz drive away from the main road and back toward the Zealand bridge, a route that took them along a country road bordered by forest on one side and fields on the other. But the snow had made progress steadily more difficult, and although Genz remained chipper, it gradually became obvious that they had to abandon the project.

Thulin's mind turns to her daughter and Aksel. The school party must have finished ages ago, and she decides to call and reassure them she is on her way home.

"Have you seen my phone?"

She gropes around in her coat pockets, but no matter how deeply she digs she can't find it.

"No. But I do have a theory about how the chestnuts could have come from rare trees on Møn and still have ended up at the Hartung place. The family might have taken a trip to Møn, seen the cliffs and gathered a few chestnuts to take home."

"Yeah, maybe."

The last time Thulin took out her phone, it was to put it on the desk in Genz's lab, and she is baffled that she's forgotten it. She never normally does. She's about to rummage through her pockets one more time when her eyes happen to be caught by something on the roadside. For a moment she isn't sure, but the image remains, and then she understands what it is that has sent her mind in another direction.

"Stop! Stop here! Stop!"

"Why?"

"Just stop! Stop!"

Genz finally puts his foot on the brake, and the car skids a fraction before coming to a stop. Thulin flings open the door and emerges into the silence. It is midafternoon, but the sun is setting. To her right are the broad, snow-clad fields, sprawling into the distance until snow and sky become one at the horizon; to her left are the woods, dark and heavy-laden. And there, a little farther back at the edge of the road, stands an enormous tree. It is taller than the others. Its trunk is thick as a barrel, its height twenty, perhaps twenty-five meters, and its hulking skeleton of branches is covered in snow. It doesn't actually look like a chestnut tree. Apart from the snow it is bare and stark, yet Thulin is certain. She approaches the tree, snow crunching in the cold air, and as she walks beneath the branches, where the snow isn't as thick, she immediately feels the small globes underneath her feet. She isn't wearing gloves, so with her bare hands she digs around in the snow to pick up the fallen chestnuts.

"Genz!"

It annoys her that Genz has remained standing by the car, that he isn't as excited as she is. She brushes the snow off the chestnuts, and the icy, dark-brown spheres in her left hand look like the ones that had borne Kristine Hartung's fingerprints. Thulin tries to remember the distinguishing characteristics the expert had mentioned.

"Come and look at these. It might be them!"

"Thulin, even if they're the same chestnuts, it doesn't prove anything. The Hartungs could have come down to see the cliffs and driven along this road on the way home. Their daughter could have picked up some chestnuts here."

Thulin doesn't reply. She didn't see it when they first drove past the tree, but now she is standing underneath it she realizes that the forest isn't as dense as she'd thought. Beside the tree there is a road that twists deep into the woods, and the snow looks utterly unspoiled.

"Let's drive down here and take a look."

"Why? There's nothing down there."

"You don't know that. The worst that can happen is we might get stuck."

Thulin tramps energetically back to the car. Genz is standing beside the driver's-side door. He's watching her, but as she passes him and walks around to the other side his gaze snags on an invisible point far down the narrow road into the woods.

"Fine, then. If that's really what you want."

113

Autumn 1987

*T*he boy's hands are dirty, and he has earth under his nails. He's trying clumsily to make a hole in the chestnut with the awl, but Rosa has to show him how it's done. You don't jab, you bore. You twist the awl until it bites and pierces the flesh of the chestnut. First you make the hole for the neck in both chestnuts, then you screw half a matchstick firmly into one of them before you stick the other chestnut on top. Then you bore in with the awl again to make holes for the arms and legs—deep holes are what you want, so the matchsticks have a good firm hold.

It's the girl who gets it first. It's as though the boy's fingers are too rough and insensitive, and time after time the chestnuts fall from his hands and onto the wet lawn, so that Rosa has to pick them up for him so he can try again. Rosa and the girl laugh at him. Not to make fun, and the boy doesn't take it that way. Well, maybe at the start, the first few times, when they went into the undergrowth beneath the tall tree to gather chestnuts with Mom and Dad. Afterward they sat in the back garden, like they are now, on the steps of the old playhouse among the red and yellow leaves, and Rosa laughed at his fumbling with the chestnuts. He'd looked frightened, and so had his sister, but then Rosa had helped them both, and they'd understood her laughter meant no harm.

"Chestnut man, do come in. Chestnut man, do come in—"

It's Rosa who sings that song as she shows the boy what to do, until at last his chestnut man is finished too, and can be placed on the wooden board alongside the others they've made. She tells the twins that the more they make, the more money they can earn when they sell them at the stall by the road. Rosa has never had siblings before, and although she knows the twins won't be here forever, probably not even until Christmas, she doesn't want to think about that. It's lovely to have them there when she awakes. Early in *the morning on a Sunday or a Saturday, when there's no school, she can sneak into the guest room on the far side of Mom and Dad's bedroom, and even when she wakes up the twins they don't get cross. They rub the sleep from their eyes and wait for her to tell them what they're going to do. They listen eagerly to the games Rosa suggests, and it doesn't matter to her that the twins don't talk much and don't have any suggestions of their own. She always looks forward to telling them what she's come up with, and it's as though her imagination swells with fun ideas and inventions once she has an audience besides Mom and Dad, who usually just go "ooh" and "well" or "We've seen that one now."*

"Rosa, could you come in here a minute?"

"Not now, Mom, we're playing."

"Rosa, come in here. It won't take long."

Rosa runs across the grass and past the kitchen garden, where her dad's spade is wedged between the potato plants and the gooseberry bushes.

"What is it?"

She fidgets impatiently by the utility-room door, but her mom says she has to take off her rain boots and come all the way inside. Rosa is surprised to find her mother and father standing in the utility room, both

waiting for her with peculiar smiles, and she realizes they've probably been watching them play in the
garden for a while.

"Do you like playing with Toke and Astrid?"

"Yes. What is it? We're busy."

She's annoyed at having to stand there in the utility
room in her raincoat while the twins are waiting for
her by the playhouse. If they get the chestnuts finished
this morning, they can fetch the fruit crates from the
garage and make the stall before lunch, so they've got
no time to waste.

"We've decided to keep Toke and Astrid, so they
can stay here for good. What do you say to that?"

The washing machine behind her dad starts up with
a hum, and the two grown-ups are looking at her.

"They've had a difficult time. They need a good
home, and your dad and I think it should be here with
us. If you think so too. Do you?"

The question catches Rosa unawares. She doesn't
know what she thinks. She thought they were going to
ask her whether they wanted some rye bread snacks.
Or some squash or a few Marie biscuits. But that's not
what they're asking. So she gives the answer the smiling faces want.

"Yes. That's fine."

The next minute Mom and Dad are tramping out into the wet garden, Mom in rain boots and Dad in flip-flops. She can tell they're happy. They're not wearing their coats, not even warm sweaters, but they make their way over to the playhouse, where the twins are sitting on the steps, still preoccupied with the chestnuts. Rosa stays by the door to the utility room, where they told her. She can't hear what they're saying, but Mom and Dad sit next to the twins and take their time. Rosa can see the twins' faces. Suddenly the girl grabs Dad and hugs him. Then the boy begins to cry. Just sits and cries. Mom puts her arm around him to comfort him, and Mom and Dad turn their faces toward each other and smile in a way Rosa can't remember seeing before. The skies open. The rain pelts down, and as Rosa stands in the doorway the others huddle under the small pent roof and laugh.

"**We completely** understand your decision. Where are they?"

"In the guest room. I'll go and get them."

"How is your girl?"

"Not too bad, given the circumstances."

Rosa is sitting at the kitchen table, but she can clearly hear the voices from the hall. Mom walks past the slightly open door toward the guest room, while

Dad remains in the hall with the man and the lady. Rosa has just watched them get out of the white car in the road outside the kitchen window. The voices in the hall get quieter, vanishing into a whisper Rosa can't decipher. There's been a lot of whispering over the last week. Rosa wants it to be over soon. It started right after she told them the story. She doesn't know where she got it from—well, maybe from kindergarten, that time. She can still remember how the grown-ups reacted when a girl called Berit told them what happened in the playroom with all the cushions. She'd been playing with the boys, until one of them wanted to see her front bottom. He'd even offered her fifty øre for it. So Berit showed him, and then she asked if the other boys wanted to see it too. Lots of them did, and Berit earned loads of money from the boys. They could put stuff up there too, which cost an extra twenty-five øre.

The grown-ups had been scared, that was obvious. There'd been lots of whispering after that day in the playroom, including among the parents in the cloakroom, and not long afterward they made tons of new rules that were no fun at all. Rosa had nearly forgotten the whole thing. But one evening after Mom and Dad spent all day buying and putting together two new beds and painting the guest room, the story had come to her quite naturally, without so much as a second thought.

Through the chink in the door she sees the two small figures go past, heads bowed. She hears their feet on the steps outside the front door, where Dad has already put their bags. In the corridor she hears Mom asking the lady where the children will be sent next.

"We haven't found a new place yet, but hopefully it won't be long."

The grown-ups say goodbye, and Rosa goes into her room. She doesn't want to see the twins, because her tummy hurts. Like there's a knot inside. But she can't take back the story now, because she said what she said, and it's not okay to lie about that sort of thing. She's got to hold it in and never say a thing to anyone. Still, she feels about ready to explode inside when she sees the present they left on her bed. Five chestnut dolls in a ring, as though they're holding hands. They're held together with steel wire, and two of the dolls are bigger than the others, as if it's a mom and a dad with their three children.

"All right, Rosa, they're gone now . . ."

Rosa bolts past her mom and dad. She hears them calling after her in astonishment as she runs through the front door. The white car has just pulled away from the curb and is speeding up toward the bend. Rosa runs as fast as she can in her socks, until the car disappears. The last thing she sees are the boy's dark eyes, staring at her through the back window.

Friday, October 30th

114

By the time she turns down the road into the woods and accelerates, the daylight is almost gone. It has started snowing again, and the snow has nearly obscured the faint tire tracks Rosa can just make out in the beam of her headlights. At first she overshot, and had to dash into a house to ask for directions. She's never been to Møn before, and even if she had, it wouldn't have made a difference. Following the instructions the lady at the house gave her and driving back the way she'd come, it strikes her that she completely overlooked the big chestnut tree and the side road that turns into the woods. The road snakes through bare old trees and tall firs, one hairpin bend after another, but because she can follow the tracks she is able to maintain her speed and stay on the road.

As the tracks gradually grow fainter, wiped smooth at last by the driving snow, panic takes hold. There is no farm here. No people, nothing at all, only the road and the woods, and if she's taken another wrong turn then it might be too late.

Just as Rosa starts to doubt herself, the forest opens up before her and the road suddenly leads onto a wide farmyard surrounded by enormous trees. It isn't what she'd imagined. The description in the report she'd read at the ministry had made her picture some tumble-down place, untended and ugly, but it isn't like that. It's idyllic. Rosa stops the car, switches off the engine, and completely forgets to lock the door as she climbs hurriedly out into the snow and glances around, her breath turning to vapor every way she looks.

There are two wings to the farmhouse—two stories, thatched roofs—and at first glance it looks like a nicely renovated country house. But the white-plastered façade is illuminated by modern outdoor lights, their glow extending all the way into the yard where she stands, and in the crannies beneath the thatched roof are small glass domes Rosa recognizes as CCTV cameras. Through the white-mullioned windows she can see something warm flickering inside the front room, and not until she sees the inscription above the front door, which reads CHESTNUT FARM in tidy black letters, is she sure she's come to the right place. Rosa can wait no longer. She shouts at the top of her lungs, and when she draws in the breath and lets it out, the name echoes through the yard and up among the trees.

"*Kristine . . . !*"

A flock of crows are flushed from the trees behind the farm. They dive through the snowflakes and fly over the wings of the house, and only once the last of them has vanished does she notice the figure by the barn door.

He is tall, about six foot one. Clad in an open oilskin jacket with a blue heavy-duty bucket of firewood in one hand and an axe in the other. His face is mild and youthful, and at first she doesn't recognize him.

"You found it . . . welcome."

There is a note of acknowledgment in his voice, almost of friendliness, and after a brief stare he starts walking across the yard toward the front door, while the snow crunches beneath his feet.

"Where is she?!"

"I want to start by apologizing that the farm looks different from the way it did back then. When I bought it I planned to re-create the place so you could see it in its original condition—but the thought was too depressing."

"Where is she?!"

"She's not here. You're welcome to look."

Rosa's heart is hammering. The whole thing is surreal, and she snatches at her breath. The man pauses at the front door, opening it amiably wide as he stands back and knocks the snow off his boots.

"Come on, Rosa. Let's get this over with."

115

Rosa shouts her name through the corridors of the dark, cold house. She runs up the stairs to the first floor and searches beneath all the sloping roofs, but with the same result. There's nothing. No furniture, no possessions, only the scent of varnish and fresh wood hanging over everything. It's an empty, newly renovated house, and it feels as though nothing has ever been inside. On her way down the stairs she hears him. He is humming something, an old nursery rhyme, and when she realizes what it is her veins freeze to ice. When she walks through the doorway from the front hall to the living room, he is crouching with his back to her, jabbing a poker at the smoldering firewood in the stove. In the blue bucket beside him is the axe, and in one swift movement she grabs it. But he doesn't move a muscle. He is still crouching when he looks up at her, and her hands begin to shake, but she tries to position them on the handle so she'll be ready to use it.

"Tell me what you've done . . ."

He shuts the door of the stove and carefully fastens the hasp.

"She's somewhere nice now. Isn't that what people say?"

"I asked you what you've done!"

"That was what they told me, anyway, every time I asked about my sister. Bit ironic, really. First you lock twins in a basement and let hubby do whatever he wants while Mommy films the whole thing. Then you split them up for years without a word of contact because you think it's best for them . . ."

Rosa doesn't know what to say, but as he rises to his feet she tightens her grip on the axe.

"But *somewhere nice*, that isn't very comforting. I think the not knowing is the worst thing. Do you agree?"

The man is insane. All the ideas that had come to Rosa on her way down are unusable. There is no reasoning, no strategy or plan that can be used before those calmly staring eyes. Instead she takes a step closer.

"I don't know what you want. And I don't care. You're going to tell me what you've done and where Kristine is. You hear me?"

"Or what? Or you'll use that on me?"

He points casually at the axe, and she feels tears welling up. He's right. She'll never use the axe, because then she'd never know. Even as she fights them back, the tears begin to come, and she sees the ghost of a smile on his face.

"Why don't we skip this part? We both know what you want to know, and I want to tell you. The only question is how *much* you want to know."

"I'll do anything . . . just tell me. Why can't you just tell me . . ."

He's quick, and she has no time to react before he's standing close to her, pressing something wet and soft against her face. The sharp stench sears her nostrils. She tries to twist free, but he's too strong, and his voice is whispering much too close to her ear.

"There, now . . . breathe. It'll all be over soon."

116

The light is harsh, blinding. She blinks and struggles to open her eyes, and the first thing she registers is the white ceiling and the white walls. To her left, away from the wall, she can make out a low steel table that shines in the light, and that plus the flickering monitors on the opposite wall make her think she's in the hospital. She is lying in a hospital bed, and the whole thing has been a dream, but when she tries to sit up she realizes she can't. It isn't a bed she is lying on. It's an operating table, also steel, and her bare arms and legs are spread, tightly bound with leather straps that are bolted to the table. The sight makes her call out, but the strap that holds down her head is stretched across her open mouth, leaving her cries muffled and incomprehensible.

"Hello again. Are you all right?"

Rosa feels groggy, and she can't see him.

"The effect will wear off after ten minutes or so. Not many people know this, but ordinary horse chestnuts contain aesculin, a poison that's just as effective as chloroform if you make the right cocktail."

Rosa's eyes flick back and forth, but she can still only hear his voice.

"In any case, we've got plenty to do, so you'd better try to stay awake from now on. Deal?"

Suddenly he enters her field of view, wearing white plastic coveralls. In one hand he is carrying an oblong flight case, which he sets down on the low steel table, and as he bends down and opens the lock she hears him say that Kristine's story began the day he suddenly recognized Rosa on the news, after many years of searching.

"I'd actually started to think I'd never find you. But from the backbenches of parliament you were promoted to minister for social affairs. Just imagine the irony. I found you because of exactly that appointment . . ."

It strikes Rosa that the white coveralls are identical to the ones she's seen the police techs wearing. He wears a white mask over his mouth and a blue hairnet, and with plastic-gloved hands he opens the lid of the flight case. When Rosa forces her head hard to the left, she can just make out two hollows in the foam inside. He is blocking the contents of the first, but at the back she can see a gleaming metal rod. One end is fitted with a metal ball roughly the size of a fist, covered in small, sharp barbs. At the other end is the handle, but where the handle ended and the rod ought to stop, the metal protrudes to form an awl five or six centimeters long. She strains and jerks at the leather straps, while she hears him say that he discovered why he and his sister were transferred to Chestnut Farm when he accessed an old file from Odsherred Council.

"You were just an innocent little girl, of course, struggling to cope with delayed gratification. But your little lie got away from you, and every time you came out and started talking about the poor wee children I could tell from your smug face you'd forgotten all about it."

Rosa screams. She wants to tell him it isn't true, but the sounds that come out are like a wild animal's, and from the corner of her eye she senses him take out the object in the first hollow.

"On the other hand, it seemed too lenient to just have you die. What I really wanted was to show you the suffering you'd caused—I just didn't know how. Not until I discovered you had a daughter, one about the same age as my sister had been, in fact—and that gave me the idea. I started studying your routines, especially Kristine's, of course, and since she wasn't especially bright or original, living her coddled upper-class life, it was easy to figure her out and come up with a plan. Then all I had to do was wait for autumn. By the way, was it you who taught her to make chestnut men?"

Rosa tries to get her bearings. There are no windows, stairs, or doors in her line of sight, yet she starts systematically screaming. Although most of the sound is blocked by the leather strap across her mouth, it fills the room and gives her the burst of energy she needs to writhe in an attempt to free herself. But then the voice is suddenly much closer, and she realizes he is standing fiddling with something by her side.

"It was a very special pleasure to watch. At that point I didn't know how I could use it, but it had its own poetry, her selling them by the roadside with her friend. It actually made me hold back for a few days, before I followed her from the sports hall like I'd done so many times before. Only a few streets away from your house I made her stop and show me the way to Rådhuspladsen so I could shove her into the van. I drugged her and left her bike and sports bag in the woods so the police would have something to occupy them, and then we drove off. She was well brought up, I'll say that for you. Trusting and friendly, and believe me, you only get that way if you've got the right parents . . ."

Rosa is crying. Her chest rises and falls with the rhythm of her sobs, which force their way up her throat and try to escape. She is overpowered by the sense that she deserves to be here. It is her fault, and she deserves her punishment. No matter what has happened, she hasn't looked after her little girl.

"Now then. Funnily enough there are four chapters to this story, and that was the first. We're going to take a break now, and then I'll tell you more afterward. Sound good?"

There's a piercing noise, and Rosa tries to turn her head. The implement, steel or aluminum, is maybe the size of an iron. It has two handles, a metal plate, and a saw guide with rough, hand-welded seams, and it takes Rosa a moment to realize that the noise is coming from the rotating blades at the front of the instrument. Suddenly she understands why her arms and legs are tied so that her hands and feet protrude over the edge of the table, and when the saw bites into the bones of her wrist she begins to scream again behind the leather strap.

"Are you all right? Can you hear me?"

The voice reaches her, and the harsh white light flickers again before her eyes. She tries to orient herself and remember what had happened before she lost consciousness. For a moment she is filled with relief that nothing else has happened, but then she feels the paralysis on her left side. When she turns to look, panic rises. A large laboratory clamp made of black plastic stops the blood gushing from the open wound where her left hand was, and in the blue bucket on the floor she can make out the tips of some fingers.

"The second chapter begins in this basement. By the time you'd just begun to sense that something was wrong, Kristine and I were already here."

She listens to his voice as he moves around to the other side of her with the instrument and the blue bucket. The white plastic overalls are spattered with blood, *her* blood, all the way up to his shoulder and on the mask over his mouth.

"I knew her disappearance would turn the whole country upside down, so I was well prepared. The basement looked different back then, and I'd arranged things so that even if somebody came here and discovered the house they wouldn't find it. But Kristine was rather surprised, of course, when she woke up down here. *Frightened* is probably a better word. I tried to explain that I just needed to give her delicate little hand a quick cut so I could use her DNA to draw the police's attention toward someone else, and she took it very bravely. But most of the time she was alone, I'm afraid, because I had my job to attend to in Copenhagen. I'm sure you're wondering how she felt. Whether she was sad and afraid, and the honest answer is yes, she was. She begged and pleaded to be allowed to go home to you. It was very moving, but nothing lasts forever, and when the storm died down after a month it was time to say goodbye."

The words hurt worse than the pain in her arm. Rosa sobs again, and it's as though her whole rib cage is being torn open.

"That was the second chapter. Now we're going to take another break. Try not to lose consciousness quite so long this time—I don't have all day."

He places the blue bucket underneath her right hand, and Rosa begs him to stop, but all that comes out of her mouth are meaningless noises. The instrument begins to whirr, the saw blades rotate, and she screams in agony again as it sinks into her wrist. Her body tenses into an arc toward the ceiling as she feels it slide along a bone and into a notch, where the blades bite and begin to cut. The pain is inconceivable. And it continues even when the implement abruptly ceases and is switched off. Rosa's muffled screams are drowned out by a beeping alarm, and that's the noise that has attracted the man's attention, making him stop what he's doing. He's turned toward the monitors on the opposite wall, the instrument still in his hand, and Rosa tries to follow where he's looking. On one of the screens she can just make out something moving, and it dawns on her that she's watching the feed from the CCTV cameras. Something far away is coming into view. A car, maybe. It's the last thought that crosses her mind before everything goes black.

117

The effort makes the blood from her head wound run down over Thulin's face, and she has to take deep, violent breaths so she doesn't pass out. The gaffer tape is wound so sloppily around her head that she can only breathe through one nostril, and her hands are bound so she can't rip it off. She is lying on her side in the trunk, and as soon as she's inhaled enough oxygen she starts jabbing her knee once more into the spot in the dark where she thinks the lock must be. All her muscles are straining, her neck and the top of her back wedged against the rear wall. She keeps going, kneeing the lock again and again, as snot and blood bubble through her nostril. But it refuses to yield. Instead she feels a screw cutting deeper into the flesh wound beneath her kneecap, and when the lack of oxygen exhausts her, she gives up and collapses, gasping frantically for air.

Thulin doesn't know how long she's been lying in the trunk. The last few minutes have felt like an eternity, because all she's been able to hear is the distant whine of a machine mixed with a woman's screams. Although the screams are muffled, as though the woman has something over her mouth and the sound is coming from a ventilation shaft, Thulin has never heard such a heart-rending sound. She'd have covered her ears if she could—she can imagine all too vividly what is causing those screams—but her hands and feet are bound, her hands so tightly they've gone numb.

After she came to, she wasn't sure at first where she was. The pitch-blackness swaddled her, but by feeling along the sides and the cold metal surface above her she realized she must be in the trunk of a car. Probably the one she and Genz had arrived in. When the woods suddenly opened up and they drove into the yard, all her attention had been focused on the farmhouse. She'd climbed out into the untouched snow, observing the tall, old chestnut trees that encircled the yard, and when she caught sight of the inscription above the front door she drew out her service pistol. The thatched farmhouse was dark and inhospitable to look at, and as she approached the outside lights came on, making the

CCTV cameras visible. The door was locked, and there wasn't anyone or anything to see inside, but she knew she'd come to the right place.

Thulin began to walk around the farmhouse, searching for another way to get in, and just as she'd decided to break a ground-floor window and crawl inside, Genz appeared behind her and said he'd found a key underneath the mat by the front door. She wasn't surprised. In fact, she thought she ought to have checked for that possibility herself, and they went inside the house together. She entered first, and the smell of varnish and fresh wood met her in the hallway. As though it were a completely new house, one that had never been used. But as soon as she reached the stove in the corner of the living room, which wasn't visible from the yard, it became obvious the place was occupied. Two laptops had been left on a white desk, as well as electronic equipment, mobile phones, bowls of chestnuts, floor plans, round-bottomed flasks, and lab equipment. A couple of jerry cans stood beside it on the floor. On the wall above hung photos of Laura Kjær, Anne Sejer-Lassen, and Jessie Kvium. A picture of Rosa Hartung hung at the very top, and there were also paparazzi-like images of herself and Hess.

The sight sent a cold shiver down Thulin's spine. Turning the safety off on her gun, she prepared to search the rest of the house, and because she didn't have her phone she asked Genz to inform Nylander immediately of what they'd found.

"I'm afraid I can't do that, Thulin."

"What do you mean?"

"I'm expecting a guest, and I need to work in peace."

Genz was standing just inside the living-room doorway. The lights in the yard behind him were still on, so she couldn't see his face, only his silhouette, and for a moment she remembered the silhouette behind the tarp on the scaffolding opposite her apartment.

"What the hell are you talking about? Call him now!"

Suddenly it struck her that Genz was holding an axe. Just letting it hang, like an extension of his arm.

"It was a risk using the chestnuts from the farm. Maybe later you'll get the chance to understand why it had to be them."

For a brief moment she stared. Then she realized what he'd said, and she understood how catastrophic it had been to ask him for help. She raised her arm to point the gun at him, but at the same moment he swung the axe, handle first. She jerked back her head, but not enough, and the next time she woke it was with a thundering headache in the darkened trunk. The sound of voices roused her—Genz's, and a frantic female voice that sounded like Rosa Hartung's. They came from the yard, but then they disappeared, and soon afterward she heard the muffled screams.

Thulin holds her breath and listens. The machine has stopped. So have the screams, and she doesn't know whether the silence means it will soon be her turn to undergo the same torture. She thinks of Le and Granddad back home, and it flashes across her mind that she might never see her little girl again.

But out of the silence comes the noise of an approaching engine. At first she doesn't trust her ears, but then it sounds like a car is driving into the yard, and when it stops and the engine is switched off, she's sure.

"Thulin!"

She recognizes his voice. Her first thought is that it is impossible. It can't be him. He can't be here—he's supposed to be going somewhere far away, but the fact that he might be here after all fills her with hope. Thulin shouts back as loudly as she can. The sound that comes out is minimal. He can't hear her, at least not from out there in the yard, so instead she starts kicking desperately in the dark. Striking one of the sides, she hears a hollow thud, and she keeps kicking the same spot over and over again.

"Thulin!"

He's still shouting. Only when the sound fades does she realize he must have gone inside the house. To Genz, who must know he's arrived, or the machine would never have stopped. With that certainty, she keeps on kicking in the dark.

118

The front door is unlocked, and it doesn't take Hess long to establish that the ground floor and upstairs are empty. Pistol drawn, he hurries back down the stairs from the first floor and through the unlit house, but there is no sign of life apart from his own wet footprints on the wide floorboards. When he reaches the living room and the work space by the stove, where there are pictures on the wall of the three victims as well as Rosa Hartung, Thulin, and himself, he pauses and listens. Nothing. Not a sound apart from his own breathing, but the stove feels warm, and he senses Genz's presence everywhere in the house.

The farm's appearance has astonished him. It isn't the dilapidated, ramshackle ruin he's read about in the old police report, and the surprise has disconcerted him. He immediately clocked Rosa Hartung's car in the yard, though it was almost covered with snow, and he estimates it must have been there for at least an hour. He can't see the car Genz and Thulin drove in, however, so it must be either concealed or somewhere else entirely. Hess hopes it's the first option. He noticed the CCTV cameras when he arrived, several of them, mounted near the top of the façade, so if Genz is here then he knows Hess has come. That's why he did not hesitate to shout, first for Thulin and then for Rosa Hartung. If they are nearby—and if they are alive—there is a chance they'll hear him. But there was no answer, only the ominous silence; he's still listening to it now, breathing hard.

Although he's already been inside, he hastens back to the kitchen, trying to recall the old photo from the crime-scene archive. The two teenagers were sitting on either side of a messy table, but that isn't what interests him. It's the door he remembers from the background of the image. He assumed it must be the door to the basement where Marius Larsen and the twins had been found, but now, standing in the renovated kitchen, which looks as untouched as a display at IKEA, he can't find it. The walls have moved; the angles are different. In the middle is a large, unused kitchen island with six gas burners and a chrome hood, surrounded by an

American-style fridge, two white double cupboards, a porcelain sink, a dishwasher, and a sizeable oven still covered in plastic film. There's no door, certainly not one leading to a basement, only the passageway to the utility room.

Returning to the front hall, Hess glances up the stairs and underneath them, hoping that a basement door or floor hatch will suddenly reveal itself. But neither does. For a moment he wonders whether there even *is* a basement still. Whether Genz, or whatever his name is, has long since filled it in with concrete so it would never again remind him of what happened when he and his twin lived in the house.

A distant thud. He freezes, but he can't decipher the noise, nor where it comes from. There is nothing moving in sight, only the snowflakes falling in the lamplight outside. He hurries back to the kitchen, this time with the idea of continuing into the utility room and through the back door to the other side of the building to check whether there might be any windows or shafts, anything that might answer his question about the basement. But as he passes the kitchen island, he stops short. A banal idea has come to him. He walks over to the first white cupboard, approximately where he remembers the basement stairs in the old picture. He opens both doors, but finds nothing but empty shelves. Next he opens the adjoining cupboard, and instantly catches sight of the white handle. The shelves and rear wall of the cupboard have been removed. Instead he sees the outline of a white steel door built directly into the kitchen wall. Stepping inside the empty cupboard, he depresses the white handle, and the heavy door opens outward to reveal a staircase.

Harsh white light pools on the floor at the bottom of the concrete steps, roughly three meters below. It strikes him how much he hates basements. The basement under Odin Park, Laura Kjær's garage, Urbanplan, and Vordingborg police station, and now this one as well. Switching the safety off on his gun, he descends the stairs step by step, his attention fixed on the floor at the bottom. When he is five steps down, he sees something that brings him to a halt. There is something lying on the next step, something made of plastic, crumpled and sticky, and when he prods it with his pistol he realizes it's a pair of the blue plastic overshoes he and his colleagues wear at crime scenes. Only, this pair is bloodied and used. Looking at the steps farther down the staircase, he notices bloody footprints leading upward, but only as far as the step where the plastic had been dropped. The significance dawns on him. Wheeling around, he turns his face upward, but the figure is already in the doorway. Like a pendulum the axe comes whistling down, and the dead police-man, Marius Larsen, flashes across Hess's mind before it grazes his brow.

119

The basement underneath his grandmother's house was musty and stained with damp. The stone floor was uneven and the walls rough, dismally lit by the bare bulbs that hung from the ceiling in old, black porcelain sockets with frayed, fabric-covered cables. A tangled world of disorder and clutter, of strange rooms and corridors, a world completely different from the one on the other side of the door that separated the two levels.

On the ground floor all had been yellowed. Heavy furniture, floral wallpaper, stuccoed ceilings, curtains, and the stench of his grandmother's cheroots. Ash piled like some splendid pyramid in the Krenit bowl beside the padded lawn chair in the sitting room, where she sat until the day she was carried out and driven to a nursing home. Hess hated being there, but below was worse still. No windows, no air, no way out but the unsteady staircase, which he would always zigzag back to, darkness at his heels, whenever he'd gone down to fetch another bottle for the little console table beside Grandma's lawn chair.

It is with that same childhood nausea and sense of panic that Hess awakes in the basement underneath Chestnut Farm. Somebody is striking him furiously in the face, and he feels blood running down over one eye.

"Who knows you're here? Answer me!"

Hess has been dragged onto the floor, half propped up against the wall. It is Genz, slapping him with the flat of his hand. He wears white plastic coveralls, leaving only his eyes visible through the gap between the blood-flecked mask over his mouth and the blue hairnet. Hess tries to fend him off, but it's impossible: his hands and feet are bound with what feels like cable ties.

"Nobody . . ."

"Give me your finger or I'll cut it off. Give it here!"

Genz shoves him to the ground and bends over him. His cheek pressed against the floor, Hess's eyes scour the room for his gun, but it's on the ground a few meters away. He feels Genz press his thumb against the touch ID button on a phone, and when Genz stands up and stares at the screen Hess realizes it's his. He tries to brace himself for the rage he knows will come, but the kick to the side of his head is so violent he nearly loses consciousness again.

"You called Nylander nine minutes ago. Probably just before you got out of the car in the yard."

"Right, yeah. I forgot about that."

Hess takes another kick to the same side of his face, and this time he has to spit the blood out so he won't choke. He promises himself he'll stop with the sarcasm, but the information is useful. If it's been nine minutes since he drove into the yard, recognized Rosa Hartung's car, and called Nylander, then it won't be long before Brink and a squad of police cars from Vordingborg arrive. If it wasn't for the snow.

Hess spits again, and this time he becomes aware that the pool of blood at his feet can't be his. Following the trickle on the floor with his eyes, he finds himself staring at the gaping wound at the end of an arm. Rosa Hartung is lying lifeless on a steel table as though in an operating theater, her wrist in a plastic clamp where her left hand was. Her right wrist, too, has been sawn into. Only halfway, but on the floor beneath a blue bucket stands ready. Hess glimpses the contents of the bucket, and his nausea surges.

"What have you done with Thulin?"

But Genz is no longer in sight. A moment earlier he chucked the phone into Hess's lap and walked to the far end of the room, where Hess can hear him clattering around, while he himself tries to get to his feet.

"Genz, give up. They know who you are, and they'll find you. Where is she?"

"They'll find nothing. Have you forgotten who Genz is?"

The smell of gasoline is unmistakable, and Genz reappears with the jerry can. He's already started to slosh the liquid up against the walls, and when he reaches Rosa he splashes it all over her limp body before continuing around the room.

"Genz has a bit of experience with forensics. There'll be nothing left of him when they get here. Genz was invented for one purpose, and by the time they figure that out they'll have missed the boat."

"Genz, listen to what I'm saying—"

"No, let's skip this bit. Clearly you must have lucked into ferreting out what happened here back then, but don't bother telling me you feel sorry for me, that I'll get a milder punishment if I turn myself in and all that bullshit."

"I don't feel sorry for you. You were probably a psychopath from birth. I'm just sorry you ever got out of that basement."

Genz looks at him. He gives a slight smile, surprised, and Hess has no time to prepare himself before his third kick to the face.

"I should have stamped you out ages ago. Definitely by the time you were standing with your back turned, goggling at the Kvium whore at the community gardens."

Hess spits more blood, feeling around with his tongue. The taste of iron, and a few of the teeth in his upper jaw are loose. The killer was in the shadows of the community gardens, and Hess hadn't even considered the thought.

"Frankly, I thought you were irrelevant. They said you were a failed, egotistical asshole who'd slid downhill at Europol, but then you suddenly show up dismembering pigs or wanting a chat about Linus Bekker, and I realized it wasn't just Thulin I had to keep an eye on. I saw you, by the way, playing happy family before your little jaunt to Urbanplan. I bet you've fallen for that little slut, haven't you?"

"Where is she?"

"Well, you're certainly not the first. I've watched quite a few visitors to her apartment, and I'm afraid you're not her type. But don't worry—I'll tell her you said hi before I cut her throat."

Hess feels the gasoline spill over him as Genz empties the jerry can. It stings his eyes and the old and fresh wounds on his head, and he holds his breath until it stops pouring. He shakes his head to get the drops off, and when he opens his eyes Genz has removed his coveralls and flung the white bundle, the mask, and the hairnet onto the floor. He's standing in front of a white steel door at the end of the room, probably the one that leads to the concrete steps and the kitchen. In his hand he has a chestnut man, and as he holds Hess's eye he strikes the head of the doll's matchstick leg against a matchbox. It sparks. Once the flame is big enough, he throws the doll into the liquid on the floor and shuts the door behind him.

120

The back of the seat gives a loud crack and shifts forward, creating a gap into the interior of the car. At long last Thulin can see light. She lies there a moment, sweaty and exhausted, her body in the trunk and her head in the gap. She turns her face, and upward to her right she can see through the rear side window: a narrow, vertical strip of light from the lamps in the yard tells her the car is parked just inside the barn.

The lock had proved impossible to open. Instead she'd noticed the back wall starting to give when she braced with her knees, and she'd kept using the top of her back as a battering ram. Now she braces again, this time to push herself farther onto the backseat. If she can find something to cut the gaffer tape around her hands and feet, then it isn't too late. The silence from the house is unbearable, but if she can only get inside, maybe even find her gun, it will be two against one. And Hess isn't stupid. If he's made it down here to the farm, it must be because he's discovered it was Genz all along, so he'd know to be careful. It is the last thought she has before she hears the sound of flames kindling with a snap. Like a sudden gust of wind inflating a sail to breaking point. It isn't far from Thulin. Probably somewhere inside the house; maybe from the same place the screams came from, though they've long since gone quiet.

Thulin holds her breath and listens. Yes, that's fire rumbling, and she's beginning to smell smoke. As she wriggles, trying to get her whole body onto the back-seat, she racks her brains to work out what the fire means. Suddenly she remembers the two jerry cans on the table in the front room. She noticed them in a split second as she entered the room, but then her attention was diverted toward the wall, and Genz. But if fire is part of the scenario Genz has planned, then it bodes disaster for Hess. She shimmies her torso farther onto the backseat, heaving her lower body around so that she is lying on her side. Using her elbows, she manages to sit up, and is about to reach for the door handle with her bound hands. In her mind she's already found a tool to free herself so she can run into the house, but then she catches sight of him through the chink between the barn doors.

He is coming out through the front door with one of the jerry cans in his hand, and he doesn't stop pouring the liquid until he is at the bottom of the steps. Chucking the can back through the door, he lights the match and throws it before immediately turning to face the barn. He makes straight for her. Behind him she senses the fire spreading through the house with remorseless speed. By the time he reaches the doors, the flames in the windows have already reached the ceiling, and he is visible only in silhouette.

Thulin flings herself behind the driver's seat at the very moment both barn doors are tugged aside. The wild, flickering glow streams in, and she makes herself as small as possible. The front door opens, and through the seat she feels his weight against her cheek as he climbs inside. The key is inserted, the engine switched on, and as the car begins to move across the snowy yard, Thulin hears the first windows exploding in the heat.

121

Hess had long thought of death with indifference. Not because he hated life, but because existence was painful. He hadn't sought help, nor had he gone to the few friends he'd had. He hadn't taken the advice that had been given to him. Instead he'd fled. He'd run as fast as he could, the darkness chasing him, and sometimes it had worked. Small havens in foreign corners of Europe, where his mind gave itself over to new impressions and new challenges. But the darkness always returned. Along with the memories and the dead faces he gradually accumulated. He *had* no one, he *was* no one, and the debts he owed weren't to the living, so if death did come it was no skin off his nose.

That's how he'd felt, but it isn't the emotion he is left with in the basement.

When the door slammed behind Genz and the fire began to spread, he immediately crawled across to the bloodied instrument he'd seen lying on the floor behind Rosa Hartung. It was easy to guess what it had been used for, and with the diamond-blade teeth it only took him a moment to slice through the cable ties at his wrists. He also used the blade on the ties at his feet, and by the time the fire had reached halfway around the room—now heading toward Rosa—he grabbed his mobile phone and gun and staggered to his feet. Clouds of black smoke were already surging beneath the ceiling, and as he watched the flames encroach he unfastened the leather straps one by one as swiftly as he could. Just as the fire leapt from the floor onto the steel table, he managed to heave Rosa's limp body aside and carry her into the corner where Genz hadn't poured the gasoline.

But it is a brief respite. The fire has gotten its teeth into the fiberboard on the walls, and soon the ceiling too, and both he and Hartung have been doused in gasoline. It's a matter of seconds before it spreads to their corner, or before the temperature in the room gets so high they both spontaneously ignite. The only exit is the door through which Genz has vanished, but it's impossible to open, the handle already so hot that the jacket Hess has taken off bursts into flames when he tries to use it to protect his skin. The black carpet of smoke near the ceiling is steadily thickening, but then he notices the small, coiling vortexes of smoke being sucked toward a joint in the fiberboard panels on the wall directly opposite. Snatching up the saw, he presses the diamond blades into the joint and uses it like a crowbar. At his first attempt he manages to break off a corner of the panel so that he can get his fingers around, and then he tugs at it until it snaps.

Hess finds himself staring up at a basement window with two iron bars on the inside, and in the darkness outside the rear lights of a car sweep across the yard. He jerks and tears hopelessly at the bars, and as the car vanishes into the shadows the thought crosses Hess's mind that this is when he is going to die. He turns toward the flames and Rosa Hartung, who is lying at his feet, and it is the stump at the end of her arm that gives him the idea. Grabbing the saw, he whirls back toward the window, and his first thought is that luckily the bars don't look any thicker than the bones it has been used to cut. The blades slice through the first bar like a knife through butter, and after three more cuts the bars are gone. Hess unfastens the window and pushes it open.

The skin burning on his back, he lifts Hartung onto the windowsill, hauls himself up, and crawls past her. As he rolls backward out of the window, dragging her with him, he feels the flames at his neck and in his clothing, but then he lands on his back in the wet snow outside the window.

Coughing, he gets to his feet and begins to tow Rosa Hartung across the yard. His body feels like it's on fire, and he wants to fling himself into the snow and cool himself off while he hacks up the rest of his lungs. But when he's made it about twenty meters away from the burning farmhouse, he leans Hartung against a stone wall. Then he begins to run.

122

Everything inside Thulin is screaming for her to act. Curled up in the dark behind the driver's seat, she pays attention to the speed and especially the motion of the car as she tries to recall the road through the forest, trying to gauge when Genz will be most distracted. The snow and murk ought to be on her side. Genz has to focus on the road—it is black as ink, and there are at least five or ten centimeters of snow. She tries to work out her chances of overpowering him while her hands and feet are still bound, but every second she doesn't do something is a waste of time. She needs to get back to the farm as soon as possible. Although she didn't dare lift her head and glance through the window as the car left the barn and crossed the yard, she sensed the ferocity of the blaze.

Suddenly Thulin feels the car slow down. It is as though it is beginning a broad curve, and all the muscles in her body tense. She realizes they must have reached the long bend roughly halfway to the main road. She sits up abruptly, determinedly lifting her bound hands and hurling them toward the driver's seat like a noose. The eyes in the rearview mirror, which is faintly illuminated by the dashboard, see her too quickly. It's as if he is prepared, and his hand parries with a hard blow that forces her arms back. When she tries again, he lets go of the pedals and steering wheel and turns toward her, and she feels the punches rain down onto her head. At last the car rolls to a standstill, the engine idling while she lies unmoving on the backseat, gasping for air through her nostril.

"To your credit, you were the only one on the murder squad I really felt I needed to keep an eye on. Of course, that means I know everything about you. Including your scent when you've been exerting yourself and sweating like a little pig. Are you all right?"

His question makes no sense. He's known all along she was there, and when he slips a knife into the gaffer tape over her mouth, she thinks for a moment he's going to thrust it in. Instead he cuts a slit in the tape so that she can finally loosen it with her bound hands and inhale.

"Where are they? What have you done with them?"

"You know that already."

Thulin is still lying on the backseat, panting for air and picturing the burning farm.

"Hess didn't seem all that keen on breathing, actually. He asked me to say hi, by the way, before I slit your throat. If that's any consolation."

Thulin shuts her eyes. There is too much stacked against her, and she feels the tears begin to flow. She cries for Hess and for Rosa Hartung, but especially for Le, who is at home and has done nothing wrong.

"The Hartung girl. That was you too . . . ?"

"Yes. It was necessary."

"But why . . . ?"

Her voice is thin and fragile, and she hates it. For a moment there is silence. She hears a deep exhalation of breath, and when she turns her eyes toward his silhouette it's as though he is staring pensively out into the dark. Then he shakes off his reverie and turns his shadowed face toward her.

"It's a long story. And I'm busy, and you need to sleep."

The hand holding the knife begins to move, and she throws up her hands in front of her.

"*Geeeeeeeeeeenz . . . !*"

The cry tears through the silence, but she doesn't recognize the hoarse voice. It comes at a distance, as though from the depths of the woods or some place far beneath. Genz tenses, then whirls at lightning speed toward the cry. She can't see his face, but it looks like he's staring disbelievingly at something. Thulin struggles into a seated position so she can see out through the windshield toward the end of the beam of light across the road. And then she understands why.

123

His chest is about to burst, and his heart slams against his aching ribs like a hammer. Into the air before him his breath tumbles from his mouth in white, arrhythmic clouds, and his arms shake in the cold as he tries to aim his gun at the car in front of him. It's a good seventy-five meters away, and Hess is standing in the middle of the road at the edge of the headlights' beam, exactly where moments earlier he'd come lurching out of the coal-black forest like the living dead.

The first stretch through the forest was lit by the burning farm behind him. The flames cast a wild radiance after him, and he ran in the same direction as the trees' long shadows. Remembering that the road from the farm wasn't straight, but instead formed an arc like a gigantic letter *C* before it met the main road, he'd hoped to cut through and get there before the car. But as soon as he'd run deeper into the woods, the light of the flames had grown fainter. The snow's luminosity helped a little, but as the forest closed around him he was running virtually blind. There was darkness everywhere, although the contours of the trees were a blacker shade, and he decided to stick to one direction no matter what obstacles he met. Several times he pitched forward into the snow, until at last he had no sense of where to run. At that very moment he glimpsed a weak light far to his left. The light had been in front of him, far in front, and it was still moving. Abruptly, however, it had slowed, and by the time he finally made it to the road the car was behind him, engine idling, lights still on.

Hess doesn't know why the car has stopped, and he doesn't care. Genz is somewhere behind the windshield, and Hess isn't about to move now. He is standing doggedly in the middle of the road, his gun pointed straight ahead while the wind whistles softly in the trees, when he hears the unreal sound of a ringing phone. It dawns on him that it's his own. Staring at the car, he notices the faint light of a screen on the driver's side. Hesitantly, he takes his phone from his pocket, still keeping his eyes on the car.

The voice is cold and toneless.

"Where is Hartung?"

Hess can see the outline of a figure behind the wheel. The question reminds him that Rosa Hartung's torture is the only thing that really matters to Genz, and he tries to get his breathing under control so he sounds as calm as possible.

"She's fine. She's sitting in the yard, waiting for you to tell her what happened to her daughter."

"You're lying. You never managed to get her out."

"That saw you made cuts more than bone. A good Forensics tech would have thought of that before he left it behind. Don't you think?"

There is silence on the other end. Hess knows Genz would be spooling through the interior of the basement and what had happened there, weighing up the truth of his words, and for an instant he fears Genz will drive back to the farm, even though the police are on their way.

"Tell her I'll be back to pay her a visit some other day. Move, I've got Thulin."

"Couldn't give a fuck. Get out of the car and lie down on the ground with your arms at your sides."

Silence.

"Genz, get out of the car!"

Hess aims at the car and the only point of focus he can see inside it. But the glowing screen behind the wheel vanishes, and the line goes dead. At first Hess isn't sure what that means. But then the car growls. The engine revs violently, as though the accelerator has been slammed to the floor. The wheels whirr in the snow, and the exhaust fumes billow in the red glow of the taillights, but then the tires find purchase and the car shoots forward.

Hess flings the phone aside and aims. The car is headed straight for him, picking up speed with every meter. He fires one shot, then another, then a third. The first five shots he fires at the radiator, but nothing happens, and his shaking hands tell him why. He tries again, clutching the grip in both hands, firing again and again, his confidence dwindling. It is as though the car is protected by an invisible shield, and when it's about thirty meters away he realizes he risks hitting Thulin, if she's inside. His finger stiffens on the trigger. Standing on the road with his pistol raised, he hears the roar of the engine, but his trigger finger still doesn't stir. It occurs to him he is about to be hit—there is no time now to fling himself aside. At the last moment he glimpses a movement behind the windshield, and the car jerks off course. He feels the warmth of the hood as the car hurtles past his right hip, and when he turns around he sees it fly across the road. There is an explosion of sound. Metal crumples, glass shatters, the noise of the engine elevates to a shrill, strident frequency, and the car horn starts to blare. Two tangled figures are thrown through the windscreen and into the trees like helpless dolls. It looks like they're holding each other tightly as they twirl in the air, but then they slip out of each other's grasp, and one continues its arc while the other strikes the trees with a thud and becomes one with the darkness.

Hess runs. The hood is wrapped around a tree stump, but the headlights are still on, and the figure in the big tree is the first thing he sees. The thick, crooked branch jutting through his chest. Legs trembling in the empty air beneath him. When he sees Hess, his expression focuses.

"Help . . . me . . ."

"Where is Kristine Hartung?"

The wide eyes are fixed on Hess.

"Genz, answer me."

Then life fades. He is hanging close to the trunk, fused almost with the tree, his head lolling and his arms at his sides like one of his dolls. As Hess glances desperately around, calling for Thulin, he feels the chestnuts crunching in the snow beneath his feet.

Tuesday, November 3rd

124

The little convoy of three cars drives down the ramp and leaves the ferry terminal as the sun begins to rise. Rostock is cold and windy. The convoy sets off toward its destination, a few hours away. Hess sits behind the wheel of the last car, and although he can't foresee the outcome of the trip, it feels nice to get away. Over the past few days the prevailing mood at the police station and its various departments has been one of dismay, as people hurriedly washed their hands of the situation, but on the autobahn the November sun is shining, and he can safely switch on the radio without being press-ganged into the domestic mudslinging and scapegoat hunting.

The revelation that Genz was the Chestnut Man came as a shock to everyone. As the head of the Forensics Department, he'd been a guiding light to his coworkers, and there were still disciples in the cube who struggled to believe he'd abused his office and had several lives on his conscience. In the opposite camp, his critics argued that Genz had wielded too much power. But the criticism and soul-searching didn't stop there. Certainly not in the media. The Major Crimes Division—which had made use of Genz and his skills while harboring no apparent suspicions about him—had come under heavy fire. So had the top brass, of course, who had been responsible for his promotion in the first place. So far the beleaguered justice minister had withheld any consequences for these mistakes, at least until they had an explanation of Simon Genz's actions.

With the media buzzing, Hess and the other detectives had concentrated on tidying up loose ends. What had struck Hess was the degree to which Genz had managed to steer the investigation: how from the very beginning he'd guided Thulin and Hess toward the little chestnut man with the fingerprint, so that Rosa Hartung was brought into play; how he'd made Thulin and Hess pursue the package containing Laura Kjær's mobile phone to Erik Sejer-Lassen, while Genz himself was attacking Sejer-Lassen's wife at home in Klampenborg; how he'd broken into the database at the

Rigshospital's pediatric department and found reasons to study Laura Kjær's, Anne Sejer-Lassen's, and Jessie Kvium's children—it had turned out that Olivia Kvium had also been hospitalized there after an accident at home—before sending the anonymous messages to the council, so that the police and other authorities would be confronted with the incompetence of the system; how alert he'd been to the trap set for the killer at Urbanplan; and how he must have felt pressured by Thulin's and Hess's visit to Linus Bekker, which was why he'd planted the severed limbs on Skans and Neergaard's property when he went to examine the scene in his official capacity. Last but not least, how Genz had followed the young couple into the woods using the tracking unit in the rented van, and how he must have killed the two suspects *before* he called Nylander and told him where to find them. They were all unpleasant discoveries, and there were probably others in store. Especially because they weren't finished investigating the role Genz had played in Kristine Hartung's disappearance the previous year.

When it came to Genz's personal history, the information Hess had found in the database had been examined and expanded. The orphaned twins were separated after their stay at Ørum's farm, and when the authorities ran out of foster families for Toke Bering, then seventeen, they sent him to a boarding school in West Zealand. Evidently fate smiled on him. An aging, childless businessman who had previously set up a foundation to benefit the school's more deprived children ended up adopting the boy. The man, whose last name was Genz, gave him the chance to start afresh at an elite high school in Sorø, now under the adopted name of Simon Genz, where the boy distinguished himself with astonishing speed. Yet only on the surface was the man's social experiment a success: at twenty-one, while studying business economics and IT at the university in Aarhus, Genz apparently came into contact with the lab assistant from the Risskov case. On closer examination of the case files from the Aarhus Police, it emerged that "Simon Genz, a student living in the halls of residence opposite, was interviewed concerning the possible sighting of the victim's ex-boyfriend on the day of the murder." In other words, Genz had lived opposite the victim and offered his help in solving a killing he'd almost certainly committed himself.

When his patron died of a heart attack shortly afterward, Genz inherited a considerable sum, and he used his newfound freedom to move to the capital and transfer to the police academy with the modest goal of becoming a Forensics tech. His talent and dedication to the subject were soon noticed, but evidently one of the first things he learned was how to hack his way into the national database of ID numbers and change his data so that he could no longer be connected with Toke Bering. His subsequent rise up the career ladder made for impressive yet appalling reading, given that another two unsolved murders of women between 2007 and 2011 now had to be reopened because chestnut men had been observed in the crime-scene photographs.

From 2014 onward, by then a renowned expert, he worked with the German Federal Police as well as Scotland Yard, but left both posts when he was offered the job of head of Forensics in Copenhagen roughly two years ago. The real reason he applied was presumably to exploit the role in his plans for Rosa Hartung, who had just become nationally famous when she was made minister for social affairs. Genz immediately bought Chestnut Farm, renovating it with the money left over from his inheritance, and as soon as the leaves began to fall from the trees last autumn he was ready to put the first part of his strategy into action and avenge himself. As head of Forensics it was easy for him to control the various pieces of evidence in the investigation: first, the evidence that placed the abduction of Kristine at the wrong location, but soon also the evidence that convicted Linus Bekker. Examining Genz's computer at the lab over the weekend, Thulin had discovered that he knew about Linus Bekker and his access to the crime-scene archive long before the police became aware of it. Not that he mentioned it to anybody. Genz must have realized that in Linus Bekker he'd found the scapegoat he needed, and it would have been a piece of cake to plant the bloodied machete in the garage at Bekker's block of flats before anonymously tipping off the police. That Bekker had subsequently decided to confess to the crime must have been an amusing bonus for Genz, if an unnecessary one—after all, there was already ample evidence.

For Hess, the overarching problem was that nowhere in Genz's vanishingly small number of possessions was there any trace of what had *really* happened to Kristine Hartung. All of it had apparently been deleted, destroyed, or incinerated, as the burned-out shell at Chestnut Farm testified. Initially he'd pinned his hopes on the two mobile phones found in the wrecked car in the woods, but both had turned out to be brand-new, used only on the day they were found. The car's GPS history, on the other hand, had revealed a number of visits to a particular area southeast of Rostock in northern Germany. It hadn't seemed significant at first, given Genz's past work with the German Bundespolizei, but when Hess had contacted the terminals where the Danish ferries from Falster and Lolland docked the previous afternoon, the Rostock trail had started to look interesting. A dark green rental car was still waiting to be picked up at the ferry terminal in Rostock, and had been since Friday—the day Genz had died impaled on a chestnut tree. By contacting the German rental company, Hess learned that the car was rented in a woman's name.

"*Der Name der Mieterin ist Astrid Bering,*" the voice on the other end had said.

The investigation then picked up speed. Hess swiftly used his contacts in the German police, and after a few detours it turned out that Genz's twin sister was now registered as living in Germany, which they narrowed down to an area outside a small village, Bugewitz, approximately two hours' drive from Rostock and not far from the Polish border. From the database, Hess remembered that all trace of the twin sister had vanished when she'd been discharged from a psychiatric institution just under a year before, but if she and Genz had been in touch in the intervening period—as the GPS history in Genz's car indicated—the sister might well be the only person who knew anything about Kristine Hartung's fate.

"Thulin, wake up."

A phone has begun to ring in the bundle on the seat

beside him, and Thulin pokes her bleary-eyed head out of the quilted jacket she's drawn over herself.

"Might be the Germans. Since I'm the one driving, I asked them to call you if they had anything, but just pass it to me."

"I'm not an invalid, and I speak excellent German."

Hess grins to himself as Thulin fumbles the phone out of the jacket pocket, still grumpy at having been woken so early in the morning. Her left arm, broken in two places, is in a sling, and in combination with her bruised face she looks like a walking traffic accident. Hess doesn't look much better, and they made a lovely couple at the breakfast buffet on the ferry half an hour earlier. Once they were back in the car, she asked if he minded whether she took a nap, and he had no objection. They'd been at the grindstone since Saturday afternoon. Both had been granted a few days by their respective employers to wind up the case and recuperate, and Hess guesses Thulin hasn't had much sleep. He is also still deeply grateful, because if she hadn't kicked Genz in that car he would probably have been run down and killed. He found Thulin's unconscious body in the snow some distance beyond the tree where Genz hung, and he wasn't able to tell whether her injuries were serious. At the first sound of approaching sirens, he picked her up and carried her out onto the road toward the emergency vehicles, sending her to the nearest hospital in the first one that stopped.

"Yes . . . *gut* . . . I understand . . . *danke*."

Thulin hangs up, and there is life in her eyes.

"What did they say?"

"The task force is waiting for us at a parking lot five kilometers from the address. One of the locals says there's definitely a woman living in the house, and the description fits someone of Astrid Bering's age."

"But?"

Hess can tell from Thulin's face that there is more, but he can't decode whether it is good or bad.

"The woman keeps to herself, mainly, but apparently a few times she's been seen going for walks in the woods with a child about twelve or thirteen, a child they assumed until now was her son . . ."

125

The sun shines behind the frosted glass. The bags rest on the coir matting at her feet, and Astrid waits uneasily in the hallway for the family on bikes to get a little farther away from the house so that they won't see her when she opens the door and darts out. It is only fifteen or so steps to the garage and the small, battered Seat, but she is shifting her feet impatiently: she wants to get back to the house and pick up Mulle before another cyclist or car comes past.

Astrid hasn't had much sleep. Most of the night she lay awake, her mind whirring with thoughts about what might have happened, and at about quarter past six that morning she decided to defy her brother's orders and get out of there. She unlocked the pantry, shook Mulle gently awake, and told her to get dressed while she made breakfast. Only a few pieces of crisp-bread with jam today, and a single apple for Mulle—she hadn't dared risk a trip to the shops since last week. Their bags have been packed since Friday evening, when her brother had told her they should be ready to leave when he arrived. But he hasn't. Astrid waited and waited, and from her spot by the kitchen window above the sink she stared out at the country road with bated breath, peering at the headlights that occasionally appeared in the darkness. But each time they drove past the lonely house surrounded by fields and forest. She felt equal parts fear and relief, but didn't dare do anything besides wait another day. Then another, and another. Normally he phoned like clockwork, morning and evening, to make sure things were as they should be, but there'd been no calls since Friday morning, and she couldn't call him because she didn't know his number. It would be too dangerous, he'd told her ages ago, and she'd put up with the arrangement. As she put up with almost everything he suggested, because he was the strong one, because he knew what was best.

Without her brother, Astrid had long ago succumbed to drugs, alcohol, and self-loathing. He knocked tirelessly on the doors of homes and treatment centers so they could try again to heal her, to come up with new strategies. Time after time he sat and listened to doctors and therapists explaining the damage to her mind, and she didn't understand that her suffering was also his. She knew, of course, what he was capable of, because she saw it with her own eyes that day at Ørum's farm, but she'd been so swallowed up in her own pain for so many years that she didn't notice his until it was too late.

About a year ago, when she was at yet another institution, he picked her up one day and took her out to a car. They drove to the ferry then down to somewhere south of Rostock, where there was a little cottage he'd bought in her name. She was bewildered, but the place and the autumn colors were enchanting that day, and she was so overwhelmed and grateful for his love. Until he told her why he'd bought the house, and what it would be used for.

It had happened at night, him bringing back the little girl drugged in the trunk. Astrid was horrified. She recognized the girl's face from the TV in the common area at the institution the month before, and he reminded her triumphantly who the girl's mother was. When Astrid objected to his plan he burst into a fit of rage, saying he'd have to kill the girl immediately if Astrid wouldn't look after her. Then he put her in the specially adapted pantry and left, but not before telling Astrid that the house was fitted with enough cameras so that he could observe every little thing they did. She was afraid of him then, suddenly much more than when he stood in the basement with the axe over the corpse of that policeman.

At first she'd largely avoided contact with the girl. She was only near her twice a day, when she opened the pantry door to give her food. But the sound of crying had been unbearable, and the girl's distress reminded her of her own imprisonment. Soon Astrid was letting her come out and eat in the kitchen with her. Or letting her watch a kids' TV show in the living room on one of the German channels. Astrid felt like they were both prisoners under the same roof, and the time didn't go quite as slowly when they were together, but when the girl tried to make a run for the door, Astrid had to block her path and lock her back in the pantry. There weren't any neighbors, so the noise didn't matter, yet it was still unpleasant, and it occurred to Astrid that she felt sorry for the girl. So just after Christmas and New Year, which she hadn't had the energy to celebrate, she'd decided to introduce fixed routines, so they could use the time in a meaningful way.

The day began with breakfast, then schoolwork. On a trip to one of the bigger towns nearby, Astrid had bought a pink pencil case as well as math and English textbooks, and she did her best to teach the girl at the kitchen table. Astrid used a website she'd found online to teach her Danish literature, and the girl seized the initiative gratefully. Mornings were split into three lessons, followed by lunch together, which they both helped to make, and then another lesson, which was always makeshift PE in the living room. It was there they first shared a laugh together, because they both looked so silly as they tried to run on the spot and do high knees. That was at the end of March, and Astrid felt happier than she'd been in many years. She'd started calling the girl Mulle, because it was the sweetest name she could think of.

When her brother came to visit, which he did at least once a week, the atmosphere changed. Astrid and Mulle fell timid and silent, as though a hangman had entered the room. Her brother sensed the bond that had arisen between them, and he'd upbraided Astrid several times, including on the phone, when the cameras betrayed how much freedom she allowed the girl. When the three of them ate together, usually in silence, he often sat watching Mulle with a somber expression as she cleared the plates and did the washing up, and Astrid kept a vigilant eye on his movements. But nothing ever happened. Only after another escape attempt during the summer had he hit Mulle, and only with the flat of his hand.

Before that episode the heat had made it unbearable to sit indoors, so they'd moved their lessons onto the patio behind the house, including PE. One day Mulle asked whether they could go for a walk in the woods. Astrid foresaw no danger in that. The woods were vast, and she rarely bumped into anybody in them. In any case, they were far from Denmark, and Mulle looked different from when she'd arrived: hair clipped short, clothes that made her look like a boy. But on one of the walks, her brother having graciously given his permission, Mulle bolted. As usual when they saw other people strolling through the woods, they turned back toward the house, but Mulle tore herself free and tried to catch up with an older couple. Astrid had to drag the hysterical girl all the way home, and it was obvious on the cameras that something had happened. A few hours later her brother arrived, and her punishment was a month's quarantine: for thirty days, the girl was only allowed out of the pantry to go to the toilet. Once the punishment was over, Astrid took her out on the patio and gave her the biggest ice cream she'd been able to buy. She explained how disappointed she was, Mulle apologized, and Astrid hugged her frail body.

After that things went well: they stuck to their lessons and workout routine, and Astrid wished it could last forever. But then the autumn came—and with it her brother, bringing the chestnuts.

"Stay here, Mulle. I'll be back in a minute."

The family of cyclists has gone, and Astrid opens the front door and goes out into the cold, clear air with a bag in each hand. She hurries across to the garage, wondering how far they can get today if she drives quickly. She's had no time to make a plan; usually it is her brother who takes care of such things, but now she's left to her own devices. Still, as long as Mulle is there, everything is fine. She's realized they belong together, and has long since stopped thinking that the girl has ever had any home besides this one. Perhaps it's actually a good thing her brother isn't around. Deep down Astrid has been afraid he'll do something to the girl once the whole thing is finished.

It is the last thought that crosses her mind before she turns into the garage and a gloved hand is clamped over her mouth.

"*Wie viele gibt es im Haus?!*"

"*Das Mädchen, wo ist sie!?*"

"*Antworte!*"

The bags are ripped from her hands, but Astrid is too shocked to reply. It is only when a tall, bruised man with two different-colored eyes speaks to her in Danish that she starts stammering that they can't take her girl. She feels a lump in her throat, and the tears begin to stream, because he isn't listening.

"Where is she?" he keeps asking. Only when she realizes they are about to storm the house with their rifles and sinister masks does she tell him what he wants to hear, and then she collapses on the tiles beneath him.

126

The kitchen is empty in a way that tells her she is never coming back. She sits in her coat on the stool by the blotchy linoleum table and waits for her mom to come and fetch her, because she isn't allowed to go out by herself.

It isn't her real mom, but "Mom" is what the woman has said to call her. Instead of Astrid. Especially when they are outside the house. She can still remember her real mother and her father and her little brother, and she dreams about seeing them every day. But dreaming hurts, and she's taught herself to do as she is told until the day she can make a run for it. She's tried so many times, in reality and in her imagination, but it has never worked out. Yet now a strange hope arises inside her as she sits looking alertly out of the window toward the garage.

Perhaps it had started a few days ago, when the man didn't show up. Mom had been all packed, and she'd been told to sit ready with her on the stool where she is sitting now. But he didn't come. Nor the day after, or the day after that. There had been no phone calls either. Mom seemed more nervous and uncertain than she usually did. And when she woke her up this morning, she heard at once in her voice that she'd made a decision.

Getting away *might* be a good thing. Away from the house she hated, from the man and the man's cameras, which were always following her. But where, and to what—maybe to something worse? She hasn't dared pursue that thought all the way to the end yet. So that isn't what the hope has sprung from—it springs from the sliver of daylight through the open front door, and the fact that Mom still isn't back.

Placing her feet carefully on the floor and standing up, she keeps her eyes fixed on the empty space outside the garage. Maybe this is her last chance. In the corner of the ceiling the camera's red light blinks, and she moves one foot tentatively in front of the other.

127

Nylander *hates* the fact that he is standing on the edge of a wood with a German task force, waiting to find out whether Kristine Hartung is inside the little wooden house or not. Gradually everything seems to be spiraling out of his control; ever since last Friday, in fact, when the rug was pulled out from under him. On top of that, his humiliation has been broadcast live. Egged on by the communications consultant, the same one he'd been thinking about seducing in a hotel room, his bosses twisted his arm into acknowledging he'd misjudged the case. And, of course, into giving credit for solving it to Hess and Thulin.

In Nylander's eyes, they might as well have cut off his balls and nailed them to the wall outside the police station. But he did as they'd commanded, and afterward he had to watch his own people and experts seizing on Genz's few possessions in the hope of finding a trace of the Hartung girl, whose case Nylander had finally put to rest before whirring cameras only a few days before.

He feels, in other words, that he is up to his ears in shit, yet he still schlepped down here in the three-car convoy, which left Copenhagen Police Station at the crack of dawn that morning. It won't be long before the tension breaks, and he'll know whether the fatal blow is going to fall. If Kristine Hartung *isn't* in the house, then the damage can be handled, and her case will probably remain a mystery—he can ramble on about that to the press. If Kristine Hartung *is* in the house, then all hell will break loose. Unless, of course, he manages to pass the buck by arguing that his error is entirely understandable, that it is due solely to the fact that someone—someone other than himself—had committed the mother of all howlers by giving a psychopath like Genz so important a job.

The German task force has surrounded the house, and the men are beginning to edge toward it in groups of two. Then, abruptly, they stop short. The front door has swung open, and a skinny figure shoots out at high speed. Nylander follows it with his eyes. When it reaches the middle of the long, dew-damp grass in the overgrown garden, it stops and stares at them.

Everyone freezes. Her features are different. She's grown, and her eyes are wild and dark. But Nylander has seen her picture a hundred times, and he recognizes her at once.

128

It is taking too long, and Rosa senses it's a bad sign. They can't see the cottage from the main road where they are standing, but they've been told it is only five hundred meters away, on the other side of the field and the wild copse with the tall trees and bushes. The sun is shining, but the wind is bitingly chilly, even though they are sheltered behind two large German police vans.

When they were told the night before that the police were investigating a lead in Germany, Rosa and Steen had insisted on coming. The killer's sister apparently lived in a cottage close to the Polish border, and there were signs he'd been on his way to see her before he was killed on a forest road not far from Chestnut Farm. There is a real chance, it seems, that the sister is an accomplice and might know something about Kristine, and since there are no other leads to pin their hopes on they insisted categorically on joining the convoy. Especially now that the murderer can no longer speak for himself.

That was Rosa's first question when she woke up in the hospital after the operations. She looked into Steen's tearstained face, and when she realized where she was—in a proper hospital and not in the nightmarish white basement—she asked whether the man had said anything. Steen shook his head, and she saw that it didn't matter to him at that moment. For him it was a relief that Rosa was alive, and she saw the same relief in Gustav's eyes too. They were also distressed, of course, because of the way she'd been tortured and mutilated. The clamp at the end of her left arm had helped save her life, preventing her from losing too much blood, but the severed hand had been devoured by the flames. The doctors had told her the pain would diminish. At some point she would be given a prosthesis made specifically for her, and she would get used to it, and not keep being surprised whenever she briefly forgot the pain and glimpsed a reflection of herself and the bandaged stump at the end of her arm.

Oddly enough, it doesn't bother Rosa. She isn't crushed by it; instead, she finds herself thinking it is a trivial sacrifice. She would give everything. Her right hand too, which has been stitched back together, both her feet or life itself, if only she could turn back time and save Kristine. Guilt overwhelmed her in her hospital bed, and in tears she reproached herself for the sin she'd committed long ago, when she herself was a little girl. It *was* her fault, and although she'd spent most of her adult life making amends, it hadn't helped. Instead Kristine had suffered for it, although she'd done nothing apart from being her daughter. That knowledge was horrifying. Steen tried to make her see she shouldn't torment herself, but Kristine was gone, and so was the man who said he'd taken her, and not a moment passed when Rosa didn't wish it was *her* the man had taken instead.

Amid the sorrow and self-reproach they received word of the lead the night before, and they were given a place in the convoy of cars, which left for Germany before the sun rose. A few hours later, arriving at the parking lot where the German police vans had been waiting, Steen gleaned from an exchange of information between the Danish and German officers that the woman who lived at that address had been seen over the summer walking with a child. Possibly around Kristine's age. The Danish officers wouldn't confirm anything, and Rosa and Steen were left by the cars with two German officers as soon as the operation was underway.

Suddenly it strikes Rosa that she doesn't dare believe Kristine might be alive. Once again she has built up a hope, a dream, or a castle in the air, which might shatter at any moment. That night, when she got up to dress for the journey, she caught herself choosing clothes she knew Kristine would be able to recognize. The dark blue jeans, the green sweater, the old autumn jacket, and the small, fur-lined boots Kristine had always called "teddy bear boots." She made excuses, telling herself she had to wear *something*, but she'd chosen those clothes for one reason only— because she'd started hoping that today might be the day she sees her child again, the day she runs toward Kristine and squeezes her close and overwhelms her with all her love.

"Steen, I want to go home. I think we should go back now."

"What?"

"Open the car door. She's not there."

"They're not back yet . . ."

"We shouldn't be away long. I want to go back to Gustav."

"Rosa, we're staying here."

"Open the door! You hear what I'm saying? Open the door!"

She jerks at the handle, but Steen won't take out the key and let her in. He's caught sight of something behind her back, and she turns to look in the same direction.

Two figures are coming toward them from the copse of trees and bushes. They are approaching across the field, making for the road and the police vans, lifting their feet extra high, probably because the mud from the field is clinging to their shoes. One is the policewoman, the one called Thulin. The other, holding Thulin's hand, seems at first glance to be a boy about twelve or thirteen. He is short-haired and scruffy. His clothes hang off him like a scarecrow, and he keeps his eyes fixed to the ground because it is hard work trudging through the mud. But when the boy looks up and peers searchingly toward the cars, where Rosa is standing with Steen, she knows. She feels the deep jolt in her stomach, and when she glances at Steen to check whether he is seeing the same thing she is, his face is already cracking, and the tears are running down his cheeks. Rosa begins to run. She runs free of the cars and out into the field. When Kristine lets go of the policewoman's hand and she too breaks into a run, then Rosa knows that it is true.

Wednesday, November 4th

129

The cigarette doesn't taste like it normally does, and Hess is in no rush to enter the international atmosphere, fond of it though he usually is. He is standing at the airport outside the entrance to Terminal 3, and despite the pelting rain he waits to see whether Thulin will show up.

The emotions of yesterday are still with him, and if he forgets them for a brief moment he is reminded as soon as he catches a glimpse of a news screen on a mobile phone or an iPad. The Hartung family's reunion with their daughter has supplanted the articles on Simon Genz, and it is the big news story of the day, surpassed in font size only by the possibility of a new war in the Middle East. Even Hess had struggled to hold back tears when he saw the parents standing there in the wind, embracing the girl on the field, and when he collapsed into bed at Odin late last night, he slept for ten hours at a stretch for the first time in years.

With a forgotten feeling of well-being he got up and drove with Thulin and her daughter, who were on a belated autumn holiday, to the institution where Magnus Kjær had been taken. Magnus's former stepfather, Hans Henrik Hauge, had been found and arrested that weekend by traffic officers at a rest stop in Jutland, but that wasn't why Hess wanted to visit Magnus. The two children, Le and Magnus, had quickly bonded over a shared interest in League of Legends, while the head of the department told Thulin and Hess they'd found a good foster family for the boy. The family was from Gilleleje and had ten years' experience, as well as a foster son who was slightly younger than Magnus and could do with a brother or sister. The meeting between Magnus and the family had apparently gone well, although afterward Magnus had said that if he could choose he'd rather live with "the policeman with the eyes." It made no sense, of course, but while Thulin went for a walk with Le, Hess and Magnus played for a while. The haul was one conquered tower and the eradication of a horde of minions plus a single champion before Hess gave Magnus a slip of paper with his phone number and left. He reassured himself one last time with the departmental head that the foster family was good enough, and then finally he went outside.

At the Science Museum he ate the catch of the day with Thulin, and while Le was busy getting back into the Labyrinth of Light, they stayed sitting in the café among all the families with children, among the shouting and screaming. They both knew he was leaving for Bucharest, but the intimacy and naturalness that had been between them the past few days suddenly gave way to awkward conversation. Hess got lost in her deep eyes and tried to say something. Just then, however, her daughter came running back to drag them off to the Lion's Den, where you could measure the strength of your roar by sticking your head through a hole in a box and yelling as loudly as you could. Afterward it was time for Thulin to go, but in parting she said she would drop by the airport to say goodbye. With that cheering thought, he hurried back to Odin Park, where he was supposed to meet with the caretaker and real estate agent.

The agent, however, was a defeated man. The buyer had pulled out, having found something "safer" in Østerbro. It seemed to upset the Pakistani caretaker more than it upset Hess. Hess thanked him and gave him the keys, and on the way to the airport he felt so full of energy that he asked the taxi to make a stop at Vestre Cemetery.

It was the first time Hess had visited the grave. He didn't know exactly where it was, but at the cemetery office they pointed him down the paths toward a little wood. The grave site looked as sad as he'd feared. A mossy stone, some greenery and pebbles; it made him feel guilty. Hess placed a flower from the forest onto the pebbles, then took off his wedding ring and buried it beneath the gravestone. She would have wanted him to do it ages ago, but even now it was difficult. Standing at the graveside, for the first time in years he let his memories flow freely, and as he walked back toward the exit he felt lighter than when he went in.

Another taxi sloshes past Terminal 3, and Hess stubs out his cigarette and turns his back to the rain. Thulin isn't coming, and maybe it's better that way. He lives like a homeless person and not a thing in his life has got its act together. He sticks his hand in his pocket and takes out his mobile phone to find his boarding pass. On his way toward the escalator to Security, he realizes he's received a text message.

"Have a good trip" is all it says. Seeing who the text is from, he clicks on the image attached.

At first he can't tell what it is. A strange childish drawing of a big tree with branches and glued-on pictures of himself and a parakeet and a hamster. And then he laughs. With all his heart. By the time he reaches Security, he's looked at the picture several times, and he still can't stop laughing.

"**Have you** sent it? Has he seen it?"

Le watches as Thulin puts down her phone and casts around for a kitchen drawer where she can put the poster.

"Yup, sent it. Now go and open the door for your granddad."

"When's he coming back?"

"No idea, now go and open the door!"

Le plods out into the hallway toward the ringing doorbell. For Thulin, sending the picture was the culmination of a weird day. Visiting the Kjær boy with Hess and Le was emotional, and it didn't get much better when Le persuaded them into a trip to family hell at the Science Museum. In the middle of the café, amid screaming youngsters and lunch boxes, she suddenly sensed the danger of a life in the same rut as the families around them. She knew Hess wasn't like that, but then he looked at her with something on the tip of his tongue, and she couldn't help but think of detached houses, pensions, and the whole fat lie of nuclear-family life. Seconds later she said she would drop by the airport, but only to get the hell out of there and safely home.

Back home, Le had insisted on printing out one of the photos she'd taken on her phone of Hess at the Lion's Den. What's more, she wanted to stick Hess onto the school poster of her family tree.

Thulin was very reluctant. But once the photo had been glued on, Hess looked almost as natural as the animals that flanked him, and it is this picture of the family tree Le insisted on sending.

Thulin hesitates by the kitchen drawer and can't help smiling. As she hears Le letting her granddad into the hallway, she decides she will let the poster be pinned to the kitchen wall. Not somewhere prominent. Just next to the hood of the stove. For a day or two, anyway.

130

Linus Bekker is breathing fresh air, but above him the clouds hang dark and heavy. The platform at Slagelse Station is deserted, and the small rucksack with the possessions he'd wanted to bring from the secure unit rests at his feet. He's just been released, and he ought to be happy and relieved, but he isn't. Freedom—but now what?

Something in Linus Bekker is considering his lawyer's suggestion about seeking compensation for pain and suffering. He's already done more than enough time for the only offense he's actually committed: hacking into the archive. Money is fine, he thinks, but he senses that money won't change how disappointed he feels. The Chestnut Man case didn't reach the conclusion he'd hoped for. Ever since he realized during an interview last year that he was an important cog in the machine, he'd been pleased. At first he had no clue who could have put the machete in his garage, but when the detectives tried for the millionth time to make him confess by confronting him with the image of the sharp weapon on the shelf, he noticed the little chestnut doll in the background. Linus had put two and two together. He confessed, and every day in the hell of the secure ward he looked forward to the coming of autumn, when the Chestnut Man would unveil his next step. It was worth the wait, once news of the killings had begun to trickle in, but then the party had fizzled out, and the Chestnut Man turned out to be a bungling amateur undeserving of his faith.

The train pulls in, and Linus Bekker picks up his rucksack and climbs aboard. As he sits down in the window seat, life's tedium still casts its pall—until he notices the single mother sitting diagonally opposite him with her little girl. The mother smiles and nods politely. Bekker returns her civility, smiling back.

The train pulls away. The dark clouds scatter, and Bekker thinks he might find a way to make the time pass after all.

Acknowledgments

THANKS TO: Lars Grarup, who first encouraged me to write a crime novel five or six years ago, when he was senior digital editor at Politiken and no longer head of media at the Danish Broadcasting Corporation, where I got to know him.

Lene Juul, head of Politikens Forlag, who, alongside Lars Grarup, talked me around. When I finally accepted the challenge, I got stuck halfway through, but Lene kept the faith and gave me the time and space I needed.

Emilie Lebech Kaae, producer and lover of literature. For her fantastic support and optimism when I most needed both.

My friends Roland Jarlgaard and Ole Sas Thrane. For reading the earliest draft and for continually inspiring me to keep writing. Special thanks to Ole, because he also contributed with his incredible knowledge of IT.

Scriptwriter Michael W. Horsten, for lending me an ear at the first tentative beginnings. Nina Quist and Esther Nissen, for helping me with the research. Meta Louise Foldager and Adam Price, for their patience with me every day in our shared space.

My sister, Trine, for her wonderful support and confidence.

My agent, Lars Ringhof, for his enormous experience, acumen, and all the good advice.

My editor at Politikens Forlag, Anne Christine Andersen. Sharp, exacting, and absolutely brilliant.

Suzanne Ortmann Reith, for her coaching and infectious humor.

The biggest thanks go to my wife, Kristina. For her love, and because she never stopped believing in *The Chestnut Man*.

About the Author

SØREN SVEISTRUP is an internationally acclaimed scriptwriter, creator, and film producer of several TV series. From 2007 to 2012 he was the creator and writer of *The Killing*, which has won several international awards and been sold to more than a hundred countries all over the world and remade for AMC by Fox Television Studios in the US. He lives in Copenhagen.

HARPER LUXE

THE NEW LUXURY IN READING

We hope you enjoyed reading
our new, comfortable print size and found it
an experience you would like to repeat.

Well – you're in luck!

HarperLuxe offers the finest in fiction and
nonfiction books in this same larger print size and
paperback format. Light and easy to read, HarperLuxe
paperbacks are for book lovers who want to see
what they are reading without the strain.

For a full listing of titles and
new releases to come, please visit our website:

www.HarperLuxe.com

SEEING IS BELIEVING!